Ramsey Campbell is ...or writer. He has received the World Fantasy Award twice and the British Fantasy Award five times – more awards for horror fiction that any other writer.

He was born in Liverpool in 1946, and still lives on Merseyside with his wife Jenny and their children, Tammy and Matty. After working in the Civil Service and in public libraries, he became a full-time writer in 1973. He also reviews films for BBC Radio Merseyside, and is president of the British Fantasy Society. His pleasures include good food, Laurel and Hardy films, and walking, and he uses music from Hildegard von Bingen onwards as an aid to his writing. His books have been translated into French, German, Italian, Spanish, Finnish, Japanese, Swedish and Dutch. He is much in demand as a reader of his stories to audiences.

Books by Ramsey Campbell

RAMSEY CAMPBELL

INCARNATE

Futura

FOR MATTY:
some day, son, all this
will be yours
– with my love

A Futura Book

Original edition © Ramsey Campbell 1983
Revised and expanded edition © Ramsey Campbell 1990

First (abridged) edition published in Great Britain in 1984
by Granada Publishing

This (complete) edition published in Great Britain in 1990
by Futura Publications, a Division of
Macdonald & Co (Publishers) Ltd
London & Sydney
Reprinted 1991

ISBN 0 7088 4395 6

Printed and bound in Great Britain by
HarperCollins Manufacturing, Glasgow

Futura Publications
A Division of
Macdonald & Co (Publishers) Ltd
165 Great Dover Street
London SE1 4YA

A member of Maxwell Macmillan Publishing Corporation

Among the people I could not have done without are my wife Jenny, for continuity

George Walsh, for improving the structure

John Owen, for allowing himself to be taken to a Spiritualist meeting

Carol Smith, for insights into television

Norman Shorrock, for philatelic pointers

Christine Ruth, for London locations

Dave Drake, for reminding me of Chapel Hill

Jim Walker, for cinema backgrounds

John Williams, for legal advice

John Thompson, for help in post-production

'. . . dreams you might have dreamed yourself . . .'
— ROBERT ROBINSON, on classic horror fiction

'I have walked a city's street where no man else had trod.'
— ROBERT E. HOWARD, *Recompense*

'I ask you to think on the hours when one sleeps. Do you know what happens then? The body may lie still in bed, but what happens to the thoughts – the spirit? With what ancient demons does it spend its time? And in what deeds?'
— ARDEL WRAY AND JOSEPH MISCHEL, *Isle of the Dead*

'I am forever dreaming of strange barren landscapes, cliffs, stretches of ocean, and deserted cities with towers and domes . . . All this dreaming comes without the stimulus of *Cannabis indica*. Should I take that drug, who can say what worlds of unreality I might explore? . . . I have travelled to strange places which are not upon the earth or any known planet. I have been a rider of comets, and a brother to the nebulae . . . Surely the strange excrescences of the human fancy are as real – in the sense of real phaenomena – as the commonplace passions, thoughts, and instincts of everyday life.'
— H. P. LOVECRAFT, in letters
(27 September 1919, 21 May 1920)

When they let her out of the room at last, she'd forgotten what she had to say. The sky outside the window told her it was evening, the sunset descending a smouldering ladder of clouds above the Oxfordshire hills, and she could hear voices in the corridor. But apart from those details, her mind was blank. Above the clouds the August sky was a deep calm blue, calm as the sleep her whole body ached for. Maybe the voices weren't in the corridor after all but in the pincushion that her wired head felt like. She had just realized that her speculations had driven what she had to say out of her head when the door opened and Stuart Hay came in.

Whatever it had been, she didn't think she would have been able to say it to his round, young, constantly flushed face that always looked incredulous. 'Still here then, are you?' he said, scratching his mat of cropped red hair. 'Having a lie in?'

'There isn't much else I can do, is there?'

'There is now.' He pulled back the cuffs of the redundant lab coat that he wore like a sceptic's uniform and began to peel the taped wires off her forehead. 'You can meet the others.'

So she would meet them at last, but just now that was only another distraction, something else to make her forget what she had to remember. 'Is it over?' she said.

'Disappointed?' He had removed the last of the contacts; the patches of her skin where they had been felt moist and cool, as if his fingertips were lingering. 'What were you expecting?' he said with a grin that seemed patronizing.

'What were you? It was your idea.'

1

'Dr Kent's, not mine.' He was smiling, pleased that she'd been sharp with him. 'But no, we haven't done yet,' he said, bringing her her dressing gown from the hook on the door. 'She thought it was time for you all to meet one another.'

She swung her disused legs out of the sheets that felt untidy and clammy, and wondered if she could stand up. 'How long now, do you think?'

'You've only been here five days, you know.'

'It feels more like twice that,' she said, matching his sharpness. She'd listened to at least that many playbacks of her voice that sometimes sounded as if she had been muttering drunkenly in her sleep. 'I can't even read now, I can't concentrate with waking up so much.'

'You could go stir crazy in here, at that,' he admitted, with a glance around the pale green room that was almost clinically bare, but his tone seemed to say that not only had she volunteered, she was being paid as well. She tidied her hair in front of the mirror and gazed at her wide mouth, her bright green eyes, her long blonde hair spilling over her shoulders. He took her arm as she limped on her prickling legs towards the door, and that contact let her ask, 'Have you found out anything about me?'

'Too soon to say.' He halted, gripping the doorknob. 'Just one thing before you meet the others – please don't talk about any of your dreams. I don't need to tell you why.'

The smell of paint in the corridor caught at her throat, the indirect lighting that trailed down the green walls made her feel half-asleep. She could hear several voices now, in the lounging area at the far end. Though Stuart was leading her slowly toward them while she got used to her legs again, she felt she was going too fast to think. Had she had a dream that she'd forgotten to confide to the microphone over her bed, or was that her exhausted imagination? Had Stuart been in it, or was that her imagination too? The more she tried to grasp it, the less real it seemed, and in any case it was too late now, for they were at the end of the corridor. As she stepped off the linoleum onto the island of green carpet, everyone turned to look.

She didn't take in their faces at first. She had let go of Stuart too readily. The carpet seemed to give way under her feet, and she sat quickly on the nearest chair, almost missing. She had a confused impression of a crowd of seated people and large-boned Dr Kent alone on her feet, the empty socket where a television should have been plugged in, tables bare of newspapers and magazines, smoke streaming jerkily up from an ashtray. But there were only a few people, one of whom came over and sat next to her. 'We've been looking forward to meeting you, Molly. I'm Joyce.'

She was a small woman in her forties, grey eyes bright as steel in her square face behind her pale blue spectacles, whose case was clipped into the breast pocket of her candy-striped summer dress. She snatched off the spectacles as if that would help her get closer to Molly. 'I'll introduce you. Freda, Helen, Danny. Stuart and Guilda you know, of course.'

Guilda must be Dr Kent, whose long face, with its pale, almost invisible eyebrows, looked amused by the way Joyce had taken over. She came round the circle of low chairs to Molly, her large hand fingering the row of pens in the pocket of her lab coat, and Joyce rounded on her. 'Now we're all here, what can you tell us?'

'Not a great deal. I thought I made that clear. Nothing that might influence your dreams.'

Joyce looked furious at being put in her place by a woman several years younger than herself. 'Will you give us your word that you'll tell us everything if we agree to continue?'

'Eventually, when we've analysed the results.'

'Very well. We put our trust in you.' She was taking her role of spokeswoman rather for granted, Molly thought in the midst of her frustration at trying to remember. 'Just so long as you make sure,' Joyce was saying to Dr Kent, 'that people know what we've seen before it's too late.'

3

'Famous.' That was Danny, a bullnecked man in his twenties, whose head looked too small for his neck. Perhaps it was the multitude of pimples that stood out against his pasty complexion which made him avoid looking directly at anyone and keep his voice so low that they had heard only the last word. 'We'll be famous,' he said now that everyone was listening.

'I don't care if we're famous or not.' Joyce put on her spectacles to stare at him, her grey eyes glinting in her square face. 'We could be useful if only the world would acknowledge it, that's what matters. That's what I expect Guilda to achieve.'

'They must think we're important,' Danny mumbled, 'or they wouldn't be paying us so much.'

He couldn't earn much if he was impressed by the nominal fee they were receiving. He broke the embarrassed silence himself. 'It's funny,' he said, forcing a laugh to prove it, 'I used to dream I'd be famous. That shows it works, doesn't it? That'll show them. Once I dreamed – '

Dr Kent was behind his chair so fast that he shrank away. 'Please remember what I said,' she murmured.

Freda took pity on him. She was a lanky woman in her forties who sat stooped forward as if to hide her tallness. Above her full lips and long nose, her eyes looked wistful. 'I know how you feel,' she told him. 'Sometimes I wish I could have seen the future. I don't usually dream ahead, I dream – ' She smiled quickly and covered her mouth.

'Dreaming ahead isn't what counts,' Joyce said. 'It's preventing what we see that matters.'

'That's what I meant I wished.'

But Joyce had already turned back to Guilda. 'Have you any idea how it feels to see these things and not be able to do a blessed thing to change them? It's worse than being paralysed, it must be. It's like being the only one who can see in a world full of blind people. It's like seeing a child on the edge of a cliff and not being able to do anything because

4

you're too far away and the people who could save the child can't see and won't believe. And not just once, night after night, dream after dream. And every time it's worse because you know nobody will listen.'

Danny was gazing at her as if she'd read his thoughts. Certainly she'd given voice to discouragements Molly hadn't fully realized that she felt herself. That unresolved feeling in her mind was still there, distant and vague. If the others stopped talking she might be able to grasp it, and it seemed important that she should.

But Helen was trying to speak, a plump young woman perhaps still in her teens, whom Stuart's gaze kept straying to: long black hair glossy as sealskin, eyes very dark in her pale oval face, curves filling her jeans and t-shirt, and Molly scoffed at herself for suffering a twinge of jealousy, as if Stuart's opinion mattered. Joyce interrupted before Helen had got out a sentence. 'You can tell us this much,' she said to Dr Kent. 'Have any of us had the same dreams?'

'It's rather early to say,' Dr Kent said and smiled at Joyce's immediate fierce frown, 'but there do seem to be suggestive similarities, yes.'

Perhaps their murmur of triumph drove Stuart away, through a pair of swing doors. Molly had joined in, but she was wondering which of her dreams someone else might have shared: her sailing ship as long as the horizon, her trying to sing 'I'm only a cross-eyed octopus' to an auditorium full of priests, her endless clamber up a sloping roof in a blizzard to get to her parents' bedroom? More likely it had been one of the dreams she had forgotten by now.

'Some people won't believe you dream,' dark-eyed Helen said, now that she had the chance. 'My husband won't believe he does. It's like he won't admit to that part of himself. It's very strange.'

'My Geoffrey has to believe in mine,' Joyce said. 'Has to put up with them. Not that he can do anything about them, any more than I could.'

5

'David must be wondering how I'm getting on.' Helen sounded as if she hoped he was. 'I wish I could call him. I know I can't,' she said quickly as Dr Kent made to speak. 'He'll just have to wonder a bit longer. Do him good. Keep him guessing.'

'I'd like to know how my Geoffrey's coping. I can't leave him with a can of beans unless I leave instructions with the opener. Men are such babies, all of them.'

'I think some people are afraid to think too much about their dreams,' Molly said, changing the subject for Danny's sake. 'I expect they feel they're at the mercy of their dreams. We all are.' Certainly she felt at the mercy of the one she had forgotten; it made her feel ponderous and prickly and stupid. Just then Stuart wheeled in a trolley laden with food on moulded plastic trays.

So there must be people in the long concrete building who she hadn't seen, someone to cook and someone to read the scribbling of brain waves, perhaps, unless a computer took care of the latter. Stuart passed out trays and plastic cutlery, lingered beside Helen and then beside Molly. Danny was peering suspiciously at his knife as Freda said, 'Tell us about yourself, Molly. You haven't had a chance.'

'I'm in my last year at university before I go out into the big wide world. I'd like to work in the media. I was working for a magazine when I heard about this.' No need to say it was a sexology magazine, it made her feel so stupid. Concocting readers' letters had sounded like a fun way for her and Stephanie to spend the vacation, but two weeks of inventing variations had left Molly and her imagination exhausted. The day she'd found herself writing about buttered breadsticks she had known it was time to quit, even if she hadn't seen the call for subjects for the Foundation for Applied Psychological Research. 'I'd like to work somewhere,' she said, suddenly realizing, 'that would give us a voice.'

Joyce was a nurse, Freda worked in a department store in

Blackpool, Helen was at library school, Danny was a cinema projectionist and said so resentfully when Helen asked if he was a student too. Molly was surprised how happy she felt just to be with people like herself, people who didn't regard her as a curiosity or an embarrassment. Her parents had always behaved as if it wasn't quite nice of her to say that she'd dreamed last night of the morning's news; even if it were true it was something you didn't talk about, like her periods, and she had learned not to mention either as she had ceased to be a child. Since then she'd seldom woken with that sense of having seen a photograph that was waiting to be taken, but perhaps now, as she found out about herself – Now Stuart was stacking the scraped plastic trays and collecting the empty beakers, and all too soon Dr Kent was saying, 'I think it's time to continue.'

They were standing up when Joyce demanded, 'What was the idea of bringing us all together for tea?'

'Why, to see if meeting each other affects your dreaming.'

The others were heading for the bathrooms, Freda stooping a little, Danny brushing back his spiky hair that looked as if he kept losing his temper with it, Stuart watching Helen's blue-jeaned bottom swaying. Molly glanced back at the circle of empty chairs, and suddenly she felt as if she'd dreamed the meeting. Had the photograph been taken without her noticing, or had it yet to be? For a moment she felt breathlessly apprehensive. She couldn't tell Dr Kent, for it was too late for her to know if she'd had the dream or was just imagining that she had. She trudged away to the bathrooms, to her room, back to bed.

She filled her tumbler with water from the jug on the bedside table and lay down, gazing at the microphone. Dr Kent's last words were troubling her somehow, mixed up with the dream she didn't know if she had had and the distant frustration that had seemed, for a moment when Dr Kent had finished speaking, close enough to grasp. There was no point in saying any of this to the microphone when it might not be switched on, but perhaps she could tell Stuart when he reached her on his rounds.

The thought of how he would react kept her quiet as he taped the wires to her skull. Damn his scepticism, he was here to listen. He was tucking in the sheet now, and she felt his hand under her breast through the mattress, as if he wore a huge clumsy glove. 'Anything else I can do?' he said.

'You'll be lucky.' He reminded her of the obscure contempt the sexology editor felt for his readers.

'Be like that, then.' He sounded offended. He gave her and the room a curt glance from the doorway before he closed the door.

She dragged her paperback *War and Peace* off the bedside table and tried to read. She didn't feel like closing her eyes just yet. If the idea of dreaming had begun to make her uneasy, that was information too. Perhaps it was rather the thought of having to wake up at the end of every dream that was troubling her; she knew by now that she would. Soon all this would be over and she could write about it. Perhaps that might even help her get a job.

She took out her tasselled bookmark that was cracking the fat spine. 'What did I come here for?' Rostov was wondering. 'Who are they? Why are they here? What do they want? When will all this end?' Not for another thousand pages at least, and the prospect made her eyelids droop. She closed the book on her finger so that she wouldn't be tempted to give up entirely, and let her eyes close.

She felt Tolstoy settle beside her. She felt warm and safe, no longer troubled by frustration. Sleep must be the answer, and she hadn't realized how much she needed it. Fish never sleep, she thought, sharks never dream, and wondered what these dreamy thoughts looked like as they swarmed along the wires, spiders of the mind, swarming out of the other rooms to their lair. Was anyone dreaming yet? What *did* Freda dream? It frustrated Molly not to know, but now she was drifting again, Little Nemo piloting the *Nautilus* deeper and deeper through the chambers of the subconscious but nobody was at the controls . . . little nobody . . . nobody in the passenger area with its pale green walls and its low chairs on the island of carpet . . . except that now something was: a circle of seated figures that were altogether too pink, that were turning their blank heads to her. She jerked awake and muttered a description to the microphone, though she wasn't sure where her sleepy thoughts had turned into a dream. Usually she liked this state, the stream of thoughts and obscure correlations that reminded her of the pages she'd read of a digest of *Finnegans Wake*, but now it felt uncontrollable, sweeping her toward the precipice of dreams. There was nothing to fear, everyone dreamed, but why did they? Whenever I feel afraid I hold my head whenever I feel afraid I hold my head whenever I feel afraid, over and over an' dover Andover, an Iron Age settlement near London, but she wasn't sitting a history examination now, she was back in the sexology office and faking letters as fast as she could, for Danny Swain in stained trousers to collect. That woke her momentarily, wondering why she should have thought that was his name, but now she was in a lecture hall where Joyce was haranguing the audience while Dr Kent heckled, shouting, 'A blind man needs no crutch.' That seemed profoundly meaningful as Molly woke, she would have told the microphone except that she was sinking again into the dark, which seemed impatient now. It was all right, she had the microphone, she could keep in touch as she ventured into the dark.

She looked up as she took the first step. Either the walls met overhead, high up in the dark, or the sky was utterly lightless. Though the walls were full of windows, not a window was lit, and she couldn't see a single face in the crowd she was struggling through. Their bodies felt puffy and yielding, they smelled of sodden musty cloth, but she

9

could wake if she had to, if their hands should seize her and drag her back into the dark. Waking was the best means of escape, the only one – but suddenly she was out of the crowd, in a narrow street lit by lamps that dripped black rain. She was in front of a door.

She mustn't go in. This was the photograph that was waiting to be taken, the red door where green paint showed through the top left-hand corner of the upper right-hand panel, the dog-faced knocker canted slightly to the left, a brass ring in its mouth. There were six doors in that house, but if there were more – She was shuddering and reaching for the microphone in the hope that telling it would help her understand why she was so afraid, and then she remembered that it could do much more: it would let her find her way back. She raised the microphone to her face and glanced back along the cord. It had snapped.

The frayed end lay in the gutter, the exposed wires twitching in the water that was streaming toward the drain. She flung away the microphone, which struck the foot of a streetlamp with a hollow tinny sound. She couldn't find her way back. There was only one way to go, for someone had opened the door.

She wanted to turn and run, it didn't matter where. Worse than nightmare waited beyond the doorway. But the distant frustration was suddenly close, urging her forward, and when at last she managed to make her legs move she found she was stumbling into the house, along the hall, past the staircase where she didn't dare look up. The knob of the door beyond the stairs felt like a lump of ice in her hand. When the door opened, it seemed to drag her into the room.

It was a back parlour. A tasselled lampshade turned the walls and floorlength curtains a smoky brown. Antimacassars drooped over the chairs and settee that huddled around a gas fire, its orange flames stuttering. China dolls lined up neatly, the tallest in the middle, on the mantelpiece beneath an oval mirror. The room was stifling, she could hardly breathe. Then she saw the figures in the room, and she couldn't breathe at all.

They must be life-size dolls. What else could they be, with their blurred pink faces? But they were moving toward her, and so was the man who couldn't close his eyes, another man with something nodding on his shoulder, and yet another who was armless, staggering about and crying at his incompleteness. Worse, she was moving toward them. She was suffocating with panic and the heat of the room, she would wake if only she could scream – and then she saw her terrified face in the oval mirror and realized that she could do neither. She had made things change at last, by going through the doorway of the house. The frustration that had urged her forward was satisfied, and now she knew that it hadn't been hers, nor Joyce's, nor anyone's. For one appalling, endless moment, everything was clear: both what would happen, and what she would have to do to prevent it from happening.

Her convulsion tore all the wires off her skull. One adhesive pad pulled out several strands of hair. She was sitting upright in bed, staring at the pale green room, but she felt as if she hadn't escaped the stifling brownish room. Her head was pounding, her whole body ached with jerking upright. She felt she was being dreamed.

She went stumbling toward the door, though she wasn't sure which door it was. Someone was crying out, but it was so distant that she could hardly believe it was her voice or that anyone else could hear. She ought to have used the microphone to cry for help, but now she was at the door, clinging to the knob without knowing if she meant to turn it or to hold the door shut. If the bare green hall was out there it would be no relief, for it led to Joyce and the others. She didn't know why that terrified her – she had already forgotten what the dream had revealed. She knew only that the door was opening as, too late, she struggled to hold it closed.

11

Stuart was there. Behind him she saw Dr Kent, who looked baffled. Now that the door was open, Molly was able to distinguish that the cries weren't her own after all. She couldn't tell whose they were, which room they came from, but they sounded like the cries of someone unable to wake. At once she was sure that someone was still in the stifling brownish room.

She was beginning to tremble as the implications of that thought grew clear. The door opposite hers laboured open. It was Danny. He clung to the doorframe and seemed to be trying to focus his eyes. When he saw Dr Kent, he lurched at her. 'You made it happen,' he shouted, in a blurred voice that sounded as though he had never raised it before.

Dr Kent stepped back, and Danny saw Molly. His eyes widened. He staggered toward her and halted himself by grabbing the wall outside her room. The hatred in his bloodshot eyes felt like a blow in her face, and looked very much like madness. He couldn't be about to say what she feared he would. It wasn't true, she cried within her panic. Please don't say it, please.

'And you did,' he said.

Eleven Years Later

The rain came slashing across Hyde Park and plastered the traffic at Marble Arch with the leaves it had ripped from the trees. Above the rotary choked with traffic, the November sky was a tidal wave. Bayswater Road was a mass of black roofs that the spiky rain turned pale, taxis full of businessmen stuffed with expense-account lunches; tented cyclists wobbled between the buses on Oxford Street, early Christmas shoppers struggled along Edgware Road behind the shields of their umbrellas. Molly gazed down at all this from the window of the office on the fifth floor of Metropolitan Television and couldn't hear a sound.

In six months she hadn't got used to the silence. It made her think of those moments when she would remember something so intensely that her surroundings slipped away without her noticing. She tried not to have those moments any more, they felt too much like losing control. She turned away from the window, to the accounts Ben had dumped on her desk.

Their programme had gone over budget last month, if she could call it hers as well as Ben's, or wanted to. Surely not even his dining could have gobbled up several thousand pounds. She skated a ruler down the columns of figures while typewriters chattered in the adjoining offices, and at last she found the culprits, though she had to phone Accounting to be sure what the secretive computer meant: the film extracts Ben had used in his programme about corruption in the unions, Peter Sellers as a shop steward, Richard Attenborough suffering the silent treatment for breaking a strike. Ben had said he had contacts in the film companies who would let him have the extracts cheap, but it seemed he had run out of favours.

She sat back feeling justified, staring at his desk opposite hers. It was bare except for programme schedules and the afternoon's memos, two piles of paper flanking the telephone at the exact centre of his desk. Her desk was crowded with everything else: newspaper clippings, In and Out trays, an IBM typewriter, the telephone, which had to pass all his calls; there wasn't room for anything of hers. It must be essential to his image of himself that his desk always be clear, as essential as the calendar girl above his swivel chair, her hip turned just enough to show a hint of curly pubic hair. The trouble was that the calendar was hanging where Molly would see it whenever she looked up, and she knew all too well what that was supposed to achieve. This was where three years at university and eleven in broadcasting had got her. She was sighing fiercely when he came in from lunch with the head of Programming, a lunch that had lasted most of the afternoon. 'My God, you sound frustrated,' he said. 'You can stop now.'

He looked like his own image of perfection: black blazer with polished gold buttons, steel-grey knife-edged trousers, a polo shirt so white it was fluorescent, blue just-shaved jowls, clipped black moustache, sleek hair combed back. She couldn't help but enjoy saying, 'Your bits of film cost too much.'

'You're joking. What, that old stuff? They ought to be paying us for the publicity, if any of them are still alive.' But he looked pleased with himself. 'Dig out your maps. We're going North tomorrow.'

When she spread the map on his desk he reached across her to run his finger up the motorway, and she could hardly breathe for the smell of haircream. 'We'll be staying here overnight, so you'll need to book rooms for us and the crew. Adjoining if possible.'

'I shouldn't think it will be.'

16

He straightened up, and the back of his hand touched her breast – back-handed but no sort of compliment, she thought wearily. 'Look, Molly,' he said as if he hadn't noticed, 'we have to work together. Why behave like this?'

'I don't think you can complain about my work, Ben, and that's all the advertisement said you were hiring.'

'And your personality.' He was trying to be gentle, but that was even more oppressive than the smell of haircream. 'We have to get on with each other when we're together so much of the time.'

'Then try treating me like a person instead of a dictaphone. You want me to book these rooms and I don't even know why.'

'Sorry, my mistake. I've been talking to one of the protesters who got inside the nuclear base. He can prove they were, whatever the Navy says.'

'Thanks.' She folded the map and went back to her desk. 'Now I know.'

'Friends?'

'I suppose so.'

'Fine. That's what I like to hear.' He began to leaf through the programme schedules. 'Adjoining rooms then, yes?'

'Not for us, Ben. Not now or ever.'

He gave her a long expressionless stare and looked away, as if he'd seen nothing worth seeing. 'Just do your job, then. Get the hotel.' He pretended to ignore her as she dialled, but she knew he was listening intently, and it was stiffening her words even before she spoke them. So this was the prospect Leon had found for her, the opportunity he'd convinced her she was looking for.

That wasn't fair to him. Metropolitan had looked to both of them like her chance to achieve something at last. Six years in parochially local radio had helped her sleep at night without starting awake in a panic, but the experience hadn't been much use when she'd moved to London and television. She'd worked two years as researcher for a chat show hostess whose sole distinction was to sound less intelligent than any of her guests, and nobody in the audience knew that was the truth. Thank heaven for BBC and the job assisting Leon! She'd enjoyed those years once she had got used to him. She had been as disappointed for herself as she was pleased for him when MTV had offered him his own arts programme but wouldn't keep her on as his assistant, and then he'd found her the job as assistant on the news programme. The show was going to be independent and fearless, it had sounded like her chance to be that too. And by God she was, as far as Ben Eccles was concerned. Thinking about her ambitions while she waited for the hotel receptionist to answer made her want, however sadly, to laugh.

So did what the receptionist said. 'If there's only one single then of course I must have that,' Molly said, smiling sweetly at Ben. 'Mr Eccles and his crew will sort out the doubles between them.'

Ben made to speak, but glared at the schedules instead. He ignored her when she said, 'Anything else I can do?' Perhaps he meant her to feel useless, which, infuriatingly, she did. She had been reduced to gazing out at the lake, a slab of jagged slate amid the sodden park, by the time Leon came up from the studio.

The sight of him, of his chubby good-natured face beneath its ash-blond hair and the rest of him bearlike in his sheepskin coat, cheered her up even before he said innocently, 'How are you, Ben? What are you investigating now?'

Ben clearly wanted to ignore him but couldn't resist a retort. 'Maybe I should be investigating you and your bloody silly titles.'

'Oh, Ben, I didn't know you cared.' Leon's campy wriggle was barely a glimpse, a throwaway joke. 'Nothing wrong with a bit of irreverence. We shouldn't take ourselves too seriously in this game.'

'Irreverence? You call calling a programme *Arty Farty* irreverent? Infantile, more like. If I'd had my way you wouldn't have got away with it, and I don't mind telling you I let them know upstairs. There's enough gossip about us as it is.'

'Don't tell me you've been reading *Private Eye* on the newsstands again.'

'I wouldn't wipe my arse on it.' Ben's face was darkening, and Molly found she was wishing once again that she'd read the magazine's lampoon of him before she had applied for the job at MTV: 'Ben Eccles, investigative journalist noted for his closeup investigation of any female staff who stray his way . . .' 'I'd like to know where they're getting their information about us,' Ben said with a glare at Leon.

'Not guilty, your honour.' Leon raised his eyebrows, which made his chubby face look even more amiable. 'Why, I thought you were a champion of investigative journalism.'

Ben's glare went blank. 'Did you want something here, Leon?'

'Molly, when she's ready. We're due at the London Film Festival.' He glanced at his watch. 'I can wait a few minutes if you like. I'll chaperone you two and Molly can chaperone us.'

Ben looked down, dismissing them both. 'She can go. She's done enough for one day.' As they left, Molly buttoning her quilted Finnish raincoat, he muttered, 'About time you went back to the BBC and wasting the taxpayers' money.'

He meant Leon, not her. She was stuck with working for a man she didn't like at a time when jobs were growing scarcer. The weight of six months of Ben and who knew how much longer suddenly made her feel exhausted. 'Would you mind very much if I don't come with you this time?' she said as the lift took them down to the lobby.

'I really would appreciate your company.'

He looked so disappointed and anxious that she gave in.

19

'But I don't want to hang around after the film. I know you, you'll be talking for hours.'

'I won't make you hang around unless you have a reason to,' he said, so slyly that she would have asked what he meant if the lift hadn't opened just then. The lobby was deserted except for Mr Wick the commissionaire, who wished them good-night in a voice thick with shag. Everything around his circular desk – back-to-back chairs, thick carpet, even the welcome mat big as a single bed – was green: the colour of expectation, she had felt at first, until she'd learned what working with Ben involved. She turned up her fat collar as she followed Leon out through the revolving doors.

There were new graffiti on the nine-storey concrete façade, Iranian with English subtitles. Green light swept repetitively over the rainy forecourt from the rotating sign on top of the portico, the 'M' sharing a leg with the 'V' and sprouting the 'T' like an aerial. A taxi swung into the forecourt in response to Leon's wave.

Queues were forming outside the National Film Theatre for tonight's last performances, a Nigerian fantasy and an American independent film called *Bierce*. 'SOLD OUT' was plastered across a poster for the restored print of *Greed*. She hurried after Leon through the black-walled corridors, past the bowls of sand and cigarette butts, into NFT 1.

The lights were still up. A film reviewer from the BBC gave Leon a copy of his novel about John Wayne, a woman next to Molly was complaining that nobody knew how to trim a poodle these days, an Australian was holding forth behind her: 'The only vertigo I got from Hitchcock was falling off my seat from boredom; *The Big Sleep* was one big yawn . . .' Molly skimmed the programme notes. All she knew about *The Spin* was that it was a documentary about Las Vegas, but now she realized that she'd seen another film by Martin Wallace, *The Unamericans*. She remembered its fierceness, the shock of a scene where a march of draft dodgers had been clubbed down by police. 'Wallace is wiser

20

than Wiseman,' the *Village Voice* had apparently said. 'He confronts Las Vegas without fear or loathing . . .' It was hoped that Mr Wallace would answer questions after the screening, and now the lights were dimming.

The film was powerful enough for her eventually to turn on the Australian and tell him to shut up. It wasn't so much the technique that impressed her – the intercutting of small-town penny arcades called Las Vegas with the real thing, a tracking shot through deserted Las Vegas streets from church to silent church, a protracted panning shot around a casino that picked up winners and losers at random – as it was the people in the film. The faces of the heavy losers looked as if they'd collapsed inside themselves; the eyes of children were bright as Christmas; the gamblers talked to the camera as if they couldn't stop, any more than they could stop gambling. A woman traded jewels from her throat and her liver-spotted arms for chips, lost, came back and tried to trade her watch, turned to the camera and begged whoever was behind it to lend her money, just a hundred dollars, okay, fifty, she'd pay it back in half an hour – she knew this time she was going to win. Her voice began to fade until there was only the withered colourless face, lips still pleading, and then, abruptly, darkness. No sound, no music. The dedication – 'For my parents' – appeared and faded, and the lights came on.

The silence gave way to applause, but at first Molly was too moved to join in. 'You liked it, obviously,' Leon said, and when she nodded, 'Now that you've given me your unbiased opinion I can tell you the good news. MTV has hired Martin Wallace to make a series.'

'They're welcome to him,' the Australian muttered as Molly stood up quickly – she would feel rude if Martin Wallace saw her leaving. 'Thanks, Leon,' she said, and ruffled his ash-blond hair. 'See you tomorrow.'

The people between her and the aisle were getting up. Leon shook his head, gestured her to sit down so that he

21

could whisper. 'Ladies and gentlemen', the director of the festival said into a microphone, 'Martin Wallace', and it was too late for her not to feel rude – but that wasn't why she sank back into her seat. As Martin Wallace came on stage, she took slow deep breaths to calm herself, as she'd learned to do at meditation class eleven years ago. She couldn't leave until she knew why the sight of Martin Wallace had brought her so near to panic.

Martin Wallace didn't look like the director of his films. His thick black eyebrows were the fiercest thing about him. His broad smile looked surprised and even a little uncomfortable between his small nose and large chin, as if he hadn't been prepared for such applause. His hair was rumpled, his complexion dark; he was tall and slim and dressed in a suede jacket, high-necked black sweater, black corduroys. When he spoke, there was a touch of the American South in his voice, and a cold.

'I hope you can all understand this Colonial accent. I guess your English weather makes it more of a language barrier.' The microphone squealed, and he sat back while the festival director adjusted it for him. 'Okay, well, all I really wanted was to thank you for being kind to my film. I felt good when I'd finished editing, but I never know if I should until I know how people feel.' He paused. 'Any questions?' One timid hand went up. 'Yes?'

'How did you set up that shot of the churches? Are the streets really ever that empty?'

'There's a story behind that,' Martin Wallace said, but Molly wasn't really listening; she was trying to cope with her sense that something was going to happen. She'd thought she was rid of those feelings and the panic that came with them. She tried to breathe as she prayed she was.

'What about Hollywood?' a girl with rainbow hair said after Wallace had finished his anecdote.

'I did get invited, but I guess I prize my independence too much. But listen, independence can lead you to compromise, it puts so much pressure on you sometimes . . .' He wasn't a slow speaker, once he got going; he just kept running out of breath in the middle of syllables, hyphenating like an inexpert printer. Molly was almost calm now, for she'd managed to explain away her panic: Leon had made her feel conspicuous in exactly the way she was trying to avoid. Of course that must be all.

Wallace fell silent, and sneezed. 'Just a few more questions,' the festival director promised, and pointed straight at Molly. 'Yes?'

She was opening her mouth with no idea of what she might say when she realized he was pointing at the Australian. 'What were you trying to say up there today?' the Australian asked.

'Well,' said Wallace, 'I hope the film speaks for itself. If it doesn't, uh, I'd say I've failed.'

'You reckon it's a failure?'

'I didn't say that. I'd say it was up to you out there to judge.'

The Australian persisted. 'You're telling us you have no opinion of your stuff?'

'Of course I have an opinion. I'm saying that mine is the least worth knowing.'

Wallace was staring at his shoes as if he hoped the man, who was clearly enjoying his embarrassment, would go away. Perhaps he was trying to keep his temper. Molly's face was growing hot in sympathy. Wallace looked toward her, and before she knew it she had raised her hand. 'Yes?' the festival director said.

What could she ask? 'You dedicate all your films to

someone, don't you,' she said, thinking out loud. 'This one is for your parents, the one about draft dodging was for Larry.' But that wasn't a question. 'Who's Larry?'

She would have liked to crawl under the seat when she saw his reaction, a lopsided smile that couldn't quite mask his pain. 'He was my brother,' he said.

'One more question,' the festival director said quickly, and a young man wearing a bowler hat asked about influences. Molly closed her eyes as if that might make her invisible, as she'd thought it would when she was little. She'd made things worse for Martin Wallace than the Australian had, intruded where she shouldn't have. When Leon squeezed her hand, she clung blindly to him.

'Martin Wallace, thank you very much.' Applause merged into the thunder of upturned seats. A few people made their way to the stage, where Wallace was chatting away from the microphone. 'Oh, Leon, I wish I'd kept my mouth shut,' Molly whispered. 'I'd apologize if I knew how.'

'Why don't you? Come on, before we lose him. If you don't you'll only go home and brood.' He made for the stage without looking back to see if she were following, and she was so annoyed with him for being right about her that she almost didn't.

'Martin Wallace? I'm Leon Bardin. And this is Molly Wolfe, the best production assistant I know.'

'Hello, how are you?' He mustn't recognize her, for he was smiling. 'It's good to meet you,' he told Leon. Close up, his thick eyebrows stood out even more, despite his dark complexion, and so did his large, deep blue eyes. 'I hope I can live up to your faith in me.'

'Met's, not mine. All I did was make them look at your work.'

'It's lucky they didn't see me up here today.'

'You were fine. Especially considering the bug.' Leon was leading them past rows of empty seats draped with abandoned programme notes. 'What you need is a little medicinal alcohol. Let's take a stroll and avoid the film buffs.'

A neon sculpture stained the misty air above the Hayward Gallery; the spotlighted Houses of Parliament looked trapped in amber. Molly accompanied the others as far as Waterloo Underground, and then she blurted, 'I'm sorry I asked you that question. I was only trying to shut the cobber up.'

Martin blinked at her. 'Which question was that?'

'About your brother.'

'Oh, was that you? That's all right, it was a legitimate question. I mean, I put my feelings up there.' He smiled at her and looked away, murmuring, 'That's all right,' to himself. Of course it wasn't, and she wanted to reach out and touch him, say she was sorry that way. Instead she turned toward the ticket office. 'Thanks very much for the film,' she said to both of them.

'At least have one for the road on a night like this,' Leon cried. 'Besides, you wouldn't leave Martin at my mercy, would you?'

'Yes, please do join us, won't you?' Martin said, and she wasn't sure why she felt unable to refuse.

Leon found a pub off Waterloo Road. He was always for walking until he found somewhere new. The barmaid, a squat woman with a yellowing perm and a pugnacious lower lip, took her time in coming to them, though nobody else was waiting to be served. They carried their drinks from the low smoky bar into a back room where workmen in overalls rested their muddy boots on the guard in front of a coal fire, and Molly couldn't help feeling that the workmen were eavesdropping as Martin began to talk about himself.

He was from Chapel Hill in North Carolina, but he'd attended university in the south of the state – 'the Baptist belt', he said with a jokey shudder. His parents still lived in Chapel Hill and seemed to trouble him, for he went on quickly to describe how he'd become a filmmaker, first

25

making a half-hour fiction film with a group of actor friends before deciding that film was so exacting that it ought to be about something more substantial. He'd made six features now and was satisfied with none of them. 'Sometimes I think I need to work with someone who'll head me off from getting too polemical,' he said.

Something had occurred to Molly. 'You were saying you valued your independence and yet you're going to work for MTV.'

'Well, because they're giving me total freedom. That's what won me over, and also I needed to work outside America.'

'Really.'

'Absolutely,' Leon said, a little sharply. 'I had to fight for it. I knew we wouldn't get him otherwise.'

'No,' said Molly, 'I meant I wondered why you feel the need to leave America.'

'Because I feel too close to my material. Here maybe I can stand back, not get so worked up about things all the time.'

'But feelings are what your films are about,' Molly said. 'That scene in *The Unamericans* where the peace march was attacked, I felt angry for days because I couldn't do anything.'

'A film about peace made you want to beat up those cops, right? That's what I mean. I got so angry I made too much of that incident, kept cutting back to it, remember. Well, I've made better films since then.'

It seemed to distress him, or perhaps it reminded him of something that did. Sensing so much about him so soon made her feel uneasy, on the edge – of what, she didn't know. 'So what do you plan to make for us?'

'Well, that's what I have to find out.' He moved a loaded ashtray to another table. 'One thing I'd like to look at is how your country has become Americanized. It's changed a lot in just a few years.'

'You've been here before?' she asked.

'For a while. I wasn't looking for subjects, I just had to get away.'

Again she sensed distress, again she wanted to touch him. 'It'll be good to get away from American subjects,' he went on. 'Sometimes I think all I do is take the lid off America's garbage.'

'So he comes over here to do it to ours,' one of the workmen said.

Martin blinked at the table by the fire. None of the workmen was looking at him, so he wasn't sure if the remark had been about him. 'Well, I didn't quite mean that,' he said, and sneezed.

'Finish that Scotch and I'll get you another,' Leon said, breaking his untypical silence at last. He lingered when Martin had drained his glass. 'If you need someone to show you round,' he said, 'it ought to be whoever assists you on the series. You'll need a production assistant on the team.'

Martin smiled wryly. 'I can use someone who'll keep an eye on me when I get out of hand.'

'Here she is,' Leon said.

So that was why he hadn't told her sooner that Martin was to work for MTV. He must have been planning this for weeks, a surprise to make up for Ben Eccles. Martin gazed at her, and she couldn't grasp what she was feeling, she was growing so tense. 'That's fine with me,' he said.

'Drinks all round,' Leon said, and stood up. 'To the start of a fruitful relationship.'

All the workmen burst out laughing, not with humour. 'Queer and a pimp as well,' one said.

'I don't think I care for this pub,' Martin said.

Still the workman, a stocky youth whose hand left muddy fingerprints on his glass, didn't look at him. 'Then fuck off back where you came from.'

A piece of coal exploded in the fireplace. 'Let's find somewhere else,' Molly murmured. Leon nodded, Martin

27

picked up his gabardine and slipped one arm into the sleeve. 'Let's do that,' he said.

'Let's do it,' the stocky workman said, 'before I have to show you ladies where to go.'

'It's okay,' Martin said to Molly, but she saw he was trembling. 'We have these in America too.'

The workman swung round, and the fireguard clanged on the bare boards of the overheated room. 'What have you got in America, honey-bunch?'

'Assholes. Arseholes, you'd call them. People, who, when they open their mouths, shit comes out because that's all that's in their heads.'

The workman stood up with a thud that shook the boards. His stool fell like an echo. Martin got up slowly, his gabardine dangling by one sleeve, and Molly made to step between them just as the barmaid got there. 'I'll not have language like that in my place,' she told Martin. 'Get out and take your friends with you or I'll call the police.'

She blocked the doorway of the snug when the workman tried to get past her. 'They're not worth dirtying your hands on, Bobby. Go and sit down quietly now and there'll be a drink on the house.'

A chill wind that tasted of fog blustered along Waterloo Road, jingling the streetlamps. Molly and Leon linked arms with Martin as they strode into the gusts, and after a while he stopped trembling. 'You see what I mean about getting out of hand,' he muttered. 'I get people thrown out of pubs.'

'I'm surprised you kept your temper as long as you did,' Molly protested.

'Sometimes I don't. Anyway, now you've some idea of what you'll have to put up with if you work with me.'

She took time to think what to say; she had already distressed him enough. 'I do appreciate being asked, and I do think I could be some use. It's just that I didn't know Leon was going to suggest me. Would you mind if I thought about it for a day or two?'

Leon stared at her. 'What's there to think about?'

'Call it female indecision.'

'Christ preserve us from stereotypes.'

'All right, it was a stupid thing to say.'

Leon rushed them into the wind and it snatched at her breath. She had to slow down, she couldn't think. 'All the same, I need time to decide,' she said.

'What's the problem? You aren't sure if you want to leave Ben Eccles?' Leon was growing angry. 'This is your big chance, Molly. You don't want to work for this outfit for the rest of your life.'

'You ought to take your time, Molly,' Martin said. 'I don't want to feel you were forced into anything.'

She felt so grateful that she almost blurted out that she would work with him. She headed for the Underground instead, before she could. Trains squealed in their burrows, and at last one emerged. She had to change at the next station, and so she was on the Circle line, in an empty carriage lit like a hospital corridor, before she was able to think.

Perhaps she could work with Martin. He would be the perfect reason to leave Ben, since it would be clear that she was moving on to better things rather than away from Ben. Yet the idea made her nervous, perhaps because she already seemed so much in tune with Martin, almost as if she had met him before – as if she had dreamed of him. If she had, she didn't want to know. Surely the explanation was that she'd sensed what Leon had in mind. A good night's sleep would cure her nervousness.

She came out onto Bayswater Road a couple of miles west of MTV. A sodden oak leaf flapped on the railing above the steps. She turned left at the estate agent's and up the hill. A minute's climb past the white four-storey Victorian terraces brought her home. She closed the gate in the railings and went down the glassy steps. She found her key in the dark niche that the pavement walled in. A car door slammed farther up the hill, a disco light pulsed red and green at a fourth-floor party across the street. She slipped the key into the lock and then hesitated. For a moment she had expected someone to open the door from within.

She switched on the light in the hall. Nobody there, nobody in the mirrors that faced each other across the hall but her own twin image striding forward: wide mouth, high cheekbones, bright greenish eyes, clipped blonde hair. Wind chimes tinkled as she entered her flat. Nobody in the living room with its thick rugs, its plump seats snug in the corners of the room, the shelves and table she had built from kits with incomprehensible instructions; nobody had stolen her video recorder. Nobody in the bathroom that smelled of Sea Jade talcum powder, nobody in her bedroom except her old toy monkey on the pillow. His behind was ragged and shiny now; he looked more like the real thing than he had when she was little. She drew the curtains to shut out the pulsing party light, then she lay beside him on the bed. Nobody had been in her flat. No time to wonder why she should have thought someone had. She still had to decide what to do about Martin Wallace.

The estate agent's black moustache looked as if it had been drawn with a marker pen. Susan didn't feel rude for staring fascinated at it, not when he had ignored her ever since she had sat down, even when she'd asked him where he lived – to give herself the chance to talk about home. Now he unclipped his pen and tapped the desk as if to wake Mummy up. 'Is that the kind of thing you had in mind, Mrs Verney?'

Mummy gave him back the handful of typed pages she had been sorting. 'Haven't you anything nearer?'

'Nearer to what, madam?'

'Here.'

'I gathered that, madam. I meant to say, what do you particularly want to be close to?'

Mummy frowned at him and gestured round herself. 'Here.'

'Forgive me if I'm being obtuse. You want to be close to this office, do you mean?'

'Yes, if you like.' Mummy's dark eyes stared at him from her pale face. She was frowning harder, which made her face seem even older. She always looked over forty when she was worried, though she'd turned thirty last month. She pulled her plaid skirt over her knees, the way she did when she was talking to a man she didn't like. 'Have you anything?'

Susan might have felt sorry for him – he didn't know that Mummy was often like this – except that she was too nervous. She noticed that he gave a tiny shrug as he sorted through another bunch of pages. 'This is over there,' he said, pointing past the couples who were looking in the window at the photographs of houses. 'But I must say that it isn't as attractive as the others you've been considering.'

Mummy read the page and handed it to Susan. 'It sounds quite homey, doesn't it?'

Living room with gas fire and fitted carpet, bedroom, kitchen, bathroom/WC. It didn't sound at all like home to Susan, and how could it to Mummy? London felt like getting lost, it was so big, and the flat sounded like having no home. 'I don't know,' she said miserably.

'You could have the bedroom. I don't mind sleeping on the couch.' Mummy stood up, looking eager. 'We'd like to see it. Can we go now?'

'By all means.' He called his partner out of the inner office once he had found the keys. 'I'm just taking this lady over the way.'

Lorries halted gasping at the lights, and he ushered

Mummy across. A West Indian wearing an ankle-length coat and headphones pushed past Susan as she hurried after Mummy, the November wind biting her ears. A cut-out lady stood in the window of a W. H. Smith's and invited them to book their summer holidays, but how could they if Mummy spent all she had on the lease? The estate agent was leading them away from the main road, and Susan felt the bookstore dwindling behind her. It was the last thing that seemed at all familiar or comforting. When she caught up with Mummy and held on to her hand, Mummy didn't even give hers a squeeze.

Perhaps Mummy was secretly daunted by the houses too. They were so big, many of them five storeys high; even the trees in their front gardens couldn't reach higher. Crescents curved away from the side road, more and more white terraces that looked as if they might never end. The porches were tall as double-decker buses, giants' porches. If she lived here she might as well be lost in a land of giants. The white façades beneath the cold swift sky made her think of tombs.

Perhaps there was still hope, for Mummy seemed uneasy. 'I didn't think it would be this far,' she murmured.

The estate agent took her elbow to lead her into a crescent opposite a weeping willow. 'Here we are,' he said, but the side road was out of sight before he turned along a garden path through a gateway without a gate.

The house looked just like all the others with four storeys to Susan, and she could imagine not being able to find it, wandering the maze of streets until it was too dark to see. Someone had been painting something on the patchy lawn, for there was an oblong yellow outline on the grass. Apart from that and the cars parked nose to tail alongside both pavements, there was no sign of life in the street. 'I suppose that isn't too far,' was all Mummy said.

When the estate agent unlocked the door, a smell of dust and cats came out of the house. Circles of black water marked the linoleum in the gloomy hall, the stair carpet turned into another carpet halfway up the first flight, under bare lightbulbs that hung on crooked cords. Mummy strode in. 'It's the second floor, isn't it?' she said.

All the stairs creaked. The first floor smelled of old boiled cabbage, the second floor stank of cats and what they did. Two doors faced each other across the narrow landing, in the muddy glow from the skylight above the top floor. Once he'd unlocked the left-hand door, the estate agent stood aside, and Susan wondered if he was ashamed to go in.

The large bare room had been made smaller by a partition wall in which a doorway was hung with plastic streamers. A cracked Donald Duck mug sat on the mantelpiece above the gas fire. Pieces of brown carpet had been stuck together to cover the floor; in places they were curling up. Apart from the partition, the walls were papered with a floral pattern. All the flowers were too big for the room.

Mummy pushed through the plastic streamers. 'Oh, look, Susan, there's a little hall.'

It was more like a box, with just enough room for two people abreast, and it was very dark. Another set of streamers hid the kitchen, a narrow room with a grimy cooker and a stained sink unit. Two shaky doors led off the hall, to a bathroom where the toilet was squeezed between the wall and the bath and to a windowless space that must be the bedroom, since the pale shape of a vanished double bed took up half the bare floor. 'It's snug, isn't it?' Mummy said, dragging at a frayed string until the bedroom light came on. 'We don't really need all that space at home for just the two of us. What do you think? Do you like it?'

How could she even ask? 'No!' Susan cried.

Mummy looked bewildered, then determined. 'Well, I'm sure you will once we settle in.'

Susan glimpsed how surprised the estate agent was in the moment before he controlled his face. She felt as she had the first time she'd realized that something was wrong with

Mummy, that all she could do was love her and pretend she hadn't noticed and hope that Mummy would get better. She'd thought that Mummy had, but now Mummy was saying, 'Can we go back so I can sign the lease?'

Wind twanged the aerials of parked cars and made the bare trees squeal. A wet newspaper with a staring face sailed across two gardens, caught on a gatepost, and struggled there until the face tore in half. As Mummy and the estate agent strode heads down into the wind, Susan lagged behind. She was trying to slow them down while she tried desperately to think of a way to stop Mummy from signing the lease.

Perhaps he wouldn't be able to find it when they got back to the office. Perhaps Mummy wouldn't have enough cash with her – there must be something to pay. If only there were someone with them to tell Mummy to think it over, sleep on it – and then she had it. 'Will Daddy have to sign too?'

Mummy glared at her as the estate agent hesitated. 'Forgive me,' he said, 'I understood you were divorced.'

'So I am.' She sounded proud of it, and furious with Susan. 'I can show you the papers next time I come down if you like.'

At least that would cause a delay, give Susan time to think of something else. She drew a shaky breath that felt like ice in her nostrils. Then the estate agent said, 'That won't be necessary. You do own your home.' He looked back at Susan. 'Don't worry, young lady, everything's in hand.'

He meant that she was only ten years old, she couldn't be expected to understand these things. All she had achieved was to make sure they would take no more notice of her. She sat in the office among posters of smiling couples with keys to their new homes and watched helplessly as the estate agent asked Mummy questions and filled in a form, passed it to her, waited while she read it, and handed her a pen. Mummy's signature was loud and scratchy. Susan felt as if she were already back in the cold empty flat, as if she hadn't left it and never would.

Mummy hired a taxi to Euston, to celebrate. Their carriage on the train was empty, which Mummy always liked. 'Lots of room,' she said, which made Susan think of the windowless space that would be her bedroom, not even half the size of hers at home. Soon the train was gathering speed toward Liverpool: the lit streets flew away, the nighttime fields flooded by like ink, until they turned grey with snow. 'You'll like it when we move,' Mummy said, 'I promise.'

'I don't want to.' She was near to tears. 'Why have we got to move?'

'Because I want a change. I don't want to be stuck in Wallasey for the rest of my life, and neither should you. London is where the opportunities are. Perhaps we won't have to stay there forever. But you'll like it, it'll be an adventure. You wait and see.'

A town glinted beyond the glowing fields and was doused by a sudden fall of snow that must have been a hill. The train was rocking Mummy to sleep. Now her eyes were closed and moving behind her eyelids, as if they were watching something Susan couldn't see. That was supposed to happen when you were dreaming – but Mummy said she never dreamed. The sight of her eyes shifting in sleep, out of control, made Susan even more anxious for her. She couldn't be dreaming, for dreaming was wrong. Susan didn't know why, but it was.

She remembered the time half her life ago, when Mummy had kept demanding over breakfast if she had been dreaming. 'I don't want you dreaming, that's all,' she'd said as if that was reassuring, but for years Susan had been scared to go to sleep in case a dream carried her away. She'd felt them waiting for her in the dark where her night-light couldn't reach. The sight of Mummy lolling as the empty carriage swayed made her feel nervous and alone. She jumped up and went to the buffet car.

The can of Coke took most of the money in her purse. She

sipped it and stared at Mummy and thought that at least Mummy was sleeping all night these days, she'd said so. Just a few nights ago she'd frightened Susan awake by shouting incomprehensibly in her sleep, and Susan hadn't dared to go in and wake her. Why, that had been the night before she'd said they were going to London, and Susan wished now that she'd wakened her, though she didn't know what use that would have been.

Susan looked out at the grey glow that was sailing by at a hundred miles an hour. It made her feel sleepy too. She gulped her Coke so that the fizzing in her nose would keep her awake, and then she was coughing and spluttering as too much went up her nose. She would have covered her mouth while she coughed, except that suddenly she hoped her coughing would wake Mummy up. Mummy didn't even stir. Susan coughed and wept and fumbled her handkerchief out of her sleeve. She drew a deep breath and gave in to a last fit of coughing while she kept her eyes shut and wished fiercely that when she opened them she would see Mummy awake. At last she looked, but Mummy hadn't moved. She looked out the window again but had to dab her eyes before she could make out the speeding fields. And the face looking in at her.

She cried out, more loudly when Mummy didn't wake. Her eyes were blurred and stinging, and rubbing them only made them worse. The face had been between Mummy's reflection and her own, but when she turned to look the carriage was deserted. The doors at either end were miles away. She made herself turn again to the window. The face was still there, if you could call it a face. Nothing was clear in the bright pink oval except the eyes.

'Mummy!' she cried, tugging at her hands. If Mummy woke, the face would go away, please let that be true! 'Mummy, Mummy,' she pleaded, tugging so desperately that she was afraid Mummy would topple off her seat. The edge of her vision was a rushing blur, but something pink was closer, hovering. Susan twisted Mummy's hands and saw her eyelids flutter, but then Mummy sank into sleep again. Now Susan thought of something that would wake her up, though she couldn't have said why it should. 'Mummy,' she cried, 'why really have we got to move?'

Mummy's eyes wavered open. If the look in them meant that she knew the answer, Susan no longer wanted to know. The next moment they closed again, and Susan dug her nails into the limp hands. 'Mummy!' she screamed.

Mummy jerked awake and snatched her hands away. 'Good God, child, what's wrong?'

'There was – ' But there was nothing. The carriage was deserted except for her and Mummy, and so was the reflection. There was nothing except a grey glow. 'Try and have a little doze if you're bored,' Mummy said, closing her eyes again. 'For heaven's sake let me get some sleep.'

The northern town was deep in snow. Molly dined in the hotel's cavernous dining room among deserted tables and echoes of the limping waiter, then went up to her room. Large slow melting flakes brushed the window. The television said it was Britain's worst November for more than ten years and predicted that December would be worse. She hoped Ben was getting soaked out there. Perhaps now he was regretting leaving her behind.

'The fewer of us who are at the interview the better,' he'd said, but she was sure he had been getting his own back for yesterday's argument about the rooms. She wished she could tell him that she was going to work with Martin, but she needed to understand her own feelings.

Ben ought to have had this room after all, for a bulge in the carpet under the bed yielded up two pornographic magazines, dated next year. She put them back and tried to read the paperback of *War and Peace* she'd bought that afternoon. The opening pages seemed familiar, yet she was certain she had never attempted the novel before. It felt like a kind of double vision and was so distracting that soon she gave up. She was sleepy, that was all.

She was in her pyjamas when someone knocked lightly at the door. 'Yes?' she called.

'It's me, Molly.'

It infuriated her that he assumed she would know who it was. 'What do you want?' she said, not moving.

'Open the door, will you?' His voice was as muted as his knock had been. 'We can't talk like this.'

The sooner she got rid of him, the sooner she could sleep. She bundled herself into her Finnish coat and opened the door a crack. 'What is it, Ben?'

'Can't you let me in for a moment? No need to have everyone listening.'

Just then Roy looked out of the room he was sharing with Ben. Roy was the sound man, small and rotund, given to showing her photographs of his prize budgies and his children. 'Were you knocking?'

'Not for you.' Ben glared at him until he closed the door. 'Well?'

'Whatever it is, please keep it short,' Molly said, and stepped back. 'I need my sleep.'

He eased the door shut like a thief but stayed by it, holding up his empty hands as if that showed his intentions were harmless. His blue jowls looked freshly shaved, his moustache and his sleek hair just combed. 'I wanted to thank you for getting us here in one piece. Thank you properly, I mean. You're a damn good driver – and it was a damn good interview.'

'All right, Ben, you've thanked me.' She was wary of

what 'properly' might mean. 'Good night now. I'm going to be driving tomorrow, remember.'

'No need for the cold shoulder, though, is there? You'd think I was your assistant instead of the other way round.' He reached back to support himself against the wall, and she saw how drunk he was. 'Damn it, that isn't what I wanted to say. You make me so nervous sometimes I don't know what I'm saying.'

'Tell me at breakfast. Now if you'll just – '

'Look, this is what I wanted to say.' He sidled against the door, perhaps for balance. 'You aren't really happy, are you? Tell the truth.'

'I'm as happy as I can be under all the circumstances.'

'Just what I thought. You can't work with someone as closely as I've worked with you without getting to know them.' He ran his fingers around the neck of his polo shirt, revealing a tangle of damp hair in the hollow of his throat. 'I know you better than you know yourself.'

'Yes, well, we won't talk about that just now. I think we both need sleep.'

'Still the cold shoulder?' His hands had let go of the shirt and were working in the air. 'You don't need to pretend with me. You're lonely and unhappy and so am I. There now, I'm baring myself to you.'

'Ben, for God's sake go and call your wife and talk to her. I'm sorry, I can't help you. Go and bare yourself somewhere else.'

'She once said that. The bitch said that to me. Not twice she didn't.' His face had turned red and ugly, and now she saw why he'd been dragging at his collar: an erection was struggling in his trousers. 'You aren't like that,' he said, and lurched at her. 'Not really, or you wouldn't have let me in.'

He was fumbling in his trousers to give his erection room. She sidestepped as he reached her, and he sprawled over the footboard onto the bed. It took him a while to flounder round and face her, one hand still down the front of his trousers. 'It's a joke to you, is it?' he spat.

'It's no joke, Ben. It's far too sad. Now please just leave.'

'Make me.' He heaved himself to his feet. 'You started this, you can finish it.'

'That's enough, Ben. The end.' Her legs had begun to shiver, but she gazed at him without moving. 'And I shouldn't try this with whoever you get to replace me.'

'Threats now, is it?' He let go of the footboard and toppled backward on the bed. 'Let me tell you, I could replace you just like that.'

'You'll have to. I've had an offer.'

She had never heard anyone grind their teeth before. 'Is this another of gay boy's bright ideas?'

'Don't you realize how much he regrets suggesting I should work with you?' She went to the door and held it open. 'Good night and good-bye.'

She couldn't tell how much of his anger was deliberate, but it was visibly exciting him. 'Time you learned a few manners,' he snarled as his excitement jerked him to his feet and drove him toward her. 'I'm not so difficult to get on with.'

She could tell he meant to slam the door and lock them in. If he had been an anonymous rapist, she would have kicked him in the crotch, but having worked with him was irksomely inhibiting. 'Don't be stupid, Ben,' she said icily. He turned away and at first she didn't know why he demanded, 'What it is now?'

'I thought I heard someone calling,' Roy said.

'I don't think it matters now. Ben was just leaving.'

Ben turned round at last, having concealed his erection as best he could. 'I'll see you in the morning,' he said with furious gentleness.

'Possibly.' She locked the door behind him and flopped on the bed, and found she was shaking with laughter. How could she have taken so long to make up her mind about

Martin Wallace? She was almost grateful to Ben for tonight, for helping her decide. She felt immensely relieved and sleep came as softly as the whisper of snow at the window.

She dreamed of an office where a young girl and a woman who looked prematurely grey were leafing through files of typed foolscap. 'I don't like any of them, Mummy. Let's go home,' the young girl said, and as far as Molly could tell, they did. She was awakened by knocking at the door.

She groped for her watch on the bedside table. It was early morning, too early for apologies or for Ben at all. 'Go away,' she croaked.

'It's Roy. Can I have a word?'

She stumbled to the door and blinked at him. 'I just wanted to say that if you don't feel up to it, I'll drive.' He glanced toward the room where Ben was sleeping and winked at her. 'It gets pretty cramped in the back of the van. You might be better off going by train.'

She wondered how much he knew: enough for her to kiss his cheek. 'Thanks, Roy,' she said, and he tiptoed away blushing.

As soon as she was dressed and had packed her overnight bag, she settled the bills at Reception and made for the station.

The rainy London streets were dazzling as tinfoil. Drying trees turned piebald in Hyde Park. Molly felt bouncy and free as she reached Ben's office. She blew a kiss to the calendar girl as she sat at her desk. 'You're welcome to him,' she called, and set about the budget for the northern expedition. The less that still had to be done when he returned, the better.

She had almost finished when her phone rang. 'Mr Gould would like to see you,' his secretary said.

She shared a lift to the ninth floor with the head of Religious Programmes, a balding, compassionate-looking man with a pop singer's smile. Jake Gould's secretary sent her straight into Gould's office, a spacious, sparsely fur-

41

nished room that smelled of sunlit leather chairs and tinny air conditioning. He sat forward as she came in, stretching his arms sphinxlike across the desk and displaying his gold cuff links. 'Miss Wolfe.'

'That's me.'

He frowned, though she hadn't meant to be facetious. 'I understand that all is not well between you and Ben Eccles.'

'It depends what you mean,' she said cautiously.

'I mean, as an example, a programme underbudgeted by several thousand pounds. I mean leaving him and his crew to find their own way back this morning.'

So Ben had beaten her to it, by phone, of course. 'The budget was based on information he gave me,' she said as calmly as she could. 'And I had good reasons for coming back by train. For one thing, I was too tired to drive.'

'Do sit down if you feel the need.' He gazed at her while she did. 'Are you finding the responsibilities of the job more than you bargained for?'

'Not the job, no. Just fending off Ben Eccles.'

'Of course one hears tales about him, mainly in the press.' His gaze grew keener. 'One wonders who might have been gossiping, and why.'

'I don't know why, but as to who, I should think it could be any woman who has ever been alone with him.'

Gould was unwrapping a cigar. The crackling of cellophane rasped Molly's nerves. At last he looked at her again, as he shook out the match. 'Well,' he said between puffs, 'no doubt you know that Martin Wallace wants you. Frankly, on your present showing I don't know what to tell him.'

'I won't work with Ben Eccles.'

He applied another match and blew out smoke that seemed for a while to be endless. 'How do you feel about working with Wallace?'

'I'd like to. Very much.'

'Much as you felt about working with Eccles, I suppose?

How can I be sure you won't let Wallace down?' Abruptly he ground the cigar into rags in the ashtray. 'Well, it's his responsibility. You're clearly no more use to Eccles. But I give you fair warning,' he said, standing up to terminate the interview, 'I shall be monitoring your performance.'

The next Molly knew she was at the lifts, knuckling the call button until her skin started to flake. At the fifth floor she shoved the doors aside and strode blindly down the corridor to Ben's office. She hoped he was there and by God she would tear him to pieces. But the office was empty now that Martin and Leon were emerging.

Her rage drained away. She felt weightless as a dream of flying, and yet on the edge of something; one step and she might fall, not fly, fall and never wake. 'Gould says we can work together,' she said.

'That's great, Molly. I'm really pleased. Leon's been telling me how good you are when you're given the chance.'

'Pubs are open. I propose a toast,' Leon said, and Molly thought that a drink might be just what was needed to get rid of this vague apprehension that wouldn't quite go away. Feelings like that were no use to her, they never had been. If she had dreamed of Martin, it must have been years ago.

6

It took all day to film the Heathrow introduction, since Martin seemed to think on film. After the last shot of the morning – of Martin descending by escalator into the international crowd – he said, 'That's enough of me, too much, probably. Let's eat.'

He and the crew ended up in the airport snack bar.

Planes turned ponderously beyond the double glazing and rose silent as clouds into the sky. 'Maybe I shouldn't appear in the film at all,' Martin said.

Terry Mace sat forward and his motorcycle jacket creaked. He was assistant to the cameraman. 'What did you want to put yourself in for, anyway?' he said.

'Well, I'm in there whether or not you see me. I figured appearing in it would be taking responsibility for it, saying it's my view of things. Maybe I'm too visible already.'

'What, because you were in *Private Eye*? Don't let those buggers get to you. They're just out to get MTV because a couple of the backers sued them years ago.'

'I guess they let me off relatively lightly.' But he sounded as if he wished he knew what he'd done to deserve their attack. ('News from Empty Vee: Leon "Call me Lane, love," Bardin, winner of the Worst Programme Title By A Gay Producer Award, is importing Martin "Instant Controversy" Wallace, a film director with an international reputation for bothering needy old ladies and policemen doing their duty. What is the relationship between Lane Bardin and Marty the Menace? We think we should be told . . .') 'Back home we have the *National Enquirer*,' Martin said.

'Just don't let that shit put you off making the kind of film you make.' Terry brushed his long hair out of his eyes and stared defiantly at a woman who had turned to frown at him.

'Well, Terry, maybe you're surer than I am what kind of film that is.'

'Right, maybe I am. I think your best film was *The Unamericans*, fantastically powerful. You ought to show up our police the way you did yours. About fucking time someone did.'

Martin was smiling at his vehemence. 'Aren't your police pretty reasonable overall?'

'What? Tell Lenny Bennett's mother that after the pigs got him in a cell and killed him.'

Molly spoke for the first time. 'Well, that's one version,' she said.

'Right, there's the official version and the truth. No prize for guessing which one MTV broadcast. He died just up the road from them and they didn't even go to investigate.' She had been trying to calm Terry down but had only infuriated him. 'What do you think the pigs were going to do to a black militant who'd been criticizing them, after they got him in by planting explosives on him? Bake him a cake? I've seen the inside of one of those fucking cells. They could have worked on him all night, nobody would have heard him scream.'

The cameraman, Andy Butterworth, spoke low. 'Watch your language, lad, or they'll have you back inside.'

'I bet they'd love to. Didn't even charge me in the end, just wanted to shut me up.'

Mace had been kept overnight in a cell for chanting slogans in front of the police station and buttonholing everyone who passed. 'You should investigate them,' he told Martin. 'You've got the power to make people look.'

'If you feel so strongly about it,' Wallace suggested, 'maybe you should tell people yourself.'

'Think I haven't been? Do I look as if I sit on my arse doing nothing?' He pointed to the badges on his jacket: Troops Out Of Northern Ireland, Free Iran. 'I've been playing a policeman in a street play about Lenny Bennett. We'd do it in front of the station if there was room. Make the bastards think Lenny had come back to haunt them.' He seemed about to say something but changed his mind. 'You've got the power to take it into people's homes,' he said fiercely. 'Things won't change unless they know.'

Martin had finished his lunch and looked restless. 'Come on, lad,' Andy said. 'Finish your milk and let's get going. Time enough to tell folk how to make films when you've made a few yourself.'

After they had filmed a few impressions of Heathrow,

Martin wandered for an hour or so before saying abruptly, 'That's it for today.' He was silent on the drive back. As Molly steered the van into Connaught Street for the car park under MTV she thought he seemed to be gazing at something inside himself.

His office was on the fourth floor, down the corridor from Leon's. Its personality was mostly Molly's: a calendar of English landscapes, an old percolator she had managed to fix, the binoculars she took whenever she drove into the countryside. He leafed through the reviews of *The Spin* she had brought him to read, but he was obviously ill at ease. He kept rumpling his already untidy hair, pinching the skin between his thick eyebrows.

'I'm sorry about today,' she said.

His deep blue eyes widened. 'Why should you be sorry?'

'I should be making sure you aren't put off your work.'

'Christ, I can fight my own battles.' That brought him back to himself. 'I didn't mean that. You've been a tremendous help. I only meant I should be able to handle Terry. He reminds me of the Baptists. The university was overrun with them.'

'Oh?'

'Sure. Anyway, you don't want to hear about my student days.'

'I don't mind, if you feel like talking.'

'Snapping me out of it comes with the job?'

'You could say that.'

'Well, it's fine with me,' he said, smiling suddenly. 'How about dinner? Do you like Indian food? I haven't had any since the last time I was here.'

'I'll take you to the Standard.' She was startled by how pleased she felt that he had asked her out. 'We can walk there,' she said.

The night was growing colder. A few stars glittered like ice above the lamps on Bayswater Road. 'So tell me about your student days,' Molly said as they crossed a side street.

He took her arm. 'My baptism of fire. All the time I was at college the Baptists were trying to get evolution taken off the syllabus. Evilution, they called it. I guess it's pretty funny,' he admitted as she laughed, 'but they could get to you if you weren't careful. For instance, they'd say God created all the fossils to test everyone's faith in the Bible. You'd find yourself arguing back that maybe the world was created just a moment ago, our memories and all, because how can anyone prove different? There's a born-again millionaire in Texas who's offering fifty thousand dollars to anyone who can prove evolution to him. A few years around that kind of thinking can loosen your grip on reality, believe me.'

In the Standard Molly ordered for both of them. 'I was just thinking,' Martin said as the waiter marched away, 'the last time I met any of the Baptists was after I'd made *The Unamericans*. This girl came up to me on the street in Chapel Hill. Right there in front of some people she said I should have dedicated it to Satan instead of to Larry.' He was staring at the table. 'You asked me once about Larry.'

'I didn't know you then.'

'So ask me now.'

Something had made him need to talk. She squeezed his hand. 'Tell me whatever you like.'

He was silent for a while. 'I really think he was jealous of me,' he said at last, uncomfortably. 'He was two years older, you see, and I think he'd had time to get used to being king of the hill. I don't mean he ever took it out on me. Maybe it would have helped if he had. No, he looked after me all the time. Really,' he said, taking a deep breath, 'all he wanted was to make our father proud of him.'

He paused while the waiter brought a bottle of wine and struggled with the cork. 'You have to understand my father,' he said. 'Maybe you know there are Southerners who are still fighting the Civil War. Sabres on the wall and all that. Really what they're doing is preserving the old

47

ways. You look around and see why they might want to. There aren't many gentlemen left – you couldn't call me one.'

'Who couldn't? I would.'

'You wouldn't if you were a Southern lady.' He smiled wryly and touched her face, a gesture that seemed so intimate she felt dizzy. 'What am I saying? I don't mean you aren't a lady, not at all. But our Southern ladies wouldn't think much of a guy who got them into a pub brawl.' He put his fingers on her lips when she made to protest. 'Want to hear a bad joke? Your people wanted me to call my series "A Yank in England." That would really have improved my father's opinion of me.'

Before she knew what to do about the glimpse of his pain, he said quickly, 'The trouble was he needed us to be like him. He taught Southern history at the University of North Carolina, and so he wanted us at least to go to college and know more than him about something. Well, Larry knew more about cars than anyone else I know. He was fixing them before he was old enough to drive them, he was planning to open his own repair shop just before he went to Vietnam, but none of that was any good to my father. And neither was I.'

He stared into the distance while the waiter unloaded a trolleyful of food. 'He thought I was. I mean, I read all the books in the house and went to college. Then friends of mine started refusing to go to Vietnam and I went with them on the peace marches. The Baptists went round wearing stars and stripes in their lapels and saying we should be proud to fight God's war against communism. I filmed the police at a march and they smashed my camera. Some of that footage is in my film.'

His eyes clouded over, and he gave a short sour laugh. 'Sometimes I wonder if that's what made me committed – getting my camera smashed, not my friends dying in Vietnam at all.'

'I expect it was both.'

'Maybe. Anyway, my father heard about the marches and ordered me home, and we had the argument that must have been happening all over America just then, me saying I might die for my country but wouldn't kill for it, him saying he'd go himself if he was younger, I was the first coward in the family, he was glad his father was dead and couldn't see how I'd grown up, other stuff you don't want to hear. It wasn't as though I'd even got my papers. I really think he would have backed off if I'd said I might think of enlisting. So eventually we finished yelling at each other and I started upstairs to my room, and Larry was telling my father he'd talk to me when my father said, "Whatever gave you the idea he'd listen to a goddamned dumb mechanic when he won't even listen to me?" That was the last time they ever spoke to each other. The next day Larry volunteered.'

Belatedly he realized he was eating. 'This is very good,' he said, but Molly doubted he was tasting it; she was beyond tasting much herself. 'He wrote to me and my mother a couple of times,' Martin went on. 'He was never much good at writing – used to say that was one thing his hands weren't good for. He said he was glad he'd gone instead of me, he could look after things out there while I got on with learning, there were enough of us dying. He wanted me to promise my mother I wouldn't go, and her to make me promise. A rocket killed him in the jungle near some place I never could pronounce.'

He dabbed at his mouth with his napkin, and then at his eyes. 'I was home for the funeral when my draft card came. As soon as the funeral was over, I skipped to Canada and spent two years making my film.' He dug his fork into a piece of meat so hard that the tines screeched on the plate. 'As if making it could wipe out what I'd done.'

'I don't see why you should feel guilty.'

'Don't you? I must have expressed myself badly, then.'

Or had he left something out? He was withdrawing behind his smile. 'This is wonderful,' he said. 'Let's eat.'

She felt as if she'd missed a point somewhere, but he encouraged her to talk about herself, and she told him about her childhood near Plymouth, about the smugglers' coves and the inns with secret passages; Winston the bulldog who sat in the middle of the village street and would move just enough for a car to pass; about the summer day she'd lain on Dartmoor and watched the clouds until she had felt the world turning and the night she'd seen sailing ships in the moonlight (but that must have been a dream). And then she was on the edge of telling him about her dreams, but she held back. 'Were your parents pleased you dedicated this last film to them?' she said.

'My mother was. My father, I guess not, if she even told him. I don't hear from him. I know from her he's pretty ill by now, his heart and too much booze. Something else I can take the credit for.'

'You shouldn't be so hard on yourself,' Molly said, but she felt she wasn't reaching his pain. She wished she could confide more of herself to him, reach him that way, but all she could think of to share were her dreams.

After the meal he walked her home. Queensway was crowded as a bazaar, Bayswater Road was almost deserted except for a turbaned cyclist and a few cars. A stone eagle on a pedestal guarded a private square, a crow like a tatter of the night flew into the park. As they turned the corner by the estate agent's, she made up her mind not to invite him in for coffee; she would be too conscious of not being able to tell him about the dreams she used to have. She had forgotten how much it meant to her.

'Thanks a lot, Molly,' he said when they reached her gate. 'I had a fine time. You're good company. I'm lucky to know you.' He smiled and turned away quickly, up the hill toward Kensington and his flat, which MTV was paying for. She bolted the gate behind her, feeling oddly disappointed, and was at her door when suddenly she wanted to call him back. Instead she strode furiously in to discover who was in her flat.

She snatched a letter from the doormat and stalked along the hall, shoving doors open and switching on lights. She'd find them this time, whoever they were, however they had got in. Wind chimes whispered phrases, her monkey gazed from the bed, the serving hatch gaped. Hadn't she closed it last night? Apparently not, since nobody was in her flat. The secretaries from the second floor must be making her paranoid with their incessant borrowing – why, just the other day they'd banged on her door to borrow her phone directory, they'd rung the doorbell and thumped on the windows in case she couldn't hear – but if that were the explanation, she wished it would start to be reassuring, for her nervousness reminded her too much of the time she hadn't been able to sleep for fear of dreaming. She slammed the serving hatch and sat down to read her letter, and then she saw the name on the return address. As she stared at it, her heart pounding, the room seemed to darken with a panic that she hadn't experienced for years.

7

By the time Geoffrey left the auction, it was fifteen minutes later than when he had meant to start back. If anyone but Mr Pelham had stopped him on his way to the rostrum, he would have made his excuses, but Mr Pelham had the worst stammer Geoffrey had ever heard. It had taken him five minutes to tell Geoffrey that one of his c-customers had a s-s-s . . . a s-s-s . . . 'A stamp collection,' Geoffrey had suggested, since it had to be, but even then it had taken them five minutes to establish that the lady lived in Pett

Bottom near Canterbury and wanted Geoffrey to price it next time he was in the area. It was all right, Geoffrey had minutes to spare, except that then he had to wait by the rostrum. By the time he was able to settle up for the collection he had bid for, his hands were sweating. Most of all he hoped Joyce wouldn't start to worry about him.

He swerved the Mini out of the car park in front of the mansion and drove through Windsor to the motorway. Boys in tailcoats trooped across the bridge to Eton, the college red as a robin beneath the clear blue November sky, no threat of sleet for days. A helicopter rose from the grounds of Windsor Castle, and stags raised heads like shrubs to watch.

On the motorway he made himself put his foot down, gradually as if he mightn't notice. As the speedometer crept toward seventy, the Mini began to vibrate. He didn't like driving so fast, but Joyce must need his support, otherwise she wouldn't have asked him to be there. Today was crucial to her, that was why. She was all right now. He mustn't let himself be troubled by how like eleven years ago this was.

He caught sight of himself in the mirror, his long almost rectangular face. 'I love your wrinkly eyes,' Joyce had said in the days when they'd said such things, but the wrinkles were mostly of worry by now. It was no use, he couldn't put the drive to Oxford out of his mind, the glare of his headlights on the interminable roads, his anxiety for Joyce. She had looked almost herself when the young man in the lab coat had taken Geoffrey to her, sitting with the others who'd looked lost and shaken and blank-faced with tranquillizers, something she would never let herself be fed. They had been well on their way home before she'd started glancing at the back seat as if she were afraid someone was behind her, and actually home when she'd demanded, 'Where are we? Where is this?' She was better now, that was all that counted, and he tried to adjust the mirror so that he wouldn't see his anxious eyes.

The motorway gave out at Chiswick. Traffic lights began to hold him up. Long before he reached the day centre, the streets were narrow and dilapidated, with pedestrians and parked cars to make them narrower. In the distance above the precarious chimneys he could see home, the village on the hill. He parked in a side street and hurried back, past a video library displaying posters for *Kindergarten Rapist* and *They Eat Your Eyes*, to the day centre.

Joyce wasn't there. Her presence was, in the bright yellow walls, the paintings of dogs and cats and children, the check tablecloths on the long tables, the semicircle of easy chairs around the electric fire set into the far wall. But the walls were visibly damp now, for rain seeped in from the adjoining shops, which were boarded up and beginning to lose their windows. An old woman warming the stump of one leg by the fire picked up her crutch suspiciously as Geoffrey came in, an old man stumbled away from a table toward him. 'Are you the police? Thank God you've come. I want you to tell the people to get out of my flat. They keep turning all the switches upside down. There are dozens of them. I don't know how they dare. They won't even let me get into bed.'

Fat, freckled Sally the ex-nurse intervened. 'You threw them all out, Tom, don't you remember? You told us they were so offended they said they would never come back.' She led him away as Geoffrey turned to Mark, Joyce's other helper, a young poet who'd told Joyce he needed to do social work in order to grow. 'Mrs Churchill is at the public enquiry,' he said. 'She hasn't been gone long.'

The enquiry was being held in a school hall up the road. Geoffrey wished he'd gone straight there. He hadn't been to the day centre for months; the old people always made him scared of ending up like that himself. Joyce almost had, eleven years ago. If the two of them couldn't age with dignity, he would rather that they didn't age at all.

The school yard was crowded, though it was half-term.

Pickets marched back and forth, waving placards – 'SAVE OUR SHOPS,' 'THE PLANNERS ARE THE VANDALS' – and chanting slogans. 'Out! Out! Out!' was all that Geoffrey could distinguish. Shouts and an interrupted voice that kept beginning the same phrase led him past the empty class-rooms, in one of which an orphaned exclamation mark stood on a blackboard, to the assembly hall.

The hall was full of people, many of whom were shouting at the three men on the stage. 'The purpose of this meeting,' the man on the left began yet again. Geoffrey peered through the chalky air and saw Joyce at the end of a row of four of her old folk, her square face and bright grey eyes intent on the stage. She snatched off her spectacles as he came up. 'We haven't had a chance to speak yet,' she whispered. 'Just you wait.'

She was wearing her blue suit with slacks, she smelled of the cool sweet perfume she always used, but her face was drawn, the wave in her grey hair looked nothing like permanent now. Perhaps she was wondering if she had been right to bring the old folk: one old lady was rearranging the contents of her handbag, all wrapped in cellophane; one old man was nodding off. He started awake as the right-hand man on the stage shouted 'Order!', cutting off his colleague in the middle of his phrase. 'May we please take your points one at a time.'

Joyce stood up so quickly that Geoffrey, squatting beside her, almost lost his balance. 'I run a day care centre for elderly people,' she said, jamming her spectacles back on her nose and folding her arms. 'Some of them have nowhere else to go. Some of them are afraid to be at home by themselves. I don't think you can realize that you're proposing to close down the only place these people have to meet their friends, or do you just not care?' Her voice was rising, and Geoffrey wished he could take her hand, to calm himself as much as her. 'We've had no offer whatsoever of alternative accommodation,' she said.

'I believe many of the local churches have provisions for the elderly,' the left-hand man said, and the chairman nodded. 'Thank you for putting your point, Mrs Churchill.'

'Not so fast. It's time you heard from the people whose lives you'll be damaging.' Joyce was beckoning the old lady with the handbag to stand up. 'That's it, Mrs Madden. You tell them.'

Mrs Madden jumped up when she heard her name, and dropped her handbag. Pension book and hairbrush and purse spilled over the floorboards, cellophane rustling. 'Oh, my things,' she cried, and fell to her knees. Joyce's fingers began to clutch at the air as if she had been robbed, and Geoffrey was reaching for her hand when the old man beside Mrs Madden sprang to his feet. 'I'll tell them.'

For a while it seemed he would only shake his finger at the stage. 'You listen, you,' he shouted as the chairman made to acknowledge someone else. 'Mrs Churchill looks after us Methuselahs when the rest of you would like to have us put to sleep. You give her somewhere and be quick about it, she's doing a job you ought to be doing. I'm one of the lucky ones, I've a home to go to, and do you know where? Fifteen floors up a tower block, thirty flights of stairs that stink of piss and none of the lifts ever working. They want to knock it down now and about time too, but where are they going to put me?'

'That's fine, Arthur. Sit down now,' Joyce hissed, but he wasn't listening. 'Going to leave me in there,' he shouted, 'while they knock it down, are they?'

The old lady next to him joined in. 'That's right, they don't care a toss about us. They let the muggers and the rapists roam the streets and tell them not to be such naughty boys. You aren't even safe in your own bed any more. I *beg* your pardon, Mrs Churchill, I won't be quiet, you brought me here to talk.' Half a dozen people were shouting now, and the one who shouted loudest won: a barrel of a man who turned out to own the video library. Joyce sank into her seat as he accused the planners of letting the area run down until half the property was beyond repair, so that they could buy it cheap. 'You did well,' Geoffrey murmured, gripping her hand, dismayed to find it so cold and shaky. 'You made your point. I'm sure it will be in the papers.'

She let go of his hand and helped Mrs Madden retrieve her things, and was placating the old people when the meeting came to an abrupt end. 'Look after them for me while I talk to the reporters,' she said, and was gone before Geoffrey could speak. He sat uncomfortably next to Mrs Madden and said, 'We'll just wait for Joyce,' and hoped that would be all that was required of him. He marvelled yet again that Joyce had taken on this work and wondered yet again if she had taken on too much. Thank the Lord, she was coming back.

He didn't feel they were on the way home until the car had climbed the hill above the shabby roofs. A bridge carried Hornsey Lane a hundred feet above the ravine of Archway Road, and then they were on the summit, in the High Street of Highgate, where the wind blew the rumbling of London away. There was the wine bar that had once been Geoffrey's shop, near the steep dark slope of Swain's Lane that led to the cemetery, the forest prying open the graves. He turned the car past Castle Yard, where cottages brandished fenders at the traffic, and parked in front of their Georgian house.

He followed her up the path between the neat flower beds. She hurried into the house so hastily that she trod on a letter without noticing and almost tripped over the vacuum cleaner. He had to struggle with the albums he'd bought outside Windsor as he closed the door, and so he had time to read the return address on the envelope. He snatched it from the mat and stuffed it into his pocket just as she emerged from the kitchen. Thank God, she must think the letter was for him. 'What was wrong?' he said.

'I thought I heard the kettle boiling.' She grimaced at her

silliness. 'I don't know what I could have been dreaming of.'

'It isn't worth worrying about.'

'I didn't say it was.' She frowned at the vacuum cleaner and wheeled it back to the hall cupboard. 'Don't get too engrossed,' she said as he carried the albums upstairs. 'I've put the stew on. Half an hour.'

His office was next to the guest room. Windows were lighting up on Muswell Hill like sparks reviving a fire; the gutted shell of Alexandra Palace was a dark blotch. He laid the albums on his baize-topped desk and took out the letter. It was unthinkable that he should open a letter addressed to her. He locked it away in the safe and tried not to wonder what it said.

He leafed through the first of the albums and wished that he hadn't made so much of her hearing the kettle. She never left the vacuum cleaner out, but she must be worrying about the day centre, that was all. He stared at the dark wallpaper and the Gibbons catalogues that always made him feel cosy, at home, and wondered what she was doing downstairs. He was glad when she called him to dinner.

Her mother's Wedgwood gleamed through the glass of the dresser in the dining room. She seemed happier now, ladling out the stew while he poured chilled apple juice from a jug. 'We'll find somewhere,' she said. 'They can't just close us down without giving us somewhere else.'

'I'm sure you won't let them.'

'They'd better believe it,' she said with a fierce grin that looked more like her. 'And if we should be closed down before they give us somewhere, I'll just have to bring my old folk round here.'

He almost choked on a piece of potato. 'I hope that won't be necessary,' he said as soon as he could.

'I only said *if*. They wouldn't be in your way, they'd stay downstairs. I suppose you could put up with them using the toilet when they had to. I should think you'd want to help.'

'You know damn well I'll help you if I can.' Why, he'd sold his shop in order to buy her the lease on the disused butcher's because she'd once told him that she'd dreamed of looking after the old folk down the hill, it was a scandal that nobody did. He would have done anything to bring her back to herself, he would have given her a child if he had been able. 'If you have to bring them here,' he said, 'I won't stand in your way.'

She was suddenly laughing. 'You are a sport, there's not another like you, but oh, I wish you could see your face! It isn't doomsday yet, not quite. I'll be at the planning offices first thing in the morning and I won't leave until I get some sense out of them. If they're going to be difficult, they'll find I can be difficult too.'

After dinner they sat reading. No doubt the old folk would like the paintings of cats and curly-haired infants, the china animals next to the photograph of her parents as a young couple, but how could they all fit into the living room? It wasn't half the size of the day centre. That troubled him as he tried to read *Philatelist's Weekly*, her not thinking of it did too, and so did her reading one Agatha Christie while another lay next to her chair. Soon she began to nod. 'I'm going up,' she said the third time her head jerked.

'I'll be up shortly.' He waited so as not to overhear her on the toilet, then he strolled through the house, trying the windows and outer doors. She wasn't quite asleep when he eased himself into bed. 'We'll have somewhere by next year,' she said, her words slurring. 'Sally and Mark can look after things for a couple of weeks. How would you like to drive across America? Love to. Keep us young. You're only as young as you feel,' she mumbled, and was asleep.

He lay and stared at the bar of dimness opposite the gap between the curtains. The sky was murmuring, an aeroplane was dwindling among the stars. Surely she would find somewhere before she grew frustrated; he didn't dare think what that might do to her now. He was remembering the day she had told him about her dreams, not long after they were married: remembered sitting on a bench outside a pub on Jersey, watching sheep flock toward the coast of the tiny island, the white wall at his back so hot that he'd had to sit on the edge of the bench, and suddenly Joyce had said, 'What would you do if you knew that ship out there was going to sink?' He'd had no proper answer to that, then or now – certainly not once she'd made him realize how frustrating it must be to know that there would be a fire, a train wreck, a motorway pileup, and never to be able to convince the right people in time. Almost always she didn't even know who they might be, and when she did they wouldn't listen. That frustration had led her to Oxford, and now he said a silent prayer that she would never dream again.

He was turning uneasily in bed, reliving that desperate time and wishing that he could sleep. All their doctor had been able to give her were tranquillizers and a lecture about getting mixed up with that sort of thing. He'd advised Geoffrey to sue the Foundation for Applied Psychological Research, but that would have meant reminding her, when all Geoffrey had wanted was for her to come back to herself. It had been days before they'd had a conversation that pretended she was mending, weeks before she had gone out shopping, but suddenly one morning she had pushed the breakfast tray back at him. 'Look at you taking care of the old crock, I should be the one who's taking care of someone.' And she had been Joyce again, not a promise or a hope; she had even survived the ordeal of going back to nursing only to find that they no longer trusted her. She was whole now, that was what mattered, and he wouldn't let anyone touch her, especially not Stuart Hay, whose letter was locked in the safe. No, Joyce must never see that. His resolve made him feel that everything was under control. He would sleep as soon as whoever was padding along the street went away.

A draught stirred the curtains, and he felt as if the room

were shifting. He turned on his side, slipping an arm around Joyce's waist. He dragged the blanket over his ear just as he heard a stair creak.

He was out of bed so quickly that the blanket tugged at Joyce. 'What's wrong?' she mumbled. 'Where are you?'

'Won't be long. Go back to sleep.' The possibility that she might hear almost caused him to panic. The sounds were going downstairs; they sounded less like footsteps than lumps of fat plopping on the carpet. Two stairs creaked one after another. Joyce turned back on her side, and he tiptoed onto the landing, closed the door, switched on the light above the stairs.

Now the sounds were in the street. He must have been half-asleep to believe that they had been anywhere else, especially since none of the stairs creaked as he crept down. They never creaked. He unchained the front door and slid back the bolt.

The street was deserted. All the Georgian houses were dark. A sliver of moon was hooked in the glass of some of the upper windows. The sounds were vanishing beyond the bend that led downhill, and for a moment he saw a figure that made him think of a baby that was just learning to walk. If it looked like a baby at that distance, it must still be larger than he was, which was nonsense, especially since he'd thought it was naked – naked and fat and doughy white. Of course there had been nothing at all.

He bolted and chained the door, and stopped halfway upstairs to check that he had. The public enquiry and the letter from Oxford must have made him nervous. He slipped into bed again and squeezed Joyce's waist. Hay and his kind were what she must be protected from, not half-awake nonsense. In a few minutes he felt calm, and was asleep.

He woke before Joyce did. He bathed and shaved and dressed, then he brought her a cup of tea. He had to say 'Joyce' several times before she woke and peered at the alarm clock that had failed to wake either of them. 'Why did you let me sleep? I told you I wanted to be out first thing.'

'Well, I thought – ' He didn't want to imply that he needed to be concerned for her. At last he said, 'I overslept.'

'Oh, never mind.' She gulped a scalding mouthful as if that would wake her up. 'You can be getting the paper while I make breakfast. Let's see what they have to say about us.'

A van was dumping a bundle of papers outside the newsagent's on the High Street. Geoffrey waited while the newsagent found a razor blade and cut the string around the newspapers. He read the morning edition as he walked home: nothing on the front page, but even Joyce couldn't have expected that; nothing on the first six, seven, eight pages . . . He was beginning to crumple the pages as he turned them, and one tore. He almost missed the item, it was so insignificant. 'Uproar at meeting' said the tiny headline on page ten. There was no mention of any of the points Joyce had made.

He wished he could throw it away, but that would never do. Nevertheless he stood for a while on the garden path listening to the mutter of London down the hill before he took her the paper. Breakfast was in the oven, and she was watching the midmorning news on MTV. 'Nothing,' she said, gesturing at the television, and barely glanced at the report when he handed it over. 'That's all they think of us, is it? They'll sit up and take notice before I've finished. I have to get going.' But he could tell that she was battling frustration, for all her refusal to be disappointed. She switched off the television. 'You should just see the stuff they broadcast as if it's important news. It isn't how important you are that matters, it's who you know. If only I knew someone there,' she said.

61

8

The flat was crowded before the men brought the table upstairs. There was hardly space between the piles of cartons for them to carry Susan's bed to her room. She retreated to the kitchen and peered over the frosted glass of the nailed-down sash. Chimneys taller than she was stood against the empty sky, a woman shook a duster from a window and stared down at her. She ran to open the bathroom door as the removal men struggled to manoeuvre the bed. When they managed at last to sidle it into her room, the doorway shook.

'These are your sheets,' Mummy said, dragging a carton away from the window. 'You can be making your bed if you like.' She hurried after the removal men – she had been following them up and down the stairs, to make sure they didn't damage anything – and Susan was alone in her new home.

It didn't feel like home. Mummy's photographs were standing on the mantelpiece above the gas fire, her herb chart and the calendar with Susan's painting of the Mersey from the window of their old flat were hanging in the kitchen. But the calendar made Susan want to cry, and the photographs – Susan in her first school uniform, Mummy before she was married, with long black hair that Susan wished she had herself instead of her babyish auburn waves – only reminded her of the photograph Mummy had torn up. The flowers and scraps of flowers on the walls dwarfed her, a draught from the landing made the plastic streamers rattle, and then she knew what the flat felt like – the removal van, not meant for living in at all.

She unpacked the folded sheets one by one and stacked

them by her bed. The smells of clean linen and new carpet cheered her up, almost made her forget where she was. Mummy had had the green carpet fitted throughout the flat, but that made it seem unreal, the same feeling underfoot whichever room you were in, even in the lightless shaky hall. Mummy had been in London all half-term, getting the flat ready and making sure of Susan's place at school and, Susan presumed, finding out where her new job was, while Susan had stayed at Arabella's house on Seaview Road. She'd used to tease Arabella because her house didn't have a view of the sea at all or even of the Mersey, but she wished she had Arabella's view now instead of the view from the main room of the tall, cold, white houses, the porches whose pillars looked like sticks of chalk.

She was making her bed when she heard the men leave. The outer door closed, and Mummy came to find her. 'That's a good girl. I'll see if I can find your other things for you to put away.'

Susan's little bookcase had to stand on her dressing table, in front of the mirror. She oughtn't to complain, Mummy didn't even have a proper bed now, only a bed-settee. She unpacked her annuals and C. S. Lewises and Alan Garners and arranged them in the bookcase, and saw herself staring out through the gap before the last few books fell into place. It made her think of the face she had seen at the window of the train. It must have been a daydream, and she was glad she didn't usually have them; Mummy had warned her against them years ago. She propped her dolls against the wall at the foot of the bed – Rapunzel with her golden hair and Repulsive the witch with her long, green nose and chin – and then closed the door and pulled the frayed string and watched the patterns of light that came rushing into her eyes, filling her vision and fading away to the edges to make room for the next wave, until she realized fully how dark it was; she had never been in a place with no windows before. She groped for the wobbly door-handle and fled into the main room.

'You can be taking the empty boxes down,' Mummy said. 'The bins are at the back.' Susan jumped on the cartons to flatten them and carried them down through the smells of dust and cats, the light like stagnant water beneath the unlit bulbs. Eventually the rusty bolt of the door beyond the stairs scraped out of its socket and let her into the yard.

The high walls were spiky with glass. A few weeds poked out from beneath a collapsed outhouse and two mattresses, a sandwich full of springs. 'Flat 4' was painted on a dustbin near the gate, but it didn't seem worth using in the midst of all that mess. She was dumping the cartons on top of the mattresses when a voice said, 'Oh dear no.'

It was an old man in a beret at the kitchen window under theirs. 'Sorry,' she said, blushing, and stuffed the cartons into the bin, but before she could retreat upstairs he'd scurried out to her. 'Tidy up, giddy up,' he gabbled. 'Gee up, get your lid off, let's see what you're made of.'

He was rummaging in her and Mummy's bin when a tiny woman with bright red hair and a face like crumpled paper appeared in his window. 'Out of it before I call the police,' she shrilled at Susan. 'And stay away from him if you know what's good for you.'

'I live here,' Susan had to say.

'Do you now. Well, God help you and whoever brought you.'

The old man who might be her father or her husband was at his own bin now, digging out an empty bottle and stuffing it with rubbish – banana skins, a tangle of string and sealing wax. 'Watch and learn,' he cried, but Susan fled upstairs to find Mummy staring at the cartons as if she couldn't quite recall what she had sold to make room. 'Just keep an eye on the flat while I make sure there's nothing left in the van.'

'Let me come with you,' Susan pleaded.

'Why?'

'I don't want to be on my own. Not just yet,' she said, hoping against all her instincts that it would be never, not here.

'Susan, I hope you aren't going to start that kind of silly nonsense. You're a sensible girl, you don't imagine things, and if you do you can just get rid of those books. You know the ones I mean. And the dolls. I mean it, Susan. You start imagining things and I'll throw them out myself.'

Susan bit her lip. 'I want to see if they've left anything of mine in the van.'

Mummy must know she was lying, but she softened. 'All right, I know, it must all be a bit sudden, moving when we've never moved before. Come on then, we'll both go down. I expect we're being overcautious, but it never hurts to check.'

The street was deserted. The houses looked glossy and brittle under the colourless sky. Susan lingered by the flaky gateposts, for the removal van reminded her how empty it had made her old home. Her footsteps had echoed as she'd walked through the flat to say good-bye, and she'd hardly been able to see for tears. She had almost forgotten to take the plaque that said 'Susan's Room' off her bedroom door, and she didn't think she would ever put it up. 'Hello, Eve,' said Mummy from the back of the removal van. 'I wondered when we'd see you.'

Susan's heart seemed to stall and start again. Was this part of what was wrong with Mummy, was it getting worse? The street shivered around her as if its glassy surface were cracking. But when she went to Mummy there was someone after all: a girl of about Susan's age was sitting on the step at the back of the empty van, a girl with hair almost as long as Rapunzel's and as black as Mummy's in the photograph. 'Susan, this is Eve who lives near us,' Mummy said. 'I told you about Susan, Eve, my little girl.'

Eve turned her small face, delicate as a doll's, up to Susan and smiled shyly. 'Will you be my friend?'

Susan couldn't help resenting that Mummy had told Eve about her but hadn't bothered to tell her about Eve. 'I'm sure you will,' Mummy said to both of them.

Eve turned to her with a grateful smile, and her hair swayed away from her face. Her left ear was red and swollen. 'Whatever have you done to yourself?' Mummy cried. 'Did someone do that to you?'

Eve pulled her hair over her ear and shook her head, too quickly. 'If someone did, they should know better,' Mummy said. 'Hitting people on the head is very dangerous. If I were you, I'd tell your mother who it was.'

Eve seemed frightened, and Susan closed her eyes. The space behind Eve didn't look like a van, it looked like a tunnel, huge and dark and endless. It must be how her eyes went funny sometimes when she was nervous.

'Have you moved in now?' Eve asked. 'Can I see?'

'Of course you can. You don't mind, do you, Susan?'

'No.' It wasn't Eve's fault that Mummy hadn't mentioned her. Nevertheless Susan felt resentful all over again as Eve ran upstairs without waiting for her. Eve's duffel coat flapped as she ran, displaying a hole in the seat of her jeans. She waited by the open door for Susan, then skipped in, almost tumbling over a carton of last-minute packing. Eve was turning round and round, clapping her hands. 'Isn't it big!' she cried. 'It's much nicer than ours.'

'It is nice now, isn't it, Susan?' said Mummy. 'It'll be even nicer when we've unpacked.'

'I can help you, can't I?' Eve was already unfastening the toggles of her coat; one was missing. Underneath she wore a pink cardigan with holes in the elbows. 'You tell me what to do.'

'You can help Susan. These need to go in the kitchen.' Mummy pointed out two cartons, and Eve stooped to the larger at once. 'Be careful,' Mummy called as they struggled into the hall, stumping like camels.

Eve made unpacking seem like a treat. Didn't her mother

let her do anything? They unwrapped the plates and stacked them, and Mummy showed them where to put the plates away. 'You're both good girls,' she said and retreated a step, for a large black beetle was ambling out from under the sink unit, rocking from side to side as it walked on the pile of the new carpet. Before Susan could run for the dustpan – Mummy hated insects – Eve picked up the beetle and squeezed it in her fist. Susan heard it crack and squish and saw a black leg twitching helplessly between Eve's fingers. Eve stared at her for a moment, then she went to the toilet and flushed the beetle away. 'Well done, Eve,' Mummy said, but she sounded as queasy as Susan felt, and hurried away to bring them the last carton of kitchen things.

As she put away the cutlery, Susan was wondering if Eve had helped Mummy clean the flat. She wished she had been here to help Mummy – it might have made the flat feel more like home to her – but staying at Arabella's saved the train fare. Mummy was always saying that librarians weren't paid enough.

The girls began to flatten the cartons, competing to see who could jump highest, giggling. They didn't stop until Susan was out of breath and Mummy called, 'Don't make too much noise.' Susan felt as if she had been jumping on the old man's head downstairs and couldn't stop giggling. 'I'll take these down if you like,' Eve said.

Susan took a breath that made her head ring and her vision begin to flicker. 'There's a horrible old man down there.'

'He won't mess with me,' Eve said as if she already knew.

Susan was lining up the plastic bottles on the windowsill and listening to hear if he caught Eve when Eve came back. 'Is this your bedroom?' she said from the hall. 'Can I see?'

'Go on then,' Susan said, and hurried through the streamers in case Eve couldn't find the light cord and tripped over something.

'Haven't you a lot of books. I read too,' Eve said. 'We can lend each other books.'

'If you want,' Susan said, though she didn't like lending books; half the time they came back damaged, if at all. She cringed inside when Eve chose her favourite Alan Garner, the horsemen riding into the sky and Susan in the story falling behind, though Susan reading always hoped that this time she would go on riding, into the sky and the magic. She pulled the frayed cord and followed Eve into the main room.

'Oh, isn't it lovely!' Eve cried.

Susan had to admit that the room looked improved. Mummy's streaky pottery squatted on the bookshelves among the junior encyclopedias and Mummy's books about librarianship. Mummy's plants and Japanese trees in their pots helped the room to look green, the green settee and the chairs sat near the gas fire, waiting for the television to be switched on. Mummy was underneath the dining table with a screwdriver, fixing the round top to the pedestal.

'More empties,' Eve said, jumping on the cartons. 'I'll take them.'

'I will too.' As they dumped the cartons on the mattresses, Susan felt brave and a little wicked. When they ran back upstairs, Mummy said, 'I think we all deserve a cup of tea or would you like something else, Eve?'

'I've got to go now. I said I'd lend Susan a book.'

'I'll come with you while Mummy makes the tea.'

Mummy and Eve exchanged a glance. 'Stay and help me,' Mummy said. 'Eve won't be long.'

Mummy served the tea in brand-new mugs. Mummy's had a green flower on the side, Susan's had Snoopy. It must be meant to cheer her up, and so she did her best to seem as if it had. The gas fire grew orange and filled the air with the smell of burning dust, and Susan sipped her tea to wash away the tickling in her throat. After a while Mummy said, 'We'll try and go back for Christmas if you like.'

'Oh, yes please,' Susan said, and wished she hadn't sounded quite so eager. They were both staring into their tea when the doorbell rang, making them both jump. Susan went to the door and there was Eve with a book and a carrier bag. The book had a witch with a nose and chin like horns on the glossy cover. Eve handed it over, and then the bag. 'My mummy said I had to give you this.'

The bag contained fish fingers and frozen chips. 'You'd better tell my mummy,' Susan said.

'No, I've got to go now. I'll see you tomorrow.'

'I'm going to school tomorrow. Just round there, Mummy says.' Susan pointed to the curve of the street, where four young blacks were sharing a cigarette under a streetlamp. 'Do you go there too?'

'No. I'll see you after school,' Eve said, and was gone. Susan fled upstairs before the grudging time-switch could leave her in the dark.

Mummy was in the kitchen. 'Do you know what I've forgotten? We've nothing at all to eat,' she said with an embarrassed laugh.

'Eve brought something.'

Mummy looked in the bag. 'Well, that's kind of her mother, I must say. I must be sure and find out where she lives so I can thank her.' All the same, she was frowning. 'Between you and me, Susan, I don't think Eve's mother treats her very well. You saw her ear. I have my suspicions. Maybe if I meet the mother I can help.'

Susan liked it when Mummy talked to her like this, it made her feel grown up. 'It'll be better for Eve now that she has you to play with,' Mummy said. 'I got the impression she roams the streets at night because she's afraid to go home.'

'She can come and play after school. She said she wants to.'

'That's right, you look after her.' Mummy was opening the packs of frozen food. 'Don't get the idea it's all her mother's fault. The father left them years ago. Eve hardly remembers him, but you can tell she misses him. I'd like to get my hands on him.' She was talking to herself now. 'That's marriage for you,' she said, 'a snare and a delusion. Something men believe in as long as it's convenient for them.'

Susan took Eve's book into the main room. She never liked it when Mummy talked like that, and just now it reminded her of the photograph of Daddy she had found when they were packing. Mummy had snatched it from her, smashed the glass and torn the photograph. 'You'd love to come with us, wouldn't you?' she'd cried at the pieces she was tearing up. 'Would you like me to tell Susan how you left us just when I needed you most? There, that's what we think of you.' Susan sat by the gas fire and tried to read Eve's book, but found herself looking at the pictures – misty forests with eyes between the trees, castles with turrets that poked the clouds – while she listened to conversations shouted across the roadway and big portable cassette players turned up full. The street was waking up.

Soon Mummy brought dinner through from the kitchen, and milk in the new mugs. It must have been the gas fire that made the food taste dusty. When they'd washed up, Mummy said, 'Bed now, young lady. School tomorrow and I'll go hunting jobs.'

Susan stared at her. 'I thought – '

'No need to look at me like that, Susan. Jobs aren't quite so easy to come by as I thought they would be. Maybe you'll find that too when you grow up.' Her smile was warning Susan to keep quiet. 'We aren't completely penniless, you know. We won't starve while I look for a job.'

Susan washed herself with her Snoopy soap and brushed her teeth in front of the bathroom mirror. A face much like her father's in the photograph and not at all like Mummy's gazed back at her, a long face with a large nose and eyes that were almost black. She shouldn't think of him as Daddy, Mummy never let her call him that. She looked squashed against the wall above the bath, the room was so cramped.

She pulled on her pyjamas and hurried across the draughty hall, yanking at the cord to remind herself of the layout of her room. 'Good night, Mummy,' she called, and Mummy came to tuck her in. 'Good night, darling. You're my best girl,' Mummy said and gave her another kiss before she pulled the cord and left her. The dark felt cool and soothing. Susan was on her way to sleep when the day's events crowded in. The things Mummy hadn't told her nagged – Mummy's lack of a job, her having met Eve already. She remembered the squish of the beetle and shuddered, remembered how Eve had watched her and thought for a moment that she had met her before, seen Eve's eyes watching her. She must be jealous of Mummy for having met Eve first, she told herself, and with that she was asleep.

9

'Soho,' Molly said. 'Why not Soho, Martin?'

Leon grinned at her inspiration. 'Can it wait until we've finished?'

'I was only thinking that's one way Britain's changing,' she went on. 'People finding that all of a sudden they're living in the sex centre of the country, above porn shops instead of delicatessens. It's never been done on television, not from the inside.'

'Sounds possible,' said Martin. 'Especially if we can find aspects that are specifically British so that people don't think they're looking at Times Square. Maybe we can go along there later and prowl around.'

'I'll take a look now,' Molly said.

'Well, maybe you shouldn't go by yourself. We'll only be an hour or so, right, Leon?'

'Don't be such a Southern gentleman,' Molly said, patting Martin's arm. 'I'll steer clear of the white slavers.'

'Okay, make sure you do.' He turned back to her as Leon ushered him away to be interviewed. 'I mean it, look after yourself.'

After the relentless central heating of MTV, the open air felt like a cold shower. A single lemony cloud hovered where the western sky grew pale, a lorry piled with Christmas trees held up traffic on Edgware Road. In Oxford Street windows half a mile apart displayed placards that seemed to prove Father Christmas could be in two places at once.

She was at Wardour Street in fifteen minutes, and turned toward Soho. Film companies exhibited posters for Christmas treats and next year's hopes, but it was the neon of Soho that drew the eye as the street grew darker. She mustn't walk too slowly, in case someone thought she was plying for trade. When she glanced behind her, a man turned quickly to look at the Columbia posters.

Lights chased around the borders of neon signs in Old Compton Street, cards bearing women's handwritten names were tacked above doorbells in shabby alleys. Spiky rubber penises stood in shop windows, masked women brandished whips on glossy covers, women bared breasts like a baby's dream, improbably muscled young men looked made of bronze or chocolate. Women with faces that made sure nobody thought Soho had anything to do with them were hurrying home through the narrow crowded streets. Molly strode through the neon flood, trying to ignore the feeling she was being followed, and read the signs. Ram Books, Curious Bookshop, Lovecraft, and here was one of the kind she had been looking for, that could hardly be more British. She went in.

Two men left at once. Perhaps they had been leaving anyway, with purchases hidden in their expensive briefcases. That left five men, leafing through magazines or pacing past viewing booths the size of toilet cubicles, and as she ventured down the narrow shop their awareness of her was almost suffocating. She scanned the glossy magazines on the racks, the promises of spankings on the covers, spankings of schoolgirls old enough to know better, nurses and traffic wardens and schoolmistresses and wives and air hostesses and policewomen, while cries of simulated Cockney anguish came from the booths, and somewhere cries that sounded unnervingly real. Molly was sure that all the men saw her as a threat to be imagined as a victim. She turned. No wonder she felt she was being watched.

It was the shopman. His counter and the stool where he was perched looked too small for him, as did his short-sleeved red shirt from which his hairy arms protruded – arms, she thought, like Popeye's. He stared at her for quite a time before he went on talking into a phone, and then she turned hastily to the magazines, to the sprawled women who were trying to look penitent or apprehensive or just to keep a straight face, and felt as if she'd walked into a Gents' by mistake. 'They're both under twenty,' the shopman was saying. 'They're ready whenever you want to start filming.'

All at once she was sure of herself. They couldn't turn her into a victim of their fantasies, she was here to do a job. She went to the counter and waited until the shopman put his hand over the mouthpiece. 'How would you feel about letting someone watch you make your films?' she said.

'All right, if you were going to be in one.' He stared at her and added, 'When you were younger.'

He wasn't getting away with that. 'Seems to me you know some pretty elderly schoolgirls.'

'Hold on a moment,' he said to the phone, and pointed the earpiece at Molly. 'You looking for work?'

'I'm looking for material.' She felt in control now. 'For a television documentary.'

'Can't help you there, love. Can't have cameras snooping around in here.'

73

She nodded at the phone. 'Hadn't you better ask him?'

'What do you know about it, love?'

As he leaned toward her, his sleeves pulled back and hairs sprang up on his arms. Again she felt that everyone was watching her, but she wasn't going to be daunted now. 'Isn't he the owner of the shop?'

The hairy man was smiling. 'Don't be so sure.'

'Well, why don't you just find out if he wants to speak to me. MTV would pay quite decent money if we can use him.'

Perhaps the mention of MTV impressed him. He stared at her as he said, 'Got a reporter here from the television wants to make a film about us. Want a word?' He listened, then passed Molly the receiver. He was smiling oddly. 'Here she is.'

'I'm not actually a reporter, I'm a researcher.' The phone answered that with silence. Molly had to think aloud. 'I understand that you're making a film. If my director is interested, would you let us film you filming?'

'Come off it, dearie. They wouldn't let you show a corporal punishment film on television and you know it.'

Molly had to take a breath, for the throaty voice was unmistakably a woman's. 'I think they would. I think it's the only kind of pornography we might be able to show.'

The silence lengthened as Molly resisted an impulse to look round, to make sure the man who had last come into the shop wasn't watching her. 'What's your game, dearie?' the woman's voice said.

'We're thinking of making a film about Soho. I believe my director would want to include your point of view. He's Martin Wallace,' she said, and wondered why she should expect that to mean anything in Soho. 'There's nothing to prevent you from appearing, is there? Your kind of film isn't against the law.'

Silence. Then: 'I'll tell you what I'm going to do,' the voice said. 'I'll give some thought to what you've said and

74

call you back at wherever you work. I can do that, can't I?' The voice was all at once sharp.

'Of course you can. I'm at MTV,' Molly said, and gave the number. 'Ask for Molly Wolfe.'

'I might just do that. Put Desmond back on now.'

Molly handed over the receiver. She was suddenly anxious to leave, however irrational that was. She had a vivid impression that the man who had come in last had turned when she'd given her name, had perhaps even said something. She went quickly to the door and glanced back. Her fists clenched. She had seen him before.

She dodged into the crowd at once. She was heading for Chinatown, to be out of Soho more quickly and onto Shaftesbury Avenue. She glanced back and saw him in the doorway, neon turning his spiky hair and his pimples green. He'd followed her from Wardour Street, where he had been pretending to look at the Columbia posters. As he caught sight of her and lurched out of the doorway, his eyes glaring like traffic lights at go, she struggled away, yearning for space to run.

But the street was narrowing. She seemed to be heading deeper into Soho; dim staircases led upward beyond doorways without doors, shops reverberated with amplified orgasms. The street was hot, suffocating. An endless one-way train of cars prevented her from stepping into the roadway. Now men were starting to try to detain her, and she shoved them out of her way.

Beyond the dazzle of the mouth of a neon side street, she looked back. She couldn't see the man who'd followed her, and she wished she had confronted him at once. Had he slipped past her in the crowd? She dodged into the side street. The next turn left should bring her to Chinatown. She couldn't understand why she wasn't already there.

The next turn left was narrow and unlit. Nevertheless she stepped into it, for the side street had come to a dead end. Her neon shadow jerked ahead of her, and then she was in the dark, heading for the lights at the far end. She was halfway down the narrow passage before she began to glimpse the walls. There were open doorways here and there with staircases beyond, and many windows overhead, all dark. How could she have thought she was halfway down the passage? She was nothing like halfway, and all she could do was hurry forward, ignoring her impression of figures coming down the staircases and along the hallways, figures that looked pink and naked. Perhaps she should run back to the bright streets rather than stumble onward, but when she turned it seemed that the passage behind her was crowded. Where had the crowd come from? She was wishing desperately that she had something in her hand besides her handbag, which contained the letter that dismayed her as much as anything here in the dark. She fled past doorways in which figures loomed, almost certainly naked as babies. She couldn't see their faces, nor did she want to. Some of them were close enough to touch now and so, she sensed, was the crowd at her back.

Panic must have blinded her, for the end of the passage came as a shock. So did the noise of the bright street, and she realized that she hadn't heard any sounds in the passage, or if she had, they had been very soft and vague. More neon signs and bookshops, and she was struggling through the crowds before she realized she was out of Soho and at least a quarter of a mile from where she had meant to emerge. She was on Charing Cross Road, and there was a taxi, thank God.

By the time she reached MTV she felt calmer. Leon and Martin were still in the studio, working out which clips to use before they concluded an interview. She scribbled a note for Martin about the Soho possibility. It infuriated her that she had been so anxious to escape that she had neglected to get the woman's name. She mouthed at Martin through the glass that she had left him a note and then made her way home to try and sleep off her panic.

She couldn't help glancing round when she reached her gate, and when she found she was wondering if anyone was in her flat, she swore aloud. She stalked through the rooms muttering nobody, nobody, nobody. Nor was there, but it disturbed her that she wished she had company.

She switched off the lights and lay down on the bed. Just breathe and rest and then she would be calm. A car's lights brushed her curtains, an aeroplane shrieked overhead. She hoped Martin would like the Soho proposal, if only because watching the film being made ought to defuse Soho in her mind, give her back her confidence that she should never have lost at all. The aeroplane was gone, and she felt as if she were following it into the quiet dark. If a pimply man had followed her through Soho then that was his problem, not hers. It didn't matter whether he had overheard her name, there was no way he could trace her. Suddenly she realized what she'd thought he had said.

Panic seemed to jerk all her muscles. She felt as if her body was out of her control, for she couldn't find the dangling switch. It didn't matter, she wasn't alone, she had only to call to her parents and they would come, they would open the door and drive out the dark, they would tell her that what she thought she recalled wasn't real, just her imagination again, they were real and it was a dream. Then she had the light switch and was staring at the door, trying to inhale her lost calm, get hold of her thoughts, wake up.

Her parents were in Devon. A phone call would prove that, but she didn't need to phone. She was alone in the flat, which was the way it ought to be. She flung open her bedroom door to give herself no chance to be nervous. She was awake now, she knew what was real. The mirrors on the hall walls multiplied themselves as she switched on the lights. Coffee was what she seemed to need, not sleep. Or perhaps she should go back to MTV, except that Martin and Leon might have left by now. Her parents weren't here and she ought not to want them to be, she would be staying with them over Christmas. Their presence had been a dream.

She halted halfway between the kitchen and the front door. Had the pimply man whose moustache seemed to have decided that it didn't want to come out after all really spoken to her, not today but years ago? Had he really said that she had made it happen, whatever *it* was? She mustn't think that, the world was full of pimply men with spiky hair, Soho especially. It was ridiculous to think he was the same man or that she could recognize him after eleven years. She didn't know his name, she told herself. She didn't know . . . She had only dreamed that it was Danny Swain.

Danny hadn't realized it was so far to Chelsea. By the time he reached Sloane Square he was already late. Birds exploded from crusts of bread on the spattered pavement under the plane trees as he ran across the square. Danny's shirt was sticking to his armpits, the trousers of the suit he hadn't worn for thirteen years were squeezing his stomach like corsets, but he didn't care. He was sure that he was going to get the job.

A girl who wore a dress composed of veils ran ahead of him on the King's Road, smelling like spring. A silver car that he thought was a Rolls-Royce waited outside an antique shop where a tall woman was examining mirrors, and he wondered where the chauffeur was. Everyone on the street and in the boutiques looked bright and young and full of life, not at all like the noisy young people and grumpy old folk who came to the Hercules. They made him feel sure of himself. Perhaps he'd dreamed he would get the job, perhaps he could still have those dreams after all.

He almost ran past the side street where the Royal was. By

now he was ten minutes late by the Mickey Mouse clock that he glimpsed in a boutique. It didn't matter, the manager could be interviewing whoever else had applied for the job. Danny was sure they wouldn't have as much experience as he had. His thirteen years at the Hercules were worth something after all.

He stood and admired the Royal before he went in. A red carpet held by polished golden bars led up steps that looked like marble, past posters for a week of Fred Astaire. That was the kind of films his parents liked, and they would be able to get in here free if they didn't mind travelling so far. Perhaps he and his parents could move to Chelsea to help his mother get well. He would certainly be earning more than Mr Pettigrew paid him at the Hercules.

The small foyer smelled of metal polish and carpet cleaner. Life-size stills of Chaplin and Bogart faced each other across the thick red carpet beneath a whispering chandelier. A young woman in dungarees was cleaning the window of the paybox. When he told her he was a projectionist, she said, 'Go straight up to the manager's office.'

The carpet was so thick he couldn't feel the stairs. He was climbing the black mirrors of the walls in his suit that he'd worn when Mr Pettigrew had interviewed him. This time his mother wasn't with him, he would be able to speak for himself. He knocked at the manager's door. 'Come,' a voice said.

The only person in the room was a woman. She wore a black suit and white blouse, and was sitting behind a heavy desk. She was about his mother's age. For a moment he felt tricked and nervous, but why should he care? She must be seeing how smart he was as she glanced at him through the glittery frame of her spectacles, not how his head was too small for his neck or how his moustache would never grow properly. 'Mr Swain?' she said.

'Yes.' He closed the door quickly – a blue suit with a brooch on the jacket swung back and forth on the hook –

and sat down at once. 'Yes,' he said again in case he hadn't said it loud enough, remembering his mother's admonition: 'Go on, Danny, speak up for yourself.'

'I'm Miss Astaire.' He was almost sure that was what the manageress said as she lifted bags of money into the safe. He thought of making a joke in case she had said Mrs Tare but decided not to. She closed the safe and spun the wheel before she turned to him. 'Did you have much trouble finding us?'

'No.' His voice seemed very loud in the small room, but better too loud than too low. 'Just walk along King's Road like you said,' he added to show that he had taken notice.

'I asked you that because you really should have been here half an hour ago.'

'Not half an hour.' It couldn't have been twenty minutes since he'd seen the Mickey Mouse clock, not even ten. 'Not that long,' he said at the top of his voice.

She was looking oddly at him; you couldn't call it a smile. 'Do you remember what time I said?'

'Half past ten.'

She pulled back her sleeve. 'And what time does this say?'

'Oh.' The Mickey Mouse clock had tricked him. 'I'm sorry,' he said, 'I didn't think it would be so far.'

'I wonder if you realize you would have to make that journey every working day.'

'I don't mind,' he said, but he felt trapped in the office with the small barred window; how late would he be at the Hercules this afternoon? 'I'm sorry,' he said again to make sure she believed him. 'I thought you would be interviewing the others.'

Again she gave him her odd, not quite smiling look. 'You're the only applicant today.'

He smiled at her, he couldn't help it. He didn't even have to compete for the job, it no longer mattered if he was late at the Hercules. 'Oh, good.'

She sat back, tugging her cuff over her watch. 'So tell me about yourself. How much experience have you had?'

'Thirteen years.' When she didn't react he said it again at the top of his voice; he never knew when he was speaking too low. 'Thirteen years.'

'I heard you the first time. No need to shout.' She was staring past him. 'You've always been a projectionist, have you?'

'Not always,' he said, in case she was testing his intelligence. 'Ever since I left school.'

'Well, I assume so.' Again the odd look. 'What drew you to the job?'

'The films. I only liked the good ones, ones like you show, I mean. Old ones.' He was hoping that would please her, but her expression didn't change. 'My dad was a projectionist, so he let me help him in the box when I left school. He got me the job.'

'You've worked there ever since, have you?'

'Yes.' He wondered whether he should say, 'Except on my days off,' but she didn't seem to care that much about words.

'Where?'

He should have been ready for that. He was going to get this job, it was his dream come true, but he didn't want Mr Pettigrew to know he had been for the interview, just in case. 'How do you mean?'

'I mean,' she said patiently, 'which cinema?'

'Just near where I live. Down Seven Sisters Road.' Surely he didn't have to name it. But she was staring at him, less patiently. At last he mumbled 'the Hercules' as indistinctly as he could.

'The Hercules, did you say?' She was smiling and shaking her head, and he thought she was impressed until she said, 'Is that still Sidney Pettigrew's cinema?'

'Oh, I don't know.'

'You don't know the name of your own manager?'

'Yes, I do. It's Mr Pettigrew.' He hadn't been cunning enough. 'I don't know what his first name is.'

'You don't know – ' She was staring past him again. 'Well,' she said slowly. 'Why do you want to leave the Hercules?'

Again he felt trapped, for he hadn't realized she might ask. He couldn't say he hated Mr Pettigrew for treating him like a dog, not when Mr Pettigrew might be a friend of hers. He couldn't say that he wanted a job he had got for himself instead of the job Mr Pettigrew had given him as a favour to his father because it was clear nobody else would employ him, just because he wasn't very good at speaking. He wanted to be somebody, that was all, somebody more than the schoolboy who had never been able to speak up when the teacher had said, 'Got a bone in your throat, Danny?'; more than the teenager who'd locked himself in the toilet to hide from the girls who said, 'Got a bone in your trousers, Danny?'; the girls kicking the toilet door and telling him what they were going to show him, until he hadn't dared go out when the afternoon bell rang because the girls would be waiting for him in the classroom. He couldn't say any of this, he mustn't get confused, mustn't let his enemies confuse him. His trousers were hurting his crotch, his stomach felt squeezed and he was afraid he was going to fart, and suddenly he realized he didn't know how long she had been waiting for him to answer; he couldn't see her watch as she glanced at it. All at once he had an answer, and it came as a shout. 'I don't like the films at the Hercules.'

'I see.'

'Really,' he said, thinking of the trash he often had to show.

'All right, if you say so.' She stood up and held out her hand. 'Thank you for coming.'

He jumped up and shook her hand, and held on to it when she tried to let go. 'Have I got the job?'

He couldn't see why she looked uneasy: Mr Pettigrew

82

had told him at once. 'I really think you must wait to hear from me,' she said.

He couldn't go back to the Hercules without knowing, not when he was going to be so late. 'Can't you tell me now?' he said as she pulled her hand free.

'I think it would be unfair to the other applicants.'

'You said I was the only one.'

'The only one today, I said. You're the last.' She looked a little nervous, his voice had been so loud and harsh; he could still feel it in his throat, a soreness that was growing. 'Well, perhaps in your case I should make an exception,' she said. 'You've a good secure job at the Hercules. I should hold on to it if I were you.'

His throat felt as if he had swallowed her soap, the smell of which was choking him. 'Haven't I got the job?'

'Yes, at the Hercules. Not here, I'm afraid.' She was stepping round the desk. 'Now if you'll excuse me, I have to get ready for opening.'

He turned toward the door so that she wouldn't see his face. He ought to have told her his mother was ill, that he needed the job so that he could afford to have his mother looked after properly, but it was too late now, and anyway she wouldn't care. When he jerked the door open her suit leaped off the hook toward him. 'It's all right, I'll see to that,' she said, but he wasn't trying to catch it. He wanted to trample it, grind his heels into it, but she caught it in midair. He shoved the door out of his way and strode blindly out past Chaplin and Bogart and Astaire, his eyes stinging with daylight, with the air that was sharp and bright as knives.

King's Road looked cheap now, full of girls with tired eyes dressed in flimsy clothes that would be worth nothing in six months. He snarled as he ran past the boutique with the Mickey Mouse clock. The car outside the antique shop wasn't a Rolls-Royce or even silver. As he ran across Sloane Square, slithering on droppings, his armpits felt like sponges, cold and soaked.

The man in shirt-sleeves behind the ticket window made him wait because he asked for Finsbury Road instead of Finsbury Park. 'No such place, mate,' he kept saying until Danny felt as if he no longer knew where he lived. Eventually the woman behind Danny in the grumbling queue told the man what he meant, and Danny ran down to the trains.

Ten minutes dozed by before a train came, and then he had to change at the next station, Victoria. He wouldn't even have time to change out of his suit now. He felt as if it were squeezing him smaller, smaller. The train carried him beneath the West End, past King's Cross and into the long darkness that came before Finsbury Park, a tunnel four stations long on the route map but full of nothing except roaring dark. He tried to understand how he could have been tricked out of his job at the Royal when he was sure he had dreamed he would succeed. Had the dream been a trick as well? Had they managed to harm his mind after all this time, when he'd fought them off for eleven years?

He ran up the sloping tunnel at Finsbury Park and onto Seven Sisters Road. Nothing seemed familiar; half of the Greek signs on the shops didn't even bother to explain themselves – he was surprised the numbers on the clocks weren't foreign too. The clocks agreed on how late he was, he mustn't go home to change, and then he realized that he must, otherwise Mr Pettigrew would see that he'd been for an interview. He turned off Seven Sisters Road, along the concrete path.

The flats were concrete terraces on top of terraces on top of terraces. As he panted up the stairs to the second balcony he struggled to pull out his key so fiercely that he almost tore his hip pocket. The postman had been to Danny's, for his father was limping away down the hall, stuffing a letter into his pocket. 'Back already, are you,' he growled without looking, and slammed the parlour door behind him.

Danny had to lie down on his bed before he could squirm

84

out of his trousers. He heaved the mattress up and laid the suit underneath. He peeled off his sodden shirt, and then he heard his mother's asthmatic wheezing in the hall. She had opened the door before he could shout, and he felt as if she'd caught him playing with himself. 'Are you home for lunch?' she said, covering her eyes and retreating into the hall.

'I can't,' he said nervously. 'I'm late.'

'Promise me you'll have a proper meal. We've two ill people here, we don't want you ill too.' Her wheezing laboured away down the hall, and he was glad that at least she hadn't asked why he had worn his suit, for he would have had to admit he had failed.

A wind met him on the balcony, and he felt the spikes of his hair spring up. He couldn't do anything about that now, though it made his scalp crawl. A clock chimed somewhere: half past twelve. He ran alongside the giant white arrows flattened on the tarmac of Seven Sisters Road. Everyone was trying to confuse him, the manageress at the Royal and the man in the Sloane Square ticket office, trying to make sure he couldn't get away from where his enemies wanted him, make sure he was too anxious about his mother to be able to think. But they wouldn't stop him thinking, that was one thing they couldn't do to him. They must be worried now, to have made sure he didn't get the job. They were worried because at last he was sure who their leader was.

A giant crutch that was propping up a five-storey terrace stood in the market opposite Hercules Place. Headless men were queueing in the market, or dwarfs in coats too big for them, and then he saw they were empty coats, hanging on the wire mesh. He turned his back on them and hurried up the cracked steps of the Hercules.

He was showing zombies this week, though the poster called them zombeys. Mr Pettigrew wouldn't change the printers, they came too cheap. Pictures of hot dogs were peeling off the stained oven on the sweets counter in the foyer, beneath the buzzing fluorescent tubes with their blackened ends. Suddenly he understood what had been going on today, saw the pattern of events. He was smiling when the office door opened beside the sweets counter and Mr Pettigrew saw him.

He stared at Danny while he finished tying his bow tie. He was already dressed in his black suit with the shiny lapels, his frilly shirt, his shoes that his wife polished every morning. His clipped moustache looked like part of a uniform too, and so did his shiny black hair, combed straight back from his glistening temples. 'You look pleased with yourself,' he said at last. 'I hope you've got a damned good reason.'

When Danny didn't answer, he fished out his pocket watch on its chain. 'What time do you call this?'

I call it the watch you got out of lost property, Danny almost said. He shrugged to show he was sorry, tilted his head as if that might hide the smile he couldn't quite get rid of. Eventually Mr Pettigrew snapped the lid over the face of the watch. 'If your father wasn't ill with his leg I'd fire you now,' he said. 'Go on, get in your box where you're some use. I'm taking a pound off your wages. Maybe that'll give you less to smile about.'

He stood in the doorway of his office, hands on hips, while Danny climbed the seven faded stairs to the door of his box. The usherettes were snorting with mirth. 'That'll be enough,' Mr Pettigrew said with a kind of leering indulgence. 'Now his highness has arrived we can let in the queue.'

Of course there was no queue. Danny closed the door behind him and climbed onto his high chair, then down again to switch on the single bar of the electric fire. He was grinning. He didn't have to hide his triumph now. He glanced at the time sheet, spotty with dots where Mr Pettigrew had rested his pen, and peered out through his window to check the clock above the toilets next to the

86

screen. Whoever had altered the Mickey Mouse clock must have had their instructions. That was when his enemies had begun to try to confuse him.

The audience was trickling in now, unemployed hooligans and pensioners who must be hoping that the heat was on. They reckoned without Mr Pettigrew. Danny watched them for a while, enjoying the knowledge that they didn't realize they were being watched. Then he dimmed the houselights, made the curtains open, and switched on the projector. The zombies came trudging toward the credits, all of which looked like misprints, and the hooligans began to pass a bottle back and forth. They must think nobody could see them. He grinned at them out of the dark. They were just as plain to him as the tricks of his enemies were.

He switched off the electric fire, then he sat up to watch through the window. The projector was already hot, the extractor fan wasn't taking out enough of the heat of the carbon arc, but Mr Pettigrew said he couldn't afford to have it fixed. 'If you're too hot you'll be able to do without your fire,' he'd said. Danny watched for the zombie with the maggots in its eyes and thought about the leader of his enemies, thought that she must have realized when she'd seen him that she hadn't managed to destroy his mind with whatever she'd made happen eleven years ago after all. That was why she was making mistakes now, ever since she'd let him see her in Wardour Street. She hadn't been able to lose him before she'd gone into the shop to phone, and it didn't matter that she'd managed to lose him afterward by making the streets become confusing: that simply proved she was afraid of him, to play her tricks so openly, to give away so blatantly that she was responsible for everything that had been happening to him in the last eleven years. He only wished he had been close enough to the phone to hear what she had been saying about him.

Here came the zombie, maggots pushing out its eyes. Danny grinned as the hooligans began shouting, trying to pretend it didn't bother them. He was surer every time he saw it that it was a real decaying corpse; they could do anything in films these days. He touched the projector and snatched his hand away, enjoying the blaze of pain. He was stronger than she was, and cleverer. He was going to enjoy making her pay for all that had been done to him. He was sure he would find her again, now that he had her worried, now that he knew her full name was Molly Wolfe.

Freda turned for a last look at her department and could almost hear the children. Holly wreathed the security cameras above the empty aisles, fold-out Father Christmases with expanding paper bellies stood guarding the toys, and she thought of the hordes of children who would soon be overrunning the Toy Fair, children wanting this and this and this while their parents said, 'We'll see,' or, 'Be good or Father Christmas won't come.' She went back, past the toy guns she wouldn't stock if the store directors gave her a choice, to help a teddy bear as big as a six-year-old to sit up straight, and suddenly the emptiness reminded her of Doreen. She turned quickly and made for the escalators. If she wasn't careful she might be locked in.

Walking down the dormant escalators seemed unreal, even though her boot-heels were loud as a child's drum. On the second floor the empty beds in their hints of bedrooms made her think of Doreen too. She stepped down away from them as Mr Harvey shouted up, 'Miss Beeching.'

'I'm coming now.' She met him in the hosiery department, among the sauntering pairs of tights. 'I'm sorry if I kept you waiting.'

'No trouble. Nowhere to go in particular.' He was

settling his trilby on his high forehead and taking his pipe out of the pocket of his fur coat. 'May I give you a lift home?'

She was fond of him – his shyness when he wasn't being the assistant store manager, his unobtrusive praise when he was. He always looked at her as if she were no taller than she ought to be, as if he liked to look at her moist eyes and her lips, which she had a habit of pursing. But she wanted to be alone just now, to think of Doreen. 'I'd like to walk, thanks all the same,' she said.

He held onto his trilby as he locked the doors behind him. He must think she was mad to walk on a night like this, when the wind felt like an invisible blizzard, or that she must dislike him. For a moment she thought of the way Timothy had looked when she had refused to marry him. 'Thank you, really,' she said. 'Another time.'

The streets of Blackpool were almost deserted. Ripples scurried across puddles, the pool of light beneath a trembling streetlamp wavered, blurring. There was nobody on the promenade. She crossed to the railing and gazed out to sea in the hope that the wind might strip her fears away like litter, leaving her able to think instead of feel.

Dark waves smashed over the Lower Walk. The night was roaring, tugging at her headscarf and her heavy coat; her face felt gripped by frost. After a while she walked past the locked piers toward the mile of stalls and fairground. The rigging of the mast that stood in the Crazy Golf course was singing in the wind. Above her the Tower was a latticed silhouette on the churning sky. She thought it was creaking. When the wind dropped for a moment, she heard the sparks of a distant tram on the wire.

The ice cream parlours, the Horror Crypt, and the shops that sold funny hats were all locked; corrugated covers were rolled down over the souvenir stalls. The fortune-tellers' booths were locked too. Freda hurried past on the opposite pavement, for they always made her think of the fortune-teller Doreen had taken her to, who'd told her she was trying to be fair to too many people and ought to be fair to herself – she had to decide what the rest of her life was going to be like while she had the chance. She'd told herself that could mean anything: she'd thrown away her chance and Timothy's as well, sent him to Germany to burn alive in the sky. It was no good telling herself that he would have died anyway, she could never be sure that he hadn't taken some risk because she had refused him. She would always wish she had known what was going to happen before she had decided that her first loyalty was to her parents, that they'd needed her more than Timothy did.

Awnings flapped in the locked fairground, cartoonish colours seemed to glow. She had almost been able to see the future once, eleven years ago, when she had misread the advertisement about dreaming. The so-called experts had persuaded her to stay to see if she could pick up the ability, but whatever had affected her dreams that last night in Oxford, the experience had been so dreadful that she had never dreamed again. If the store hadn't given her sick leave, if Doreen and Harry hadn't let her stay at their boardinghouse while she recovered, she was sure she would have gone mad.

The giant face of the Fun House leered across the fairground as if it were ready to laugh its mechanical laugh and roll its mechanical eyes. Doreen and Harry had looked after her when she had needed it most and now, when Doreen needed her, she wouldn't go. Doreen had written again yesterday, pleading with her at least to come for Christmas. If only it were just her company that Doreen yearned for! But she'd seen at the funeral what Doreen wanted of her, and she couldn't, not any more. She'd dreamed of Timothy after his death, she'd dreamed of her parents after they had died in their beds halfway through the war, but she'd had nobody to dream of since then. In a way she had been grateful for that, even before Oxford; it had once occurred to her that people had to die before she could dream of them. Now even the thought of it made her insides feel loaded with ice.

The wind almost overbalanced her as she reached the end of the fairground wall. It shoved her round the corner, towards Central Drive and her rooms. She mustn't go to London, not when she felt like this: Doreen's yearning would be too much for her, even if Doreen never spoke of it; just being there would make her feel she had to dream of Harry. What did Doreen expect him to say? The dead never had much to say for themselves, even in dreams – just that everything was fine and nobody should worry about them, they would all be together again one day, though Freda had always felt on waking that they'd told her much more that she had forgotten, that she would have to wait to learn. Couldn't she tell Doreen she had dreamed of Harry, that he was happy and wanted Doreen to be? Certainly she would write to Doreen as often as she could, phone her every day, perhaps.

She was past the far side of the fairground now, and entering the complex of streets that led back to the prom-enade. You couldn't get lost, not with the Tower to guide you. She would call Doreen as soon as she got to her rooms, tell her that she couldn't take time off before Christmas or after, she was needed at the store. It wouldn't be worth going to London for just the Christmas break. In fact Tess could take over the department for her, she had done so last summer, but it wasn't really fair to ask her, and besides, Freda had made up her mind. And all at once she realized that she was as afraid of London as of dreaming.

She halted at the crossroads. Terraces led away from her in all directions. Unbroken rows of houses opened straight onto the pavements – homes or shops or guest houses. There was nobody in sight, hardly a window was lit, and she couldn't see the Tower. Why was she afraid to go to London? She wasn't going, she didn't need to know, but not knowing made her nervous. It made her feel as if some hidden part of her mind was lying in wait for her.

She was hurrying in the direction where she felt the Tower should be. None of the streets seemed to be parallel to any other, and the smudgy black sky wouldn't help her locate the Tower. A dog barked in an unlit house, a cat lay on a butcher's counter, an empty front room was lit only by the bars of an electric fire. She wanted to be in her rooms, where she might be able to think.

She wasn't expecting to see the promenade, but there it was suddenly, at the far side of a crossroads. The tide must be rising, for the glittering fringe of a wave fluttered above the edge of the promenade before it was torn away by the wind. She made for the promenade at once. That would show her the way home.

The street beyond the crossroads was dark except for one dim lamp. She had to peer at the uneven pavement as she walked. A paving stone tilted like a Fun House floor as she stepped on it, and she thought of the giant face with the rolling eyes. She would be safer walking on the road. She stepped onto it just at the edge of the pool of light. Something gleamed beyond the lamp, and she glanced up.

A sign over a door said 'SAGE.' At first she thought it was illuminated from within; then she saw that it was gilded, though it managed to seem brighter than the lamp. Notices covered the window beside the door: 'SAGE KNOWS YOUR FUTURE,' one said. She had stepped forward to read the small print when she realized that what had looked like a black door was an unlit corridor, and there was a light at the end. She noticed nothing else, for she'd realized where she was. She had tried to find this place eleven years ago.

She'd come back from Oxford desperate to know her future – to know that eventually her panic would end. A friend of her landlady had told her where to find a psychic who was supposed never to be wrong, but Freda had lost her way in the dark side streets – these streets. Perhaps her need for help was even greater now, since it had brought her here at last.

She stepped into the corridor at once. Suddenly she needed to trust someone else's insights, though she wished the corridor weren't so dark. When a board gave way underfoot and she reached out to steady herself, the wall felt like damp chalk. But here was the end of the corridor, here was the light beyond a doorway. She stood gazing.

The light, whose source she couldn't distinguish, was made to shine straight down on a table and two chairs; the rest of the room was in darkness. A man with an oval face so calm that it looked like a sculpture was sitting at the far side of the table. Presumably he was Sage. She was beginning to regret having wandered in, to scoff at herself – Sage knows his onions, she thought wildly – when he said, 'Please come in.'

His voice was soft and gentle. It made her think of a calm, moonlit sea. He stood up. He was taller than she was. Timothy had been; for the first time in years she didn't feel the need to stoop. He was reaching out to her with his long fingers, white and smooth as marble, like his face. Either he was bald or he had the highest forehead she had ever seen. She stepped forward to the black table, and then she felt as if she were falling into a well. The top of the table was a black mirror, though she couldn't see him in it, nor herself. If she fell she would never stop.

His hands caught hers across the table. His fingers were as cool as they had looked. She thought of her mother's cool fingers, stroking her forehead when she'd had a fever. His hands and hers were reflected in the mirror now – it must have been a trick of the light that had made her unable to see them before – and she had an impression of restrained strength, of a deep calm that could be hers. 'Will you sit down?' he said. 'I can help.'

She was scarcely aware of sitting down, since his face stayed level with hers all the way. She wondered what the smell was that reminded her of fallen plaster, she wondered how large the room was – and then she was aware only of him. When she made to speak, he shook his head and smiled. 'You need tell me nothing,' he said.

She had no idea how long he gazed into her eyes. She felt oddly that he was gazing down into the mirror as well. Peace seemed to be flowing into her through his fingers, which were still holding hers. At last he said, 'You are troubled because someone else is.'

'Yes.'

'She has lost someone dear.'

'Yes,' she said, and felt as if she didn't need to speak, that her secrets were passing to him through her fingertips in exchange for peace.

'She is unable to accept the death because it seems so pointless.'

She hadn't thought of that, but it must be true, not only because Doreen and Harry had been planning their second honeymoon, to see a few of the places they had always felt they couldn't afford, but because Harry's death had been so unnecessary. It seemed impossible that he could have lost his way in the streets near the boardinghouse, that he could have been so preoccupied that he had stepped in front of a lorry. 'Yes,' she said, since the man called Sage appeared to be waiting.

'She would accept it if she heard of him.'

'I suppose so.'

'You can do so, you want to, but you are afraid.'

Could he read all her secrets? Yes, she wanted to, but the idea terrified her. She felt like a blind person who was horribly afraid to see. Even his peace couldn't reassure her now; she was afraid where it might lead.

He must have sensed that she couldn't speak. 'There is nothing to fear,' he said. 'You can help her. Only you can.'

If that was true, she didn't want to know. It wasn't only dreaming that she feared, it was going to London. Could she invite Doreen to stay with her for Christmas? But then she might have to dream. 'I can't,' she pleaded. 'I'm afraid of where she lives. I can't go there, I don't know why.'

A frown passed across his forehead, a single ripple. 'Perhaps you have painful memories.'

Of course she had. Timothy had come from London. He'd worked at Harrods and all over London there were places that would remind her of him. She was struggling within herself, for the man called Sage was robbing her of all her reasons not to go to Doreen, making her afraid that she would have to go. Suddenly the dark around her seemed as limitless as the dark in the mirror. Just as she thought of pulling her hands free of his, he took hold of them more firmly and looked down into the mirror. He gazed and gripped her hands until she had to look down too, however afraid she was. Down there in the dark, so distant that she couldn't understand how she could make it out, was Harry's face.

She would have fled, if the man called Sage hadn't been holding her. His peace was flooding her, washing away her panic, and she saw that Harry's face was luminous; Harry's eyes were gazing into hers, telling her something beyond words, something of what she had always forgotten when she woke from her dreams. The light that was his face was growing brighter; every feature was microscopically perfect, made of light that was still brightening, until she had to close her eyes.

She didn't know how long she sat there, blinded. If the long cool fingers hadn't kept hold of hers, she felt she would have been lost forever in the dark. When she opened her eyes, Harry's face had gone. She gazed at the man called Sage. 'You see what you can do,' he said. 'You must not waste that. Few have your vision.'

She felt drained, almost weightless, but no longer afraid. The vision of Harry's face was an aspect of the peace that had washed away her fear, and she wished she could see it again. 'Will you help your friend now?' he said.

She said 'Yes' without thinking, from deep in her peace. But had she been coaxed into giving a promise that she would be unable to break? How would she feel when she went away from him into the dark? 'Can I come and see you again?' she said, trying not to be nervous.

'I think you will find there is no need. I shall be moving on. I've finished here. There is no reason for you to be afraid,' he said, and paused. 'Should you ever need me, perhaps you will see me again.'

She realized that was a dismissal, and she let go of his hands and stood up. In the unlit corridor she looked back. He raised one hand in a gesture of farewell and of promise, too, she hoped.

She felt peaceful, if she would let herself do so. She didn't even realize she was walking away from the promenade until suddenly she found herself in sight of the locked entrance of the Tower, almost home. She let herself into her rooms and made for the phone, clapping her hands to chase Grimalkin away from her knitting, which he'd pawed out of the basket, and back to his cat food. This time she wouldn't try to know better than the advice she had been given. Why had she been afraid to go to London? If there was one thing she could be sure of, it was that she was unable to predict her own future.

She dialled quickly and waited while the phone rang and rang, until she began to grow anxious for Doreen. Then there was silence. 'Hello?' Doreen said.

She sounded hopeless, lifeless, unconvinced that the phone was worth answering. 'It's Freddy, Doreen,' Freda said at once, seeing Harry's luminous face and the eyes of the man called Sage, wondering if the vision had come from those eyes rather than from the dark mirror. It didn't matter, the vision was part of her now, if only she could communicate it to Doreen. She must communicate that peace. 'I'm coming to stay with you for Christmas,' she said. 'Keep your chin up until I get there. You won't be alone much longer.'

The young woman who played the victim of the corporal punishment film couldn't get a university place or a job. Martin interviewed her while the film was being made, since he was given so little time. By no means all of the corporal punishment was simulated. Terry Mace grew furious when the woman directing the film, who was a partner in a firm of solicitors whose office was disguised as a headmaster's study that Sunday, refused to talk to Martin for the camera.

'About time you stopped chasing awards and got back to making films you care about,' he said afterward to Martin, and Molly knew she must get Martin on his own to find out what had really been troubling him.

At Kensington High Street baskets of flowers like vegetable spiders hung under the roof of the station arcade, beneath the frosted glass that the afternoon sky turned to gold. Martin Wallace lived opposite, in a turn-of-the-century block of mansion flats white as china. As they went up in the lift, a cage of polished bars and mirrors, Molly saw the buttons for the servants' bells next to each door, brass sockets gleaming. His apartment was on the top floor, six rooms with a bell push in every one, antique furniture as elaborate as the plaster vegetation that sprouted all the lights, a four-poster bed in the bedroom. 'VIP treatment from MTV,' Martin said as if he didn't know what else to say. 'I just hope I'm worth it.'

'You know you are.'

'With your help, maybe.' He hurried across the densely carpeted hall and opened the outer door. 'Come up and see the view.'

He pushed the bar on the door at the top of the last flight

of stairs and they stepped onto the roof. The cold was exhilarating. They made their way between the skylights and the craning insect aerials to the edge. A silenced crowd streamed homeward along Kensington High Street, and the muted brass of traffic drifted up. The rooftops were a different city – weathercocks dozing for the moment among the turrets and highbrow windows and rooftop green-houses; flags stirring among the shrubbery of a roof garden. Beyond the sunset roofs, Chelsea looked carved out of amber. A breeze lifted a hint of bells from the spire of St Mary Abbot's. Molly gazed down at the coping stones above the apartment windows. 'They look as if you could just step down to the street,' she said, and suddenly she was swaying at the edge of the roof, flailing her arms. Martin grabbed her shoulder. 'Nearly lost you there,' he said.

She was squeezing his waist as if she would never let go. Her grip seemed to mean paragraphs she couldn't speak: I want you to know what I am, I don't want to be alone with it, I *would* tell you except I'm afraid that would bring it all back, don't let go, don't say anything . . . Then he turned and kissed her. They kissed hungrily, and quite a time passed before they thought to move back. Then they were on the stairs, in the flat and the bedroom. They undressed mutually and urgently and made love so fiercely that the four-poster canopy shook.

Afterward they lay embracing. His penis was quite small, she noticed now. He grinned at it as if it were an oddity he was rather fond of and told her about the girls it had taken aback: Marsha at high school who'd held it and complained, 'Is that all you've got?' as if it were a donation to a charity, Sharon who'd seemed to regard it as the best you could expect at a Baptist university. Molly laughed, and they made love again, more gently, and she knew that if she told anyone it would be Martin, but not now. She felt so safe, drifting away into the evening dark, going to sleep in his arms. . . . Suddenly she jerked awake: she might dream if she fell asleep now – she might dream of *him*. It made her panic. She groped for the light switch and her clothes.

He'd promised her dinner but she didn't feel up to it now. Eventually, to his amusement, she managed to persuade him to go down and get her a Big Mac. As soon as she'd eaten the hamburger out of its squeaky container, she wiped her mouth and kissed him. 'You don't mind if I go now, do you? I've things to do at home.'

'Sure.' But he seemed disappointed. 'Go ahead.'

'It isn't true, I haven't. I just don't want to sleep here tonight, all right?'

He smiled wistfully and took her face in his hands. 'I understand.'

In the frosty High Street a car drove over a McDonald's carton that crunched like ice. Plaques glittered on houses in Holland Street, where the ladies in waiting at Kensington Palace had lived two hundred years ago. Smells of cooking hung around Queen Elizabeth College, a peacock cried sleepily in Holland Park. She went quickly down the steps to her flat, trying not to feel disappointed by knowing nobody was there.

She'd taken a shower and made herself coffee before she remembered Martin's TV interview. Had he been hoping she might watch it with him? There he was now, talking to Leon about his work with a kind of shy self-questioning enthusiasm. She wondered if he were watching by himself or if he would be too embarrassed. Had she simply been afraid that if she dreamed she would have to tell him? She switched off the television and went to bed, hoping to sleep.

Soon the dark began to shift and whisper, but that was only rain; she heard the splash of a passing car, imagined rain flooding down her steps. The rain was outside, her flat wasn't underwater. That was just a momentary dream, like the pimply face that was on the pillow when she turned over, the face of the man who'd followed her in Soho, the face that pressed into hers whenever she closed her eyes.

She floundered out of bed away from it, the blankets clinging to her then floating away through the room, she swam to the door and dragged at it, but the weight of the water that filled the room was too much for her. If her parents were out there they must have drowned by now, but the thought drifted away into dreamless sleep.

She towelled herself briskly after her morning shower to get rid of the damp, shivery feeling. She dropped bread into the toaster and switched on the percolator, then, on impulse, called her parents. 'Hello, sweetheart,' her mother said. 'Do you mind if I call you back? We're flooded out this morning. Burst pipe.'

At least it had actually been raining. Water was still dripping from the steps and snaking over the windscreens of parked cars. A woman on the corner by the estate agent's looked as if she had been standing there all night; the shoulders of her hooded coat were black, her grey hair looked like fluid congealing in the hood. Molly dodged around her, thinking that her dream was nothing special, she could have guessed that her parents' home might have suffered a burst pipe, it was so cold in Devon just now. All the same, she wanted to see Martin. She had just passed the woman in the hooded coat when the woman grabbed her arm.

She let go at once and looked bewildered. For an instant she'd made Molly feel they knew each other, but the thin anxious face seemed wholly unfamiliar. She was holding a sodden street map, the pages stuck together in a solid mass. 'Are you lost?' Molly said.

'I might as well be.' She seemed to be trying to place Molly. 'I'm looking for a job.'

'I see what you mean,' Molly said, thinking of the unemployment figures. 'Anything in particular?'

'I was a librarian.' She frowned and added, 'I still am.'

Darkness loomed over them, the sounds of Bayswater

Road were fading. 'You ought to be able to find something, then,' Molly said.

'I need to work near here.' It sounded like a plea. 'You wouldn't know where there's a job, would you?'

'There might be one where I work. That's MTV.'

'The television station?' The woman looked awed. 'Could you put in a word for me?'

'Be better if you got in touch yourself. Say you've heard they need a librarian. The person you want is Jake Gould. He's in charge of staffing.'

'I will. I'll do it right now.' A large drop of rain emerged from the grey hair at her temple, wandered across to the bridge of her nose and trickled down to the tip, but she was too intent on Molly to brush it away. 'What's your name, in case I get the job, so I can thank you?'

'Molly. Molly Wolfe.'

The woman frowned, then shook her head. 'What's yours?' Molly said.

The woman hesitated, almost as if she were listening. 'Nell.'

'Good luck, Nell,' Molly said and hurried away, glad that Nell wasn't following. She couldn't help feeling uneasy about the encounter.

Glassy buds of rain grew on the trees in the park. As she passed the police station where Lenny Bennett had died, she thought of Martin and by the time she reached MTV she was almost running. Ben Eccles came striding toward the lift and looked furious when she didn't hold it for him. She restrained herself from calling to Martin as soon as she reached the fourth floor. But he wasn't in his office, and there was nothing to show he had arrived for the day.

Leon's office was empty too. There was a chance he'd be in editing. She waited patiently for a lift to take her to the seventh floor. Editors pored over moviola screens in the long room: a tiny Pope blessed a crowd and trotted backward off the balcony, came back and tried again; a bomb sprouted like a mushroom in a nature film, a mushroom hardly large enough to poison anyone. Martin and Leon were huddled over the screen at the furthest bench. 'What's so interesting?' Molly said, and then she faltered as she saw their faces.

Leon waited until she reached them, and even then his voice was low. 'Unless I'm dreaming,' he said, 'we've been watching the police beat Lenny Bennett to death.'

Eventually Mr Rowley unbuttoned his transparent bluish raincoat and his crumpled jacket and took out his folding glass to examine the album more closely. He'd clucked his tongue appreciatively at the sets from all the Japanese occupied territories, and now he was looking at individual stamps: the Medieval Postman's Bell, the Girl Plucking Tea, the Sea-God Palace Gateway, the Rice-Eating Rat of Kanazawa . . . He brought his hands together once, applause so polite it was almost inaudible, but all he said to Geoffrey was, 'Everything all right?'

'Oh, you know how things are.' As Geoffrey closed the safe belatedly, he glimpsed Hay's letter. 'Many folk worse off than us.'

'Can't argue with that.' Mr Rowley was using Geoffrey's tweezers to turn over the Benefits of Irrigation. 'And Mrs Churchill, is she carrying on the good work?'

'She does her best.'

'And a good best it is.' He frowned, having noticed that Geoffrey was gazing at the tweezers. 'Do you mind if I use these?'

'Of course not. Why should I?'

'Well, one doesn't like to presume.' He was putting

Loyalty and Filial Piety back to its chronological place in the album and leaving Geoffrey to his own thoughts. Before she'd gone out this morning, Joyce had wanted to know what he'd done with the tweezers she used to pluck out her white hairs whenever they dared to appear. They had been on the dressing table, under a perfume bottle he had seen at once was tilted. Of course, she was entitled to be a little distracted while the future of the day centre was in doubt – hadn't she been infinitely worse eleven years ago? Nevertheless he was grateful when Mr Rowley closed the album with a gentle thump and recalled him from his thoughts.

'Splendid,' Mr Rowley said. 'First-rate. Thank you.'

'I thought of you as soon as I saw the auction catalogue.'

'I must be on my travels soon, before the weather intervenes. Will you be going to Oxford tomorrow?'

'I certainly am.'

'I hope it proves worth the journey.'

'It will be,' Geoffrey said, thinking of Hay's letter. He needn't open it – he already knew Hay's address in Oxford.

'Well then, Mr Churchill.' Though they'd known each other for twenty years, they never called each other by their first names, perhaps because they never met outside their offices. 'We should discuss a price,' Mr Rowley said.

They haggled politely for five minutes, saying 'Well' before each sum. Mr Rowley made the final move, and they shook hands briskly. Mr Rowley was taking out his large pictorial chequebook when the front door slammed downstairs.

'We're up here, Joyce,' Geoffrey called.

Mr Rowley completed the cheque, and then Joyce appeared in the doorway, snowy glitter melting on her shoulders and headscarf. Her face was so eloquent that Mr Rowley blurted out, 'Oh dear, what's wrong?'

It reminded Geoffrey of the day she had gone back to nursing. She'd come home far too early, looking very much as she looked now – concussed, that was the word. It had been her first and last day at the hospital, and she had only ever told him one thing. 'They said,' she'd told him, whoever they had been, 'I should be a patient, not a nurse.'

'My day centre has been knocked down. My centre that you bought for me, Geoffrey. They've left us nowhere to go.'

'Good heavens!' Mr Rowley cried. 'I saw them doing it on my way here. I thought I must have mistaken the street.'

'How can they? How can they get away with it?' Geoffrey said angrily.

'They said the contractor had made a mistake.'

Her face looked as if only her fierceness was preventing it from crumpling. 'If you'll excuse me,' Mr Rowley said hastily, 'I think I should be going before the roads get worse.'

A gust of pure white forced them back into the house from watching him drive away. The snowflakes were growing; they looked as if the Georgian houses were shedding their plaster, a stone autumn. 'What will you do now?' Geoffrey said as casually as he could.

'You wait and see. I haven't even started. Some of my old folk say they'll picket the planning offices every day until we're offered somewhere acceptable. I'll take them to court if I have to, I will.' But her anger was flagging. 'My old folk won't be picketing if the weather stays like this, they'll be off to the church halls and staying there.'

'At least they'll be looked after.'

She stared at him as if he were being obtuse. 'But I'd lose touch with them.'

'That doesn't matter, does it? There will always be people who need looking after.'

'But these are *my* old folk, Geoffrey, can't you understand? They know me. They need *me*.'

He thought of the people at the day centre, the one-legged woman and the flabby lady who'd thought he had come to take her home, and had never admired Joyce so much: she wasn't merely caring for them, she was genuinely fond of them. She'd see it through, he knew she would, and he could help by dealing with Hay, though she must never know. 'So what will you do?' he asked again.

'I'll have somewhere down the hill by Christmas, before my old folk have time to forget me. I will, or I'll make sure the whole country knows what's been done to them, and to me.' He had to believe her: if anyone could do it, she could.

They had stew again for dinner. By then the snow had stopped without settling, though there was the threat of another fall in the overcast with its ominous brassy glow. Early Christmas trees sparkled in windows on Muswell Hill, dots of light which, if you squinted, resolved into several colours.

After dinner he went to his office and listened from the door until he was sure that Joyce was reading. He unlocked the safe and left it open while he took Hay's letter to his desk. He ought to know what Hay had written, hadn't he, in order to confront him?

His face grew hot as soon as he read the first words. 'Dear Joyce Churchill,' the letter began, without even the courtesy of a Madam or a Mrs. 'You may recall that I helped run the experiment in which you participated at the Foundation for Applied Psychological Research. I am writing to enquire if you have experienced any after-effects which you consider to be attributable to the experiment, particularly recently. Please include anything which you feel to be in any way unusual and describe it as fully as possible. It may be important to both of us for me to have this information. I look forward to hearing from you . . .' He wouldn't for much longer, Geoffrey thought with a grim smile, and slipped the letter inside the jacket he would be wearing to Oxford. He locked the safe and went downstairs.

Joyce was asleep. The Agatha Christie had lodged face down on her instep, glossy cover curling. He sat by her and stroked her face, which looked older when she was asleep, and eventually woke her so that they could go to bed. He felt peaceful as he lay beside her, secure in the knowledge that each of them had something they must do.

He woke to the soft, vague thuds of snow at the window. It was daylight, and he was alone in the room. The faded hands of the luminous clock told him he should have been up an hour ago. At least the snow wasn't settling, but if he was short of time when he reached Oxford he would simply have to miss the auction. He hurried downstairs. Joyce's boots were by the front door, and she was in the kitchen. 'Why didn't you wake me?' he said.

'I was going to leave your breakfast in the oven and write you a note.' She hung a tea bag in a cup for him and turned to frown. 'I certainly hope you won't think of driving in this weather.'

'It isn't as bad as it looks. You're going out, aren't you?'

'Are you telling me I have a choice? My old folk can't be expected to picket in this, though I wouldn't be surprised if some of them try.' She was gripping the handle of the boiling kettle. 'Don't make me waste time talking. I have to go, but you haven't. And I won't be driving.'

'The auction is important too.' He was sure he would have to miss it now. 'Don't worry, I'll be careful. I'll take it slow.'

A nerve was twitching beneath her left eye. 'You never drive in this kind of weather.'

'Then it's about time I learned,' he said desperately. 'One day I may have to in an emergency.'

'Won't you stay at home when you can see how much it means to me?' There seemed all at once to be many more lines on her face. 'Do you want me to be tormented all day when I should be looking for somewhere for my old folk? I'm not getting any younger, Geoffrey. I can't take worry like I used to.' She turned away, her shoulders hunching up then drooping. 'I've got to go now. If you care at all for my feelings you'll stay in.'

106

He heard her stamping to put on her boots. Must he lie to her? He had to go to Oxford to deal with Hay before he wrote another letter that Geoffrey mightn't intercept. She was opening the front door; he heard the hiss of snow. He would promise not to go and hope that he got home before her. 'Oh, Geoffrey, look,' she cried.

He was out of his chair so quickly that his slippers almost tripped him. Joyce was stepping coatless onto the pavement, her hair whitening. He followed her and snow began immediately to trickle into his slippers. The figure Joyce was running to might almost have been some stray Father Christmas; it was wearing the largest duffel coat he had ever seen. 'What are you doing all this way from home in this weather?' Joyce cried. 'Don't you know me? It's Joyce. You come with me, now. Help me, Geoffrey.'

He went reluctantly to them, his slippers cold and soaking. As they guided the old man toward the house he leaned his weight first to one side and then to the other, so that both of them staggered. It was like trying to move a heavy piece of furniture through the snow.

There wasn't room for either of them to go through the doorway beside the old man; they had to support him from behind. As soon as the snow was shut out, Geoffrey heard a sound like a baby's first thin squeals. 'Lie down,' it said.

'Of course you can.' Joyce guided him toward the stairs. 'Come on, Geoffrey. Don't let me down now.'

It was too sudden. There was an intruder in their home, and he felt he hadn't been consulted. Joyce mouthed 'Geoffrey' furiously at him, but he might have refused to help if he hadn't seen that she was supporting the man's entire weight. As she stumbled backward, he went to her aid. Before he could consider what he was doing, they were supporting the old man upstairs. At every step the duffel coat brushed the wall and the banisters, the stairs creaked.

Geoffrey leaned in the guest room doorway and watched Joyce draw the curtains. The old man sat down so heavily that the mattress sagged. He struggled out of his coat and kicked his boots across the room. 'That's right, you get out of those wet things,' Joyce said.

He shook his head to get rid of the duffel hood, and Geoffrey saw that he was bald except for a few strings of grey hair. His scalp looked like old white cheese. Under the coat he was wearing pyjamas. He leaned forward groaning and managed by lifting his ponderous legs to grasp the sodden cuffs, which he rolled to the knees up calves that made Geoffrey think of giant pale tubers. When Geoffrey noticed that the wrists and ankles were half the thickness of the arms and legs, he had to turn away. An enormous creak made him look back. The bald man was in the bed, he was a mound that the bedspread barely covered. Only his great slumped face was visible, a mass of pouches hanging from the cheeks, the chin, the closed eyes.

Joyce beckoned Geoffrey out of the room. As they reached the landing the thin voice piped, 'Don't leave me.'

'Someone will be in the house with you, don't worry,' she called. 'I'll leave the bedroom door open.' She gestured Geoffrey to keep quiet until they were downstairs. 'She's just nervous in a strange place,' she whispered then. 'I'll be back as soon as I can.'

He didn't know if he found it more distressing that the bald intruder was a woman or that Joyce expected him to stay with her. 'You don't mean to leave her here, do you?'

'Yes, until I come back and can sort things out. What do you want me to do, take her with me on a day like this?'

'But I can't look after her.' He was rubbing his hands on his dressing gown and couldn't tell if it was soaked with sweat or snow. 'Suppose she falls ill?'

'She won't. She's never any trouble. All she wants is to rest in the warm. You don't begrudge her that, do you? You may be like her one day yourself. Just let her rest and know you're here if she needs you.' She looked squarely at him. 'It isn't as if you were going anywhere.'

When he didn't answer, she tied on her headscarf and zipped up her long quilted coat, then impulsively she kissed him. 'Dear old Geoffrey, I can always count on you.'

He watched her until she vanished downhill. The slow deep breathing upstairs seemed to permeate the house. At least that ought to mean he would be undisturbed. He went up, treading lightly in case the stairs creaked, and felt foolish. He paused outside his office to listen to the long, slow breaths, and then a kind of fascination he hadn't felt since early adolescence made him creep along the landing and peer around the ajar door.

The window and the mirror opposite streamed with white. The bald head was so deep in the pillow that the linen bulges on either side were higher than the nose and chin. He couldn't imagine what the face had looked like when it was younger, even in middle age, for the features seemed lost in porous dough. His fascination urged him forward, the hinges gave a faint squeal as he edged the door open, and then he flinched back, closing his eyes. He didn't open them until he was in his office with the door shut tight behind him. It wasn't that the bald head had risen as the hinges squealed, it wasn't the sight of her white face turning towards the door as if she could see through her closed eyelids; it was that as he had retreated and the head sank back, still breathing regularly, the face had seemed to flatten as if it had no bones to hold it up.

Of course he couldn't have seen anything of the kind. Briskly he unlocked the safe and took out the sheets of yesterday's issue that he had collected from the post office before Mr Rowley was due. All at once a thought made him smile: for now he could deal with Hay by ignoring him and, more important, as long as Geoffrey was at home, Hay couldn't get to Joyce. He took Hay's letter from the jacket he had meant to wear and locked it away. Snow flurried over Muswell Hill, and Geoffrey was glad not to be driving. As he turned over the first sheet of stamps to search for imperfections, he felt so calm he thought if the breathing slowed any more it would put him to sleep.

As soon as Molly gave the desk sergeant her name, Inspector Maitland stepped forward. His face looked younger than he'd sounded on the phone, though above his protruding ears his fluffy hair was greying. 'You're the lady who wouldn't take no for an answer,' he said with a droll smile that pushed his lower lip out, and turned to Martin. 'And you must be the victim of the press.'

Martin forced a smile. 'You could say that.'

Maitland gave them chairs in his office and walked to his desk with an easy gait that looked like the product of physical training. Close up he smelled of mints. 'Well now,' he said as he crossed his legs and leaned his chair back, 'tell me what you're looking for.'

'I usually don't know until I see it,' Martin said.

'A tour of a typical London police station, eh?'

'Maybe.'

'A cautious talker, isn't he?' The inspector swivelled his chair to face Molly. 'I suppose one learns to be careful with the American police. Never know when they might pull out a gun to settle the argument.' He pivoted back to Martin. 'We aren't like that here, my friend. We just try to do one of the more difficult jobs in the world the best way we know how. Those who can't don't stay. What can I show you?'

'I was wondering if we could see behind the scenes,' Martin said.

'Of course you can. We've nothing to hide.' He was leaning back again, enjoying his balance. 'Just tell me one thing,' he said carelessly. 'Why did you choose this particular division?'

'I told you on the phone,' Molly intervened. 'We want – '

'I know what you said, but I want to hear from the man in charge.'

'We looked on the map and found you were closest to MTV.'

'Thank you, Mr Wallace. Just what Miss Wolfe told me.' Now his smile was meant for himself. 'So what might there be behind the scenes that you think you ought to see?'

'Maybe the cells.'

'The dramatic approach, eh? Well, why not. They're empty just now, but let's visit them by all means. Perhaps we can arrange for them to be in use when you come to film. We can always lock up a drunk or two, it's just that we don't always bother.' His smile was fading. 'I'm sure you know that it's only the untypical that's news. Unfortunately that means it's the least typical incidents that everyone hears about.'

'You mean Lenny Bennett,' said Martin.

'I do indeed.' His smile looked sad, as if he'd expected that. 'But I don't mean only him. I mean a child of just about my little daughter's age who was raped so hard by three young blacks not a mile from here that she may never walk again and can't eat for thinking of what they made her swallow. That isn't typical either, but it's what we have to deal with.'

'Do you think it would have been less of an ordeal for her,' Molly said before she could stop herself, 'if her attackers had been white?'

'Dear me, I must watch my language if I'm to be scrutinized that closely.' He was holding the door open for them. 'No, I don't suppose it would have done her any good if they'd been white, but they weren't, were they?' He collected a bunch of keys from the desk and went to a heavy door at the end of the corridor. 'Maybe you should realize that we don't lock up many blacks, and those we do aren't here for very long.'

Beyond the door a few steps led down to a short corridor across which two pairs of cells faced each other. Walls and cell doors were pale green, and Molly couldn't think why that should make her nervous. Martin was silent. Who wouldn't be preoccupied, she thought. The jiffy bag with the film of Lenny Bennett's death was addressed to him. He was involved. And even if the film turned out to be fake, he couldn't walk away from it now. 'Why is that?' she said to Maitland, since Martin remained quiet.

'Now, why do you suppose? You must know that we can hardly stop a black in the street without some bush lawyer complaining of harassment. That's why the stories about Bennett are so patently ridiculous, even though he had been such a naughty boy.'

Martin spoke without warning. 'Which cell did he die in?'

'He didn't die in a cell at all. I wonder who told you he did.' The inspector had selected a key and was stroking it with his fingertips. 'He died in hospital. He ran out of here when we brought him in for questioning, straight in front of a car. I can give you my word that is what happened, even though I wasn't there. He couldn't have done that if we had been treating him rough, now could he? I'm not telling you anything that wasn't in the papers. You could have read about it in the *Telegraph* instead of listening to propaganda.'

'You brought him in for questioning at three in the morning?' Molly said.

'Certainly, since that was when we found him. He wasn't very anxious to be found, you know. Hardly surprising, since he was concealing explosives in his flat. Which, I may say, we didn't discover until after his death, so you see we had even less reason to lose our tempers with him.'

Perhaps he was telling the truth. Perhaps the film was a fake – could a film really have been shot here unnoticed? 'But you did put him in a cell,' she said.

112

'That's so. This one.' He was unlocking it. 'I admit that was an unfortunate mistake, very unfortunate. The driver and his passenger brought him in off the road before they could be stopped, and the officer who dealt with it wasn't as experienced as he might have been. This was the only place he could think of for Bennett to lie down. Of course Bennett should never have been moved at all.' He stood aside from the open door. 'Go ahead, look around. Take your time.'

Martin went in first, and Molly glanced around the pale green corridor. A peephole glinted bulbously at her from the door opposite. The film was replaying itself in her mind: the door of Lenny Bennett's cell looked warped by the peephole through which the camera was spying, the warped door kept opening on glimpses of Bennett – or someone who looked very like him when he took his hands away from his smashed face to scream for help. The film jerked from shot to shot of the door as it opened to admit policemen whose faces one never quite saw, and beyond them one glimpsed Bennett, spitting out a tooth in one shot, lying on the cell floor in the last shot, unable to raise himself to protect his face with his broken fingers as a boot went in . . . The film was barely four minutes long; half of it consisted of shots of the closed door. There was no sound, and nothing else to see except the beginnings of a graffito on the wall above the bunk, 'LE' in large broad strokes that might have been scraped with the heel of a shoe. She glanced toward Martin, who had turned away from the bunk that was the only furniture except for the seatless lavatory, and saw that the wall was unmarked. She went in then, surprised to find how much she had been dreading the sight of those two letters on the wall. 'Yes, do go in,' Inspector Maitland said.

Now that she was closer to Martin she noticed that his hands were trembling slightly. 'Did you get the name of the driver who ran into him?' Martin said.

'We should have, for speeding. But no, I'm afraid we let him get away.' Maitland moved into the doorway, which was little wider than his shoulders. 'Just goes to show how concerned we were about Bennett.'

He was making the cell feel smaller. The pale green glare of the wall made her anxious to get out of the cell. She started to turn away from the bunk and then saw what Martin's shadow had obscured, what he had already seen, why his hands were trembling. The light picked out the faintest trace beneath the new paint of the first two letters of Lenny Bennett's name.

Maitland blocked the doorway, smiling peacefully. All at once, with a vividness that made her throat feel stuffed with paper, she saw the first shot in which the door of Lenny Bennett's cell was open, a shot of a policeman whose shoulders almost filled the doorway as he went in. She stepped forward quickly, willing Martin to follow, but the policeman didn't budge. 'Perhaps you ought to stay in here,' he said, 'while you decide what to film.'

Molly closed her eyes: the green seemed to be advancing like fog. 'I'd like to go up now,' she said. 'I don't feel very well.'

'Claustrophobic?' The inspector's tone was sympathetic, but she heard his smile. 'Then you really shouldn't have come down here.'

His voice hadn't moved, he was still blocking the doorway. Martin took her arm. 'I guess you want to stand aside,' he said.

She made herself open her eyes. Maitland was stepping back, looking amused. 'You mustn't take me too seriously. You ought to know that we don't lock up people in your line of work unless they've been very irresponsible.' As he locked the door at the top of the steps he said, 'Would you care for a drink, Miss Wolfe? Just a cup of tea, I'm afraid.'

'No thank you.' She swallowed painfully. 'I need fresh air.'

He looked disappointed. 'You'll let me know when you intend to come back.'

'You'll be hearing from us,' Martin said.

The wintry air outside went through her like a shudder, and at first she thought she would be sick. Cars spattered the pavements of Bayswater Road with grey slush beneath the ominously luminous sky. When Martin wiped a dripping bench dry in Hyde Park she realized that he needed to sit down as much as she did. She could see Lenny Bennett's mother, a thin middle-aged woman, gazing at the film as if she couldn't close her eyes, sobbing, 'Oh, Lenny, they did it, oh, sweet Jesus,' over and over as tears streamed down the lines in her face. Molly huddled close to Martin on the bench. 'It was him, wasn't it?' she said.

'In the film? Sure. He was the first one into the cell, he must have been in there all the time. Christ, I don't know how I managed not to knock him down.' He was clenching his fist. 'Okay, I'll give the film to your news people and they can interview me saying I'm convinced it's real. Who do I give it to?'

'Ben Eccles.'

'But isn't he the guy who – '

'That doesn't matter. It's over. It's his programme, and he's good at his job.'

'I guess it must be true if you say so. Do you mind if we get back right away?' He was hugging her and staring at the trees that were trickling snow. 'You see, the thing is, Molly, I would have told you sooner except for all this about Lenny Bennett, but I need to go home.'

'You mean home home.'

'Right, North Carolina. I have to fly out tomorrow morning, that's the earliest they could give me.'

They'd only made love a couple of times, she thought, she had no right to expect him to let her know what he was doing. She could see how troubled he was; he had been concealing it until they'd finished their investigation. 'It's your father,' she said.

'Right.' His fist was open now; his hand looked helpless.

'My mother called last night. He had a heart attack a few days ago but he won't stay in bed or stop drinking. That's my father,' he said and looked as though he wished he felt entitled to think affectionately of him. 'She says he mentioned me. I don't know what he said or even if he really said anything, but I have to go back, don't I? I ought to take the chance.'

'Of course you must.' She kissed him and stood up. 'Come on, let's get the film out of the way.'

She couldn't watch it again. She turned away amid the faint oppressive hum of the moviola while he did. 'Introduce me and I'll do the rest,' he said as they went down to Eccles.

He was in his office with his new and proudly lesbian assistant, Laura Box. The pubic calendar still hung, an emblem of lecherous defiance, behind his desk. 'What can I do for you?' he said to Molly, with an emphasis on the last word that felt like the grinding of a heel.

Eventually Ben accompanied them grudgingly to the seventh floor. He watched the film, watched it again while Martin told him about Maitland and the writing on the wall, watched a third time while he heard about Lenny Bennett's mother. He looked suspicious when he learned that Molly had been at the police station. 'I may want to use it, I don't know yet,' he said at last. 'I'll want to do some checking. At any rate, we can record what you've told me in case you aren't here.'

By the time Martin had spoken his piece to the camera, it was dark outside. The Christmas lights made Oxford Street look like a fun fair. The slush was lumpy poster paint, splashed everywhere. In the Korean restaurant on Poland Street, he murmured, 'Will you come back with me to-night?'

'If you want me to.' She hoped her eyes told him how inadequate her words were. She wanted to be alone with him, to tell him about herself before he went away. The restaurant and the taxi to Kensington were too public, the lift was too deserted and echoing, and they hadn't been in the flat long before they were making love, enjoying each other's bodies like tactile sculptures made of flesh and muscle and bone and salt skin until they could no longer take their time, digging their nails into each other's shoulders as they came. Then they lay in each other's arms, and Molly said sleepily, taking herself unawares, 'The first time we met I felt as if I'd dreamed of you.'

He stroked her breast and cupped it in his hand. 'I'm glad.'

That wasn't how she'd meant it, she had to start again. 'It frightened me. I nearly refused to meet you.'

His small sleepy frown looked slightly resentful. 'Why, what did you dream?'

'I didn't dream anything that I know of. It was the idea of having dreams that frightened me.' She wasn't making herself clear. 'I used to dream of the future,' she said, and grew tense.

'I guess most people do sometimes.'

'Sometimes. With me it was often. I used to dream that someone was going to die, and they did.'

'That's pretty common, isn't it? I seem to recall the Rhine Institute back home went into all that once.'

'I took part in some research years ago,' she said, and felt as breathless as she had in the police cell. 'Near Oxford. They had several of us under observation to see if we dreamed the same thing.'

'Did you?'

'I don't know. I've managed to forget what I dreamed, and now I feel as if I shouldn't have.' She stretched out her arm for her handbag. 'I'd just about forgotten the whole thing when I got this.'

He held Stuart Hay's letter above them to read it, and she read it again, though she knew it by heart. '. . . the experiment in which you participated . . . any after-effects

. . . anything which you feel to be in any way unusual . . . may be important to both of us . . .' Despite that no doubt inadvertent hint of intimacy, it read like a form letter to her, the kind of letter that opinionated self-important Hay would send. It had no right to disturb her as much as it did.

Martin folded it and handed it to her. 'So?' he said as she replaced it in her bag. 'Any after-effects?'

'I don't think so. No,' she said defiantly. 'I thought I saw someone the other day in Soho who took part in the experiment. I could have, I suppose, but it doesn't count. And I've been dreaming again, strange dreams. Too strange to be the future, anyway, that's something. Maybe they're after-effects of his letter.'

'I take it he ran the experiment.' When she explained, he held her gently as if to soften what he had to say. 'If that's all that happened,' he said, 'why does it bother you so much?'

'I suppose because it reminds me.' Her heart was pounding unpleasantly. 'Reminds me how much I've forgotten and makes me wonder why. And reminds me how I used to feel. Frustrated, mainly, knowing that someone was going to die and not being able to do anything. I wanted to change things, I wanted to so much.'

He was smiling and nodding, satisfied. 'It's good we've talked this out before I leave.'

'How long do you think you'll be gone?'

'I wish I could say. I'll call you from Chapel Hill, okay?'

She wished she felt calmer. She felt as if she had left something crucial unsaid. She tried to recall the experiment while she was safe in his arms, but there wasn't much left: a sense of thundery frustration, pale green walls and doors, a blur of faces whose names were clearer than they were, Joyce and Stuart and Guilda and Freda – and Danny, whose name she'd only dreamed was Swain – and the student whose name was, wait a moment, Helen. The sense of frustration led her back towards the dreams she'd had as a child, to her parents' gentle rebukes that she shouldn't say that kind of thing, it only upset people for no reason. Perhaps they had been right after all. She was dozing in Martin's arms, she felt ready to dream without being afraid even if she couldn't change anything, and then she jerked awake so violently that Martin gasped. 'Are you all right?' he demanded.

'I think so. I've remembered something.' She was hardly aware of clinging to him while she tried to recall. 'I had a nightmare about changing things. I must have been quite little, before I can remember dreaming of the future. I dreamed my bedroom was changing into something else, and it would stay like that if I didn't wake in time. I knew somehow it was changing because I was dreaming. When I managed to wake up I didn't dare look.'

'Sounds like it might have been a good thing for you that you weren't able to change things.'

'You don't understand.' She was so frustrated that she punched his shoulder. 'How could I *want* my dreams to change anything after I'd had a nightmare like that? How could I forget it so completely? I've never remembered it until now, don't you see?'

'It's pretty common, forgetting stuff that disturbed you when you were young.' She sensed that he was willing her to calm down; he had his own troubles. 'You're all right now, Molly.'

She wished she were. She wished she could forget again, forget how she had opened her eyes at last and glimpsed her bedroom reshaping itself around her, presenting its familiar appearance just a moment too late, a movement so subtle that eventually she'd been able to persuade herself that she hadn't seen it at all, or else she would never have slept in that room again or anywhere else, perhaps. Now all she could think of was the headachy frustration of not being able to change what she foresaw, and Terry Mace saying they had the power to change. Hadn't he said something

119

else that she ought to remember? Struggling to recall it only drove it further into hiding. Perhaps Martin could remember, but when she turned to ask him, he was asleep.

An arctic wind had left the streets deserted. Under the streetlamps the slushy pavements were shivering. Alone in bed, she wished she had stayed with Martin. She woke in daylight, orange through her eyelids, and wondered if Martin had left by now. She stretched out her arm and bruised her knuckles against a bony object that shouldn't have been there beside the pillow. Her eyes sprang open. She wasn't in her flat, she was in the four-poster bed.

It was as though she'd dreamed herself back into Martin's flat. The place was too quiet; it felt like the times when sounds withdrew from her. Then she saw the note propped up next to her handbag. *Didn't want to wake you but I had to catch my flight. I'll call you when I'm on the ground. Look after yourself while I'm away. Love, Martin.* She saw that he'd hesitated after writing 'Look after yourself' and wondered if he had thought of adding 'for me.' So she had only dreamed that she'd gone home; she realized now that she hadn't felt her steps. Nevertheless the flat and its antique furniture seemed unreal, a museum exhibit she had strayed into by mistake. As she used the shower, she wondered when exactly she had started dreaming.

She was still wondering as the cage glided through the floors, as she closed the street door behind her and stepped onto the crackling frozen slush, as she slithered into the station arcade, beneath the hanging flower baskets. Had she already been dreaming when she had turned to find Martin asleep? And what had she wanted to ask him?

Trains rattled her to Marble Arch. In the office she felt disoriented and lonely, at a loss for work. At the edge of her vision, the blue corridor kept seeming to have turned pale green, and made her feel as if someone were going to appear. When someone did, she started and then stared, wondering who the woman was.

'Remember me? Nell. I just wanted to thank you. I only got the job upstairs because of you.'

'You got it? That must be a relief,' Molly said distractedly.

'You've no idea. Anyway, I'd better not be seen chatting on my first day at work.' A minute later she came back. 'We can walk home together, can't we?'

'Yes, if you like.' Yet Molly wished she hadn't said so, which seemed absurd and unfair. Perhaps the visit to the police station was still troubling her. Or telling Martin about her dreams. Or his sudden departure. Working on the budgets ought to help her get hold of herself. She should be pleased that she'd helped find Nell a job. Perhaps Nell was a little odd, but it was wholly unreasonable of Molly to wish she had never met her at all.

The further you ventured into the Moonlight World, the darker and hotter it grew. At first all Susan could see as she peered into the cages were her own dim face and Eve's, flattened on the glass. The glass seemed to melt away as her eyes adjusted, and here were harvest mice no bigger than her thumb, restless foxes the colour of moonlight, the black and white explosion of a porcupine, a loris climbing as if it weighed nothing. Two sleepy fat-faced rats sat together on a log and watched her as she copied the labels on the cages into her school notebook, and then she found her way through the dimness and the chorus of flapping and scuttling to Eve.

Eve was in front of a cage in which washleathers hung from a branch, pegged there by their feet, for they were bats. Susan copied their label and watched their fluttering.

The movements seemed mysterious, so secret that they didn't know themselves that they were making them, and she knew they were dreaming. It wasn't only the enclosed heat that turned her throat dry. She cleared her throat and blurted out, 'Do you have dreams?'

A blur peered out at her between the bats: Eve's face. 'Don't you?' Eve said.

'No, I never.'

'You do, you know. Everyone does.' Eve turned away from the bats, and they stopped fluttering. 'If you don't have them when you're asleep you must have them when you're awake.'

'How do you mean?'

'Some of the things you think you see must be dreams.'

'That's stupid,' Susan said, to get rid of the idea; it made her feel feverish, and so did the oppressive heat and the dimness. 'Everyone doesn't dream. My mummy doesn't.'

'Oh, yes she does.'

'She doesn't. I should know. She's my mummy, not yours.' But Eve looked so sure of herself that Susan demanded, 'Why did you say she does?'

'Because she told me.'

'She never.' Eve looked calmer still, and Susan wanted to push her, kick her, pull her hair. 'When?'

'Before you came.'

Was it possible that Mummy could have told Eve a secret she had kept from Susan? 'What did she say?' Susan said resentfully.

'I can't remember. She didn't say what she dreamed, if that's what you mean,' Eve said when Susan glared at her, and headed for the steps. 'Come on, there's lots more zoo.'

Faint grey stains were spreading over the white sheet of the sky. The light made Susan blink and sneeze as she picked her way between islands of slush that were shrinking in miniature lakes. Soon Eve began sneezing too, though Susan had thought it was only yawning that you caught from other people. She pinched her flapping notebook between her icy fingers and went to an enclosure where tortoises big enough to ride on were poking out their old men's necks. She wrote them down, and was listing a crocodile like a scaly watchful rock when someone called, 'Hey, Susan.'

It was Chloe and Zoe, who didn't rhyme. Mrs Cranfield, the teacher, had written their names on the blackboard just yesterday when she was talking about words. Susan liked her, liked the school even though it was so big, liked the way Mrs Cranfield's class had welcomed her on her first day with paintings and lemonade and homemade cakes. 'They're in my class,' she told Eve.

Chloe's hair was plaited like a basket, Zoe's skin was blacker, her lips plummier. 'How many have you got?' Zoe said.

'Lots.' Susan displayed her list. 'How many have you?'

'More than you.' Zoe was turning Susan's pages. 'I got all the insects.'

'Insects don't count,' Chloe protested.

'They do too. You wait until Mrs Cranfield sees you didn't write any insects.'

'Don't care. They don't count, do they, Susan?'

'I didn't think so.' She would have liked to have spent more time watching the beetles like walking jewels. Eve was peering over Zoe's shoulder at her notebook. 'What's that?' she said as Zoe glanced warily at her. 'They aren't insects, are they?'

'They're a tongue twister,' Zoe said scornfully. 'Try it, girl. Say it ten times fast, go on.'

'Gwyneth's useful Aberystwyth thesaurus.' It had been Mrs Cranfield's tongue twister that nobody could say, but Eve said it ten times without stopping. 'There,' she said, not even breathless.

'Get her,' Chloe said, so sarcastically that it reminded Susan she hadn't introduced Eve. 'This is Eve. She lives in my street,' she said, then wondered if Eve did.

'Susan has to list some more animals now,' Eve said. 'You can come with us if you like. We don't mind, do we, Susan?'

'We're going to the Moonlight World. You've been in already. Come on, Zoe, move your arse or we'll be late for the disco.'

They'd had enough of Eve, of her frayed coat and droping socks and her black eye. Perhaps that was unfair of them, but Susan couldn't help resenting Eve for driving them away; no wonder Eve seemed to have no friends to play with. A mynah said 'Wotcher,' a lion gave a meaty yawn, camels like patchy carpets stalked about, and Susan listed them all. She hoped her list would be the longest and win Mrs Cranfield's gold star.

Though it had been Eve's idea to come to Regent's Park, Susan didn't speak to her until they had left the zoo and were on their way to Baker Street through the darkening twilight. It wasn't only that she had driven away Susan's friends, it was her saying that Mummy had dreams. That was why, as they stood on the down escalator with the ink from their tickets printing itself on their hands, Susan said, 'Does *your* mummy dream?'

Eve had stepped onto the next stair down to let a father run past with his little boy on his shoulders. 'I don't know,' she said, not looking up.

'You said everyone does.'

'Well then, you don't need to ask.'

She wasn't getting away with that. Susan waited until she could see Eve's face. 'What do you think she dreams?'

'I don't want to know.'

They were running for the train. 'Why are you scared of her? What does she do?' Susan said as the doors closed and the train lurched forward.

'This.' Eve pointed to her black eye with the hand that wasn't clinging to the strap overhead. 'Don't make me tell you what else. I'm frightened to.' She gazed at Susan over

124

the heads of grown-ups squashed together on the seat, and Susan wondered how many of them were listening. 'That's why I'm glad you're my friend,' Eve said.

Susan wasn't sure why. 'Can't someone stop her? Doesn't anyone know?'

'I don't want anyone to try. They'd only make her do worse things.' She gave Susan a wide-eyed pleading look as the train stopped at Edgware Road, jerking them loose from their handholds. 'The people who know her are frightened of her too.'

They struggled to the doors and ran toward the District Line. Susan was growing used to London, except that it seemed to take so long to reach anywhere she wanted to go, and almost everywhere felt like the rush hour all day. Perhaps she didn't want to see where Eve lived after all. They found seats on the train, and she was wondering what else she could ask about Eve's mother when Eve said, 'Do you want to dream?'

It sounded like an offer. 'Why?'

A flood of darkness swept the station away. ''Cause I can show you how to,' Eve said.

'You mean sniffing something.' Just the other day a policeman had been to the school to tell them all how dangerous glue was.

'Oh, no, you don't need that. You just have to let the dreams come.' Eve was giggling at her suspiciousness. 'They're there all the time. You shouldn't try to stop them.'

The train rocked in its cradle of darkness. 'Do you want to?' Eve said.

Susan was remembering the times Mummy had demanded if she'd dreamed, until she had made Susan afraid to sleep in case she did. She had always thought that Mummy stopped herself from dreaming too. 'I'll think about it,' she said, feeling at the mercy of the dark.

Night had reached Bayswater Road. Drops of water on

the buds of a shrub in a garden were unlit Christmas lights, drops turned a drooping clothesline into an abacus and Susan felt she could slide them along.

She unlocked the door. The smell of cats and cabbage met her as she poked the time-switch and she and Eve raced upstairs. Her footsteps clattered, Eve's were softer. She was turning the key when the light above the stairs went out. 'Mummy,' she called. But when she pushed the door open she found the flat was dark.

Her feet sank into the new carpet as she groped for the switch. In the dark they seemed to sink further than they should. The light came on, and somehow Eve was at the mantelpiece. 'She's gone out,' she said, handing Susan a note.

'Won't be long' was all it said, except for a line of kisses. Surely she couldn't be working late on Saturday. Perhaps she was buying Christmas presents, but Susan felt let down, not only because she had expected Mummy to be home but also, more so, because Mummy always wrote Susan's name on notes. The way Eve had got hold of it first, it was almost as though Mummy had meant it for her.

'Do you want me to show you how to dream, then?' Eve said.

All of Susan's resentment made her say 'Yes.'

'Come on then, before she gets back. We'll use your room. That's the darkest.'

After the streamers that slithered over Susan's face and hands, the dark felt soft and soothing. She pulled the cord, and there were Rapunzel and Repulsive sitting together like old friends. She was growing apprehensive. 'What have we got to do?'

'You haven't got to do anything. Just stop trying not to dream.' Eve stood by the light cord. 'Lie down, go on.'

Susan climbed on the bed but sat against the headboard. 'Can't we leave the light on?'

'No, it's got to be dark.' Eve came to her and pushed her

126

gently down. 'I'll be with you,' she said, and went quickly to the cord and pulled.

The dark took Susan's breath away. She felt she was drowning in it. When she felt Eve lie down, a soft weight beside her, she managed to draw a breath. One reason she spoke was to hear herself; the dark was silent as the bottom of a pool, her ears were throbbing. 'Now what happens?'

'Breathe slowly, like when you go to sleep,' Eve whispered in her ear. 'Let yourself float and see where you go.'

Susan was having enough trouble reminding herself where she was, for she felt as if the dark were growing. The shifting patches of dimness must be in her eyes, but they made her feel that the dark was like the Moonlight World, full of activity that she would see as soon as her eyes adjusted. Closing them was no help: light seemed to flare up from her cheekbones, two regular flares that fanned across her vision and faded away. Her breathing was slowing down into their rhythm, it seemed to be the only way she could breathe. 'That's right,' Eve whispered.

If this was dreaming, drifting helplessly through the dark while the lights in her eyes made her feel even blinder, Susan didn't want to dream. She would have got up at once except that Eve might laugh at her. She dug her fingers into the mattress through the blanket and hung on. She thought of holding Eve's hand but somehow didn't want to. When her ears stopped throbbing, she heard the television in the flat next door.

She tried to hear it clearly so as not to drift, but it made the dark seem even larger. She was listening across a dark river, very wide. It was the Mersey, of course it was; she could see it at the feet of streets as she ran home, down past the shop with the rising sun on the awning that said 'Every Morn Think of Vaughan,' down past Vale Park and the tree that bore a mossy toilet seat, the mark of a fallen branch. Now it was night and the misty dockyards were hooting like a ship as long as the far bank, a ship carrying dozens of cranes and chimneys twelve floors tall and the Liver Clock with the stone bird tied on top, a long thin misty ship lighted by sodium streetlamps and the pinpoint windows of tower blocks, a ship that was sailing away under a fairy-tale moon like a fat banana. High tide was rushing in, children came racing down the ramps from the promenade to see who dared stay longest on the beach, and Susan sang 'Girls and boys come out to play, the moon does shine as bright as day.' She went back along the pipe, above house bricks that the sea had smoothed into oval red stones, and headed for the ramp at Egremont, where the streets to the promenade were so steep they had handrails. 'Leave your supper and leave your street,' she sang, 'and join your playfellows in your sleep,' which seemed so odd that it made her shiver. 'Don't try to see things,' Eve said beside her. 'Just let them come.'

Had Susan been singing aloud? If that was dreaming, she wished Eve hadn't interrupted. She lay and waited and hoped she could go back. Surely hoping didn't count, but now there was only the dark that might be huger than the sky or close enough to touch. Suddenly she couldn't move. She remembered asking Mummy what death was. It was like going to sleep and just not waking up, Mummy had told her, which had sounded reassuring until Susan had realized that if you never woke up you might never be able to stop dreaming. She couldn't move, for the coffin of darkness was holding her tight, the darkness which was how it was once you were dead, a dark in which you were no longer any size and so couldn't measure the dark, the dark in which there was movement, the flares blooming in her eyes, light opening like hands and passing out of her, great luminous hands that kept letting her go. They were playing with her, but not forever. The next time they might not open, they might keep hold of her as their face leaned down between them, a huge blurred glowing face that she could almost see. Once she saw it clearly, the hands would never let her go.

She opened her eyes but could still see the blurred face, growing huger and closer. She was clutching the blanket, but that didn't seem real enough to help. She was really lying on the bed, the dark was her room, she could roll off the bed as the face that was almost not blurred filled the dark above her, as the hands closed over her. She dodged at the last moment and slipped breathlessly under the hands, which missed her shoulder but touched her hand as she shoved herself off the bed, soft fingers that felt huge but shrinking. Of course that must be Eve's hand, and the rest was a dream. Susan knocked a book off the shelves on the dressing table as she plunged through the dark. The thick carpet seemed to be drowning her feet until she pulled the cord. She stood gaping, trying to breathe. The bed was rumpled but deserted. She was alone in the room.

She fled into the hall. The streamers at both ends were still, the bathroom was empty. When had Eve left her? As she ran into the main room, she called 'Eve' so loud that the window vibrated. There was no sign of Eve except for her book on top of Susan's encyclopedias. Susan ran between the plants to the window to see if Eve was out there, under the streetlamps that were beginning to shake in the wind. She hadn't reached the window when someone knocked at the door.

She hoped it was Mummy, too burdened with parcels to use her key. Just now she hoped it wasn't Eve. But it was a woman in a housecoat, her hair in curlers under a net. It looked like dust in a carpet sweeper. The woman demanded, 'Was that you?'

'Yes.' Susan recognized her now: she lived across the landing – beyond the open door cats slept on faded chairs in front of a gas fire. 'I was calling to my friend.'

'You admit it, do you? Well, we'll have less of it. This is a quiet house.'

'I wasn't making much noise.'

'The cheek of it.' She turned to her cats and shouted,

'Just listen to her, will you. Not much noise, she says.' She swung round to glare at Susan. 'I suppose you'd call that singing all day yesterday not much noise, would you?'

Susan stared, forgetting not to be rude. 'It couldn't have been us. I was at school and Mummy was at work.'

'I'll bet she was. You wouldn't have been making all that row if she'd been here.' She reached out and thumped the door with her fist, and Susan smelled the cats on her. 'Don't you be saying it wasn't in here. I stood right here listening and telling you to stop. You're the only child here, aren't you? Haven't got another family hidden in there, I suppose?'

'There's just me and Mummy,' Susan said, but her thoughts were louder.

'I should think so. No call for us to do it just because the darkeys do. Half of them don't know what a proper house is for. No wonder, with all that stuff they smoke. Never mind that,' she growled, dragging herself back to the subject. 'It was you singing and getting me so I couldn't hardly think. Don't you ever do that again or you'll have something to sing about, I'll set the truant officer on you.' She was shuffling back to her flat, her slippers clapping under her heels. As she shooed a cat back onto its chair and slammed the door, Susan heard her mutter, 'I wouldn't even call it singing. Raving, more like.'

Susan closed out the dark landing and stood by the door. She didn't want to think, but she had no choice. Eventually she turned on the gas fire and watched from the window for Mummy. The streetlamps shivered, shadows roamed the street. Eve must have been in here yesterday when she ought to have been at school, however she had got in, but there was more to it than that. Eve had made her dream. That wasn't the worst problem either, that wasn't what Susan had to deal with. If Mummy were dreaming, after all that she'd said about dreams – and it was Eve who said she was – then Eve must be doing that, too.

Molly was almost nodding off when the phone rang.

It was Ben Eccles. So you've found out where I live at last, she thought, much good may it do you. 'What's the problem?'

'Martin Wallace.' His voice was savage and something else – triumphant, perhaps. 'Is he there?'

'He went back to the States this morning. Why?'

'Because his film that we broadcast tonight is a fake.'

She didn't quite believe him, not when she disliked him so much, not when it sounded almost as if he were accusing Martin of having faked the film. 'Who says so?'

'I'll tell him, not you. Where is he?'

'I don't know his number.'

She hoped he would tell her what he wanted to tell Martin, but he only gave her his home number. 'You tell him to call me as soon as he gets in touch with you,' he said.

She couldn't believe him when he had offered no proof. She paced through her flat, past her aimless army of reflections. Even the sounds of the wind chimes above the doors rasped her nerves. When the phone rang again she vowed that she would get some sense from Ben, if there was any to be had. But it was Gould, the head of Staffing. 'I understand you may know where we can contact Martin Wallace.'

'I'm afraid not.'

'You surprise me. If he contacts you, please ask him to call me at once.'

'Has Ben Eccles been saying things about him?'

'No, the police have. About him and the film he claims was sent to him. The film is bogus. There is no question of that.'

She wrote down his number, which was more than she'd done for Ben Eccles.

She put down the phone and wished she had asked him what proof there was. She was still wondering whether to call Martin when he called her.

She told him everything except Gould's request. She didn't want to give him any more to deal with. She could tell that he wanted to stop talking and think, and she said good-bye as soon as she decently could.

Afterwards she lay feeling exhausted and wondering what the police had said. Suppose they had faked their proof and the film was real after all? It seemed impossible that Lenny Bennett's mother could have been fooled, even though by the time you saw the face of the man in the cell it had been beaten almost shapeless. Her thoughts were blurring, she was falling asleep – no wonder after such a night. For a moment, then another, she couldn't even hear the silence. She was stepping down through the gaps in her consciousness to a place where there might be no anxiety.

But there was. She was watching the film of the cell, though it was in colour now instead of black and white, as Inspector Maitland's voice said, 'There, there, there.' He was holding her head still, his hands felt capable of crushing her skull if she didn't see what he wanted her to notice. She would if she could, there was no need for him to thump on her skull and ring bells in her ears. She woke and felt as if her skull were still caught, more so when she realized that the thumping and the bell were at the front door.

She tied her dressing gown around her as she hurried down the hall. The two blurred figures beyond the frosted glass must be the secretaries from upstairs. This time they'd get what they were asking for. She was past the mirrors so quickly that she didn't even see herself. She threw open the door and was folding her arms when she saw that the two figures weren't the secretaries, but police.

One stooped to pick up her bottle of milk. 'Molly Wolfe?' his companion said.

'Yes?' She glanced from one to the other of the rigid young helmeted faces and wondered what could have brought them here so early. Had something happened to her parents? 'What's wrong?'

'Inspector Maitland wants a word with you.'

'Why?'

'You know,' the policeman with the bottle said.

She resented having been made needlessly anxious. 'Tell him I'll be in to see him later,' she said, and held out her hand for the milk. 'Thank you.'

He moved the bottle out of reach and stared at her. 'Inspector Maitland wants to sort this out as soon as possible,' the other policeman said.

A postman whose bag was stuffed with Christmas cards glanced down through the railings and looked hastily away. She was damned if she'd have a row out here over a bottle of milk. 'Then you'd better come in while I get dressed.'

She took the milk. One policeman followed her into the kitchen while she stood the bottle in the refrigerator. When he followed her into the hall, she said, 'I want to get dressed now.'

'Please don't mind me,' he said. The other policeman was outside her bedroom window when she picked up her clothes to take into the bathroom. 'If you were looking forward to the show you're out of luck,' she said under her breath, but his expression made her go cold all over. She wondered if he could read lips.

At least his companion didn't try to make her leave the bathroom door open. She hoped he heard her use the toilet, hoped he was blushing. She took her time in the shower until she wondered what they might do if they thought she was taking too long, and then was towelling herself before she stepped out of the bath. 'I won't be long now,' she called, hating her nervousness.

When she unbolted the door they were both in the hall. One insisted on holding her coat, though she didn't like turning her back on him. Outside the overcast glowed like a pall of smoke in front of a fire. Her open gate met the open door of the police car, and there was nowhere to go but in.

The police car smelled of seat leather and boot polish. In no time it squealed to a halt in front of the police station.

Christmas cards and holly were taped to the wall behind the desk. She wondered who had sent the cards: grateful criminals, victims of crimes? As the policeman with the cheerful eyes tapped on Maitland's door, she heard church bells far away. 'Yes, yes,' Maitland said.

He gazed at her for quite a long time once they were alone. Whatever his smile meant, it made her nervous. Her bladder was aching and she'd had enough of waiting for him to be courteous. She was about to sit down when he said, 'You should have let me say no in the first place.' He was shaking his head, with its fluffy grey hair and protruding ears. Part of her wanted to laugh. 'You should have looked elsewhere for your typical London police station.'

She felt like a child who'd been found out for lying, and it made her furious. 'Don't look at me like that, miss,' he said. 'You're in enough trouble as it is.'

Did he think he was speaking to one of his children? 'I was doing my job,' she said. 'I'm sorry I didn't tell you the whole truth, but surely that isn't a crime.'

'Oh, is lying acceptable now? Perhaps in your line of work.' His ears were turning bright red. 'In itself it isn't a crime in law, no. But wasting police time is, and so is behaviour likely to cause a breach of the peace. And I hope you realize you could be charged as an accessory to falsifying evidence.'

'You mean the film?' That sounded too much like admitting guilt. 'I still don't know how it was proved to be faked.'

'Which is to say you don't believe me? I suppose that's part

134

of your job too.' He stood up and opened the door. 'Let's hope we can convince even you,' he said, ushering her along the corridor, one hand lightly on her elbow, to the cells.

She felt she had to go down or he would be suspicious. The echoes of her footsteps made the pale green corridor seem longer than it looked. He joined her at the foot of the steps, and she smelled his minty breath. 'Do you remember which one?' he said.

'That one.'

'Indeed. One can't fault your powers of observation. A pity that you aren't with us.' He was selecting the key to the cell. 'Out of interest, can you tell if these cells are empty?'

She went quickly from door to door. Each fish-eye peephole contained a distorted bunk and a lavatory. 'Yes, they are,' she said.

'Could you have seen that from any of the other cells?'

'Yes, if the cell I was watching was open.' She wondered why she couldn't just have said no.

'That would certainly be convenient, wouldn't it?' He was waiting for her to follow him inside the cell he had unlocked. 'Now then, just tell me what persuaded you that film was genuine.'

Though the closeness of the pale green walls made her breathless, she moved until she could see the letters under the paint. 'The writing on the wall,' she said.

'A pity that you couldn't read it.' He was smiling at his wit. 'Now tell me this. Who do you think scratched those letters there?'

'Lenny Bennett, presumably.'

'We brought him in to beat him up then left him alone to write his name? Or was that while we were taking a break from the good work? Before or after we're supposed to have smashed his hands?' His shadow blotted out the letters as he stepped between her and the door. 'Perhaps we can excuse you for seeing what you wanted to see, but make no mistake, those letters were put there after Bennett's death.'

135

'By whom?'

'By one of two demonstrators who picketed us after Bennett died. We locked them up for causing a disturbance and blocking the traffic. If we'd seen which one, we'd have had him for defacing public property. I wouldn't be surprised if they both did, one hand each. You know what the comrades are like.' He was watching her eyes. 'Still don't believe me? Then believe this. The cell was inspected after Bennett's death, as soon as the accusations started flying. No evidence of violence and certainly no writing on the wall. That was put there a month later, and it was seen by the painters when they came to smarten up the accommodations.'

Her own breath tasted of mint by now. Her nerves were jerking the walls of the cell, which flickered forward, glaring. She wanted to ask him to let her past, but she heard herself saying, 'Who inspected the cell?'

'Dear me, you are difficult to convince. Someone whose word even you would accept, I think.' He wasn't smiling as he closed the door and leaned against it. 'Just take my word for now if you will, to save time. I can understand how you feel, believe it or not. You thought Wallace was justified in what he was doing.'

'I still do. Now can we please go upstairs?'

'Soon, I hope. That's up to you.' As he folded his arms, they made his shoulders against the door even huger. 'You really think that Wallace was justified in falsifying evidence when the event never took place?'

'He didn't falsify anything. Someone sent him the film and he thought it was genuine.'

'Sent it to himself, did he? And made sure someone saw him receive it, am I right?' He was shaking his head, and looked almost sympathetic. 'I realize that your relationship with him isn't merely professional. It's for precisely that reason that I think you must have known what he meant to do.'

'He used that film in good faith.' The glare of the walls was making her eyes sting. 'Now will you please let me – '

'Listen to me.' The first word was a shout, too big for the cell. 'By the time my children get to school on Monday morning, some of their classmates are going to be convinced that I helped murder Bennett. It doesn't matter that we have proof to the contrary, half of them won't understand that, too many adults won't either. Some of them will carry on believing that film.' He was rocking on the balls of his feet as if about to move toward her. 'But your testimony might convince them, and it better had. Either you can tell me the truth about Wallace because you see it's the proper thing to do, or you can tell me because we make you. Your choice. Take your time.'

Her legs were shaking, but she mustn't sit down, she had to get out of the cell. She seemed to be able to feel all her nerves individually. 'I'd rather not say any more until I've made a phone call.'

'Picked that up from watching television, did you? Use the phone if you can find one by all means.' He pointed to the seatless lavatory. 'Have a look in there.' He opened the door and stood in the doorway until she ran forward, then he put one hand on her breasts and shoved her back. 'If I were you I really should decide to talk before we come down to see you.'

The edge of the bunk folded her legs up, the wall thumped her shoulders. She was up and running at the door as the key turned in the lock. A dwarf with Maitland's face swelled up in the fish-eye, and then there was only the empty section of corridor, the cell door opposite bulging like a barrel, the lingering smell of Maitland's breath.

She mustn't lose control. He was trying to scare her into saying what they wanted to hear. They wouldn't dare touch her, not when she was with MTV, though if they did and she reported them, would she be believed now that the film had been discredited? She mustn't think that, mustn't wonder if Maitland had. If he imagined that refusing her a phone call would undermine her, he was wrong, for who could she have called? Leon was in Belfast, her parents were in Devon, and now she felt abandoned, buried in the windowless room where she couldn't even hear the heavy traffic less than a hundred yards away. That was all the silence was, the soundproofing of the cell; she mustn't let the silence frighten her, the silence or the pale green walls. She was pacing back and forth to hear her footsteps, though her legs were aching where the bunk had bruised her. The sooner Maitland came down again the better, for she couldn't be forced to say what she didn't know. It wasn't Martin who had faked the film, that was all she knew. It needn't even have been anyone at MTV.

She halted, not quite knowing why she had thought that, and then she knew. 'Oh, good God,' she whispered. Panicky cramps seized her stomach so painfully that she pressed her hands against it. Perhaps she did know who had faked the film, for she'd remembered what she had been struggling to recall the night before Martin had gone home: Terry Mace had said he'd been locked up here for picketing outside, that films had to be used for change, that if they had performed their street play here, the police would have thought Lenny Bennett had come back to haunt them. How closely did the actor who played Bennett resemble him? She couldn't be sure, she mustn't let the police scare her into giving away what she suspected, but now she was concealing information after all. Maitland did have a reason to work on her, even if he didn't know. The thought cramped her stomach until she had to use the toilet. The porcelain was so cold it seemed to bite into her thighs. She hadn't finished when the key turned in the lock.

A policeman with close-cropped hair and Maitland stared at her. 'Perhaps you could leave me alone until I've finished,' she said, shivering with cold, with helpless rage.

'Have you decided to tell us what we need to know?'

'I've already told you the truth.' She reached for the

138

toilet paper; let them watch if it turned them on. 'If you insist on having me watched,' she said through her stiffening mouth, 'you know it ought to be a policewoman.'

'None on duty.' Maitland let the skinhead policeman precede him into the cell, then leaned against the door. 'Besides, they don't like doing what you're making us do.'

His colleague sat on the bunk and put his legs up. 'Get on with it,' he complained, staring at her as he might have stared at an incontinent puppy. 'This place stinks.'

She stood up furiously and wiped herself. 'Happy now?'

'Looks as if she is,' he said to Maitland. 'Likes us watching her, the dirty bitch.'

She almost tore her clothes as she dressed herself. Like her head, her hands felt hot and swollen; rage that was very like panic had clamped her mouth shut. She dragged at the handle of the cistern, tried again, but nothing happened. 'Can't even clean up after herself. We ought to make her clean it out,' the skinhead policeman said.

'This is getting us nowhere,' Maitland said, and she turned to him. She was beginning to feel relieved until she saw his face. 'Stand there,' he told her, 'and put your hands on your head.'

'Don't be ridiculous.'

'Do it.' His shoulders lifted from the door. 'Do it or by God we'll make you.'

'If you hurt me you won't be able to pass it off as a car accident.' She was frightening herself, but couldn't stop. 'You wouldn't dare hurt me.'

'What, because you'd go and show yourself on telly?' the skinhead said behind her, sniggering. 'You wouldn't believe the things we can do to you without leaving a mark.'

'He doesn't like your audience being told lies about him any more than I do. Just put your hands on your head.' Maitland said wearily. 'You'll get tired of that soon enough. Tell us the truth about Wallace and you can go.'

She heard the skinhead's boots strike the floor as

Maitland shoved himself forward. She put her hands on her head and sobbed furiously inside herself. She'd stand here as long as they wanted, it was stupid and humiliating but would do her no real harm. She had told them the truth about Martin, she mustn't think about Terry Mace, they didn't know about him. Surely Maitland wouldn't see her harmed to make her talk.

She didn't know how long she stood there, but it felt like hours. Soon her arms were aching, her legs felt as if they would be agony to move. There was the threat of new cramps in her stomach. The pale green walls jerked forward again, and she thought she was falling. Every time the green closed in she was close to forgetting where she was.

Maitland had been watching her patiently, a man who didn't care for some of the things his job required him to do, but now his eyes were growing blank and indifferent and tired. Perhaps he was thinking of turning the skinhead loose on her. She was searching frantically for words that would make them let her go, trying to think what she hadn't already said. Suddenly she thought she knew. 'It couldn't have been Martin. You can't believe he made the film after we came here, he wouldn't have had time. If he made it before, who told him about those?'

She had turned to point at the letters on the wall. 'Keep your hands on your head,' Maitland said.

'Yes, but listen to me.' She turned back, planting her feet further apart so as not to fall, raising her hands to her head, almost clawing at her scalp. 'Why should anyone have wanted him to make the film instead of making it themselves? It isn't as though his name is on it. Besides, he hasn't been here long enough.'

'Long enough to get you into bed,' the skinhead said. 'Mind you, I reckon that's not saying much.'

She must ignore him, but all she could think of to take her mind off him was Terry Mace. 'I suppose it's just possible that we're mistaken about your relationship with

Wallace,' Maitland said. 'Have you had sex since he went back to America?'

She had been closing her eyes to shut out the encroaching green, but now she glared at him. 'No.'

'She must be gasping for it,' the skinhead said.

'Indeed.' Maitland was staring at her parted legs. 'Miss Wolfe does seem confused about sex. That was something I learned when she was here asking questions to make sure our American friend didn't miss anything – that she doesn't know if it would be preferable to be molested by blacks or whites.'

'Must have had plenty of experience, the way she looks.'

It didn't matter what they said about her, it didn't matter that her arms and legs were jerking like the walls, that her mouth was stiffening shakily. Maitland was smiling and looking past her, she thought he was about to give the skinhead the nod. If only his wife and children could see him now, she thought, and before she knew she was going to speak she said, 'Would you like someone to treat your daughters like this?'

His face darkened, his wide shoulders stirred. 'Leave my family out of it.'

'It was you who told me about them.' She'd reached him, she had to go on. 'The worst you suspect me of is lying, though I give you my word that I've told you the truth. Suppose one of your daughters was accused of lying? Would you want someone to – ' Shut up, she screamed inside herself, don't say another word in case he sees that you know. He was gazing quizzically at her.

'Well?' he said.

But she couldn't go on. She remembered what he'd said: that his children would be led to think he was a murderer. He wouldn't fear that unless he had been here the night of Bennett's death. He'd told her that he hadn't been, and there was only one reason for him to have lied: Bennett had

141

been killed here after all, the film was true even if it wasn't genuine. 'Well?' he said, impatiently now.

'That's all,' she said through her stiff shaky lips. 'I'm not a criminal, I've told you the truth. Please let me go now. Let me go before you do something you won't be able to hide.'

His shoulders pushed him away from the door. 'Such as what?'

She mustn't show fear; the appearance of dignity was all she had left. 'Such as letting him touch me,' she said, and prayed that would suggest to Maitland that she trusted him.

'I'm afraid you haven't made a conquest, Randy.' He gazed at her breasts, her aching legs, finally her face. 'I take it Wallace will be away for a few days. Perhaps we can give you time to reconsider.'

He was opening the door. As she stumbled forward the skinhead policeman stepped in front of her and shoved her back toward the bunk. She wondered how she could have imagined that Maitland meant to let her go. A stomach cramp made her whole body clench.

When Maitland reached the corridor, he looked back. 'That's all right, Randy. Let her come. She can help us further with our enquiries when she's had time to think.'

He unlocked the door at the top of the steps and waited for her. As she inched past, scraping her shoulders on the corner of the wall so as not to touch him, he said, 'Expect us any time.'

She hardly noticed the desk sergeant as she stumbled out. The roar of traffic on Bayswater Road seemed not only to deafen but also to blind her. When she came to herself, she was shaking so much that people were watching her. She was closer to her flat than to MTV but she didn't want to go home, that would be no help. She wished there were more people as she hurried past the police station, on the opposite side of the road. At least her legs weren't aching so much, and by the time she reached MTV she had almost stopped shaking.

Terry Mace was at the round reception desk. When he saw her and opened his mouth to speak, she said, 'You bloody sod.' She left him staring after her as the lift carried her to the ninth floor and Oliver Boycott, MTV's lawyer. If he wasn't in his office, she would get his home number. Maitland and his randy crony wouldn't find her so easy to intimidate once Boycott had been to see them. She could hardly wait to see their faces. She felt almost incandescent with fury, which made her think of Martin. It was a good thing he was in America. God only knew what his temper might have caused him to do if he were here.

More than anything else – more than Mummy's new dress in its box under Susan's bed, or trying to guess where Mummy had hidden her presents, or the classroom party next week – the snow made her feel close to Christmas. She took a chair to the window and knelt there, gazing at the endless silent flock of snow beneath the darkly glowing sky. Large flakes thudded like loose snowballs on the window and trickled down the pane, veils glided past the house, veils that grew more solid in the distance until they merged into a sheet of white. She couldn't follow the patterns that the snow made in the air, she could only let them happen. They made her feel peaceful and outside herself, almost ready to dream. She wondered if she dared. Perhaps when she got the courage to ask Mummy if she dreamed.

The snow was settling. Parked cars rose like cakes, gateposts grew cotton flowers; penguin people with white fronts that they kept slapping to dislodge the snow waddled through the drifts between the cars and the vanishing gardens. White Christmas, Susan thought, and wondered if the snow would stop the trains. Perhaps she wouldn't mind not going back for Christmas. She had new friends now.

A student postman whose bag looked heaped with snow came trudging along the street trying to find the pavement. He turned in at the gate below her window, and she heard the clank of the letter slot deep in the building. She was pushing herself away from the chair to go down when she saw Eve, clutching her duffel hood around her face as she came up the path, then she was out of sight and the bell was ringing. 'It's Eve, Mummy,' Susan called and ran to let her in.

The prickly mat in front of the door was scattered with envelopes. Susan dragged the door open, shoving the envelopes aside. Eve came huddling in. Snow that felt like a memory of itself brushed Susan's face while she gazed at the path, at two sets of the postman's footprints and one of Eve's. What else was she expecting to see? She closed the door and found Eve sorting the letters onto the shelf above the gas meters. 'These are yours,' Eve said, handing them over, 'and these are for your mum.' Before Susan could take those as well, Eve ran upstairs.

'Thank you, Eve.' Mummy didn't sound at all surprised that Eve had brought her the cards.

'I came to see if you wanted a snow fight,' Eve said.

'Why don't you, Susan, until dinner's ready? Just make sure you wrap up warm.'

Susan hurried to her room for her coat and hat and mittens. This was the chance she needed, to talk to Eve by herself. She wished the woman with the cats would come out and see Eve, but the landing was deserted. Halfway downstairs Susan said, 'Do you go in our flat when I'm not there?'

Eve turned to her as the light went out. 'How could I?'

Susan didn't bother with the time-switch, she knew the stairs by now. 'Maybe you've got a key.'

'Better ask your mummy.' Eve's voice seemed distant,

though her footsteps were close. 'Anyway, why would I want to?'

'To hide from your mummy.'

'Who says I do?'

'The woman who lives on our floor,' she said.

Eve opened the front door, letting in the snow's twilight and a flurry of snowflakes. She was shaking her head. 'You shouldn't listen to her, she's crazy.'

'How do you know, if you haven't been coming in?'

Eve stepped onto the path, from which her footprints and the postman's were already vanishing. 'Because I've lived round here longer than you, that's why.'

Somehow Susan knew Eve was lying. What could that mean? Just then she noticed the corner of an envelope sticking out of Eve's coat pocket. She was almost sure that pocket had been empty when Eve had come into the house.

The kerb had vanished. The toothy track of a single car broke the snow on the road. Snowflakes danced in the cones of light beneath the streetlamps. Eve ducked as Susan flung a snowball, and the envelope emerged a little further. It was slightly too large for her pocket. If it had been there when she had let Eve in, Susan was sure she would have seen it.

Eve dodged away between the cars. In the dreamy hush of the street, the snow squeaked underfoot like icing sugar. Susan followed her, running though it felt like plodding. She had to see the envelope, whether it was addressed to her or Mummy or even perhaps Eve at their address. She realized suddenly that she didn't know Eve's last name.

Perhaps she could make Eve slip and fall. She gathered snow from the plump roofs of cars, squeezed it into a ball, and threw it as hard as she could. It thudded against a car's feathery windscreen. 'Hey,' Eve cried, her face glistening with snow from the windscreen, 'not so hard.'

Then she ducked, for someone else was throwing snowballs, three children coming from the direction of Westbourne Grove. Her movement pushed the letter half out of her pocket, and Susan was afraid the address might be washed away before she had a chance to look. Perhaps not, for Eve was retreating toward her – but before she came abreast of Susan, she dodged between the cars.

The children were following. Susan threw a token snowball at them and slithered back toward the house, since that was where Eve seemed to be heading. She managed to struggle as far as the gate just as Eve veered toward it. It might be Susan's only chance. She slipped deliberately and fell.

She was almost too convincing. One hand clawed the snow off the bonnet of the nearest car; she felt rust scraping her fingertips as snow trickled into her sleeve. Her other hand grabbed Eve, tugging at her pocket, at the envelope. Her fingers were so stiff with cold that she couldn't keep hold of the envelope. It jerked out of Eve's pocket and fell in the snow at her feet.

The moment seemed to turn into a photograph. A snowball had just thumped the windscreen of the rusty car; thick slabs of snow skated down the glass and piled against the wipers. Eve was watching the children and she hadn't seen the letter yet. The envelope lay face up, the address was already spreading but still clear. It was addressed to Mummy and had been sent on from Wallasey. As Susan struggled to her feet she stuffed the envelope into her pocket. 'I'm going in now.'

'Play a bit longer.'

'I can't. I heard Mummy calling.'

Eve turned, ignoring a snowball that shattered into white spray and lumps on her duffel hood. 'No, you didn't,' she said.

There was something in her eyes and in her voice that made Susan back away, clutching the envelope in her pocket with one hand while she fumbled for her key with the other. 'I did,' she stammered. 'Anyway, I've hurt my leg.'

She was praying that the children would keep Eve busy as she struggled through the tangle of footprints up the path. She had to hold the key with both hands before it would fit into the lock. She swung round, suddenly expecting Eve to have crept behind her to snatch the envelope back. But there was no sign of her.

Enormous whiteness rushed at Susan as she slammed the door. She couldn't see where she was going as she ran upstairs. She felt for the lock on the apartment door, shook the key into the slot, and then there was the flat, too green to be blotted out. The afterimages on her eyes were shrinking as Mummy brought in cutlery and table mats. 'I was just going to call you,' Mummy said, and then, 'What's wrong?'

'Eve took your letter, Mummy.'

Mummy dumped the handful of cutlery in front of her. 'Go on, set the table. What letter?'

'This one.' Mummy was turning away. 'Look, Mummy!' Susan cried.

'She put it in your pocket, did she?' Mummy shook her head sadly. 'Just give it to me, Susan. No need to look like that if you took it by mistake, I won't punish you. Just don't tell fibs.'

She dropped the crumpled letter by the table mat and headed for the kitchen. Susan followed her through the rattling streamers. 'She really did take it. She stole it, Mummy.'

The streamers in the kitchen doorway slapped her face as Mummy turned on her. 'Susan, why are you being like this? Why should Eve want to do anything of the kind?'

That was what Susan wanted to know. 'Well, open it and see.'

'Don't you speak to me like that, young lady. Don't you say another word. Get the plates and behave yourself.'

Susan towelled her feet before she put on her slippers, then she carried the plates to the table. Her face was hot with resentment that made her unable to see anything properly. Mummy had never spoken to her like that before, she'd always encouraged her to talk to her like a friend. The streamers sounded as if they were sniggering. Mummy carried in the casserole with her padded oven glove and ladled chicken onto the plates. Susan was cutting her meat up neatly when Mummy said, 'Just what have you got against Eve?'

'What do you mean?'

'You know perfectly well what I mean, or you should. You were grateful enough to have her as a friend when you didn't know anyone here. Now you've made friends at school you don't want to know her, do you? You ought to be ashamed of yourself.'

'I still play with her.'

'Yes, and then you come home telling tales about her stealing. She looks like a thief to you, does she? Do you know, Susan, I think if we aren't careful you'll be turning into a snob. Eve can't help the way she looks. I'd buy her clothes myself except that might make life worse for her. You know what it's like for her at home.'

Susan wondered suddenly if Eve had stolen the food she'd brought them on their first day here, but it was too late to find out. 'Mummy, do you let her hide from her Mummy in here?'

'Yes, there she is, under the settee. Or maybe she's under the carpet. What are you babbling about, you stupid child?'

Susan knew she would make her more angry, but what else could she do? 'She comes in when we aren't here.'

Mummy stared at her for quite a time before she spoke. 'I'm warning you, Susan, if you can't control your imagination, I'll give away every one of your books. I'll give them to Eve to make up for the way you're treating her. And if you keep on I'll have your mind looked into. No, I won't, it was people like that who nearly gave me a breakdown, they won't get their hands on you.' She was talking to herself and

148

staring at the Oxford postmark on her letter. 'Now just shut up and eat your dinner before you put me off eating.'

Susan ducked her head and ate, and watched. Mummy was forking food into her mouth and chewing more and more slowly as she gazed at the envelope. She dug her fork into a chicken leg and let go. The fork keeled over into the gravy as Mummy snatched the letter, so violently that Susan thought she was going to tear it up. 'Don't,' she cried.

'Why don't you want me to read it? What do you think you know?' Now she was in that strange mood Susan always tried to ignore until it went away. She ripped the envelope and dragged the letter out, read it in a few seconds. 'That's all it is, and the answer's no, no, no. Won't you be disappointed, Mister Psychologist, wouldn't you be, except you don't know where I am and you never will.' She held up the letter. 'Hardly worth stealing, was it?'

It was from someone called Stuart Hay, with a tiny signature above his typed name. Susan only glimpsed words and phrases – 'experiment in which you participated,' 'after-effects,' 'anything unusual,' 'may be important' – before Mummy folded it impatiently. 'Why am I letting you read it after what you did? I must want my head examined.'

'I didn't take it, Mummy.'

'Oh, no, of course, Eve did. Evil Eve who comes in here without a key and wanted you to be her friend. Anything else you can accuse her of?'

Susan ought not to have responded, not when she could see how nervous and strange Mummy was. 'She says you dream.'

'What?' Mummy had been stuffing the letter into the envelope, but suddenly she crumpled them in her fist. 'What did you say to me?'

Susan had to ask, she mightn't dare again. 'You used to say you never had dreams. You do now though, don't you?'

'What are you trying to do to me, you little bitch?' As

149

Susan flinched back, Mummy grabbed her hand, crushing her fingers together. 'Do you want to help them drive me crazy? You want a crazy mother, do you?'

'You're hurting me. Mummy, you're hurting me.'

'I'll do more than hurt you.' She flung Susan's hand away from her. Plates rattled, gravy slopped over the table. 'Who's been talking to you? If I thought – ' She snatched the letter from the table and waved it in Susan's face, spattering her with gravy. 'Has he been talking to you? Don't you dare lie to me.'

'No, Mummy.' Susan was trembling. 'I don't know who he is.'

'And you better hadn't. He'd better stay away.' She looked disgusted. 'Wipe your face. Look what you made me do. I don't know why I bother cooking for you at all.' When she came back through the streamers with a kitchen towel, she said, 'You'd better have told me the truth. If he hasn't been talking to you, who has?'

'I told you. Eve.'

'Oh, of course, Eve's responsible for everything. If you say one thing more to me about her . . .' She mopped the table and grabbed the letter, and as she marched into the kitchen Susan heard paper tearing. The streamers scraped like litter in a wind and then exploded outward. Mummy came at her so quickly that Susan almost fell out of her seat. 'One more thing, and look at me when you answer. Are you having dreams?'

'No, Mummy.'

Mummy stooped and peered into her eyes. 'Are you telling me the truth?'

Susan was afraid to do so. 'Yes, Mummy, truly I am.'

'You'd better be, by God you had. There are pills for children who can't control their imagination, you know. Don't kid yourself I need to get them from the psychologists, either.' Her face was inches from Susan's, who felt as if she couldn't breathe. 'Now you listen to me. I don't dream,

I never dream, and I never will. Don't you dare ask me ever again if I do, don't even mention the word.'

'I won't, Mummy. I promise.'

'Just do it once and see what you get.' At last Mummy sat down. 'Now eat your dinner.'

'I don't want any more.'

'Oh, am I supposed to feel guilty? The poor child's too upset to eat, is she? Well, I don't want any either, what do you think of that? So all this is for the bin. That's what your lying and your stupidity cost.' She stalked back from scraping the food into the pedal bin. 'You won't make me feel guilty and you won't make me dream. And don't you look at me like that, young lady, or I'll knock you down. That's just how your father used to look.'

'But Mummy,' Susan wailed, 'I'm not looking like anything.'

'You don't look like much, right enough. There you are, you're doing it again, that pitying look – will we have to have Helen put away. Just like him. Get in the kitchen!' she screamed, and Susan fled, sobbing.

Snow floated past the window as she washed the dishes and dabbed her eyes with the backs of her soapy hands. Her face was out there in the drifting night, she couldn't help it if it looked like Daddy's. At last she had to go back in the big room. 'Just don't say anything,' Mummy said. 'If you ever make me lose control like that again, you'll wish you had never been born.'

She was watching television – MTV, now that she worked there. They were apologizing for having shown some film or other about the police. Susan went to the window to look at the vanishing tyre tracks and the mounds that were parked cars. It must be litter that made the shape of footprints in the snow of the garden under the window; there couldn't be just two footprints with none leading there or away. Her imagination had got her into enough trouble, and she turned away and went to her encyclopedias. 'I don't know if

151

I should let you read that after the way you've been behaving,' Mummy said.

She meant Eve's book on top of the encyclopedias. Susan hadn't wanted to read that, but now, perversely, she did. When she put her hand on it, Mummy said, 'Go on,' gruffly. Susan took it to her chair and tried to get engrossed so that she wouldn't hear the television, but the stories she knew had been changed, which annoyed her – when the prince climbed up Rapunzel's hair to take her away, he found it was growing out of the witch's head, the witch had been wearing a mask all the time; and when the woodcutter opened up the wolf to let out Red Riding Hood, the wolf turned into her grandmother – and she began to look at the pictures instead. She didn't like them very much now she looked closely. If you looked at them for long, they changed: the path to the open door of a cottage was a forked tongue, a lake with a boat on it had lips and rocky teeth, even a fairy-tale castle was a hand with claws, ready to seize the procession that was riding in. A thick, dim forest illustrated a story called 'The Maiden Who Wanted to Go Home,' but where was the maiden? Perhaps there was a tiny figure running where the trees were darkest, fleeing out an avenue so narrow there was hardly a gap between the trees. Susan brought the book close to her face and felt the focus of her eyes changing. The bright quick sounds of a television commercial receded, were gone. She could see the tiny figure now, and the face that the figure was fleeing; she could see nothing else. She was no longer aware of holding the book, which slipped out of her hands.

She felt herself flood back into the room, out of that microscopic focus. She grabbed the book and glanced wildly about, but the only place she could find for it was the bookshelf. Craning up on tiptoe, she pushed it onto the highest shelf, out of reach now, as if that would help. Mummy ignored her as she stumbled to her chair and gazed blindly at the television. Among the sources of her terror was the thought that Mummy would demand to know what was wrong. She had seen the eyes of the face in the book, seen them somehow though they were tinier than pin-heads. They were the eyes that had watched her through the window of the train home from London, and at last she recognized them. They were Eve's eyes, and the tiny figure fleeing down the dark avenue was herself.

Trees bulged like a child's chalk drawings against the yellow sky above Hyde Park. Cars waded through the brown slush that the weekend's uninterrupted snowfall had piled up for Monday morning. Men in fluorescent orange waistcoats scraped the pavement with spades in Park Lane, shoppers fat with overcoats picked their way between the icy hum-mocks on Oxford Street. Molly's stomach was growing cold and stiff as her frozen face, and seemed unlikely to relax until she did what she meant to do. As she pushed through the revolving doors of the MTV building, her breath swelled up grey on the glass. She dumped her things in the fifth-floor office and went in search of Terry Mace. 'I wanted to apologize for Saturday,' she said.

'No sweat, princess. I figured you'd mistaken me for someone else.'

'I'd been with the police. They tried to scare me into saying Martin faked that film.'

'Bastards.' But his eyes were wary. 'What did you tell them?'

'I couldn't tell them who had faked it.' She was rather enjoying his wariness. 'As a matter of fact, I think who-ever did may have been right to do so.'

He looked even more cautious. 'How come?'

'Because I think it was a reconstruction of the truth. I

think I know who the ringleader was the night Lenny Bennett was killed.'

His eyes were unreadable, his interrogative noise sounded as though he were wary of committing himself to words. 'I'll tell you when I'm sure,' she said.

As she emerged from the lift at the ninth floor, a large man with rimless glasses and a stately walk strode out of the other lift, and she didn't realize he was Oliver Boycott until he reached his office. He was removing his suede trilby as she went in after him. Except for furry strips of hair above his ears, he was bald. 'I'm Molly Wolfe,' she said.

'Pray sit down, Miss Wolfe.' He unbuttoned his overcoat delicately and arranged it on a hanger behind the door. 'Any developments since we spoke?'

'No, luckily for them.'

'And for you, I should think.' He sat down at his desk and placed a gold pen parallel to the blotter. 'Did you prepare the statement I asked for?'

'Here it is. I've written down every single thing I remember.'

'Good for you. That's the style.' He unfolded the typed pages and slipped his glasses into the breast pocket of his blazer, behind a college badge. Naked, his large face looked bland. 'Really,' he said before he'd read two pages, and soon, 'Tut, tut. Dear me.' After that he read silently, except for murmuring, 'I hope you didn't think me abrupt when you rang me at home. My grandsons were playing near the river, that was why I had to cut you short.'

His Weybridge house was close to the Thames. 'I expect you enjoy their visits as much as they do.'

'Yes, when their parents are speaking to each other. My daughter and her husband started out believing each other to be perfect,' he said sadly. 'Few things are so dangerous as seeking one's ideal. Dreams do not come true, in my experience.'

She was glad when he tapped the pages together and

looked up. 'And you've signed it,' he said approvingly. 'I take it they did you no physical harm.'

'They were too clever.'

'So it seems. Well, you've done everything I would expect of you. Now we must confront the appropriate people with your statement and see what they have to say.'

'I want to confront them myself,' Molly said, and stood up. 'Face to face.'

'It may well come to that.'

'I want to now. Will you come with me?'

'I don't think that's necessary just yet.' Before she could say that it was to her, he held up one chubby palm. 'Have you told Staffing what you told me?'

'Not yet.'

'You must, you know. It relates to your professional behaviour.' He touched the phone but strode along the corridor instead. 'Mr Gould seems to be a victim of the blizzards,' he said when he came back. 'Still en route.'

Molly had been thinking. 'May I use your phone?'

'Certainly.' He opened his mail with a bone paper-knife while she dialled. He looked up sharply when she said, 'Inspector Maitland, please,' but by then it was too late. She smiled tightly when she heard Maitland's voice, and replaced the receiver. 'He's there.'

'I really wouldn't advise confronting him.'

'Don't you think you ought to see how he reacts?' She wanted Maitland to know she wasn't defenceless now and never had been. 'If you won't go with me.' she said and wished she hadn't been so final, 'I'll go myself.'

His bland face stared at her, then he stood up. 'Perhaps it will be best if I see for myself.'

At the police station the desk sergeant recognized Molly at once.

'We should like to see Inspector Maitland,' Boycott said.

'Who would?'

'Molly Wolfe from MTV,' she said, 'and Oliver Boycott, our lawyer.'

She hadn't anticipated how enraged returning to Maitland's office would make her feel. The sight of him, watching her with faint amusement across the photograph of his daughters, started her trembling. 'Well, Miss Wolfe,' he said with his quizzical, teacherish look, 'what can we do for you today?'

Her lips were stiff and clumsy. 'What do you suggest?'

'Tours of the cells are your specialty, I think.'

He must feel very safe. 'I've had enough of those, thank you.'

'I'm glad to hear it. I think we all have.' He leaned back wedging his feet on either side of the well of his desk. 'Well, what brings you here this time?'

Suddenly she knew that he thought she was here to inform on Martin, that she'd brought Boycott to ensure she didn't implicate herself. 'Miss Wolfe alleges – ' Boycott said, but she cut him off. 'What do you think I've come for?' she said.

'Could it be to apologize?'

She'd hoped he would say she meant to tell him about Martin, so that she could demand why he should expect anything of the kind. 'Why,' she said, struggling to keep calm, 'do you think I should?'

'It might seem appropriate to some. Then again, we shouldn't hold you more responsible than presumably you were. I believe Mr Wallace is still out of the country.'

He was putting on a show for Boycott, she hoped Boycott realized. 'You know damn well he is,' she said, 'and you needn't think I'm here to say anything about him.'

'I wouldn't expect you to.'

'Wouldn't you?' Much more of his game and she might fly at him. 'What changed your mind?'

'Why, nothing. I'm not sure what you mean.'

'You've had so many people down there over the weekend that you can't remember them all, have you?'

'Miss Wolfe, I do think you should tell me what you want. I really am quite busy. If you have something to tell me, as the prince said, I'm all ears.'

'Inspector Maitland,' Boycott said, 'I have a signed statement from Miss Wolfe in which she says you arrested her without due cause and subjected her to harassment in order to force her to accuse Martin Wallace of a crime.'

Maitland gazed levelly at her. If he was hoping she would look away, he would be disappointed. Eventually he sighed. 'I can see why you might want to discredit me,' he said, 'but all the same, that kind of allegation is very serious indeed. I don't think you are an unreasonable person, just hasty when it comes to issues you feel strongly about. I should like to ask you to reconsider.'

'I'm sure you would.'

He turned to Boycott. 'When is this supposed to have taken place?'

'On Saturday morning between seven and nine o'clock.'

'Indeed.' He reached for an alphabet file on his desk, then looked up at her. She didn't think his sympathetic expression would fool Boycott. 'Could you perhaps have been dreaming?' he said.

'I wonder how I could have dreamed what you said about Lenny Bennett's cell.'

'Tell me and perhaps we'll see. No? You've nothing to add?' He beckoned Boycott to his desk and flipped open the file. 'Please call this number and ask them where I was on Saturday morning.'

Boycott glanced sharply at Molly. 'I insist,' Maitland said.

She should have known that he would have covered himself after he had let her go. It didn't matter, he'd given himself away on Saturday by telling her how the film had been shown to be fake. That was in her written statement, and nobody else could have told her. 'I'm calling about Inspector Maitland – Joseph Maitland, yes,' Boycott said as the policeman nodded. Boycott asked his question, listened, said, 'Are you sure? Well, of course. No disrespect intended. Thank you.'

When he replaced the receiver he kept his back to Molly. 'It must take half an hour to get there from here.'

'Oh, at least,' Maitland said.

Molly's fists were clenching. 'Well, who says he wasn't here?'

Boycott turned, his large face sad and weary, but Maitland spoke. 'Until eight o'clock it was only the vicar who saw me at the organ.' She could see that he enjoyed the pause before he said, 'After that it was the entire choir.'

'Well, Miss Wolfe,' Jake Gould said, 'you certainly seem to like to keep everyone guessing.'

Beyond the double glazing a glacier of cloud crept across the sky. The smells of leather and cigar smoke caught in Molly's throat and made her swallow painfully, the air conditioning filled her mouth with the taste of tin. 'I'm sorry, I don't follow,' she said.

'Either you're just being a woman or you wanted to make up for your behaviour with Ben Eccles by being so loyal to Wallace that you'd risk losing your job.'

'I didn't do it for Martin. When I gave Oliver Boycott that statement I honestly believed I was right.'

'Right for you, maybe, but wrong for us.' He stared at her. 'Whose idea was it?'

'Mine. I give you my word.'

'Admittedly it's difficult to believe it could have taken two people to concoct such an incompetent lie. Just what the eff did you think you were going to achieve?'

'I wasn't trying to achieve anything. I believed what I said, that's all.'

'And now?' When she didn't reply at once, he said, 'You're surely not still trying to insist there was something in what you said?'

158

Because there was no point in telling him there was, she said, 'No.'

'I should jolly well think not. It's incredible to me that you could have behaved so stupidly and thoughtlessly. You're good at your job when you want to be, I don't understand how you can be so unstable. Frankly, Miss Wolfe, after the business with Eccles and now this, it's no longer a question of keeping people guessing about you, it's a matter of your being all too dismayingly predictable.'

She only wished she could predict herself. 'And really, all this nonsense about a policeman called Randy,' he said. 'I can only hope your relationship with Wallace helps you work out these problems you seem to have with men.'

She wanted to know what MTV intended to do about Martin, but there was a limit to the insults she could take. 'Would you like my resignation right now?' she said, and cursed herself.

'It certainly might seem appropriate. I should be interested to hear if you can think of any reason why I shouldn't fire you, other than that it's nearly Christmas.'

'Only that Martin has got used to working with me.'

'You really must have very little grasp of the situation, or else you want me to think so.' He glanced at his watch, at a desk diary, at her. 'No, the only thing I can find to say on your behalf is that it seemed rather spiteful of the police to leak the story to the press after you had withdrawn your accusation.'

Of course she'd had to withdraw it, if only to give herself time to think.

Gould closed his diary with a loud snap. 'I'm not firing you,' he said, 'but I would strongly suggest you start looking for another job, maybe one less demanding. Even if Wallace continues, and I can't decide that until I've talked to him, it's hard to see who you might work with once he finishes. I'm giving you leave of absence until he comes back. Try and rest.'

He was being compassionate in his own terms, but she would rather have stayed at work: she would already be alone over Christmas – the trains were virtually at a standstill, she would never be able to get to her parents. She was at the door when he said, 'There is one more thing.'

She turned and was dismayed by his expression. 'It's a pity,' he said, 'but I think you ought to realize nobody would have suspected Wallace of anything if it hadn't been for your attempt to discredit the police.'

It seemed pointlessly vindictive of him. Happy Christmas to you too, she thought. She took the lift down to the eighth floor.

Nell was squatting by a low shelf, indexing the books on cards. Molly realized she had never noticed the walls, which were green, for the disorder Nell had tackled by herself. 'You've done well,' she said.

'I enjoy it.' Nell stood up, dusting the knees of her plaid skirt. 'I like things to be in order. It occupies my mind.'

'Will you be staying in town over Christmas?'

'We'll have to. We can't go home – I mean, where we used to live.' She was sorting the index cards onto her desk as expertly as a casino dealer. 'My daughter's disappointed, I think.'

'I was going to say if you don't know many people yet you might like to come over for a Christmas meal.'

'We'd love to. All – ' She faltered and looked puzzled. 'All *right*,' she said, somehow inappropriately. 'Both of us would love to come.'

'How about Boxing Day?' Molly wrote her address on a blank index card and went down to her office to collect her binoculars. She'd done a good turn for herself as well as for Nell. Nell could keep her in touch with events at MTV.

As Molly walked blobs of snow dripped from trees in Hyde Park under the darkening sky. A fat woman sat

160

down in the snow and laughed helplessly at herself, a businessman picked himself up quickly, pretending someone else had fallen, not him.

She stared at the police station as she passed and felt not at all vulnerable. The sight of a policeman's helmet bobbing in the crowd ahead no longer seemed threatening – until she saw the policeman's face.

For a moment panic grabbed her stomach like a hook. It was the skinhead policeman, striding into a hotel. When he emerged, marching a young woman who wore a jacket covered with zippers, Molly strolled forward, heart jerking. He glanced at her as he shoved his captive into the police car. He didn't recognize her – he had never met her! But she recognized him.

He sat by the young woman and squeezed the zippered pocket over her right breast, squeezed the breast too. 'Girlie, what you've got in there is going to put you away for years,' Molly heard him say as the car door slammed. Even if his name weren't Randy, she thought, her dream had been right that it ought to have been.

She watched the car as it swung into the forecourt of the police station a few hundred yards away, then she walked home.

As she unlocked the apartment door, she consulted her watch and decided to call Chapel Hill.

'Am I taking you away from breakfast?'

'That's okay, we're just finishing. How are you, Molly?'

'Sorry that you won't be here for Christmas. I know you can't be, don't worry. How are things with you?'

'Oh, pretty good. Yes, pretty good, I think.'

'Martin, this is complicated, but you ought to know. I told you the film you were sent was fake. Now I'm convinced that it was faked in order to show what actually happened.'

After a pause he said, 'What makes you think that?'

This might be the hard part. 'Do you remember what I said about my dreams?'

161

'Sure, I remember.'

Did he sound disappointed? 'You did believe me, didn't you?'

'Sure, why not? It wasn't so hard to believe.'

'Well then, Martin, listen to this. I dreamed the police took me in for questioning and Maitland gave away that he'd helped kill Lenny Bennett. It was so vivid that it was only afterward I realized it had been a dream. And then, not half an hour ago, I saw proof it was more than a dream. They killed Lenny Bennett, Martin, I'd stake my reputation on it,' she said and realized that wasn't much of a wager just now.

'Can you prove they did?'

'Well, no, that isn't what I meant. I know they did but I can't prove it.'

'Then I don't see what it changes.'

'Only that you were right to go on screen about the film.' The clarity and optimism she'd felt on realizing she had cheated the future were fading. 'At least you know you were justified. Mrs Bennett wasn't upset for nothing after all.'

'I guess that's so. Well, Molly, you've given me a lot to think about.'

'Yes . . .' She'd meant to relieve him of some of his worries, but wasn't sure she had. 'Call me over Christmas if you like,' she said.

Later she went down to Bayswater Road for a Chinese takeaway. The plastic tray burned her hands as she toiled home, the hardening slush froze her feet. She played a Tom Waits cassette while she ate from a serving tray on her lap. The sad, gravelly voice filled the room, a black voice from a white mouth, and she wondered what on earth she was going to do with her time. She'd build the extra kitchen cupboards she kept wishing for.

It's a Wonderful Life was the first of television's seasonal treats, James Stewart throwing himself in the river and then being redeemed by a vision of how his town would decline

162

without him. She was enjoying it for its sentimentality and for its odd appropriateness to her until she thought: suppose Maitland had leaked the story to the press so that nobody would believe her if the police interrogated her now? Surely he wouldn't take the risk. Nevertheless, before she went to bed she double-checked all the locks on the doors and windows.

She lay in bed and watched the beginning of a new snowfall. The small flakes floating past the gap between the curtains looked gentle as sleep. Perhaps her dream of the police cell had been so intense because it had involved Martin and her unacknowledged fear for him. It didn't bother her so much now that she couldn't tell where the dream had begun or ended, for she thought she could guard against that in the future by telling herself to wake. She dozed and then woke for a moment convinced she had already dreamed something into being, but what? Sleep seemed altogether more reassuring. She dreamed for the first time in eleven years of a red door that had once been painted green, a red front door with a canted dog-faced knocker. The door was ajar, but she managed to wake screaming, bathed in sweat, a moment before she would have had to push it open. The worst thing was that she couldn't remember how she had got there in the dream.

When Geoffrey looked up it didn't help. He ought to have known not to stare at the stamps for so long, even though they fascinated him. It wasn't as if they were worth very much, though the teenager who'd sold them to him had thought they were. 'These are special, they're 3-D,' he'd said proudly, and Geoffrey had had to point out that they would be worth more if he completed the set. He must have outgrown stamps when he'd taken up motorcycling, for he'd shrugged at Geoffrey's price as he'd unstudded his pocket to lock up the cheque. It had taken quite a while for the smell of leather to follow his jingling and creaking out of the house.

Now Geoffrey looked up from the stamps that seemed embedded in the page and wandered into the bedroom for a change of scene. He sat on the bed and gazed at Hampstead Heath, where tiny skiers glided across the dazzling snow under a bright blue sky, and wondered how long the weather would keep him away from the auctions. The breathing seeped back into his consciousness, and he remembered it wasn't the weather that was keeping him in the house.

Perhaps he still had to get used to a third person in the house. He couldn't expect the old lady to walk or be carried down the hill just now, he couldn't expect an ambulance to come up here over the frozen snow. Good Lord, he had only to stay in the house; Joyce took care of the old lady's needs while he kept out of the way. The old lady had yet to leave her room or, as far as he knew, her bed.

He looked away from Hampstead Heath to rest his eyes, which were determined to make out the microscopic skiers. He couldn't be sure that he'd seen one of them fall. He closed his eyes, and then he realized he couldn't hear the breathing. He mustn't call the doctor before he knew what was wrong, if anything. All the same, it took him a while to step onto the landing and open the door of the guest room.

The room was pale with snowy light that glinted on the Christmas decorations Joyce had hung. The enormous mound of bedspread dominated the room, on the bed and in the mirror of the dressing table, doubly still. From the doorway he couldn't see anyone under the mound. As he tiptoed into the room he had the notion, so odd that he didn't know if it was a hope or a fear, that he might find nobody there at all.

He was nearly at the pillow before he saw the upturned face

164

half buried there. It looked even fatter than he remembered. The puffy eyes were closed, the mouth drooped open. He stooped to listen for breathing, close enough to see that she had no eyebrows or eyelashes unless they had sunk into the ungovernable flesh, close enough to wonder if the inside of her mouth was white as well. And then her lips moved feebly. They closed and quivered open with a snore. Her breathing recommenced, louder as he crept away, and he had almost reached the door when she piped, 'I'm not asleep.'

He couldn't help damning himself as he turned. The mound was shifting, the blankets and bedspread slipped off one enormous shoulder. He had to speak when her small eyes met his. 'Is there anything you want?' he said.

She smiled, a wide smile that looked young. He thought she had teeth until he saw that the fat white ridges were gums. 'You can stay and talk to me if you like, Geoffrey.'

Presumably she'd learned his name from Joyce. 'Do you know, I don't know what to call you,' he said, staying near the door.

She gave him a fat exaggerated pout that hinted what she might have looked like once. '*You* know,' she piped.

'No, I don't. Joyce didn't tell me.'

'She's a wonder. There's not another like her.' The small colourless eyes closed on an appreciative look. 'She's out now finding somewhere, isn't she? Out in this. She can't do it all on her own, you know. She needs someone to speak up for her.'

Geoffrey felt accused. 'I would if I could.'

'I didn't mean you. No offence. She'll find someone.'

He could only hope so. 'You were going to tell me your name,' he said.

She sat up laboriously and minutely, displaying her bald head that looked even more like old cheese with a few cobwebs. 'What would you like it to be?'

His heart sank. 'I don't mean to bother you,' he said, 'but where do you come from?'

'Not far. Or maybe you'd think it was.' Presumably she didn't know. 'Thank you for letting me stay in your house,' she said. 'You must tell me if I'm too much of an inconvenience.'

She tilted her head almost coquettishly. 'I'm sorry I don't talk much,' she piped, 'but I like to listen.'

He felt trapped and then ashamed. 'Would you like me to read to you?'

'Oh, I'd love that. Have you got the newspaper?'

He took her to mean today's, and London's. 'I'll have to go up to the shops,' he said, and felt deeply relieved when she looked grateful. At least he could get out of the house for a while.

Walking was easy at first on the frozen snow. The pavement was a mass of overlapping footprints like a dance school gone mad. By the time he reached the newsagent's he was having to hold on to walls.

He bought the evening paper and struggled back up the hill. When finally he reached home he was hot and exhausted. At least he heard the breathing as soon as he opened the front door. He peeled off his wet clothes and toiled upstairs, resenting having panicked. Her head wavered up from the pillow as soon as he stepped into the room. 'Oh, thank you,' she piped, with a smile so sweet that his resentment vanished. The smile didn't even show her gums.

He brought in his office chair and sat by the bed to read her the newspaper. More murders in London than ever, more threats of terrorism, and he wondered if he should be reading her that kind of news, but she seemed eager for more. A television researcher had accused the police of giving her the third degree only to find that the policeman she'd accused had been in church at the time – there was a photograph of her, trying to hide her face as she emerged from a revolving door. The story amused the old lady, for the bedspread was quaking, and Geoffrey couldn't help grinning. He turned the pages, he sat forward as the print

166

grew dimmer. He didn't know how long he had been reading when he heard Joyce closing the front door.

He blinked at the room, which was almost dark. The old lady was asleep. He stumbled out with the chair, then hurried down to Joyce. 'Any luck?'

'I may have found somewhere.' She straightened up from pulling off her boots. 'Only may have. Someone wants it for one of those hamburger places. You'd think we'd get priority, but they're going to make us fight.'

'Surely they'd have to let you have it if people knew what the situation was.'

'That's right, *if* they knew. I saw some of my old folk today, they're going to write to all the papers. They want to come back to me, even though they're being taken care of. I won't let them down, not while I've got two legs and a voice.' She glanced up the stairs. 'How's she been?'

'No trouble really. I read to her for a while.'

'That's my Geoffrey. I can always count on you. I'm glad you're making friends.'

'It's you she wants, you know.' He followed her into the kitchen, where she was boiling milk to lace with rum.

'You don't mind her staying, do you?' Joyce said. 'The sooner I find somewhere, the sooner she can go.'

'It's just that I'm looking after her and I don't even know her name.'

'Sometimes it's one thing, sometimes another.'

She mustn't know either. 'Where does she live?'

'Why do you want to know that?' When she turned from pouring the milk into mugs, she looked angry. 'If you want her to leave, just say so. She's frightened to stay at home during the day, but if you can't stand her, back she must go.'

'I didn't say that.' But he was suddenly wondering what Christmas would be like. He might have raised that point, except that Joyce was staring at the newspaper he was still holding. 'Where did you get that?' she demanded.

'On the High Street. She asked me to.'

'Oh, well, if she asked . . .' She looked dubious. 'Best not to leave her alone again, though.'

They left the living-room door ajar, even though they could hear the old lady's breathing when it was closed. He sipped his laced milk as he glanced through the newspaper, where he could remember hardly any of the items, before handing it to Joyce. Then she cried, 'Good God!' He jumped up.

'Are you all right?'

'Of course I am. Don't be tiresome. Look here.' She was pointing at the photograph of the woman who hadn't managed to hide her face. 'Did you read this? It's a miracle, that's what it is. I've been wanting to pray, you know. Maybe this is meant to tell me I should.'

'What, the woman who tried to defame the police?'

'Never mind that. She must have had her reasons.' She was slapping the photograph impatiently. 'I know her, that's what I'm trying to tell you. I met her years ago. Oh, Geoffrey, what luck.'

'Well, so you know her.'

'Geoffrey, sometimes you're worse than my old folk.' She smiled tolerantly at him. 'She works on television, don't you understand? She's exactly what I need. Let these hamburger people make trouble for me now and I'll go straight to Molly Wolfe.'

The Christmas lights of Oxford Street stained the snow like petrol. As Danny turned the corner into Wardour Street, a roof dripped on him, but he couldn't have cared less. He stopped at the Rank poster windows, because he wanted to read about next year's films, not because he was pretending that he wasn't going to Soho. He didn't need to pretend, he never had. He didn't need to go to Soho now, and that was why he would.

The Essential was showing films by Martin Wallace, whoever he was. Danny picked his way past, mincing on the frozen slush, to the staggered crossroads of Old Compton Street and Brewer Street, the lights of their shops throbbing. Perhaps it was because he meant to give himself a present that the lights made him think of Christmas.

Someone was laughing in a newsagent's on Old Compton Street, and he hoped they were laughing at Molly Wolfe. He'd seen her picture in the paper, and now he knew where she worked. He wouldn't have to look for her in Soho on his afternoon off. There couldn't be a better place to celebrate than Soho, not when she had made him go there in the first place.

Or at least, his dream of her had. That was all he remembered clearly from that time eleven years ago, the dream of her and another female writing sexy letters for him to take to the printers. In the dream he had been home at once, hiding in his room to read the magazine, only to find that all the letters were about him, the only man they knew who never had erections. All the photographs of naked women, and their open thighs, had been laughing at him.

He had never been able to get that dream out of his head. Molly Wolfe had put it there, with Dr Kent's help, put it in through the wires they had stuck to his face. Soon he hadn't been able to go into a newsagent's without seeing magazines that reminded him of the dream, that made him feel contemptuously watched, unable even to think unheard. He'd fought back, he'd stayed always aware of his enemies that were everywhere, unobserved by anyone but him. He'd realized just in time that they were trying to make him say they were there so that his parents would think he was mad and have him put away where his enemies would be with him all the time until they drove him mad. Sometimes as he'd strolled down Wardour Street, he'd stood on the corners of the sex streets, wondering if they sold those magazines that made his crotch feel warm. He might have bought one if he could have thought of a hiding place. When at last Molly Wolfe had led him there, he'd been too intent on following her to notice where he was going; and that had been the day after he'd dreamed a second time that she was handing him the sexy letters.

He could still dream what was going to happen. She and Dr Kent hadn't robbed him of that after all. They had only tried because they were scared of him. It hadn't mattered that he had lost her in Soho, he'd gone back there every day that there wasn't an afternoon show at the Hercules. Once, when the man behind the counter had said loudly, 'Everything's for sale, gentlemen,' Danny had bought a book called *Erotic Cinema* so that the man wouldn't know what he really liked or throw him out for not buying. He'd thought of losing it on the way to the Hercules, then just in time he'd realized he could hide it under the carpet in the projection box. As soon as the evening's film was running, he had opened the brown-paper package. But the book he had bought in his red-faced haste wasn't called *Erotic Cinema* at all, it was called *Erotic Enema*. He'd torn it up on his way home that night and scattered the pieces like a glossy paper chase. Molly Wolfe and her spies might see the kind of thing that really excited him and have their opinion of him confirmed.

But now it was Molly Wolfe that everyone was jeering at. He grinned at the thought of all those photographs everywhere of her. As soon as he reached the shop with the opaque window, he went in.

He had his pound notes ready in his hand. He'd changed the new notes from the bank for old ones, in case the bank could trace that he'd come here. The shopman gave him a handful of fifty-pence pieces and said 'Thank you, sir' so sincerely that Danny felt he was the equal of all the businessmen at the racks of magazines. Some issues of a magazine called *Janus* – two-faced, all women except his mother were – contained instalments of a dictionary of spanking films, but that wasn't what he had promised himself. He sidled toward the viewing booths, toward the sounds of cries and pleas.

Handwritten titles were taped to the doors: *Penitent Penny, Rueful Rhoda, Tearful Tess. Spanking in the Office* was the one he wanted, but the illuminated sign above the door said 'IN USE.' He could see you weren't supposed to queue, you had to stroll blank-faced as if you weren't interested. To keep himself busy, he glanced about to see that nobody was watching, then locked himself in to wait with *Penitent Penny*.

When he fed the slot, an erect penis appeared on the door. A mouth was working on it in time to a James Last record, and there was panting that made him think of his mother, though it sounded as if it were down a well. Would he look like that, swollen and purple and bulging with veins? He squeezed his eyes shut as the penis ejaculated. It made him think of a sewer outlet.

When his fifty pence ran out, he sat and waited without putting in money until the shopman banged on the door and shouted, 'Pay up, pay up, whoever you are.'

'Coming,' Danny stammered, his face burning, and wondered why the shopman said, 'Then you'd better keep it to yourself.' He stumbled out of the cubicle, and saw that the one he wanted was no longer in use.

He bolted the door and groped beside his flaccid penis for the handful of change. At first nothing appeared on the door in response to his coin. He was nerving himself to go out and complain when the picture lit up, a little askew and blurred but clear enough. A man was shaking his finger at a girl behind a desk and waving a typed letter in her face. He dragged her off her revolving chair and across his lap, he

171

was pulling up her skirt and picking up a ruler, and she was Molly Wolfe. Danny sat forward to stare at the blurred face – it *was* her, he was sure it was – until his growing penis forced him back. When the picture vanished, too soon, he fed in more money, more. His spine was grating against the wall, but he could feel nothing but his penis, unbearably sensitive, impossibly huge. Oh, God yes, this was what was meant to happen, she was struggling and trying to cover her bottom, oh, God yes, go on, that was what she'd been deserving for eleven years, oh, God, he panted aloud, oh, God . . . Oh, God, the film had stopped, and he had no more fifty pences.

He waddled bowlegged to the door as soon as he could. His penis was tingling. Hs wasn't going to leave empty-handed after having spent so much. He grabbed the magazines that contained the dictionary of films, though he was horrified by how much he was spending. 'Thank you, sir,' the shopman said, 'enjoy your Christmas,' and Danny told himself that it was just this once, to celebrate. As soon as he was out of Soho, nobody would know what the brown-paper package was. He had just stepped onto the pavement when a woman said behind him, 'Danny Swain.'

He mustn't turn. He could run before she saw the package. He had to run while his legs were still flexible, for his body was stiffening as if his blood were turning into concrete, his brain already felt like a stone. The street was lengthening, the shops were stretching like pictures on elastic, he couldn't run all that way. Of course that wasn't happening, it was one of the things his enemies were trying to put into his mind. He turned around.

She was a large-boned woman with a long face, whose expectant grin looked as if she were challenging him. Let her grin, it didn't matter that his lips were swollen hard and closed, he could stare at her while he tried to remember who she was. People shoved by him on the narrow icy pavement or stepped into the road, and suddenly he realized that all of

172

them could recognize him. They couldn't say that he had been in Soho without revealing they had been here themselves, and the same went for her, whoever she was. He glared at her to tell her so. 'Don't you remember me?' she said.

It was all he could do to shake his head. 'Well, you're not the Danny Swain I remember,' she said. 'We'll have to do something about that. Not the same articulate chap at all.'

She was using his name in the street for everyone to hear, and he was almost sure that she was taunting him. Suddenly he knew where he had met her, but the recognition jammed his lips shut as it dawned hotly on his face. 'That's right,' she said smiling. 'Guilda Kent. I'd have been offended if you really had forgotten me.'

It was Dr Kent, Molly Wolfe's crony Dr Kent, who had done her best to destroy his mind. He felt trapped yet gleeful, if he could only think why, and in danger of losing control.

'So what brings you here, Danny?' Dr Kent said.

By the time he managed to open his lips he'd thought of a reply. 'What does you?' he mumbled, but it didn't sound as clever as it had sounded in his head.

'You mean what do I do, don't you? Well, it comes to the same thing.' She was taunting him, he knew that now, but not in the way the girls at the Hercules did; she had a purpose, he thought she was still a doctor, still something to do with the mind. 'I came here,' she said, 'because it's the ideal place to find people like you.'

He wished desperately that he knew what shape his swollen lips were making. 'What do you mean?'

'Don't you know what kind of person you are? Then you need me, Danny. We'll sort you out, I give you my word. Come along.'

'Not this time,' he wanted to say. She'd tricked him once, she'd made him feel important until he'd been able to talk without stammering, talk about the things his parents didn't want to know, his dreams. He'd taken a fortnight off to go to Oxford even though Mr Pettigrew had threatened to sack him if he did, and Dr Kent had done her best to jumble up his mind so that he couldn't put it back together. 'Won't,' he said so loudly that people on the opposite pavement stared.

'What's wrong?' If her smile was meant to be reassuring, it didn't fool him. 'It won't be like last time, don't worry. We've finished with dreams. I want to bring you back to reality.' When he didn't move, her smile grew firmer. 'Follow me, Danny, or I'll have to follow you.'

He didn't know what she might be capable of. The street was threatening to change, the neon lights were throbbing so hard that he could almost hear them, a shrill discordant jagged pounding that would scrape the inside of his skull, and then all at once his head was clear, he had to stiffen his lips so as not to grin. She thought she had outwitted him when in fact she had played into his hands. She was going to show him where to find her, and he already knew where to find Molly Wolfe. Perhaps Molly Wolfe had sent her to confuse him, but he was cleverer than both of them put together. 'I'm coming,' he said loudly, and glared at two sailors who laughed.

She led him onto Wardour Street, to the block that the sex shops had reached. The frozen slush seemed not to hinder her at all. Maybe she'd walked the street so often that she knew exactly where to tread. She waited for him in the entrance to a court between two sex shops, little more than an alley. Dustbins crowned with fallen icicles stood by doorways. As he arrived panting in the court, she was unlocking the nearest door.

An uncarpeted staircase led up to a glass-panelled door. Wasn't this the kind of place that prostitutes in Soho used? But the glass panel said 'Know Yourself Ltd,' and when she unlocked the door, he saw it led not to a bedroom but to an office: a chair on each side of a flat white Scandinavian desk, a filing cabinet, two abstract paintings on the wall behind the desk. A fluorescent tube jerked alight as she closed the door, and he sat down at once, to have time to place the magazines gently under his chair while she went behind the desk. She sat down and balanced her chin on her splayed fingers and gazed at him.

She needn't think that would make him talk. He looked away, at the paintings, but their black-and-white lines began to flicker and shift as if the fluorescent tube were failing. 'Look around all you like,' she said, and made him jump. 'It may not look like much compared to where we met last, but it's all I need. It's in Soho. That's where the people come who most need my help.'

She wanted him to think he needed help. 'Aren't you going to ask me what kind of people?' she said.

'No.'

'People who are scared of other people, Danny. Especially of women. Why are you so scared of us?'

Just let her keep on and he'd show her that she ought to be scared of him, her and Molly Wolfe. 'You've no right to say that,' he mumbled.

'You gave me the right by coming up here. Are you scared because we make you feel the way you're feeling now?'

She wasn't clever enough for him. A draught was chilling his soaked ankles, and he would have moved his icy feet except that would make her think she had him worried. 'What way?' he said slyly and wondered if she'd heard. 'What way is that?'

'Cold and scared. Wondering if I locked the door. It's open, Danny, you only have to try it. But you won't, because you know you need me. You need me as you've never needed anyone, not even your mother.'

The draught was rustling the brown paper. He wanted to reach down and hush the package, but that would draw her attention to it. Was she trying to hypnotize him, was that why she kept repeating words? She had no chance. 'You leave my mother out of this.'

'Why, how do you feel about her, Danny? Does she make you feel inadequate too?'

'My mother's ill. You leave her alone.' He was shouting, partly to drown the rustling of paper. 'She shouldn't even be living where we're living, it's making her worse. If I had a better job we could afford to move.'

'And why can't you get a better job?'

Because she and Molly Wolfe and their spies were always trying to confuse him, that was why. He mustn't let her see that he knew; he must let her think she was confusing him. 'I don't know.'

'Isn't it because your mother never gave you a chance to speak up for yourself? Don't look so surprised, Danny. Perhaps you've forgotten you told me. You wouldn't have been able to talk about your dreams except your mother wasn't there for once, that was what you said.' She looked sympathetic. 'You can't get a good job because you're scared to talk. I think you're scared to communicate with people in case they see you as you are. I think above all you're scared in case your mother does.'

'You leave my mother – ' He'd said that already, she was making him say it again, but why shouldn't he? 'You leave her alone.'

'No, *you* leave her alone, Danny. That's exactly what you're doing. You know if she found out where you've been today when you could have been looking for a better job, you wouldn't be able to face her.'

Let her go on taunting him, trying to blame his mother. 'You don't know where I've been,' he muttered.

'Why, how long do you think I was watching you, Danny? What are you trying to hide down there?'

For a moment he thought she meant the way his hands were folded over his crotch. 'You might as well let me see,' she said, 'unless you mean to walk out of here right now. But I promise you that won't be the last you see of me.'

He mustn't reach down, but her eyes were making him, forcing him to pick up the package. 'What have we here?' she said, just like a teacher finding a comic book during a class.

She peeled the tape off the wrapping with her long red fingernails and shook out the magazines. Danny's face was so hot it felt raw. She was leafing through page after page of girls sprawled across knees, and he was struggling desperately to think what he could say. Perhaps he should agree with everything she said about him, except that he might start believing it of himself. She paused at an instalment of the dictionary of films. He thought of saying he needed the magazines to know about films for the Hercules, and then he had it. 'I know,' he said, but surely not aloud.

She looked up, shaking her head. 'Who do you think you're getting even with, Danny? Why do you think you need to?'

The answer was her and Molly Wolfe, but she must believe he was too stupid to realize. 'Those magazines,' he said, taking a breath to be sure he would be heard. 'They aren't for me.'

'Really?' He could see she hadn't expected that. 'Who is your friend that you're running errands for?'

'He's no friend of mine.' Saying that made him grin savagely. 'He's the manager where I work.'

'And where is that?'

'A cinema.' He didn't want her questioning Mr Petti-grew. 'He makes me show dirty films after-hours for his friends.'

'Really?' She was gazing wide-eyed at him. 'Does that bother you?'

'Yes, it does.' He remembered the veined penis. His face was burning with resentment at having been tricked into seeing that. 'He shouldn't make me. That isn't my job.'

'He makes you come to Soho too, does he?'

'That's right, he does. He likes those kind of films best. He wants a list of them.'

'Afraid to be seen round here himself, I suppose. Well, I do seem to have misjudged you.' She slipped the magazines into their wrapping and replaced the tape. 'But not really. If you weren't so scared of people you wouldn't let yourself be used that way.'

'You stop saying I'm scared,' he muttered.

'You stop me, Danny. Go on, show me you aren't scared of me. Go on, I want you to.'

He was afraid now – afraid of what he might do to her before he was ready. 'Stop it,' he mumbled.

'You're scared of me, Danny. Scared because I know so much about you. It's my job to know, Danny. That's how I help people like you. But I can't help them if they won't admit they're scared.'

'All right, I'm scared.' Suddenly he was desperate to leave before he could touch her. 'Give me those now or I'll be late.'

'Can't your manager wait?' She slapped her hand, palm down and fingers spread, on the magazines. 'Suppose I won't give them to you?'

'Then don't.' He mustn't try to get them, in case he lost control. 'I'm going,' he said, trying to turn toward the door.

'Take them, Danny. Here you are.' She stood up between the vibrating paintings and held out the package. 'You've enough problems without my adding to them. Now, when shall I see you again?'

She had taken a file card out of the cabinet and was writing his name: Swain, D. 'I don't know,' he said, his lips making shapes that got in the way of the words.

'Make it soon, Danny. Don't give me the bother of having to track you down.' As he opened the door, she said, 'If you don't come back you won't know how much I know about you.'

178

She was only saying that to make him come back, she didn't even know where he lived. He hurried down the stairs before she could call him back to ask. How could she expect him to come again after the way she'd treated him? Because she would say she'd done it for his own good, of course – he could hear her saying so, smug and patronizing. He hoped she would be surprised when he came back, but she wouldn't like it when he did. What was good for him wouldn't be good for her.

He pulled out his note pad and wrote down the address of her office, then walked towards Oxford Circus Underground. He was going home, and Mr Pettigrew would just have to wait for his magazines. On Oxford Street he started grinning, for anyone who noticed his package would think it was a Christmas present. He wished he didn't have to take it to Mr Pettigrew, he would have liked to keep it for himself.

The packed train made him feel hot and grubby, and so did the sloping tunnel that he had to climb. The sky glittered above Seven Sisters Road, surfaces that looked like pavement in the dark gave way beneath his feet. He held onto the icy handrail as he ran up the slippery steps to the flats. When he shouted to make sure he was alone, only his flattened voice came back along the boxy hall.

He went straight to the bathroom, which was cold as its white tiles, and began to unpick the tape from the wrapping. He must be careful in case Mr Pettigrew suspected it had been tampered with. He sat on the edge of the metal bath and leafed through the magazines, but something was wrong with every sequence of photographs: they were out of order, or the woman forgot to look as if she was suffering, or the beating left no marks. Every other kind of sexy photograph was real now – why not these? He wished he could take out the staples and rearrange the photographs, tell Mr Pettigrew to go and buy his own.

And then he remembered they weren't for Mr Pettigrew at all. Dr Cunt had almost confused him into thinking they were, but she couldn't trick him. He'd pay her back for that as well, her and Molly Wolfe. He'd start now. He got scissors and glue from the kitchen drawer and went to look for the photograph. He found the newspaper in the kitchen bin. The outer pages were stained with ketchup, but Molly Wolfe's face was untouched. He cut it out and glued it over the face of the photograph he liked best, a girl being held down by her mother while her father striped her with a birch. He propped the magazine against the bath taps, and struggled to unbutton his fly to let out the writhing. He had just time to free his penis before it spurted over the tiles above the bath.

He stared at what he'd done and felt empty and meaningless and spied upon. He didn't have to turn to know his enemies were watching him. They were watching to make him feel meaningless, but if he were so meaningless, why were they bothering to watch? They hadn't thought of that, he was too clever for them. He cleaned the tiles with toilet paper, then he ran the hot tap in the sink until it was steaming and held his disgusting penis under it for as long as he could, even when he screamed. They were making him do that to himself, Dr Cunt and Molly Wolfe. Let them send their spies to watch and report back, let their spies say they'd heard him screaming. It would be nothing compared to the way he was going to make Molly Wolfe and the other cunt scream.

When Freda had finished stuffing the turkey, she went into the parlour to see if Doreen was ready to walk to midnight Mass. The parlour with its gas fire hissing orange was hotter than the kitchen; the flowers on the corner table were already wilting. Doreen was watching snowflakes vanish from the window almost before they touched it. 'You've never finished already,' she cried, letting the floor-length curtains fall together. 'You're a wonder, Freddy. Maybe someday you'll be able to teach me how to cook.'

That seemed unlikely, when Harry hadn't been able to. Perhaps that occurred to her, for she started bustling about, flicking a feather duster at her wedding photograph on the mantelpiece, pulling at the antimacassars. Freda watched her friend, this small slight woman who didn't come up to her shoulder and who oughtn't to look so frail – Doreen unbuttoning the cardigan of her twin-set and buttoning it again as she tidied the room. She had so much energy, but it didn't seem to be achieving much.

'That'll have to do for now.' Doreen lingered to prop up a card on the sideboard, next to a pile of Harry's *National Geographic*s. 'Did you see that poor old Mrs Vosper sent a card? At least this Christmas we won't have to pretend we can't see how she's doing her magic tricks.'

'I remember.' Mrs Vosper had been staying here the year Freda had taken refuge. 'You can see how happy she was from what she wrote.'

'They all wrote things like that. Look, Mr Calvert says he hopes he'll be back soon. You can't blame them for leaving before the weather got too bad and they couldn't get home to their children.'

'Of course not,' Freda said, knowing that they'd stayed as long as they could to prevent her pining for Harry, that they'd left once they knew her best friend Freddy was coming, left because they couldn't stomach her cooking or her fussing, though fussing helped her not to think. Freda couldn't tell her all that, not on Christmas Eve. 'I'll just get my coat,' she said.

'I'll come up with you, shall I?'

'Yes, do.'

The women's footsteps made the house sound like a bare

room, though the stair carpet was thick. Freda was glad when they reached the top floor.

She really didn't need to be using this room now, with an empty floor between her and Doreen's ground-floor quarters. It was the room Doreen gave to her transient guests, though she'd told Freda to stay as long as she could. Of course she wanted to believe that her former tenants would come back someday – as Harry never would. All the rooms were the same: a gas fire and a patchwork quilt Doreen had sewn, a fitted wardrobe that almost did, and a crucifix on the wall, though one resident, Freda remembered, had put hers out in the hall propped up like a boot for cleaning. Freda could only hope religion proved to be what Doreen needed, since Spiritualism seemed to have failed.

She stooped to pin her hat in front of the dressing-table mirror, which swung back to reflect the sky or the heavy curtains when it wasn't propped. 'Did you sleep well last night?' Doreen said.

'Marvellously.' Doreen wasn't pleading, not even with her eyes, but her hope was so intense that Freda found it hard to breathe. 'I can't remember a thing between going to bed and waking up this morning.'

'I thought when I saw you you needed a rest.'

'I've been sleeping much better lately.' The mirror swung up, losing their faces. She couldn't lie again, she had already told Doreen she'd dreamed of Harry, that he was happy and waiting patiently for her, that seeing her lead a full life would make him even happier, and Doreen had smiled and said, 'Oh, I am glad,' so gratefully that it had been a while before Freda realized Doreen had been humouring her, knowing Freda had been lying for her sake. Didn't she realize that if Freda dreamed, the message would be just as banal? Freda would have told her about Sage except that then Doreen would want to go to Blackpool, when Sage would already have moved on. 'We'd better go down,' Freda said.

They were on the middle landing when Doreen took hold of her arm. 'You mustn't let me trade on our friendship.'

'Doreen, you could never do that after all you've done for me.'

'But that's what I *mean*.' She stamped her foot at failing to make herself clear. 'You mustn't feel you have to repay me. I've got you cleaning the rooms and cooking dinner, I'll be having you running my bath and polishing my shoes next. You mustn't let me use you, Freddy. Just your company is enough for me.'

'I'd get bored if I sat around doing nothing.'

'I should think you must be bored anyway, you poor love. Using up your leave, and it can't be much of a holiday for you. I'll pull myself together. I won't have you thinking you can't leave me.' She punched Freda's arm so hard that it hurt. 'I'll have Mr Calvert back soon, you see if I don't. One thing I can't stand is an empty house. I'm perfectly capable of cleaning all the rooms and I'll have to employ a cook, that's all. I just have to feel right about it first. You understand.'

Of course Freda did. She was doing everything for Doreen she could think of except what Doreen wanted most and could never ask for. When they went into Doreen's quarters she felt useless. In the tiny bathroom she could see Harry's shaving kit, pale with talcum powder, and she almost stumbled over his favourite chair, its right arm worn down by the way he always propped his chin when he played chess with Doreen. She remembered his soft Cornish voice saying, 'Off to bed, m'dear? If I get tired of this one I'll come knocking.' Doreen had flung a captured rook at him in mock anger, but she'd left them alone on Timothy's anniversary, Timothy ablaze and writhing in the German sky. They had gone dancing, and there in the midst of the smoky light and the couples turning in the waves of music, he'd told her that if he hadn't met Doreen first he would have hoped to meet her. His cuckoo clock gave a tentative whir as if the bird were impatient for midnight, and Freda thought helplessly that however vivid her memories were – Harry's skin that always looked suntanned, his slow grin, his strong hands on her shoulders – they could be nothing compared with Doreen's. The trouble was that if the house could be said to be haunted, as far as Doreen was concerned it wasn't haunted enough.

Doreen switched off the gas fire in the parlour and adjusted her headscarf in front of the oval mirror, and at twenty to twelve they left the house. Snow glistened on the saplings that poked through the crust of the pavement. The two-tone Georgian terrace – cream on the ground floor where keystones looked like faint frowns above the windows, two red-brick storeys above – led to Caledonian Road, where a locked gate kept out traffic. Families emerged from under the railway bridge into the sparkling light of the streetlamps on their way to church. Beyond the bridge was Pentonville, the long off-white prison building she had once mistaken for a factory. All the trees inside the prison wall looked stunted. Two nights ago she'd dreamed that every prison window had contained the same woman's face, and that had made her even less willing to dream.

The women turned along Copenhagen Street toward the Lewis Carroll Library, in the ground floor of a multistorey block. They might almost have passed the church if people hadn't been converging on it, it looked so like a small block of flats.

Doreen fell to her knees as soon as they reached a pew. Freda knelt unobtrusively beside her and hoped that Doreen's fervour was a good sign. She didn't often go to church herself, it had always made her a little uneasy since a schoolmate had told her that her dreams were a sin. All the same, she'd come away from Timothy's Requiem Mass feeling that the church believed in eternal life as deeply as she did, so how could it say that her dreams were wrong? She had never dreamed of Timothy, though she had been haunted by the image of his death; she hadn't dreamed of anyone since her parents, after they'd died of the winter and the rationing of coal and food and the doctors being kept so busy by the air raids. Perhaps she no longer dreamed because their acceptance of her dreaming as something quite natural had died with them, but she was sure they were together, sure that she would see them again. Sometimes she had gone to church to think of them or Timothy, never to ask for anything, since she didn't quite feel she belonged. Now, for the first time in many years, she was praying – praying that tonight Doreen would begin to accept her loss.

The congregation rose when the priest came in, and Freda found that almost everything had changed: the Latin had gone, the ritual was unfamiliar. She had to watch the people in front of her so as to know when to stand or sit or kneel. Christ was born, they couldn't change that, and he promised life after death. If anyone deserved that it was Harry, who had never missed a Sunday or, as far as Freda knew, done wrong to anyone. The ritual had left her behind, but it must mean more to Doreen, who was silently weeping.

After Mass Doreen knelt for a while, hands clasped until their knuckles turned white, eyes closed, lips moving, shoulders shaking. Freda watched children, bright-eyed at their first midnight awake, filing past the crib. Doreen dabbed her eyes and stood up, smiling bravely at Freda. They emerged into the Christmas morning, where families exchanged hushed good-nights and small flakes settled through the dark air, and Doreen said, 'Sorry if I embarrassed you, blubbing like that.'

'So long as it made you feel better.'

'It didn't, not really. I was thinking of last Christmas and all the ones before it. I feel so lonely, Freddy. I don't know what to do.'

At least she was talking about it. 'It'll pass, Doreen. I know you can't believe that now, but it will.'

'But I feel so lost. You can't imagine.'

'I can, Doreen. Believe me, I can.' She'd felt like that when she'd heard of Timothy's death, felt reduced to nothing by the meaninglessness of it all. She'd overcome that, she'd come back to life, and she had to make sure Doreen did too. Doreen had to be helped to accept that she wouldn't see or hear anything of Harry for a while, that it wouldn't help if she did. That was Freda's task, and already it seemed daunting. They turned the corner out of Caledonian Road, past the locked gate, and then they faltered. A tall man in black was standing on Doreen's steps.

Doreen recovered first, no doubt because she didn't recognize him. 'I'm sorry to trouble you at this hour,' he said in his quiet voice. 'Miss Beeching gave me your address. I wondered if you might have room.'

Freda felt as if a crippling burden had been lifted from her all at once. She couldn't recall telling him the address or even her name, but thank heaven he could. 'Doreen, this is Sage,' she said. 'If anyone can help you in your trouble, he can.'

'If Freddy says so, that's good enough for me.' Doreen looked tearful but trusting. Sage's calm face and long delicate hands must have made her feel as Freda had. 'All the rooms are made up. You can have whichever you like,' Doreen said, slipping the key into the lock beside the dog-faced knocker that Harry had screwed on askew. Freda noticed that the old green paint was beginning to show through the red of the door. Perhaps she could give it a new coat of paint. She could help to cheer up Doreen's house.

When Susan came out of the bathroom, where she had been allowed a touch of Mummy's purple eye shadow, Mummy was wearing her new black dress, which Susan had saved up for. 'Oh, Mummy, you look lovely,' Susan cried.

'Thank you, kind lady. So do you. Turn round and let me see.'

The hem of Susan's long skirt whispered over her glittery stockings, and she could see it in the mirrors of her shoes. 'You look very grown-up,' Mummy said. 'You'll remember to be on your best behaviour, won't you? Our host is the lady who got me the job.'

They huddled inside their coats and went downstairs arm in arm. Lions roared in the flat across the landing, where the cats must be watching their cousins. They were roaring louder on the floor below, until a woman's voice screamed, 'Turn that down, I've enough of a circus with you as it is,' at the man who'd cornered Susan at the dustbins. He no longer bothered Susan; maybe everyone was strange sometimes – that was what she wanted to believe. 'We're having a nice Christmas, aren't we, Mummy?' she said.

'I'm glad you're happy here now.' Mummy opened the front door, where a drift as tall as a thumb had gathered. 'I was worried when I thought you mightn't be.'

Susan had been hoping Mummy would say she was enjoying Christmas now. She might have thought she was if Mummy hadn't stopped on the crunchy path and slapped her forehead. 'I knew there was something. We've forgotten the wine. Get it for me, there's a good girl.'

Susan forgot things herself sometimes. She ran upstairs and grabbed the bottle of Harrod's wine from the refrigerator. Perhaps she was wrong to be suspicious, and so she hurried through the greenish dimness of the main room to the window. As soon as she parted the curtains her heart sank. She had been right after all.

She put down the bottle and gripped the curtains so hard she could feel her nails through them. Mummy was pacing back and forth on the pavement, stepping into the road to stare both ways between the cars, hurrying to the opposite pavement to peer along there. When she came back to the light of the nearest streetlamp she glanced up at the house. She caught sight of Susan in the moment before Susan let the curtains fall and dodged back.

Picking up the icy bottle made Susan shiver. It wasn't only having been caught watching that made her scared to go down, it was the way Mummy had looked guilty because she had been caught. She had been looking for Eve. Susan was sure now she had been right to snub Eve, but that wasn't at all reassuring.

She'd felt mean when she had given Eve her book back, the day after she had seen their faces in the picture. She hadn't been able to find their faces again, she'd thought perhaps she had imagined it; perhaps that was what dreaming did to you. 'I don't want to read this any more,' she'd said. 'You can have it back.'

'But you like those kind of stories.'

'I don't like these. They aren't just stories.' She'd stared into the eyes she thought she recognized. 'You know they aren't.'

'I know your mummy wouldn't like you saying that, that's what I know.'

How could she have known? 'I'll lend you something else, then,' Eve had said.

'Don't bother. I don't want anything of yours. And I don't want to play with you any more.'

'You'd better ask your mummy first. *She* likes me.'

'I don't care. She can't make me.' The new bruise on

Eve's cheek had made Susan feel even meaner, except that she'd thought Eve had turned her head to make sure she would notice. 'I don't want to be your friend any more. I never liked you anyway.'

'But I won't have anyone to play with.'

'Whose fault is that?' Susan started away but turned back. 'And just you stay away from my mummy. You leave her alone.'

That was before Christmas, and she hadn't seen Eve since. She'd kept hearing what she'd said to Eve and wondering how she could have been so mean. It didn't prove anything that Mummy had kept asking where Eve was, she could just have been worried about the way Eve was treated at home. But Mummy had spent too much of Christmas Day glancing out of the window or thinking that she'd heard the doorbell, and she seemed less and less able to sleep. Last night the muffled creaking of the floorboards in the main room had woken Susan twice. Lying in the dark, she'd had the notion that Eve had somehow been making Mummy sleep, but why? All she knew now was that Mummy had left the wine behind so that she could look for Eve while Susan was out of the way.

She went downstairs feeling apprehensive and sick. 'Whatever kept you so long?' Mummy said.

'I dropped the bottle, it was so slippery,' Susan said, wishing desperately that they could both stop pretending.

'You should have put it in a bag. Never mind, I'll carry it. Come on or we'll be late.' Mummy strode toward Bayswater Road as if she had no time to glance at anything. Nobody but Susan would have known that, surreptitiously, she was. It seemed she had no more idea where Eve lived than Susan had.

They made their way through the gaps in the banks of cleared snow at the pedestrian crossing. A few cars passed carefully over the sparkling road on the way to Boxing Day parties. Mummy turned the corner by the estate agent's where she had bought the flat, led Susan up the hill, through a gate, and down steps.

A figure grew on the frosted glass as soon as Mummy rang the bell, and a moment later opened the door. 'Happy Christmas, Nell,' she said, 'and this elegant young lady must be Susan.'

She had a wide mouth made for smiling, friendly greenish eyes, blonde hair cut short the way Susan would have liked to wear hers. 'Call me Molly, Susan,' she said, and Susan wondered why she called Mummy Nell. Of course it was another way of saying Helen.

They had turkey with all the trimmings, and quite a lot of wine. Molly talked to Susan at least as much as she talked to Mummy, and both that and the wine made Susan feel years older. Molly talked to her about London, asked her exactly where Wallasey was and what it was like, hoped she'd inherited the reading habit from her mother. 'Don't watch telly just because we work there, if I still do.'

'I don't read that much,' Mummy said. 'It's cataloguing I enjoy. I like to know everything's where it should be. I'm really not at all adventurous.'

'I'm not as much as I used to be. Safer for both of us, probably.' Molly was dousing a Christmas pudding in brandy before she passed it through the serving hatch. 'You don't know what we're talking about, do you, Susan? Life must be one long adventure for you just now.'

Susan nodded, since they were both looking at her. 'You've made friends, that's the main thing,' Molly went on. 'You know, it wasn't until I got trapped here by the weather that I realized how few friends I have in London.'

'I hope I'm one,' Mummy said. 'You can always count on me after what you did.'

'I'm sure I can. I don't mean I've no friends, you understand, I'm not complaining. I'd hate to be alone in a big city. No wonder Soho's what it is, no wonder people are strange.'

190

'We know someone like that, don't we, Mummy?'

'I don't know.' Perhaps Mummy was glancing at the window so as not to look at her. 'Do we?'

'Eve, I mean. She's strange, isn't she?'

'I really wouldn't know, Susan. And I'm sure Molly doesn't want to hear that sort of thing at Christmas.'

But it was Molly who had brought it up. Mummy started talking about something she and Molly had been discussing in the kitchen, some film that was true even though it wasn't, and Susan felt excluded and resentful until she began to laugh, it was so complicated and incomprehensible. Mummy stared at her as if she were being rude, but Molly began to laugh too.

They were all laughing, though Susan for one had forgotten why, as they cleared the dishes into the kitchen. 'Leave them,' Molly said. They sat down breathlessly in the fat firm chairs, and Molly produced a box of chocolates. She shouldn't, she said, but since it was Christmas . . . She kept glancing at the window as they talked; perhaps she was expecting someone. Susan willed them not to arrive just yet, for Mummy was saying less and saying that more slowly, nodding and blinking and then she was asleep. 'I'll wash up,' Susan whispered, 'if you show me where to put the things.'

'Don't bother, Susan, I've time on my hands just now. Well, that's very sweet of you.' Susan knew it wasn't sweet at all; she was simply trying to get as far from Mummy as she could before she started talking. Mummy didn't want anyone to know about Eve, and that was why Susan had to tell, but it made her feel disloyal and miserable, telling tales about Mummy. When she reached the sink she found she couldn't talk.

It was Eve she had to talk about, not Mummy, but if she didn't mention Mummy there was no point in talking. Was this what they meant in stories when they said someone's lips were sealed? It felt as if the glue that sealed them had got into her mind too. When she managed to open them she found that no words would come out. Then Molly said, 'What is it, Susan? Can I help?'

Susan turned quickly to the serving hatch to make sure that Mummy was asleep. The edges of the steps to the street glinted in the dark beyond the window. 'Do you think someone can have power over someone else?'

'Of course. Most of us do.'

'I don't mean just ordinary power,' Susan said, whatever that meant. 'I mean being able to make people do things.'

'That's pretty ordinary too. We all do things because we're made to, and half the time we don't realize we are.'

'I don't,' Susan said defensively, but she didn't want to get into an argument, she was desperate to make herself clear before Mummy awoke. 'I don't mean things like you mean,' she said, with no idea what those might be. 'I mean like making people go to sleep.'

'That's easy enough to do with sleeping pills.'

Molly was putting away the last of the dishes. 'Not with pills,' Susan cried.

'Not with drugs at all? Well then, hypnosis.'

'Is that the same as hypnotism? That's it, I know it. That's what she's doing.'

Molly closed the cupboard and took her by the shoulders to gaze at her. 'If you think someone's doing that to you, Susan, you should tell your mother at once.'

'Mummy won't listen.' She had to say it now, or all her efforts would be wasted. 'She's doing it to Mummy,' she whispered.

'Who is, Susan?'

'A girl. Mummy met her before we came here to live. She tried to be my friend so she could do it to me as well.' She was forgetting to whisper, for Molly's expression of polite interest made it clear how unbelievable all this sounded. 'She puts Mummy to sleep.'

'I know a few people who do that to me.' Molly's grin

vanished when she saw how it upset Susan. 'Why should this girl want to do that?'

All at once Susan knew: because then Eve could make Mummy dream. She didn't know why Eve should want to, and there was no point in telling Molly, for how could it mean anything to her? 'I don't know,' she said, and went to the serving hatch, though it no longer mattered if Mummy woke up. Behind her Molly said, 'I really think you ought to tell your mummy all this and ask her if she'll – ' but Susan cried out, so loudly that it seemed impossible that Mummy didn't wake. 'There she is,' she cried. 'That's her. That's Eve.'

Eve was at the window, watching Mummy asleep. Susan knew it was Eve, though at first she could see only eyes. As Molly ducked through the hatch to look, Eve's face seemed to form around the eyes and then was out of sight. A moment later Susan was running down the hall. She snatched open the front door and clambered up the slippery steps.

The night hit her like icy water. All of her was shivering as she peered about for Eve. The street was darker than it should be, there seemed to be windows everywhere above her and an unbearable sense of being watched. But there was Eve turning the corner at Bayswater Road. How could she have got there so quickly on the treacherous slope? By the time Susan reached the corner by holding onto walls all the way down, there was no sign of Eve or of anyone else.

She used the walls to drag herself up the hill to Molly's, and faltered at the gate, for Mummy was waiting in the doorway. 'Get your coat, miss,' she said grimly. 'We're going now.'

She followed Susan to make sure she did as she was told, and Susan had no chance to ask Molly the question she wanted to ask. She could only give Molly a pleading look when Mummy wasn't watching. 'I'm glad I met you, Susan,' Molly said. 'Perhaps we can talk again soon.'

Susan was grateful but wished Mummy hadn't heard, for it had made her suspicious. 'What were you saying while I was asleep? Why did you run out like that?' Mummy demanded as they walked through the deserted freezing streets.

'We were just talking about hypnotists,' Susan said, sending Molly her thanks for not mentioning Eve at the window, 'and I thought I saw someone from school going by.' She tried not to shiver in case that looked as if she were frightened by lying, but trying made her shiver worse. She could see that Mummy wasn't satisfied. 'We'll have to do something about you, young lady,' she said, and Susan could only tell herself that the evening had been worth it. At least she was no longer alone with her plight. At least Molly had seen Eve.

Molly wasn't sure that she had seen anything. Two days later, as she tried to decipher the instructions for building a video cabinet, she thought that anything she might have seen had been the product of her nerves, jangled by Nell. No wonder Susan had thought she'd glimpsed someone at the window when Nell had kept glancing at it as if she hoped someone would appear. She'd made Molly so nervous that Molly had begun to feel as if the view would have changed if she went to the window. At least she hadn't seen a face, as Susan apparently had.

She laid the sides and the back of the incoherent cabinet on the carpet, and had to assume the holes had been drilled in the wrong places. No wonder the wordless instructions – arrows pointing out that A should be attached to B before D, all of which looked exactly the same – made even less sense than usual. She ought to be used by now to things that didn't make sense. She wished that she knew what to do about Susan, instead of simply knowing what ought to be done.

Of course Susan ought to see a child psychiatrist. Molly would have hinted that gently to Nell, except that she felt it was Nell who'd made Susan that way. Perhaps that shouldn't make a difference, but she hadn't even told Nell why Susan had run out of the flat. So much for her attempt to brighten Nell's and Susan's Christmas – not only had she given herself yet another problem, she had to force herself not to keep glancing at the window.

Sometimes someone was there, of course. So far today there had been the postman, with several belated Christmas cards and two large bills, and one of the secretaries from upstairs had rung the bell just as Molly thought she'd figured out the cabinet. She was awfully sorry to bother Molly if Molly had been doing anything, they were going out and thought Molly wouldn't mind if they left a note on their bell to say that she would take in anything that came for them, and Molly had had enough. 'Would you like me to take in your washing as well? And just give me a shout when you want your arses wiped.' The secretary's face had frozen into the mask she must use to ward off unwelcome visitors to her boss. 'Well, I never. You'd think that at least you could be neighbourly at Christmas,' she'd said, and now there were two more people in London whom Molly couldn't count as friends.

She wouldn't miss them. Let them plague someone else. All the same, she wondered how many people disliked her without knowing her, what with the newspaper reports and the photograph of her looking furtive, and *Private Eye*'s gleeful paragraph: 'While Marty the Menace spends the festive season in the good ole coonhuntin' South of the US of A his personal assistant Molly Wolfe works off her frustration by carrying on the bad work and accusing the police of molesting her. It seems not to have occurred to her to wonder why on earth anyone would want to. Who could have played with the big bad Wolfe? Pigs, maybe . . .' Anyone who responded to that she wouldn't have wanted for a friend, and now she saw what was wrong with the instructions, they were printed from right to left. It took her less than five minutes to assemble the base, and she was so intent on fitting the shelves into place first time that she didn't even glance up to prove to herself that there had been no movement at the window. Only when the doorbell rang did she realize that there had.

Her start of panic made her furious. The figure beyond the frosted glass could hardly be the police, unless they'd taken to wearing red boots in the snow. Besides, the woman was too small, and when Molly opened the door the woman's head looked even smaller for being tied up in a headscarf. 'Molly Wolfe,' she said.

Something about her made Molly apprehensive – not just her peremptory briskness. 'Yes?'

'Don't you remember me? I didn't think I'd changed that much. I recognized you as soon as I saw your picture in the paper. No? Joyce Churchill. You knew me as just Joyce.'

Molly's apprehension grew solid in her stomach, though she wasn't sure why: perhaps all of them from eleven years ago had seen her photograph, but why should that make her feel panicky? 'You've come about Stuart's letter,' she said.

'Stuart who?'

Why was she concerned with surnames now? 'Stuart Hay. Dr Kent's assistant. The people who got us together in Oxford.'

'Don't talk to me about them. I've finished with all that, I've found my purpose in life. Of course I haven't come about them. I've come to ask for your help.'

Molly couldn't stand there with her apprehension looming overhead so darkly it seemed solid. 'You'd better come in.'

In the living room Joyce nodded approvingly at the furniture and video recorder and sections of the cabinet. 'What can I do for you?' Molly said.

'Remember how we all wanted to change things? I think I have, in my own little way. Maybe I needed that business in Oxford to teach me not to be so ambitious. What I do, you see, is look after old folk, giving them somewhere to go so they can make friends.'

'That's worth doing.'

'Yes, it is. Nobody can say different. Nobody except the planners and the people who are too interested in making money. The planners let my day centre be demolished, after my husband gave up his own shop to buy it for me. They're paying compensation, as little as they can get away with. I'd like people to know about that,' she said fiercely, 'but first there's something else. I've found an empty property that's suitable and I'm having to fight one of these hamburger chains to get it. They're doing everything they can to make it seem they would be more of an asset to the district than a place for the old folk would be. But they're afraid of public opinion, I'm sure they are.'

'So they should be,' Molly said, and wondered why Joyce was staring so impatiently at her. 'So why have you come to me?'

'Because you work for television, of course.'

'Yes, but not at the moment. I've been suspended.'

'I know that. They told me when they gave me your address.' Joyce was growing red-faced with impatience. 'You still know who I should speak to, don't you? Surely you can put in a word for me. I don't know anyone else who can help.'

'I'll do my best, Joyce,' Molly said, vowing that once she had put Joyce in touch she would have nothing more to do with her. 'Let me make a call and see who's there.'

Ben wasn't, thank God, and wouldn't be until the new year. Tessa Schuman was in charge of news, and sounded wary when she realized who Molly was. 'It's nothing to do with me,' Molly explained, 'except that the lady is a friend of mine. Just let me bring her in and the rest is up to you.' She would have sent Joyce if she hadn't wanted time to talk to her, to ask.

Joyce had overheard her and was wrapping up her head again. 'You're a brick. Look, here's my number and where I live. If I can ever do anything for you, don't hesitate to ask.'

The more Molly thought of the possibility of a reunion, the more trapped it made her feel. She closed the front door behind them and dug her mittens out of her coat pocket. 'Don't be offended, Joyce, but I honestly feel we should try to stay apart.'

'Well, of course I wouldn't dream of imposing on you.'

'You're offended. Look, it's nothing personal. I don't know why, I just feel none of us should meet.' She was beginning to resent the way Joyce was looking at her as if Joyce never had premonitions herself. 'You had a letter from Stuart, didn't you? Didn't it make you feel that way?'

'I'm afraid I don't know what you mean. I've neither seen nor heard of him in eleven years, and I've no wish to.'

'I assumed he'd written to all of us.' What did it mean if he had written only to Molly? She thought of Danny, whose name couldn't be Swain, remembered his charge that she had made everything happen. She stopped at the corner of Bayswater Road and took the letter out of her bag. 'See how it reads,' she said. 'Like a form letter.'

Joyce read it quickly and passed it back. Molly was tempted to let it be blown into the muddy slush. Instead she replaced it in her handbag, and then had to hurry after Joyce, who wasn't waiting. 'You see what I mean,' she said hopefully. 'So how about it, Joyce? Any after-effects?'

'I'm afraid not. Reality keeps me too busy to dream.'

Did her briskness disguise nervousness? 'Joyce, what do you remember from Oxford?'

'I remember feeling I'd been locked away with nobody to turn to. Just like old people who're locked up in homes because their children can't be bothered looking after them.'

'Do you remember what you dreamed?'

Joyce stared as if Molly was raving. 'Why on earth would I remember a dream I had eleven years ago?'

'I thought you might remember the last dream you had there – the one that was more than you could take.'

'Well, I don't, and I'm glad I don't. Do you?' she said with a fierce triumphant look.

'Parts of it, yes. I remember a back room full of people who looked, I don't know, unfinished. I remember getting there via a red front door with a dog-faced knocker. Have you ever seen a door like that?'

'Never, and I don't want to.'

'What bothers me is that I can't remember how you got to that house.'

'I don't remember that either,' Joyce said, and looked furious, then tried to look careless as she hurried ahead. It took Molly a moment to realize Joyce had trapped herself, but by the time she overtook Joyce, the small woman was ready for her. 'I've only one thing to say about Oxford,' she said, 'and it's this. They shouldn't have put us all together like that. They locked up all that dreaming with nowhere for it to go. They overloaded us, that's what they did. They burned out my dreaming. And I'll tell you one more thing,' she said, grabbing a railing of the park as if she wanted to shake it at Molly, 'I wouldn't tell them, but I'm glad they did. I never want to dream again. Reality is more than enough for me.'

They reached MTV without having exchanged another word. Tessa on the fifth floor seemed determined to get rid of Molly. 'I wouldn't be seen round here just now if I were you,' she told her as Joyce began her story. Molly couldn't understand why she was lingering, after she'd told Joyce they ought to stay apart, but Tessa had to say, 'I really think you ought to go,' before Molly could make herself do so, feeling a looming frustration so intense that it didn't feel like hers at all.

Of course it must be. She was frustrated by Joyce's denial of everything she had once been. At least I can still dream, Molly told herself walking home, and I mean to use that. She already had. She stopped to gaze at the police station. What had she suddenly almost remembered? The boxy, off-white building with its gutters spiky with icicles and its buried cells looked so enigmatic it seemed meaningless. Eventually she made her way through the unsteady crowd, still wondering what she had already dreamed about the police that she had overlooked and which it was so crucial to remember.

Danny got a grey suit for Christmas. His father shook his hand curtly and growled, 'Happy Christmas'; his mother cried, 'Try it on.' When he slipped his arms into the jacket he found that the breast pocket bulged. He reached in, hoping for sweets or even a radio, but the book that looked like a miniature Bible was a thesaurus. 'You take that to work and read a page whenever you can and then you won't be stuck for words,' his mother said. Danny gave her a set of pans, gave his father a book about MGM.

It was much like previous Christmases: his mother blinked forlornly at the turkey and the charred vegetables and said, 'I don't know what went wrong'; his father clapped her on the shoulder and growled, 'Nothing wrong at all.' He glared at Danny for saying, 'I'll bet you're glad now I gave you pans.' After they had gnawed their portions of dried-up Christmas pudding, they played games to cheer her up, and then finally the whisky ritual, his father producing the bottle and muttering, 'I suppose you want one too,' while his mother said, 'Don't give him too much,' and then his father demanded, 'What are you going to do if the Hercules closes?'

Danny choked. His nostrils felt afire with whisky. 'It isn't going to,' he managed to say finally.

'Listen to it. Don't you notice anything that's going on around you? Why do you think it's closing every afternoon?'

He noticed all right, noticed more than anyone else; he'd just learned to keep it to himself. 'Who says?'

'Sidney Pettigrew says, that's who. Every afternoon once the kids are back at school. Don't tell me you didn't take that in.'

Had Danny forgotten he'd been told? Mr Pettigrew hadn't bothered telling him, more like – maybe he'd hoped there would be a scene like this. His father was shaking his head in disgust. 'Look at it. The place could catch fire and he wouldn't notice.'

His mother had been wheezing in sympathy with Danny's coughing, she'd heaved herself to her feet to thump him on the back, but now she had caught her breath. 'They won't really close, will they?'

'Afternoons are the beginning of the end, you mark my words. It's those videos that are the root of it, and people being afraid to go out at night. Soon they won't go out at all. They'll ring up for their shopping and have it delivered in armoured cars.'

She was sipping her milk with a festive touch of rum. 'Well, I think it's very sad.'

'It's more than bloody sad, it's criminal. Give me wartime any day. People cared about each other then, and the Hercules was somewhere you were proud to work. Remember how I used to have to run to the Plaza with the newsreels

201

as soon as we'd shown them? Nearly lost them in the blackout once. We didn't need to advertise in the papers, just put our posters in the shops and we'd have a full house every night. After the war the rot set in,' he said, and Danny wondered if he meant that Danny had been born, if he were remembering teaching Danny to work the projector and losing his temper whenever he had to repeat himself. 'Pettigrew can see the way it's going. He's thinking of opening a video library.'

'Then I'll work there,' Danny said.

'You'll be lucky.' His father glared at him. 'You'd need to be able to talk to people.'

'Well, leave him alone and maybe he will. You do what I said, Danny, you read that book every chance you get. Then you won't always be having to stop and think.'

But he needed to, to make sure he was safe. He wished they would both leave him alone. Danny closed his eyes and woke when his mother asked who wanted a snack. He was in bed when he realized he hadn't said thank you for the suit and the thesaurus, but he couldn't even pronounce that word; it felt like a trick played on his mouth. He wouldn't be so easy to trick tomorrow, when he would be at the Hercules and could start to deal with Dr Kent.

He left home early, he was so eager to be in the projection box. Children were fighting on the steps of the Hercules, trying to pry open the display case to steal the Disney poster, writing their names on the walls. Danny chased them away just as Mr Pettigrew unbolted the doors for him. 'Never mind chasing my audience, there's few enough of the little darlings as it is,' he said, and then he saw the graffiti. 'Little swines. I should never have left Bath. We showed the better class of film there for the better class of audience. Never sent the children by themselves, always came as a family. Half the families booked the same seats every time. It was like pews in church, and they had just as much respect for them.'

Danny was wondering why he'd come here from Bath if he hadn't had to, when the manager frowned. 'Come in my office. I want a word with you.'

There was nobody to overhear, but that was Mr Pettigrew's way, like always being on the steps at the end of the show to say good-night to his audience even when they told him where to go, and wearing his black jacket on the hottest summer days. Danny wanted to be alone in the projection box. As soon as he was standing in front of Mr Pettigrew's desk, he said, 'It's all right, my dad's told me.'

Mr Pettigrew touched the tips of his moustache with finger and thumb as if to line it up with his bow tie. 'Told you what?'

'About the afternoons.' When Mr Pettigrew still frowned, he said, 'How we're going to close.'

'What do you mean, close?'

'He said how you're going to open a video place instead of here.'

'He said that, did he? I'll be having words with him. And is that why you went skulking off to Felicity there?'

Danny glanced round, expecting to see whoever she was, or at least a photograph. The sight of nobody confused him even more than the question. 'Where?'

'All the gods help us, have you forgotten already? Don't act the fool with me, lad, you're enough of one without trying. I suppose you didn't know I knew. Well, what have you to say for yourself?'

'I didn't follow what you said.'

'Sainted heavens, you get worse. They'll be putting you away. The Royal in Chelsea, does that mean anything to you? Do you happen to recall the manageress who I've known for years and always comes round for a Christmas drink?'

The syllables fell into place: Felicity Tare, Mrs Tare, who had sounded like Miss Astaire. Danny felt prickly and desperate. 'I didn't know we were closing then,' he pleaded. 'And she wouldn't give me the job.'

'You astound me. How could she have missed the chance?' He was gripping his own lapels so hard that sweat bloomed greyly from his fingertips on the black material. 'I'll tell you something else, lad, in case it hasn't sunk in. I'm the only one who'll employ you, for your dad's sake.'

Danny had never expected to feel grateful to him. 'So can I work in the video place?'

'I'm dreaming. I'm not hearing this.' Mr Pettigrew stood up slowly as the zombies had. 'Get in your box and don't come out until you're told. And here's something for you to think about: if we're closing, I promise you'll be the last to know.'

Danny climbed the worn steps to the projection box. He should have known that the manageress would tell on him, for she was under Molly Wolfe's control – even her name had been meant to bewilder him. Now Molly Wolfe was trying to get the Hercules closed while Dr Kent kept him confused, so that Molly Wolfe could sell cassettes of herself like the one he'd seen in the booth in Soho. He knew exactly what was going on, and he meant to make sure that everyone did.

He switched on the tape of music for the auditorium, songs that Mr Pettigrew recorded from the radio, editing out the disc jockey and the commercials. Children were running into the auditorium, banging all the tip-up seats and stamping their feet for the film to begin. He watched the spottily luminous clock above the purple curtains, and grunted with relief when it was time for the film. As soon as Mandy brought his cup of tea he could begin.

The first reel was over before she gave it to him, along with a dirty look. The tea was so hot he couldn't hold the plastic cup. He put it on the ledge of his window to the auditorium, he trampled on the carpet where the magazines were hidden, then he took out his pad and sat on his high chair to write.

It was the only way to deal with Dr Kent and Molly

Wolfe. Putting her face in the magazines was no good, not when the positions were already unsatisfyingly familiar and when afterward he felt disgusted with himself. Going back to Dr Kent to make her think she'd got the better of him would be to trick himself, for there was no reason to go back. Publicity was what they were scared of, you could tell from the way Molly Wolfe had tried to hide her face from the newspaper – the same newspaper that people had been writing letters to about the sex shops. That paper wouldn't let her stop it printing what he wrote.

'Dear Sirs,' he wrote, and sucked his pen. His mouth tasted tinny by the time he began scribbling. 'The people who wrote and said they didn't want any sex shops in Soho where they live ought to be told there is somewhere a lot worse there, at 8 St Quentin's Court off Wardour Street, where Dr Guilda Kent takes people she catches coming out of the sex shops by saying she'll tell people they were there.' He had to be careful now not to give away who he was; he was sure that when he'd written to the papers during all the uproar about the CIA giving people drugs, when he'd told them to look nearer home, in Oxford, they'd thrown away his letters as soon as they'd read his address on the flap. 'She uses Soho as a front,' he wrote, enjoying his succinctness. 'She is involved with Molly Wolfe who you reported, who you can see in the sex shops, so you can see that one of them is luring victims for the other.' That would make people have to think which was which, think for themselves for a change. 'If you don't believe me go and ask them and see them hide their faces,' he finished, and began to copy the letter out neatly while he thought of a name to call himself.

He stopped at 'involved' and took out the thesaurus, which was dragging at his nipple as his mother said he used to do to her. 'Implicated' sounded better, and he wrote that instead. He finished the copying and signed himself A. Mann, then he went to his window and saw that Mr Pettigrew had called the police.

Children were dodging from row to row to borrow tickets from children who'd paid to get in, while Mr Pettigrew and Mandy and the police tried to head them off and Mickey Mouse waved a wand, trying desperately to stop the multiplying magic. Danny moved his plastic cup so as to watch the show, and it wasn't until he heard the hiss of leaking tea that he realized the projector was melting the cup. When he tugged at the cup most of it came away, spilling tea down the projector and jerking the film off the screen, toward the dusty cut-price chandeliers.

Mr Pettigrew came in as soon as the police had marched away their captives. 'Why don't you set the place on fire and be done with it,' he said when he saw the base of the cup oozing down the side of the projector. Danny's throat went dry – Mr Pettigrew was treading on the magazines. 'Off tomorrow, aren't you? Allah be praised and bless all the nignogs. If I could pay your dad his rate I'd have him back full time.'

Danny hardly heard, for Mr Pettigrew had shown him that he couldn't send the letter. If he sent it without signing his real name, then Dr Kent and Molly Wolfe would be able to lie, because there would be nobody to stand up against them. If he signed it his mother might find out he'd been to Soho. He knew what to do, they hadn't beaten him.

At home he hid the letter under his bedroom carpet and was still tonguing breakfast from between his teeth to chew as he made for Soho the next morning.

Wardour Street was almost deserted. Perhaps Dr Kent was taking a Christmas break. The door at the foot of the stairs was open, and it occurred to him that he might be able to look through her files. That sent him tiptoeing across the court. When he looked up the stairs she had come out of her office and was waiting for him.

Her long face smiled as he clung to the doorway. His penis felt as if it had retreated into his crotch from cold and panic. 'Happy Christmas, Danny,' she said. 'Come right up.'

If he tried to step back he would fall on his face. That must be why she was smiling, grinning like a horse. The staircase seemed so long and steep he thought he would never reach the top. She went back into her office as if she were tired of waiting, and now he could creep out while she wasn't watching, except that he wasn't going to turn back and leave her unchallenged. She couldn't keep him climbing the stairs forever, though he was sure she was trying. The thought seemed to release him, for almost at once he was at the top.

'Close the door.' She turned from the filing cabinet with a card in her hand. He stamped his feet – grey ice pattered down the stairs – and closed himself in. The glare of the frosted glass left 'Know Yourself' in mirror writing on his eyes. 'What brought you back to me?' she said.

He had to tell her what she must want to hear, though it tasted like bile in his mouth. 'I need your help.'

'I'm glad you've come to that conclusion yourself.' But she didn't sound altogether convinced. 'What persuaded you?'

He felt his mouth stiffen. He had no answer at all. She would know he was lying, that he hadn't come for help but to get the better of her. When she sat forward, he would have shrunk back, except that his spine was already digging into the chair. 'Were you lonely over Christmas, was that it?'

He felt grateful, and then furious with himself for it. 'Yes.'

'I can see how you would be.' She was toying with his file card. 'And is your manager still making you show films you don't like?'

'Yes,' he said, relaxing, since that was true enough.

'They still don't turn you on?'

'No,' he said, more relaxed.

'It sounds to me as if he needs me too. What was the name of the cinema again? You told me but I've forgotten.'

'No I didn't,' Danny said at once, beginning to enjoy himself.

'Oh, didn't you? Well, never mind. I'm glad that sort of thing doesn't appeal to you, Danny. Anyone who reads magazines like the ones you showed me has to be terrified of women. I'd like to get hold of their subscription list, I can tell you. It would keep a team of psychiatrists busy for years.'

'It's all right reading about doing it to boys though, isn't it? All those Billy Bunter books, all the school stories where the boys get beaten. They're still in children's libraries, I've seen them. Nobody tries to have *them* stopped. I wrote to the papers about them once but they never put my letter in.'

She was gazing wide-eyed at him, and he had a sudden dreadful feeling that he'd said too much. Eventually she said, 'You see, you can talk. You shouldn't be so afraid that people won't listen.'

She was listening to make him talk. When she'd done that eleven years ago, she had nearly destroyed him. She gazed at him over her praying hands. 'Tell me something, Danny. Have you ever asked a girl to go out with you?'

Now he knew to keep his mouth shut, but the trouble was that was an answer too. 'Why not?' she said.

'Because I don't need to.'

He'd meant to say he didn't want to. He bit his tongue for playing tricks on him, bit until he heard the flesh crunch. 'Not good enough,' she said. 'You don't believe it and neither do I. Why don't you take a girl out and find out what it's like? Are you scared your mother wouldn't want you to?'

He pressed his aching tongue against the roof of his mouth and managed to say, 'You leave my mum alone.'

'You know what it is, don't you, Danny? She's scared of letting you do anything without her and that makes you scared of what might happen. You'd be free if it weren't for her.'

He was on his feet before he knew it, his knees shoving the desk into her. 'That's not true,' he screamed.

'Isn't it?' Surely the desk had hit her, he hoped wildly that it had, but she seemed unperturbed. She must be pretending. 'Show me, then. Show me what you can do.'

He almost did. Her throat was within reach, the street might still be practically deserted. She would tip back in her chair until her head smashed against the wall, her legs would kick helplessly on the desk until he climbed on top of her, pinning her down, biting at her face so that she didn't simply die, biting as the zombies had. By the time he'd imagined all that it was too late, his impulse had missed its chance. He sat down hastily, both his prickly body and his mind feeling like someone else's. 'Now show me,' she said.

The draught under the door was flapping the sodden cuffs of his trousers, yet he felt he was burning. 'Show you what?'

'How you'd ask a woman to go out with you. Go ahead.'

He was staring at his hands, forcing them apart to grip his knees. 'Don't want to,' he muttered.

'You will when you know you can. You need to, Danny. Have a try.' She snapped his card against the desk to make him look up. 'Unless you'd rather we discussed it with your mother first.'

'You don't know where she lives.'

'Don't be so sure,' she said, and his sudden triumph turned to panic: perhaps she would follow him home instead of just sending her spies. 'If you don't want me to, then you know what to do. Go on, Danny, ask me, try.'

Almost everything he'd said to her was a pretence, but he couldn't say those words. Maybe he could mouth them, that wasn't really saying, but she said, 'No good, Danny. I didn't hear a word.'

He took a breath so deep it rasped his throat and made his head throb. He forced the words out without thinking what they meant, it was the only way they would come. Half the

209

syllables stuck in his throat. 'Will yuh guh ut wuh muh,' he heard himself muttering.

'Better, but I still can't quite hear.'

He wanted to leap up, to make her flinch. 'Will you go out with me!' he shouted.

'Of course I will, Danny. When?'

Were they still pretending? Suddenly he saw that he could get her away from the office, get her where he wanted her. 'New Year's Eve,' he blurted.

'Your cinema is closed then, is it? Perfect. Shall we say about eight? We'll take my car. Give me your address and I'll pick you up.'

'You mustn't,' he said, neither must she see that he was afraid she would talk to his mother. 'All right then,' he said, suddenly cunning. 'It's 2 Thane Villas. That's where I live.'

She wrote that down and smiled at him until he smiled at how easily fooled she was. 'I really think we're making progress. For old time's sake I'm not charging you yet,' she said. 'When we've finished you can decide how much it's worth to you.'

It was already worth more than she knew. He only wished he had been able to think of an address that wasn't just a few streets away from home.

'You look happier,' his mother said when he went home, 'now you just stay that way,' and they had one of their best evenings together, playing Snap and rummy, his mother turning girlish when she won a trick and crying 'Oh, you pig' when he did. 'You're a good boy, Danny. Your father thinks so too really,' she said as he brought her bowl of boiling water full of medicine, and she was just draping a towel over her head and starting to inhale the steam when his father stalked in from work. 'What the hell do you mean, telling Pettigrew I said he was closing?'

'But you did.' Danny appealed to the steaming faceless mound. 'He did, didn't he?'

She uncovered herself gasping. 'I thought so.'

'And he goes blabbing straight to Pettigrew. And yesterday he tried to set the place on fire – not that Pettigrew mightn't be grateful, he'd make more on the insurance than he makes with showing films these days.'

Danny went to his room and wondered if his father had noticed; he'd been talking about Danny as if he weren't there. Danny was there all right, all there. He lifted the carpet to make sure of the letter to the paper. What troubled him as he climbed into bed was that Dr Kent had tricked him into saying more than he wanted her to know. Well, she might get the better of him when it came to words, but that would only make it worse for her. Now she'd made that clear, he didn't mean to waste much more time in talking.

The Spiritualist church was a house off Gray's Inn Road. Stone animals sat on the gateposts of the small square garden, but even though a snow fight had robbed them of their camouflage it was impossible to see what species they'd belonged to. A man with pale consoling eyes led Freda to the jumble sale, a room set with trestle tables full of clothes and books and dwarfish sandwiches, and Freda could tell it was the chapel from the hushed way everyone spoke. Middle-aged women who looked dressed for an afternoon's bingo greeted Doreen and said how well she looked, but all the talk was so small it seemed clear that everyone was nervous for the sale to be over, the service to begin. Freda hung back, breathing the smells of incense and old carpets, and watched the bravely cheerful faces of the newcomers, the impenetrable faithful brightness of the veterans. The lady at the clothing table, a mauve hat pinned to her head, said, 'Bless you, Doreen, that's truly generous of you,' and Freda wondered if she realized they were Harry's clothes, wondered for a móment if Doreen were relinquishing too much too soon.

Doreen seemed glad to leave. The indeterminate animals at the gate looked as if they were hatching from the snow. Prostitutes and a snowman stood in a square near King's Cross – prostitutes looking after people's bodies while they had them, Freda thought, until they were ready for the Spiritualists. Doreen squeezed Freda's arm. 'I can't believe how much better I feel, and it's all thanks to you.'

'Now you know that isn't true, Doreen. You were the one who had to face up to things.'

'I couldn't have without you. I can see how sad those people are now, I couldn't when I was one of them. Poor Mrs Scatchard, who was making the sandwiches, do you know she's been waiting since November? And people try to say it's all fake. Her husband would have been in touch by now if it was, wouldn't he?'

It might not be fake but Freda agreed it was sad, this eagerness for any message, whole relationships reduced to the level of a greetings telegram. 'Thank God I've finished with all that. Thank *you*,' Doreen said. 'The best thing you ever did for me was give Sage my address.' Freda hoped Doreen's faith was justified, that Sage could give her more than the Spiritualists had.

Of course he already had. Just his presence made the house no longer feel lacking. Every time Freda passed the middle landing it reassured her to know that the nearest left-hand door was his. The neighbours who'd come in for sherry on Christmas morning had seemed to think it was having a man in the house that had restored Doreen to herself, but Freda knew it was the unspoken promise that he brought with him. Or perhaps it had been spoken – Freda didn't know what he might have said after midnight Mass, when she had left them unobtrusively and slept more deeply than she had for years.

Above the bridge on Caledonian Road, the sky was more open. Clouds floated like melting ice in the canal. Freda bought a tin of yellow paint and as soon as they reached Doreen's she found a paintbrush in the outhouse Harry had turned into a toolshed and set about painting the front door.

Freda had almost finished the first coat when Doreen appeared at the dining-room window with a mug of coffee. 'He says it can be tonight,' she whispered.

The overcast was brightening when Freda stepped back, waving her yellow hands for balance. Except for the knocker, nobody would recognize the door. She scrubbed her hands at the sink in her room and changed into her best black dress, and went downstairs when she heard the gong. The middle floor still felt as if Sage were in his room, but he was at the dining table. 'Now we are all here,' he said.

The sight of his smooth untroubled almost hairless face, his black-clad body, his long still hands on the table, affected her so strongly that she could say only, 'Good evening.' Doreen wheeled in the serving trolley. Sage smiled at the cold cuts and vegetables and baked potatoes, then at Doreen. 'That looks just right,' he said.

She was clearly awed by him. On Christmas Day she'd even asked if he would rather dine in his room. She looked almost afraid to join them at the end of the table for eight that was laid for three, the far end from Harry's empty chair. She gazed fascinated at his long fingers as he lifted the dishes off the trolley and piled food on Freda's plate, she cried, 'Not so much for me,' and looked away, frowning at her rudeness. It was halfway through the meal before she dared to speak to him again. 'Have you always been psychic?' she blurted.

'Not the term I would use, but always, yes. Ever since I came to be.'

'As long as that!' Doreen shook her head for wonder. 'What would you call it then?'

He shrugged and gave a faint calm smile. 'Nothing.'

213

'You're in touch with the other world though, aren't you?'

'There is no other world.' He brushed away her anxiety with a gentle movement of his hand. 'There is only part of this one that too many are denying.'

'That's true. Too many people with closed minds. They're the ones I'm sorry for.'

'Closed, no. Not closed.' There was an odd look in his eyes. 'You cannot close a mind. Cutting oneself off from part of it is not the same at all. One may live in a single room of one's house, but something else will live in the other rooms. Something else will grow there.'

'You mean,' Doreen said excitedly, 'everyone is what I'd call psychic?'

'Not exactly.' The odd look made Freda think of a secret smile. 'Something simpler. In time you will understand.'

Though she trusted him completely, Freda found the trend of the conversation a little disturbing. She thought how enigmatic he was with his ageless face that seemed related to no country, his faintly foreign use of language, English heard in a dream. 'Sage, where do you come from?' she said.

Somehow she knew at once what he would say, and was smiling wryly before he said, 'Everywhere.'

'Are you satisfied doing what you do?' She was thinking of the back-street room in Blackpool, all that he had to offer reduced to a seedy tourist attraction.

'For the moment, yes.'

'Were you in Blackpool?'

'Assuredly. I met you.'

She smiled as if that might stop her blushing, and thought of Timothy, who had once said that to her, though she couldn't now recall what she had asked.

'But don't you want more people to know about you?' Doreen said. 'Don't you want everyone to be able to see what you see?'

'Perhaps they will. I am only one.'

'You mean there are others like you?'

'You could put it that way.'

Doreen was growing a little impatient with so many enigmas. 'Doing what?'

'Why, what you would call opening minds. Opening them so gently that those concerned may not realize.' He glanced at Freda. 'You know what I mean,' he said, and for a moment she experienced that panicky feeling of being blind and afraid to see. 'Many are cut off from their night side, but that only makes it stronger. It cannot be denied now. The doors are opening.'

Had she dreamed something once about doors? She could no longer follow what he was saying. But Doreen said, 'You mean religion, don't you? Religion or actually being able to see the next world. People are turning back to religion because they were missing so much.'

'The next world! I like that phrase. Not the other world, the next, except that it is already here.' He was gazing at Freda as if he expected her to understand, but his smile said that it really didn't matter whether she did. 'Your plate is almost empty. Shall I serve?'

'Gosh, no. I don't know how I ate so much.'

'From need. Well then, I think we are almost ready.'

Doreen cleared away so quickly that she almost dropped a plate. 'Have I time to wash up?'

'Of course. Take time.'

Freda followed her, both to help and to make herself move: she felt laden with all the food she'd eaten – thank heaven Doreen was too nervous to suggest Christmas pudding, which was steaming in a pan.

'Oh, Freda, watch me to make sure I don't break anything,' Doreen whispered. 'I mustn't expect too much, tell me I mustn't. Whatever he does will be all right, I know it will.'

'That's the attitude.' They left the last of the plates to drain and went back to the dining room.

Sage had turned off all the lights but one and was sitting, eyes closed, at the table, his upturned hands in front of the chairs on either side of him. Now his hands rose and indicated the chairs. The women sat down, and Doreen reached for his right hand as it settled on the table. 'That isn't necessary,' he said without looking.

It wasn't clear what was. His face had lifted now, toward Harry's empty place. Doreen turned her head in that direction as if Harry might appear, and Freda stared along the table too. The dim light made her think of Spiritualist meetings in pink-lit rooms, the desperate bereaved singing hymns and waiting for whoever would stumble round the circle touching shoulders, bearing messages for everyone. The dimness and the ticking of the clock made her feel sleepy. The meal seemed to be weighing her down until she couldn't move. If Sage could close his eyes so could she, just for a moment. There was no chance of her dozing so long as she could hear the clock.

She closed her eyes and made a wish for Doreen. It didn't matter if she saw Harry this time, so long as Doreen did. She thought of seeing Timothy and flinched from the idea of seeing him as he had died. Perhaps she would see him when she was dead – surely that was soon enough. The clock ticked, she was sinking through her own massive peaceful weight that seemed to be confined to her stomach and her eyelids. She remembered that when her parents were near death, they'd sometimes claimed to see dead friends and relatives with them in the room. That seemed reassuring, then and now, and so she wasn't dismayed to see her mother and father beckoning her into the woods. It was only a vision, she could still hear the clock in the midst of the birdsong, and she followed her parents into the green woods, not really her parents but a vision of them. She was running through the calm green summer light to catch them up, and now the birds were all she could hear. She was running too fast to slow down when she noticed that every leaf on every tree was exactly the same shape. Even her sudden shuddering panic couldn't stop her, not even the knowledge that the figures that had halted to wait for her in the depths of the woods weren't her parents or a vision of them after all, but something else entirely. The wood was growing dark and still she couldn't stop, the wood was all at once entirely lightless and yet the birds were singing, if anything more loudly. She might have cried out, but in the midst of all that song it was impossible to hear. It seemed forever before she struggled awake.

She wasn't sure what wakened her: not the dream. The sound of Doreen's bedroom door across the hall must have been part of the dream, for Doreen and Sage were still at the table. They watched as she blinked at the clock, which had somehow gained half an hour. 'Oh, I'm sorry,' she cried, and then she saw their faces: Sage was smiling peacefully, Doreen looked dazed but fulfilled. 'Is it over?' Freda said.

'Yes,' Sage said. Doreen squeezed Freda's hand as if she were unable to express her gratitude. When she made for the hall, she seemed barely able to see where she was going. Freda heard the bedroom door close and reminded herself she had only dreamed that a few minutes ago.

'Thank you,' she said to Sage.

'Thank *you*.' He took her elbow as she stood up, and she was glad of his assistance, for all at once she felt weak and frail, feathery, light-headed. 'I feel dizzy,' she mumbled.

'That can happen on these occasions. Let me help.' He supported her upstairs – she had to close her eyes, though that made her feel she was climbing too many flights – and seemed ready to put her to bed if she would let him. 'I'll be all right,' she said, more firmly than she felt, and listened at her door until she heard him go down to his room. Now the house was still as a snowscape, and so she was able to hear, faintly but unmistakably, the sound of Doreen's voice on the ground floor.

Sage had given her what she yearned for, that was all that

mattered. Freda got ready for bed. She had never been so glad to climb between the sheets. She hoped it wouldn't take her long to fall asleep. Perhaps Sage wasn't so different from the Spiritualists after all, perhaps he offered the same faith. If that made Doreen happy, who was Freda to object? Nevertheless she pulled up the covers to shut out Doreen's murmuring, for though she couldn't distinguish a word, the tone was unmistakable. Doreen was murmuring words of love.

'Well, look who we have here,' the Customs officer said with the faintest and thinnest of smiles. His blue eyes had brightened, he was fingering his almost invisible blond moustache. 'Back to cause more mischief, sir, are we?'

Martin was too weary to argue. 'I wouldn't say that,' he said.

'They never do, sir. Will you open your case.'

He nodded to an older colleague, who strolled along behind the counter and gazed at Martin's eyes. 'Are you prescribed any kind of medication, sir?'

'No,' Martin said, and realized too late where they were heading.

The older man came round the counter while the other scrutinized the contents of the case. 'Will you come with me, please.'

They took Martin into a small bare room and made him strip naked. The older man searched his clothes as if he were looking for fleas, while the younger, a thin strip of tongue squeezed white between his teeth, tugged Martin's hair, peered breathily into his ears, recoiled from his armpits as if they stank of fear, and squatted for a while in front of Martin's penis before he picked it up and let it drop. 'You couldn't hide much under there,' he said, and Martin told himself that he mustn't let them get to him, his rage in Chapel Hill had been destructive enough. The young officer was pulling on a plastic glove. 'Bend over,' he said.

Martin touched his toes and clenched his teeth while the young officer peered with a flashlight. When the gloved finger started probing, Martin began to curse him silently and fluently. He farted just as the finger withdrew, a long full-throated growl he was delighted to be unable to control. 'Is he clean?' the older man said.

The other stood back in disgust. 'He's got nothing on him, if that's what you mean.'

'Next time we may see if we can be more thorough. With your reputation,' the older man said, leaving Martin's clothes piled on the floor, 'you must expect special treatment.'

Planes that looked brittle as bone stood beneath the grubby yellow sky. The sky and the snowy fields beyond the tarmac seemed to be emitting the same yellowish glow. If it weren't for Molly he might have caught the first plane back, except that he was faced with trouble on both sides of the Atlantic. He left the unnatural light of the snowscape for the unnatural light of the Underground, and thought she might prove to be his only reason to have come back.

The Kensington flat made him feel less like a tenant than a visitor to a roped-off suite in a grand house, four-poster bed and all. He phoned Molly at once, and felt better as soon as he heard her voice.

'Martin! You sound close.'

'Closer than you think. Can I come over?'

'Oh, you're back! You know you can. I'm not going anywhere.' She added wryly, 'I expect you'd guessed that already.'

Molly opened her door as he opened her gate. They hugged each other as the door closed, parted, and hugged again. 'I'm glad you're back,' 'I'm glad I'm here' was all they needed to say for a while. Eventually they sat down. Molly gazed at his face. 'Are you back because you've made peace with your father?'

He hadn't wanted to talk about it so soon. 'No,' he said.

'He's all right though, isn't he?'

'He's alive, if that's what you mean.'

'So it isn't over,' she said, meaning to be encouraging.

'That's right, it isn't. It's still happening in here.' He tapped his forehead so hard that it hurt. 'What's over is my chance of making peace.'

'Oh, Martin, why?'

'We seemed to be getting along for a while, and then we had a fight. Christ, two grown men. Nobody ever grows up. He got to saying I'd ruined Larry's reputation by putting his name on that old film, Larry would be ashamed if he knew and that kind of crap, until I lost my temper. That's one thing you can trust me to do,' he said bitterly. 'I told him Larry went away because of the way he'd been treated.'

'Good for you.'

'Good for nothing. It isn't the whole story. I never told you I had a fight with my father the night before Larry enlisted. I actually knocked him down, and don't go thinking that achieved anything. All it did was make Larry go to Vietnam.'

'You can't tell me your father wasn't more to blame.'

'So what? I shouldn't have said it to him. He's dying, for Christ's sake, and I couldn't even leave him his memories.' He could still see his father's face closing for good against him, whether from rage or from realizing Martin had spoken the truth. 'And what the good Christ,' his father had asked in a soft voice that shook with hatred, 'do I have to do to make sure *you* get out of my house and never come back?' Martin had caught the next flight to England. 'Let's not talk about it, Molly,' he said finally. 'Tell me why you said you wouldn't be going anywhere.'

'Oh, that? I've got myself suspended from work. Better than being hung up by your toes, anyway,' she said, with a grin that was almost convincing.

'Maybe I'll be joining you. I need to call MTV.' The thought that neither of them might be working was oddly comforting. 'But how did you manage to get yourself suspended?'

'It was that dream I told you about – told you some of it, anyway. It was more like a vision, it was so real. I thought I actually had been interrogated by the police and went and accused them of giving me the third degree. I think they would have, I think I foresaw it and managed to prevent it. I know this all sounds crazy.'

'Not to me, not when you say it.'

She smiled gratefully at him, then her smile drooped. 'It wouldn't be so bad if I'd just got myself suspended, but I implicated you, Martin, they said so. They thought I was trying to discredit them to protect you. They said they wouldn't have suspected you except for what I did.'

'Hell, they must have said that to work on you. Come on, there's no way they wouldn't have suspected me. They can't pin anything on me, you said so yourself.' He gazed at her until her smile ventured back, then he stood up. 'Better get it over with.'

Gould's secretary gave him an appointment for the next morning. Molly added to the chilli con carne she'd made for herself, and later they made love. During the night she began shouting and wouldn't be shaken awake, though since she hadn't seemed disturbed, he didn't try very hard. At breakfast she demanded, 'Was I talking in my sleep?'

'You certainly were.'

'What was I saying?'

'It sounded like "Randy Rankin the wanker".'

'I *was* right.' She seemed delighted – by the inventiveness

221

of her subconscious, he assumed. 'Good luck,' she said, and kissed him as he went out beneath the gloomy, ambiguous sky.

A chill mist made Queensway and its dormant neon signs look dusty, shrank the park. Everyone at MTV seemed wary of him. Leon was still in Belfast, and Martin went straight up to Gould's office.

Gould wasn't alone in the leathery room. Another man stood up as he did, a lanky supple man whose face was as neutral as Gould's. 'This is Superintendent Fellows,' Gould said.

The policeman questioned Martin at length. What was his purpose in coming to Britain? What was the intention behind his films? Who did he know in Britain? Surely he must know other film directors . . . Eventually Fellows said, 'Why should you have been sent the film?'

'I suppose because of my earlier work.'

'It certainly looks that way.' Fellows rearranged the fingers of the gloves that were draped over his knee. 'As it would if it had been meant to.'

Gould intervened. 'Surely the last person he'd have sent it to would have been himself.'

'That would be downright stupid, I agree.' Fellows stood up. 'I gather you have a police record in America, Mr Wallace. I'm frankly surprised you found it so easy to come here. That is all for now, but if you propose to leave the address in Kensington High Street, please let us know.'

Martin was damned if he was going to draw their attention to Molly's address. 'The only police record I have is from filming peace marches.'

'Well, that's something.'

Gould ushered Fellows to the door then lowered himself into his own chair. 'I'd better say at once that we aren't happy with your work.'

Martin felt suddenly as unsure of himself as if he were just making his first film. 'What don't you like?'

'What *don't* we like? Tell me what there is *to* like. We're clearly in need of enlightenment. Seems to me you spend more time undermining other people's programmes than making your own.'

'I don't think that's quite fair.'

'Fair or not, you'd better take it seriously. The only filming you've done that could form the basis of a programme is absolutely and completely unbroadcastable. Yes, I mean this discipline film of yours. Your tastes are your affair, but you'd better keep them off our screens, I'm warning you. Maybe you don't know that pirate copies of your film are already circulating at the BBC. All we need now is for one to get into the hands of *Private Eye*.'

Martin was stunned. 'I'll be filming again soon,' he said weakly. 'We're going into Parliament next week.'

'Parliament? Either you're joking or you're mad.' Gould's face was still expressionless. 'Why, you've already been there. You've been in Hansard. In case you don't know what that is, it means there have been questions about you in the House, about why you were let into Britain at all. You won't be filming Parliament, my friend, next week or ever. And I wouldn't be surprised if you've made it even less possible for anyone else to.'

Oddly, Martin found the loss of a subject almost reassuring. 'I'm sorry. I wish I could suggest what I can do instead.'

'Aren't you assuming you will still be working for us?'

'Won't I be?' Martin said, not sure if he cared.

'On two conditions. We shall want to know in advance what you're proposing to film, and you'll need to submit draft scripts. It was always against my judgment that you were given such a free hand.'

'I've never worked that way,' Martin said, and realized that they might let him bring Molly with him. 'If those are your conditions, I can try.'

'That's one of them. The other is that you broadcast a

statement that you were mistaken about the Bennett film, that it was fake from beginning to end. Nothing to be ashamed of. After all, it fooled his own mother.'

Martin remembered what Molly had said. 'I can't do that.'

'You can't be serious. Go on then, astonish me, tell me why.'

'Because I don't believe it's true.'

'You mean you don't believe it's fake. Why?'

'I can't say.'

'You can't do all sorts of things, it seems to me. Well, you won't be making films for us until you can.' He stood up, the trace of a pout on his round face. 'I don't want to see you here again until you're ready to broadcast that retraction.'

On the way out Martin almost got past Ben Eccles. 'Leaving us?' he said.

Martin was taken aback by how sudden and savage his anger was. 'Looks that way,' he said, breathing hard and slow.

'Best news I've had all year. Here's some to take with you to our mutual girl friend.' Martin turned and headed for the lifts, but Eccles was there first, covering the call button with one hand. 'You tell her from me that she may have got to Tessa while I was out of the way, but she reckoned without me. We won't be putting out anything about her friend and her old people's centre. Even if it were worth broadcasting, I wouldn't touch anything that came from Molly Wolfe or from you either.' He took his hand away, leaving a sweaty handprint around the button, and Martin managed not to punch him in the face as he leaned close. 'If either of you manages to fool anyone in the future,' he hissed, 'it won't be me.'

'Quick, Geoffrey,' Joyce murmured through the bathroom door, 'come and see.'

'Coming.' He struggled into his dressing gown as he unbolted the bathroom door. He wondered why he had taken to bolting it – the old lady never got out of bed unassisted. He went downstairs supporting himself to find Joyce.

He heard her voice, louder than the television interviewer's, as he reached the hall. As he opened the door she switched off the television and turned to him, her face shining. 'Oh, Geoffrey, you missed it. They let me say everything I wanted to. Millions of people must have heard me.'

'That's wonderful. I'm sorry I wasn't here to see.'

'You've heard it all before. Haven't you enough of me to put up with without watching it on the box?' She took his hands and looked so pleased he thought she was going to dance. 'And all because I knew Molly Wolfe. Some good comes out of everything, Geoffrey. You don't mind if I leave you to it now, do you? I must go and see those hamburger people at once.'

'You go and give them what for.'

He felt brighter as he climbed the stairs, though the overcast above the hill was blackening. He couldn't be bothered clearing the steamy mirror to shave: his chin felt almost smooth, and besides, it wasn't as though anyone was visiting today. He dressed in the bedroom and opened the curtains, he gazed at Hampstead Heath, which looked like spilled milk in which a few houses were swimming, and then he went into the old lady's room.

She was sitting up in bed, her delicate hands at the ends

of her balloonish arms interlaced on the shapeless quilted mound of her. 'What was Joyce so pleased about?' she piped. 'She said you'd tell me.'

'She was on television, talking about the day centre. She says they let her say everything she wanted to,' he said smiling. 'It'd take more than a reporter to interrupt Joyce.'

'I expect he might just as well not have been there.'

'Exactly.' He picked up her tray and tried not to look too closely at the contents of the plates: porridge that looked regurgitated, bread and butter marked with toothless crescents, a glass of milk down which porridge was dribbling. He scraped the plates into the kitchen bin and washed them, then he went back to her. 'So it looks as if you'll have a centre soon,' he said.

'You'll be pleased.' Either she was winking at him or her left eyelid was drooping; she had to make a visible effort to raise it again. 'You'll soon be rid of me.'

'I wouldn't say that.'

'Of course not, you're a gentleman.' The other eye was closing, a slow ponderous blink as if the fat of her hairless eyebrow were forcing the eyelid down. 'Stay and talk to me until I go to sleep if you can,' she said.

'Certainly I can.' He brought his chair from the office. 'What shall I talk about?'

'Tell me how Joyce got on the telly.'

'Through a friend of hers. I don't know her. A girl called Molly Wolfe.'

'The girl who was in the paper.'

'That's right,' he said, surprised. 'Joyce knew her years ago.'

'I like reunions. It's nice to meet old friends. Here's to more of them.'

'Reunions or old friends?'

'Reunions for Joyce. And for me too,' she piped.

He felt a twinge of hope. 'You've lost touch with your friends?'

'Only for now. You see,' she said as if she were telling him something he already knew, 'they're starting to come back.'

It made him uneasy, the way conversations with her would slip awry like this, without warning. She was smiling at him as if nothing had happened, and for a moment he felt as though he was the one who was deluded – as though she was telling the truth and laughing at him behind her bland smile because she knew he would never believe her. That was dangerous nonsense. He oughtn't to be trusted to look after her if he were going to start imagining that sort of thing. He was tired, that was all, more and more so and no wonder, what with looking after her as well as trying to do his job. 'Who do you mean?' he said, hoping he had been unfair.

'The same ones as Joyce.'

Perhaps all her friends were dead and so she needed to imagine Joyce's friends were hers. But no, of course: 'You mean the other people Joyce was looking after.'

She gave him a girlish smile that looked almost mis-chievous, and sank back, crushing the pillows. 'Who else could I mean?' She settled into her nest of pillows, her eyes closing. 'Have you lost any friends?' she piped.

'A few, in the war.' Surely she hadn't meant to imply that he didn't know what losing friends was like. 'Not so many yet,' he said, almost apologetically.

'You've still got Joyce.'

'That I have. When it comes right down to it, she's the only friend I need.'

The sky was turning black. 'Don't put the light on,' she said when he stood up, and he sat down again. 'Are you still in love with her?'

'Why, yes, of course,' he said. 'Most certainly.'

'I expect she's in all your best memories.'

'I expect so too,' Geoffrey said, feeling lulled by the growing dark.

'Have you a favourite?'

'Oh, yes, I think so.'

'Will you tell it to me?'

'If you like.' He knew at once what their best time had been, and he'd just opened his mouth when he came to himself. Good God, he had been thinking of the early years of his marriage, when Joyce and he had conquered their shyness and inexperience in bed. He'd never felt so positively young as then, so agile and so passionately in love with Joyce. Surely he hadn't been going to tell that to the old lady. 'I suppose it was when we went walking in Wales,' he said.

'I went there too. It was like another world, wasn't it? Do you remember?'

'I can see it now.' He closed his eyes to recall the physical ache of climbing and forcing himself to keep on to the next view, the breath harsh as mist in his throat, the weight of the knapsack, the patch of sweat beneath it that felt as if the flask were leaking. Here was a rocky ledge to flop on, the aches in his throat and chest and legs were already fading into the sudden peace and wholeness that the landscape gave him, the diamond clarity of villages, the tiny perfect chime of a church bell, the glowing fields and valleys sweeping like waves to their jagged stony crests. He was in another world where storms prowled the crags, pathless mountains loomed out of the clouds, peak after darkening icy peak until they merged with the sky. He couldn't express what all this said to him, seemed to promise him. It didn't matter, she had been there too, she must know how it felt to realize you could never go back, you were no longer young. His body wasn't up to it now, neither climbing mountains nor climbing Joyce, and he couldn't help shuddering as he thought of their infrequent coupling, creaking bones and dry flesh scraping together, insects mating. Better to remember being young, and that took him back to the mountain, except that now the young woman with him

228

in the sparkling sunlit field above the crags wasn't Joyce but someone else, someone he should know. He was so stunned by her beauty that he hardly realized he was getting up from his chair and going to the bed, hardly dared admit to himself what he hoped. But it was true: there in the bed she was young and slim and impossibly beautiful, and he was almost at the bed and ready to take her in his arms before he wondered what had become of the rest of her, before his feet slipped on the pats of flesh that littered the floor around the bed. The floor was so thick with them he couldn't keep his balance and was falling into her outstretched arms. Somehow he managed to fall back into his chair and woke.

The old lady was asleep, her face towards him. He clapped his hands over his mouth to keep in his cry of waking. He didn't know how much he had said to her, didn't know when he had stopped talking and begun dreaming, if indeed the one had put an end to the other.

He stood up as soon as he felt able to, and tiptoed to make sure she was asleep. He couldn't help glancing down to make sure the floor was clear. Her puffy eyelids flickered, the only movement in the inflated porous face, and suddenly he had the notion that she was dreaming what he'd dreamed, that her dream hadn't ended where his had. He wanted to step back, but he was stooping closer, for what he really wanted was to climb into bed with her just as she was, while the room was bright with a gap in the overcast. As he realized what he was thinking, he recoiled so violently that his head and his joints ached. All at once he was convinced that though her eyes were closed she had been watching him.

He crept out with his chair in his arms, and couldn't breathe until he reached the landing. He sat in his office and sorted stamps, and tried not to think about himself. Perhaps he hadn't been fully awake, perhaps his feelings had been as much of a delusion as the rest of it, but nevertheless they had been his. He stayed in his office while the day darkened and lit windows stamped the houses on Muswell Hill; he didn't even go out when he heard Joyce closing the front door. 'In here,' he murmured when she called his name, though he wasn't certain that he wanted her to hear.

She came in beaming. 'The hamburger people let me have it, Geoffrey. I knew the television would do the trick. I must phone Molly to thank her.' Her eyes clouded momentarily. 'Or perhaps she would rather I didn't. She'll know how grateful I am. I'll have to clean it and paint it before we can use it but, oh, Geoffrey, we've got somewhere at last,' she said, and he had to smile in response. It wasn't just because the old lady would soon have somewhere to go, thank God, that he was beginning to feel better; it was more that he was simply grateful for Joyce. Maybe he was under stress, maybe exhaustion had almost let loose feelings he would have to control or preferably deny altogether, but he couldn't believe there was any actual danger when he had Joyce to remind him what was real. He hugged her as if they were just married and didn't mind the breathing from the guest room. 'Thank you whoever you are,' he whispered into her hair, 'Molly Wolfe.'

28

The night before New Year's Eve, Susan couldn't sleep. At first she thought the patterns of light would help, opening over and over again in front of her eyes like a hypnotist's hands, but they only interrupted the dark. She hid under the blankets where the dark was warmer and usually sleepier, but then sounds began to poke her ears like blades of grass, distant music that seemed not to have stopped since Christmas Eve. She thought how many Eves there were, Christmas and New Year's and the other one she hadn't seen for more than a week, not since Susan had given her back her fairy tales. Susan made herself a promise that, in the dark, seemed meaningful and convincing: after tomorrow there would be no more Eves. The promise and her own breath had begun to lull her to sleep, and so when she struggled awake she first felt resentment, not fear. Someone was speaking near her in the dark.

It was Mummy in the main room. She must be talking in her sleep, unless she was awake and talking to herself. It made Susan feel lonely and afraid, because it meant that Mummy was still strange. She strained her ears to hear what Mummy was saying, then reluctantly she climbed out of bed. She was sure she had heard her own name.

When she edged open her bedroom door and crept out, Mummy's voice was louder but no clearer. She kept falling silent as if she were waiting for an answer.

Susan had just reached the streamers and their cracks of dimness when Mummy said quite loudly, 'She'll have to, won't she.' The shock made Susan feel she was falling dizzily; she put out a hand to support herself. The streamers rattled, and Mummy cried, 'Who's there?'

'It's me, Mummy.' All Susan's fears made her add, 'Who did you think it was?'

'How the hell am I supposed to know, with you creeping around in the dark like that? What's wrong with you?'

Susan could just see the room now, a dimness tinged green, and Mummy was alone. She had been talking to herself. Susan searched desperately for a reason to be up, and could only think of something she'd imagined years ago. 'I thought someone was looking out of my mirror.'

'Go back to your room and don't you dare come out until morning. I'm sick of your imagination. I'm sick of you.'

At least she believed that was what had been wrong, but Susan wished she'd thought of something else. She lay in bed and thought of someone watching her out of the mirror, someone who could see in the dark. She remembered the time she had stared at her own face for so long it had ceased to be hers. She hadn't heard Mummy when she fell victim to the worst dream she'd ever had, of being so terrified to look in mirrors that she had to blind herself rather than see. Her eyes wouldn't come out, no matter how hard she dragged at the skin beneath them; they just ached, worse and worse. She woke in the dark, lay dreading sleep, and woke again in the dark, she wasn't sure how many times before she noticed the thread of light under the door.

She took her time in the bathroom. When at last she went into the kitchen, Mummy gave her her morning milk without a word. It wasn't until they were sitting down to breakfast that she said, 'Susan, don't you like your room?'

'How do you mean, Mummy?'

'I mean exactly what I say. I want to know what all that fuss was about last night. Is it too dark in your room, is that what you don't like?'

'It is dark without any windows,' Susan admitted, wondering if Mummy didn't even remember talking to herself.

'All right then, now we're getting somewhere. Do you want to change rooms?'

'Oh, I don't know.' The idea of Mummy in the total darkness made her uneasy without knowing why.

'I should think you'd be glad to. I can't see what alternative there is. Sometimes, Susan, I don't understand you at all. I'm sure you think I'm always nagging you but it's only because I worry about you. I just don't want you turning out like I nearly did.' Mummy stared at her and shook her head. Eventually she said, 'Well, what are you going to do today?'

'You said we could go to the Tower of London one day when you weren't working.'

'So I did.' Mummy's tired eyes flickered. 'Sorry, it'll have to be another day. Why don't you go and join the library? See if you can find a few sensible books for a change.'

232

'Can I go and look at the theatres and see what the pantomimes are?'

'Yes, all right, I said we'd go to one. You see which one you'd like.' An hour later, as Susan kissed her good-bye, Mummy said, 'Nothing too scaring.'

Susan walked to Oxford Circus and into Regent Street. She would have gone the quicker way if Mummy hadn't told her to stay out of Soho. The pavement in Carnaby Street was multicoloured as the boutiques, a winged stone boy with a bow and arrow hopped in the middle of Piccadilly Circus. Feeling venturesome and grown-up and very like a Londoner, Susan turned along Shaftesbury Avenue.

When she came back along St Martin's Lane, past photographs the size of doorways, she hadn't found many pantomimes. She'd crossed a busy road to look at Puss in Boots only to find it wasn't Puss but Pussy, showing at a cinema from which a man in pointed scaly shoes had chased her away. The best she could find was Dick Whittington, by which time she'd known to make sure what kind of Dick, and the ticket prices made her gasp. Mummy was hard up; Susan had seen her biting her lip over her accounts in her exercise book. Perhaps they should do without a pantomime this year. She headed back toward Marble Arch and her real reason for going out, which had been in the wings of her mind all the time.

The lobby of MTV was crowded with men in new clothes that looked forty years old. All the men had their hair cut short, back and sides. Susan went to the circular desk. 'Not here today,' the man in the braided uniform said gruffly. 'Can't tell you where to find her, sorry.' Susan knew where Molly lived, but the trouble was that she had exhausted her resolve: she'd come prepared to start talking at once about Mummy and Eve, and now that she would have to get ready all over again she wasn't sure she could.

She picked her way along Bayswater Road, watched for

233

patches that looked like frozen slush but were the crusts of puddles. She must go to Molly. Molly had said they could talk again soon. Even if talking about Mummy made her feel disloyal, she was sure that was nothing compared to what Eve was doing to Mummy. But it had begun to hail, small hard stones that stung her cheeks and the backs of her bare knees until she trod straight into a crusty puddle. She turned before she reached Molly's hill and ran home. Molly mightn't be at her flat, and Susan would be left without shelter. Perhaps she could find an excuse to sneak away after lunch.

Her drowned foot squelched as she hurried upstairs, but she faltered on her landing: was Mummy talking to herself? She stood as long as she could bear the smell of cats and the chill of her soggy shoe, long after the hail had stopped rattling the windows, but she heard nothing further. When she knocked, Mummy came to the door at once.

'Good heavens, Susan, have you been paddling? Change your shoes and socks before you catch your death.' Her concern seemed oddly mechanical, as if it were a disguise. 'Go on, get those wet things off,' she cried, but her impatience was more like nervous eagerness. 'And then I've got a surprise for you.'

There it almost was. 'What is it?' Susan demanded.

'Get changed and then you'll see. Put your slippers on, you won't be going out again.' She pushed Susan into a chair and untied the soaked laces herself. She was too eager, her eagerness seemed to be a disguise too. Susan was so intent on her face, so anxious to make out what had happened to Mummy now, that she didn't glance up when the streamers rattled, didn't look until Eve had stepped into the room.

For a moment Susan thought she couldn't speak. 'What's she doing here?'

'That was your surprise. Eve is coming to stay with us for a while.'

Eve smiled at her and then at Susan. 'I've brought your slippers.'

Susan snatched them and couldn't look at her. Speaking again was even more of a struggle. 'There's nowhere for her to sleep.'

'Of course there is. You can both sleep out here and I'll have your room, since you don't like it anyway. There isn't space in there for both of you. You can have the sofa and Eve will put the chairs together. She says she doesn't mind.' She stood up to end the discussion. 'Ready for lunch? Lots of turkey to finish. More than enough for two big girls.'

'I'll carry the plates, m——' Eve looked shyly at her scuffed shoes with their frayed laces. 'Can I call you mummy?' she said, just loud enough to be heard.

'Of course you can, love.' Mummy was blinking as she patted Eve's bruised cheek gently as a feather. 'I'd like you to.'

'I'll help you then, Mummy.' Eve jumped up and skipped toward the kitchen with Mummy. Eve carried in the plates and smiled at her, a smile that looked innocently grateful, and Susan felt in danger of shaking until she couldn't stop. Eve went through the streamers, Mummy appeared with the turkey while they were still swaying, and Susan ran to her. 'Don't let her stay, Mummy,' she whispered.

'Susan, why are you speaking to me in that silly voice? Eve has nowhere else to go, do you understand? Her mother was hurting her and leaving her alone all night, and now she's gone to live with someone Eve's afraid of. The social workers wouldn't do anything for Eve before, and all they'd do now would be put her in a children's home. Would you like that to happen to you?'

'But I don't want her to stay,' Susan pleaded, and couldn't raise her voice. 'I don't like her.'

'I'll tell you something, miss. I'm no longer interested in what you like or don't like. You're a selfish and hysterical brat, and if you don't watch out I'll have you seen to.'

235

'But she can't stay.' Susan had remembered Mummy's frown over her accounts. 'We can't afford it, Mummy.'

Mummy looked so savage as she raised her hand that Susan almost lost her balance. 'You'd better flinch, young lady. You'll do more than flinch if you ever say anything like that to me again. Who do you think you are?' As she grabbed Susan's shoulder and dragged her towards her, her hiss of a voice was lower than Susan's had been. 'Do you know who you remind me of? Your father. He behaved exactly like this when he knew I was going to have you. Much more of this and I'll feel towards you just as I feel towards him.'

She let go of Susan's bruised shoulder as the streamers clattered. 'I couldn't find the carving knife,' Eve said.

'Come in, Eve, don't be timid. We were just sorting out a disagreement. It's sorted out now, isn't it? Sorted out for good,' she said, glaring at Susan. 'Thanks, Eve. I'm glad there's someone here I can rely on. I'll get the knife.'

Eve waited until they heard the kitchen streamers, and even then she didn't speak at once. 'She wants me to stay,' she said. There was nothing menacing in her tone or in her smile; Susan might almost have thought she was simply delighted to have a new home, if it hadn't been for Eve's eyes. She was looking at Susan exactly as she had when she had crushed the beetle in her fist.

Danny looked at himself in the bathroom mirror, at his new suit and his shaved face speckled with blood, and couldn't remember ever having felt so pleased with himself. For the first time in his life he was taking a woman out, and there was no way she could get the better of him. Maybe she thought she'd tricked him into asking her, maybe she even believed he would pay her for giving him the confidence, but he'd known all along that she was trying to regain her influence over him on Molly Wolfe's behalf. He dabbed at the specks of drying blood and splashed his face with a handful of his father's aftershave. The pain made him feel clean and strong and dauntless. He was heading for the front door at a quarter to eight, with plenty of time to stroll to Thane Villas before Dr Kent got there, when his mother came out of the parlour. 'Come in here a minute, Danny,' she said.

His father was polishing a cannon the size of his hand and didn't look at him. A tropical fish gave a nervous flick as his mother picked up a magazine from her chair, and for an awful moment Danny thought it was one of his magazines. Of course they were safe in the projection box. The woman on the cover was laughing, not crying. 'Sit down then,' his mother said. 'You're making me nervous.'

He sat as far from the gas fire as he could. He was already sweating inside his heavy overcoat they'd bought him in the market by the Hercules. His mother was staring at his father as if that would make him look up and speak. Eventually she said, 'I don't often ask you favours, Danny, do I?'

'No,' he said, wondering if his father had been saying that she did.

'But I'm asking you one now. Don't go out tonight, Danny. Stay in with us and have a drink here. See the New Year in with us like you always do. It won't be the same without you.'

'I've got to go.' He was shifting inside his overcoat as if he could shrug off the heat. 'I've promised.'

'That kind of promise doesn't count. I'm sure you didn't actually say you promised.' She was leaning forward, too far away to grasp his hands. 'You wouldn't have said that when you knew we'd be expecting you to stay with us.'

'Well, I did.' The plea in her eyes was making him hotter. 'I've got to go, I've got to now.'

'You haven't got to. You mustn't, Danny. You don't know what it will be like.' Her posture looked agonizing, she was leaning forward so far. 'The streets will be full of drunks and rough behaviour, and you'll probably be drunk yourself. Anything might happen.'

'Oh, let him be.' His father looked up at last, and shook the cannon at her. 'It's the first normal thing he's done since I don't know when. You can't keep him cooped up forever, we won't always be here to look after him. It's about time he started growing up.'

'That isn't growing up. Who are these girls anyway? What do they mean by taking you out and getting you drunk?'

'Just the girls from the Hercules.' Having to repeat the lie was robbing him of clarity and resolve; for a moment, as sweat stung his eyes, he couldn't remember their names. 'Mandy and Karen,' he said.

'Usherettes.' She made the word sound like spitting. 'Can't you do better than them? I'm ashamed of you, Danny.'

He struggled to his feet. She was making him feel towards her as he'd felt towards Dr Kent in her office. 'I've got to go,' he mumbled.

'If you do, I'll know you think more of those girls than you do of your own mother.'

He thought he would never reach the door. Her words had settled on him, heavier and more oppressive than the heat and his overcoat. 'I'm telling you, Danny,' she cried, but he wrenched the door open and stumbled along the hall, onto the chill balcony, out into the glittering night.

He mustn't resent her. She only wanted the best for him. But her anxiety had fastened on him and it was trying to drag him back to her as he hurried down the echoing concrete steps. He almost ran back to tell her the truth, tell her he was going out with Dr Kent and why, except that he'd learned a long time ago not to admit to his parents anything that he was seeing, he'd learned from the way they had looked at him. He ran toward Seven Sisters Road, telling himself that he hadn't heard eight o'clock strike, and then he skidded to a halt, his breath scraping his throat. Dr Kent was waiting for him at the end of the path.

He couldn't move for rage. His mother had let Dr Kent see where he lived. He wanted to run home, whether to scream at his mother or hide from Dr Kent he didn't know. 'I didn't think it was you at first,' Dr Kent said. 'I thought you lived somewhere else.'

She was laughing at him. Her long face looked as sober as her ankle-length black coat and black trousers, but he knew when he was being jeered at. 'So this is where you live,' she said. 'No need to be ashamed of it, Danny. It isn't as though you have the best job in the world. You work at the Hercules just up the road, am I right?'

He nodded and even smiled. He would have to finish with her all the sooner now that she knew where he lived and worked. Perhaps she always had, perhaps she had only pretended that her and Molly Wolfe's spies hadn't told her, to lull him into feeling safe. Now she was keeping him talking here so that his parents would see. 'Come on then,' he muttered.

'By all means. Oh, you're looking for my car. I'm sorry, it's off the road. It'll have to be public transport, I'm afraid.'

'Where do you want to go?'

'Why, the West End on New Year's Eve, and Trafalgar Square at midnight. Where else?'

'Better take a taxi, then. It's a long way on the train.'

'Entirely up to you, Danny. You'll be paying. I haven't brought a sou. You invited me out, remember.'

She'd set another trap for him. No doubt she would be doing that all evening. Let her, it would make him hate her

239

more, help him do what he had to do. 'We'll go on the train,' he said with a grin that gritted his teeth.

Two young Scotsmen were doing their best to feed drinks to all the faces on the posters in the Underground; beer foam dribbled from a girl's mouth as long as Danny's arm. Singing echoed in the tiled corridors as the train pulled in, a conga line came kicking onto the platform and through the automatic doors as they tried to close, again and again. Dr Kent seemed shy of all this, as if she were waiting for Danny to reassure her. Of course it must be another trick, and he was glad there was too much noise on the swaying train to make speaking worthwhile.

She took his hand at Oxford Circus, kept hold of it until they caught the train to Charing Cross, and all the time he was afraid she would be able to read his feelings by the way he held her hand. He thought of squeezing it until the bones splintered. On emerging at last into the open in sight of Trafalgar Square, he stuffed his hands into his pockets.

Crowds roamed chanting past the hotels on the Strand and under the plane trees of the Mall. They seemed almost capable of waking up the aloof buildings of Whitehall, of roping in the tenants of Downing Street. Cars flashed their lights and honked their horns at anything in sight, police-men chased a band of revellers out of the bandstand in St James's Park. Danny felt poised on the edge of a flood. All he could think of to shout was, 'What do you want to do?'

'I'll make that decision since I suppose this is new to you, but that's the last one I'll make for you, Danny, under-stand?' She pointed to a noisy pub in a side street. 'That looks as good as any.'

The pub was even hotter and more crowded than the train had been. Danny unbuttoned his coat and waited for Dr Kent to go first until he realized she expected him to force their way through the crowd. If there were any tables and chairs, he couldn't see where. He managed to locate the bar by the truncheons of the beer pumps, and was still struggling toward it five minutes later when he thought to ask, 'Do you want anything to drink?'

'I believe that's the done thing in these establishments. Did you have something else in mind?' His hatred must have touched his eyes, for she said, 'Danny, you really must learn to laugh at yourself. I'll have a large gin and tonic.'

He struggled furiously to the bar, ready to claw at anyone who wouldn't let him pass. Laugh at himself! That was exactly what she and her crony wanted, to destroy his faith in himself. They hadn't succeeded in Oxford, and they wouldn't succeed now. He caught the barman's attention at last, though not before spilled beer had soaked through the elbow of his coat, and turned with her drink and his pint of beer. She was nowhere to be seen.

His fist was tightening on her glass when he saw her waving at him from a distant corner, where she had managed to find space for two on a bench. He wormed his way over, his arms held high, his shirt glued to his armpits. She gave his suit a wry nod as he laid his coat on his lap. She sipped her drink and at last she said, 'Well, are we going to sit here and stare at each other all night or are you going to tell me about yourself?'

She had taken off her coat but was still dressed in black, a jacket and a low-cut blouse. He looked away from her large breasts, which made him feel suffocated, and tried to outstare her. 'Why not you?' he shouted.

'You know all you need to know about me.'

That was truer than she knew. He gulped his beer so that he wouldn't be tempted to say so. The heat must be making him thirsty, for all at once he was holding an empty glass. 'If you're having another I will too,' Dr Kent said.

When he reached the bar he couldn't see her now that she was sitting down. Faces moved like chunks of a glacier, like the hovering smoke of all the cigars and cigarettes; no wonder the pub was growing darker. Was the barman leaving Danny until last to give Dr Kent time to search his coat? Let her, the letter about her was safe in his room. When at last he got back to the corner, she had folded his coat just as he'd left it, and both she and the people nearby were pretending she had never touched it, which proved they were in it with her. She finished her drink and raised her full glass until he lifted his. 'Here's to the New Year,' she said, 'and now back to this one. Same question, Danny.'

He'd thought of an answer. 'I told you everything once.'

'You did indeed. More than I think you realized.' She was leaning so close to him that he could feel her breath on his cheek. 'But that was eleven years ago. You must have changed since then.'

Of course he had. She'd changed him, she had almost destroyed him, but he wasn't about to give her the satisfaction of knowing. 'No must about it,' he said.

'I'm sorry, Danny, I don't believe it. Or if I do, it makes me very sad. Don't you want anything more for yourself?' She was so close now he thought he could feel her lips moving. 'Or is it that you don't know what it is? Knowing what you want is the first step to getting it, Danny.'

He knew that wasn't true, but he couldn't think why; he could only tell himself she didn't believe it either. 'Try and tell me,' she whispered. 'I may be able to help. Try and think what your hopes are for yourself, your dreams.'

He jerked away from her so violently that he almost upset the tankard the man next to him was holding. 'Sorry,' he muttered at the man, who was staring blearily at him as if he were trying to remember how to look aggressive. 'Sorry,' Danny shouted, and turned on Dr Kent. 'I never have dreams.'

'I didn't mean that kind. Sorry to stir up unpleasant memories, if that's what they are. By dreams I meant whatever you most want for yourself.'

'I don't have either kind.'

'Everyone does, Danny. Some people are afraid to admit it, that's all, so afraid that maybe they don't even realize they have them. But you never used to be, Danny. I do hope that business all that time ago hasn't made you that way.' She actually looked hopeful, almost pleading. 'I would feel responsible,' she said.

He couldn't speak. Now he saw how deftly she had tricked him: she'd manoeuvred him into asking her out when she knew he couldn't chat to her in the way you were supposed to talk to girls you took out, the way men did in films. She must have thought he would have to answer her questions; she couldn't have anticipated that he would simply refuse to speak. He drained his pint glass to block his mouth. 'Wananother?' he said, and hardly recognized his voice.

'Thanks. You're learning,' she said with a wide smile that made him wonder all the way to the bar what lurked beneath her words. The pub was growing hotter yet, everyone seemed to be swaying. Everything was shifting. Her mention of dreams must have done that, undermined his hold on his surroundings. He'd have it out with her, he'd shout so everyone could hear; surely there must be someone in the crowd who wasn't under her control. He gulped his beer as he struggled back, another mouthful as he sat down, for his throat felt clogged with the heat. She must have got ready for him, because at once she said, 'If you won't talk about your hopes, perhaps you'll talk about the other kind of dream. What do you remember from Oxford?'

He remembered how it felt: like this, like someone trying to poke around inside his head. When they'd attached the pads with their wires and left him alone, he'd felt as if an insect with wiry feelers had hold of his brain. 'Nothing,' he said.

'Are you absolutely sure?'

'Yes.' The heat and smoke made it sound more like a cough. 'Yes,' he shouted.

'Forgive me, Danny, but I don't think you're telling me

the whole truth. I know this must be difficult for you, but now the subject has come up I hope you'll be frank with me. We need to understand what happened. It may be important for both of us.'

Her gentleness made him even more suspicious. He gulped more beer, though his stomach felt heavy and uncomfortable. 'Did you foresee too much, is that what went wrong?' Dr Kent was almost pleading. 'Whatever you saw, surely it must have happened by now. It isn't as though talking about it can make it happen.'

She must be lying. Perhaps even thinking about it could. He was raising his glass, but not to drink. He could feel how it would smash against the table, how her mouth would twitch and jerk as he stuffed the broken glass down her throat to shut her up for good. If they had been alone there was no doubt that was what he would have done. He wasn't sure he wouldn't do it anyway as she took hold of his arm. 'Danny, look at me,' she said.

He managed to turn his head at last and meet her gaze, and felt that everyone was watching him. 'I asked you at the time but I'm asking you again,' she said. 'Did all of you dream the same thing?'

He couldn't remember what he'd dreamed. He'd spent eleven years not remembering, not saying a word to anyone about that day. He felt himself grin as he said, 'I don't know.'

'You didn't discuss it afterwards. That in itself shows how disturbing it must have been. You really don't remember, do you?' She looked frustrated and guilty, or would have to anyone less gullible than he was. 'There's one thing you must remember,' she said.

He was already remembering too much, remembering how it had felt as if something were both trying to creep into his brain and emerge from it. That was how he felt now. He reached blindly for his glass, but hadn't found it when she said, 'What did you mean by what you said the last time you came out of your room?'

He gripped the glass and didn't care how many people saw. They were all on her side anyway. But he rammed it into his own face instead of hers, though it still felt as if it might break. 'You said she made it happen,' Dr Kent was insisting. 'You know who I mean. What was her name, now? Yes, Molly Wolfe.'

He bared his teeth at her. There was no point in pretending now. 'Don't you know what I meant?'

'No, I don't.' She looked so puzzled that he almost thought she was. 'I really don't. If I did I wouldn't be asking.'

He drank more beer as if that might frustrate her. It seemed not to be working for him: the sense of something in his brain was growing, he felt that everyone in the crowd that was flooding upward was waiting for him to speak. Suddenly he thumped his glass on the table and was shouting. 'She started everything changing, that's what she wanted to happen. It would have too if it hadn't been for me. I've been stopping it ever since. That's why you want to get rid of me.'

'Who does, Danny? Nobody does. I give you my word.'

He was groping to unbutton his overcoat – he was so hot and sticky – until he remembered he had already taken it off. The crowd was pressing close around him, hundreds of people, and he no longer had control of himself when she said, 'If that's what you think about yourself and Molly Wolfe, what about the others who were there?'

She was trying to confuse him, trying to make him feel the way he'd felt eleven years ago, so that he wouldn't be able to stop things from changing. The others wouldn't know what Molly Wolfe was up to, he was the only one who was standing up to her and holding off the change. The insight came too late to prevent him from smashing the glass against the edge of the table.

Only the base was left in his hand. It never happened that way in films. Dr Kent was staring at him as if she were frightened and wouldn't let it show, people were shouting at him and picking splinters out of their clothes while he gazed stupidly at the jagged disc in his hand, and then the crowd that had pretended to be jammed shoulder to shoulder was parting to let the barman at him. 'That'll be all,' the barman said. 'Fun's one thing, that's another. On your way and think yourself lucky I'm not prosecuting.'

He was in it too, of course. Danny grabbed his overcoat and bundled up its flailing arms, then he staggered along the aisle that Dr Kent's crowd were happy to make for him now they'd confused him and got rid of him. When he reached the doors, he found she hadn't followed. The barman blocked his way and waited until Danny stumbled out of the pub.

She would have to come out when the pub closed. He almost tore his overcoat before he could get it on, then he folded his arms about his throbbing, queasy stomach and waited while crowds began to converge on Trafalgar Square. Each time the pub doors opened, his fingers sank into his upper arms. They and his bladder were aching when the emerging crowd forced the doors wider, when the last stragglers swayed out, when the pub went dark.

Either the barman had let her out another way or she had been able to sneak past him. Nevertheless he thought she was somewhere in the crowd that was piling into Trafalgar Square; why, she'd said there was nowhere else to be. He relieved himself in a dark alley, he pressed his forehead against the wall then shoved himself away, because the wall gave like a mattress. The dark must be on her side. He staggered back into the light and the crowd as soon as he could.

Perhaps the dark had weakened his hold, for nothing would keep still. The crowds hustled him toward Trafalgar Square. Now and then he had to struggle free, panting and swallowing, but at least they were giving him the concealment he needed. He was sure he would find her, never mind how impossible it seemed in the enormous festive crowd.

He could see Nelson on his column now, like a student who had dared to climb a chimney. Revellers were dancing in the fountain; there wasn't room to move in the square or even to struggle round the perimeter. Suddenly, unfairly, the clocks began to strike midnight, the crowd was singing *Auld Lang Syne* until the buildings seemed to shake, thousands of people were embracing and kissing, fireworks exploded in the sky. Someone was firing guns behind him in the Haymarket. No, it was the popping of champagne corks, and all around him beer cans were spitting. Another firework bloomed in the sky, and couples parted in the Haymarket to look up. For a few seconds the upturned faces were brighter than day. Before they went out Danny felt as if his head were on fire. Not a hundred yards away a tall slim man with rumpled hair had lifted his face from a woman's upturned face, and she was Molly Wolfe.

She was turning away from Trafalgar Square before Danny was able to move. He had been right to feel that the tables were turned, to follow his instincts; he'd only been wrong to think it was Dr Kent he was hunting. The crowd between him and Molly Wolfe was still facing the square. He couldn't shout 'Excuse me' too loudly in case she heard, but more than one knot of revellers turned ugly when he tried to struggle through. He lost sight of her before he reached the Haymarket, but when at last he fought his way round the corner there she was, five hundred yards away and unmistakable. This time he wouldn't lose her.

He almost did at Piccadilly Circus, among the famished chalky addicts with their bruised arms. Her tall thin friend kept waving at taxis, all of which were taken. They wouldn't get a cab tonight; her friend's waving only helped Danny to see where they were. Crowds danced in Regent Street and Oxford Street among fallen Christmas decorations and trampled hot dogs, buildings full of faces seemed to be collapsing like waves toward Danny; people dressed like Dr Kent or with faces that resembled hers kept getting in his way. Some of them didn't even look like women. None of this could distract him, not when he'd been dealing with it for eleven years. Nothing could make him look away from Molly Wolfe.

He followed them along Bayswater Road, past an estate agent's, up a hill. When she disappeared beyond a gate, he turned up his collar and scrambled up the icy hill before she could close her door. As he reached the railings she was stooping to a niche under the steps and slipping out a key. Danny saw her and her friend vanish into the basement flat. His penis was aching, he needed an alley or somewhere else dark, but his grin didn't falter even when he turned to go downhill and almost fell. He not only knew at last where she lived, he even knew how to get in.

Martin was asleep first. Molly lay awake for a while in his arms. She breathed his warmth and stroked his chest and listened to the sounds of the New Year. She no longer felt as edgy as she had in Trafalgar Square and all the way home. She was resigned to feeling that way until she resolved what she had to resolve. She had to trust the dream.

A police car blared along Bayswater Road, greeted by a variety of shouts, and she wondered if Rankin were driving. She knew his name and his face, she knew he'd helped kill Lenny Bennett, she almost knew how he would betray himself. She'd dreamed of him before she'd met him in what most people would call reality, and that proved the dream – proved that Maitland had been telling the truth in the dream when he had implicated Rankin. Perhaps people always told the truth in dreams, in Molly's, at any rate. Rankin didn't like her audience to be told lies about him any more than he did, Maitland had said, but it had taken her a while to realize that meant Rankin had been involved in Bennett's death.

She was sure of it, but what could she do? It wasn't as if she had any proof. The dream had made her feel even more frustrated than Joyce's visit had: she hadn't turned her back on dreaming as Joyce had, but she might as well have done so for all the use her dreams were. She hadn't been able to think of much else until Martin had come home and then, that very night, she'd had the next dream.

Perhaps he had made her feel safe enough to do so. She'd found herself in a playground outside the sketch of a school, a long red anonymous Victorian building under a shaky sky. Boys had surrounded the skinhead policeman, red-kneed in a school uniform that was absurdly small for him. He'd shaken his fists at them as they chanted 'Randy Rankin the wanker'; she hadn't invented his nickname after all.

If the police didn't know what he had been called at school, what use would it be to tell them? Did she really expect them to admit anything because of a dream? She needed proof, and the next night she'd realized she could get it. All she had to do was dream.

She was nearly there now. The sounds of New Year's Day were retreating. She was walking through a field and knew precisely how many blades it contained, and then she was looking out of that number of windows, somehow looking out of all of them at once. It was too momentary to bother her, for now she was in Rankin's flat, high in a tower block.

She had been here three times. Each time there had been more to see. She hardly glanced at the chest expanders hanging beside the fitted wardrobe, the reports on immigration beneath the glass-topped table with its stolen beermats, the wrestling magazines stacked on the long low cupboard that hid the rifle she had glimpsed in last night's dream, the shelf full of much-thumbed horror stories and war books. She headed for the mantelpiece, for the plate-lipped ivory figure of a native woman with large bare pointed breasts. This time Molly meant to see what was hanging round its neck.

'So that's what you were after,' Rankin said. She turned, for she had seen what she wanted to see: Lenny Bennett's identity bracelet rusty with blood. It was hanging round the figure's neck like the trophy it was. She had her proof, she could wake now, before triumphantly sneering Rankin reached her with his hands, claws ready to dig into her arms or her breasts. But she couldn't wake.

In that case, by God, she would take control. It was her dream. He must have realized, for all at once his face began working uncontrollably, he was sinking to his knees as if she had dumped an unbearable weight on him. Tears of pain or rage were pouring from his eyes. If she could do that, she could do more. 'You killed Lenny Bennett, didn't you?' she said, stepping forward to stand over him. 'You beat him to death.'

His mouth clamped shut, writhed open to let his teeth tear at his lower lip. Whatever she was doing to him, she intensified it almost without thinking. Blood sprayed from his lip as his teeth lost their hold, and she had to force herself not to look away. 'Yes, yes,' he said, almost screaming.

'You and who else?'

'Maitland. Maitland!' He was on all fours now but couldn't crawl. 'Stop, stop.'

'I will just as soon as you've told him what you've told me,' she said, and pointed behind him. But the door of the flat was shut, and nobody was there.

Someone would be. She was resolved on that now. All she needed was a photograph that showed the trophy. The lies of the police had lost Martin his series; it was only appropriate that she should have him reinstated and herself too by exposing the police. She might be able to get Joyce on the air; she would be able to keep an eye on Nell.

Filming Rankin's flat would be the solution to so much that she had to wake fully before she realized how difficult and dangerous it would be.

At breakfast Martin said, 'You look preoccupied.'

She almost told him why, except that she'd caused him enough trouble already. Whoever went with her to film, it oughtn't to be him. 'So much has been happening,' she said.

'Yeah, well, that was last year.'

'Something else happened that I didn't tell you. You know about Stuart Hay's letter and how I thought I saw Danny whatever his name is in Soho. Well, while you were away someone else I met that time in Oxford came to see me. Joyce Churchill. She's looking after old folk now.'

'She came to see you after all that time? That's strange.'

'Well, not so strange really. She read about me in the paper.'

'Strange or not, it bothers you.'

'I suppose it does, a little. All these coincidences at once, and I keep feeling there's someone else I haven't noticed. I did last night in Trafalgar Square. Of course there might have been for all we know.'

'You know what I think? I think that guy's letter has got you on edge.'

'You could be right, the way it came just like that for no reason after eleven years.'

'If you need me to find out what he wants, just say the word.'

'I don't think I want to go back to Oxford.'

'That's what I meant. I could go and question him for you.'

'You could, couldn't you?' It would keep him out of the way while she tried to trap Rankin, otherwise he might well go after Rankin himself to keep her out of danger. All the same, she felt uncomfortable lying to him, saying, 'I really need to stay in town and look for another job.'

'Maybe I can investigate your friend in Oxford.' His grin looked wistful. 'We'll see what I think of him. I'll go tomorrow.'

She disguised her misgivings by picking up the percolator. 'No need to go so soon.'

'The sooner the better. You're anxious enough.' The most he would compromise was to delay his visit until the following week. Molly went to the bathroom and turned on the shower, then she perched on the edge of the bath, to think. The mirror and the frosted glass began to turn grey as she realized how much she was attempting. She knew who she wanted to film the evidence, but persuading him might be another matter. On top of that was the problem of access. If she broke into the flat, the police would say she had planted the evidence. She would need to persuade Rankin to let her in, and that might be the least of her problems.

The journey to Liverpool took less than three hours, but to Susan it seemed they would never arrive. Every time the train slowed she was afraid Mummy would change her mind. She went to the buffet car for a drink and to get away from Mummy's indifferent stare, and struggled not to change her own mind: she couldn't plan how to save Mummy until it was safe for her to think. Passengers were saying some of the lines were flooded, and she spent the rest of the journey listening for the sound of water. She had never thought she could hate snow.

But here was the bridge at Runcorn, the Mersey sandbanks with their bad complexions, the Stanlow oil flares like matches on the horizon. The suburbs of Liverpool sped by, melting snow spilled down the overgrown walls of the cutting, and then Mummy was holding her arm as they climbed down at Lime Street Station, where pigeons murmured among the echoes beneath the glass and metal roof. The escalators were switched off for Sunday, there wasn't a New Brighton train for half an hour, but at last the train clattered out of its tunnel and Susan saw Wallasey climbing the hill to the church. When she caught sight of the waves on the bay, she felt at last she was home.

Mummy kept hold of her arm as they went down Victoria Road, along the promenade and up the forty steps to Laura's house. Laura's Mummy hugged Susan and said 'We'll take care of her' before Laura raced Susan to show her where she would be sleeping, in a bunk in Laura's room that overlooked the river. 'I can't thank you enough for taking her,' Mummy was saying along the hall. 'If she gets to be too much for you, just let me know. Or maybe it's only me she's taken a dislike to. One thing I won't put up with is a child telling me who I can look after.'

Susan wanted to run to her, to cling to her and not let go until she had convinced Mummy she was wrong. She had no chance; Mummy wouldn't hear a word said against Eve. 'Say good-bye to her for me. I'd rather not see her. I've just time to catch my train,' Mummy said, and Susan didn't want to run to her after all. She gazed out at the river and waited for Mummy to go, and wondered how the waves that were breaking above the promenade could freeze in the air like that, how they could take so long to fall back.

It didn't matter, they looked even prettier that way. They looked as if they were turning into flowers of ice. If she watched them she wouldn't even notice when Mummy went away. Something about that made her turn away, feeling she'd been tricked. She mustn't let Mummy go. She had to, she realized instinctively, otherwise she wouldn't be able to stay here herself. That wasn't important, she mustn't let herself be made to feel that it was, not when she had to save

Mummy. She heard the waves behind her, or something huge and soft and angry reaching for her, and woke.

She was lying tucked up in the blankets on the couch. At first she felt reassured that she had been able to wake, then she made out the folding bed beside her in the greenish dimness, close enough to touch. The vague pinkish oval was Eve's face. At once she was sure not only that Eve was watching her but that Eve had made her have the dream.

Eve wanted to get rid of her so that she could finish doing to Mummy whatever she had started before Susan had come to the London flat. The folding bed made it clear that Eve was staying. Susan was suddenly afraid for Mummy, afraid what Eve might have done to her while Susan was trapped in the dream.

The pinkish oval never moved as Susan crept between it and the couch. Perhaps because she couldn't see its eyes, she felt all the more that she was being watched. She picked her way around dim wavering shapes that were chairs and potted plants, and was almost at the hall before she realized that she couldn't pass through the streamers without making a noise. But there was no need. Beyond the open bedroom door she could hear Mummy's regular peaceful breathing.

At first she didn't know why she was straining her ears. She looked back at the folding bed, at Eve's vague face. She listened to the breathing in the lightless bedroom, and then she began to shiver. The more she listened, the more it sounded as if there were two sets of breathing in the bedroom, so regular as almost to merge. She was looking at Eve in the folding bed, yet she thought that somehow Eve was in the dark with Mummy too.

Susan shivered in the dimness and wondered how she would ever be able to move. She wanted to wake Mummy, except that she was afraid of the dark in there; she wanted to climb back under the warm blankets and hide there, but she was terrified of going near the face whose eyes she couldn't see. For a moment she felt she was still dreaming, that the face on the pillow was hers and not Eve's, her own dreaming face. That made her feel even more at the mercy of the dark. Nevertheless she was creeping back there, shuffling as if she couldn't stop her feet from moving. At last she slid under the blankets, holding her breath, vowing not to sleep. The next she knew, the curtains were open, sunlight had made the room bright green as summer, and Eve was smiling at her while she folded up her bed. 'You did have a long sleep. You were asleep before I was and now you're only just awake.'

Susan knew that she had to behave as if nothing were wrong. She was sure that Eve wanted her to believe that everything last night had been a dream. She managed to smile as if she did, and Eve called, 'She's awake, Mummy.'

'I thought smelling breakfast would do the trick.' Mummy brought Susan a mug of orange juice. 'Come on, slowcoach, or I'll never get anything done.' To Eve she said, 'We'll eat up all the breakfast, won't we, and leave none for sleepy-heads.'

Susan hurried to the bathroom, slipped her housecoat on, and reached the table just as Eve and Mummy brought in plates of bacon and fried bread. 'We'll have to get you a housecoat, Eve,' Mummy said, and Susan wondered how many more presents she meant to buy. She felt jealous and helpless and most of all childish, because that was what Mummy would call her if she tried to convince her that anything was wrong.

At least during breakfast she didn't need to talk. She kept filling her mouth to make sure she couldn't, even when Mummy said, 'Don't do that, Susan. Eve doesn't, does she?' Snow was melting on the roofs, but not as much as it had been in the dream. Had the dream meant that Susan could go home to Wallasey so long as she left Mummy with Eve? She would never do that, and she hoped Eve could hear her thinking. When Eve stared at her as if she could, Susan looked away.

255

Eve followed her to the bathroom. 'Let's go somewhere today, shall we?' she said.

'I'm going out, but not with you.' She didn't like leaving Mummy alone with Eve, but there was no alternative when she had to go for help. 'You can't make me,' she said to Eve's look.

'I'm telling Mummy. She told you to be friends with me.'

'Go on then, baby, telltale,' Susan said, and sneered as Eve slunk out. Was Eve really no more dangerous than this? Perhaps she just needed someone to stand up to her, and Susan knew who would. But when Susan was dressed and went into the main room, Mummy was waiting grim-faced for her. 'Where do you think you're going?'

Susan had her lie ready. 'I want to get some new pencils for school.'

'Why can't Eve come with you?'

She had no lie to cover that. 'Because I don't want her to.'

'We'll find something better to do if Susan's being like that, won't we, Eve. And we won't tell her what it is.'

Susan was so taken aback by having succeeded after all that she couldn't resist asking, 'Where will Eve be going to school?'

'Why should you care? Not with you, miss, and I expect she's glad of that.' Mummy's glare was warning her not to ask further. 'Go and buy your pencils and make sure you're nicer to know when you come back.'

Susan pulled on her coat and boots and was afraid that Eve was letting her think she could get away so as to stop her at the last moment. Or didn't she know what Susan was planning? Had Susan imagined everything about her after all? Susan said, 'I'll try not to be long,' and made to kiss Mummy, who turned her head away. Susan was opening the door when Eve said, 'She'll only be a few minutes. She just has to go to Smith's on the main road.'

So that was why she was letting Susan go: because she knew that Susan wouldn't have time to do what she planned. Or could she really not read Susan's thoughts? Susan picked her way quickly over the lumpy snow, where last week's footprints were bigger but icier than yesterday, and was already making up an excuse: Smith's had sold out, she'd had to go further. Perhaps things would happen too fast for her to need the excuse. She climbed the hill to Molly's. But Molly wasn't there.

Then she must be at work. She was the only person who could help. She'd told Susan to come and see her again, Eve would have to leave them alone with Mummy if Molly told her to, Molly would see what that did to Mummy. At MTV, Susan went to the man in the braided uniform. 'Is Molly Wolfe here?'

He'd begun to frown as soon as he saw her. 'I told you once she isn't, lass.'

'But that was last week.' Last year too, she thought desperately.

He leaned across his desk so abruptly that she shrank back. 'Listen, lass, I'm not supposed to give this out, but I will so you'll know. She isn't working here at all just now, and if you ask me I don't think she'll be coming back.'

Susan felt as if she were still dreaming. Of course Molly worked here, or when had she stopped? For a moment Susan thought of asking if Mummy worked here, Helen Verney who had turned into Nell Verney, who wasn't very much like Mummy any more; if he said no she might wake up. But she wasn't asleep. She went through the revolving doors, into the open where every breath felt like swallowing ice.

Suppose she went back to Wallasey? She could tell Mummy's old friends how Mummy was. She kicked at the slush, splashing her legs and not caring. What use was it to pretend she could get away for so long? Besides, nobody would listen to her. Grown-ups never did.

She was nearly at the police station. If she went in there they would only take her home to Mummy, that was all that policemen ever did to children who hadn't done anything wrong. If she made a scene they would probably lock her up. She made herself cross the road, and trudged along beside the park.

It was almost deserted. Red dogs chased over the snow, bare trees gleamed like new metal. Five hundred yards away someone sat on a bench behind a tree and watched the road with binoculars. Susan squinted to make sure that the woman wasn't watching her, and then the woman waved to her.

At once Susan saw who she was. She almost fell before she reached a gate. She ran along the tinselly path, past ducks waddling towards an old lady with a greenish loaf, and had to detour when Molly waved her out of the way of the binoculars. Molly didn't even take them away from her eyes when Susan joined her on the frosty bench. She didn't sound particularly welcoming when she said, 'Hello, Susan, how are things?'

Susan found that she couldn't answer the question immediately; the answer was too long and too painful. 'What are you doing?'

'My job. You'll excuse me if I'm not very sociable.'

How could she be doing her job if she wasn't working for MTV? Susan felt nervous, all the more so when she noticed that Molly was watching the police station. 'Can I talk to you?' she pleaded. 'You said we could talk.'

'About the situation at home, do you mean? To tell you the truth, Susan, I'd just as soon not right now.'

Susan felt as if she had been physically rebuffed. 'But there's nobody else I can talk to.'

'I'm sure there must be, Susan. A nice girl like you must have plenty of friends.' Molly adjusted the focus minutely. 'We'll talk soon, I promise. It's just that I can't now. This is very important. I need to concentrate, do you see?'

'But I don't know what to do,' Susan said, and hated her own whining voice.

'Now I'm sure it can't be as bad as that, Susan, can it?' Molly glanced at Susan, but frowned at what she saw. 'Well, just try to bear up for a little while longer, and I'll see what I can do just as soon as I can.'

She jammed the binoculars against her eyes. Susan could see that she was willing her to go. 'Can I get in touch with you if I need to?' she pleaded.

'If it's absolutely necessary. I don't mean to put you off, it's just that I may be difficult to find for a while.' She reached out as Susan stood up, and pushed her gently out of her field of vision. 'I'll see you again soon, I promise.'

But she wasn't seeing her now. She was just another grown-up. Susan trudged home, and had passed Smith's before she remembered the pencils. If she bought them now they would be in a Smith's bag. It didn't matter, she didn't care. She bought a packet and threw the bag under a dripping car, but she hadn't reached the gate when she had to force herself to go on, for Mummy was at the window and turning grimly away as soon as she caught sight of Susan.

Mummy met her on the landing and kept her there, outside the closed door. In the dimness Susan could just make out her teeth and her furious eyes. 'Do you know Eve is in there sobbing her heart out?' Mummy hissed. 'That's what you've done, you little wretch.'

'I never. I didn't do anything.'

'Don't you dare say that to me. Do you know what you are? You're a liar. You don't know what truth is.' She grabbed Susan by the shoulders and shook her until her teeth ground together. 'You imagine God knows what about that poor child. If I thought your coloured friends were giving you drugs, I'd have the police to you. Maybe they could show you what reality is.'

Her face lit up, a hateful mask; the woman with the cats had opened her door. She stared out at Susan and Mummy, then she retreated into her flat, nodding to herself. 'I hope she heard all that. I hope she heard how you upset Eve after all the poor child has been through,' Mummy said. 'It's a pity Eve's mother has gone wherever she's gone. Maybe she could teach you how to behave.'

She was turning the doorknob. Through the opening crack Susan could hear Eve sobbing. She fought to suppress her thoughts. There was one other person who could deal with Eve; someone had told her who, but she mustn't try to remember, not now. 'Let's get one thing clear, miss, and don't you forget it,' Mummy said, low and dangerously. 'Eve is here to stay. If anyone has to be sent away because you won't be friends with her, it won't be Eve.'

When Freda had finished packing she carried the suitcase downstairs. She stopped in the hall to catch her breath and wondered how four flights could feel like such a distance. She knocked at the door of Doreen's quarters. That was one thing she couldn't get used to, even though she had an idea why Doreen had asked her always to knock.

Sage opened the door. 'Can we really not persuade you to stay?' he said.

'You don't need me now. You've done more for Doreen than I ever could. Is she here?'

'Of course. Forgive my rudeness.' He stood aside, and she saw the chessboard with its new unfinished game in front of Harry's chair. It shocked her a little to think of Sage using the chair, its arm still sagging from the weight of Harry's elbow. 'Are you missing the sea air?' Sage said.

'No, I just have to go back to work. I've taken all my leave.'

'One tends to forget there is still that world.'

She was beginning to find his mysticism, if that was what

it was, a shade irritating. Doreen came out of her small bedroom and closed the door quickly behind her as she saw Freda. 'You're really leaving?'

'The January sales are calling.'

'I know. I'd no right to expect you to do all you've done, never mind asking for more.'

Doreen took Freda's hands. 'You've been more than a friend to me. There aren't many who would do what you've done for me, especially for nothing. I just hope it hasn't tired you out. I don't like to think of you travelling all that way.'

Freda thought she was making rather a lot of a couple of weeks' help around the house. 'As soon as you feel you need a rest,' Doreen said, 'you come straight back. There'll always be a room for you.'

'You must come back to us soon,' Sage said as if it were his house.

Certainly its peace was his. Freda hadn't fully realized how peaceful the house was now until she stepped onto the pavement. The street felt icy and unwelcoming, strangers glanced sharply at her: it was like waking in an unfamiliar place. For a moment she wanted to turn and go back inside.

When she reached the locked gate at the end of the street, she looked back. Doreen and Sage were standing together on the steps. Sage's smile looked patient, Doreen's anxious but encouraging.

Though it was only a few minutes' walk to Euston from King's Cross, she took a cab. She didn't fancy slithering along Euston Road and getting flustered to be sure of catching her train.

The train gathered speed as colours began to appear here and there through the miles of snow, but she felt unable to fasten her mind on where she was. She was wondering what Doreen was doing now, in her room that she'd kept closed since the night of the séance, or whatever it had been. At first Freda had thought Doreen sensed Harry in there, that

261

it was his presence that was comforting Doreen, but now she thought it was Sage; for not only had she heard Doreen's loving murmurs in the night, she was sure she'd heard a voice responding. The train clattered softly through the softened landscape beyond the double glazing, and she made herself think of the sales, customers elbowing to be first at the counters, skirmishes in the aisles. She was quite looking forward to feeling less redundant than she had begun to feel at Doreen's. She thought she might accept a lift home the next time Mr Harvey, the assistant manager, offered one.

She'd forgotten how cartoonish Blackpool was. The patchy snow emphasized the colours, the childish outlines of the shopping precincts, the Coral Island arcade bright as a rude postcard on Central Drive. The out-of-season street of locked gift shops was almost deserted. She let herself into her flat and put a kettle on the Belling, then went round to the landlady's rooms.

Grimalkin didn't want to know her, he was so disgruntled that she had gone away and left him. He stalked haughtily around her rooms, sniffing at her workbasket full of knitting, the windup gramophone that didn't work very well but which she kept because she had listened to crooners on it with Timothy, her sideboard full of bundles of letters and her books she'd won at school, *The Flora of the British Isles*, *Ten Great Englishwomen*. She thought suddenly how much of a spinster's flat this was with its own front door, its collection of trivia that was meaningful only to her, the only company she had except for Grimalkin – how much lonelier it was than her room at Doreen's. She thought before she could stop herself of Sage in Doreen's bed, and wondered what it would be like to be kissed by the calm smooth pale face. She drank her tea while Grimalkin deigned to settle in his basket, and then she went out for a walk.

She wasn't sure at first that she was heading for Sage's shop. She had only been there once. At least the posters might tell her something about him, if they were still there; she might be able to rid herself of this lingering unease about having left him with Doreen. She was almost sure that she was only jealous.

She hurried down the street with the uneven pavement, the paving stone that had been too unstable to walk on. A few yards beyond the tilted stone was Sage's shop. Once she passed the splintered streetlamp she could see his name and the poster that said 'SAGE KNOWS YOUR FUTURE.' At least, she remembered that was what it said. The faces on the posters weren't his, they must be his clients, but why did they look so dramatic? She almost stepped on the rickety paving stone as she noticed that the houses on both sides of the shop were derelict. Now she could see that the posters weren't about Sage at all.

She stared at them while the wind stabbed at her ears. She felt as if its chill had seized her mind. She'd begun to tell herself that these posters – for funfairs and stage shows – must have been put up after he'd left, but all of them were at least six months old. The poster she had thought said 'SAGE KNOWS YOUR FUTURE' didn't say that after all, it said that the future lay in Revolution Now. Not only did it look like the style of printing she remembered, she was sure it occupied exactly the same position on the window.

She hadn't looked closely at the posters the night she had met him. Of course he had been preparing to move on. She went quickly to the doorless doorway and stepped in. It didn't matter that the shop immediately within the doorway was littered with fallen plaster and old newspapers, it was only the room at the end of the passage that mattered. But the walls of the passage were streaming, sodden wallpaper carpeted the floorboards, and the room at the end was in a worse state than the shop. There was no floor, just a pit of glistening earth.

Freda stared about in the hope that she had mistaken the room. The well where a staircase had once been gaped overhead. There was no other room on this floor. Someone must have taken out the floorboards after Sage had moved on. This was the place, Sage's name above the doorway proved it was. She stumbled out onto the pavement and stared up at his name, and then she began to shake. She wasn't sure if she was laughing or sobbing, or both. Now she could see the letters from which the gilt had flaked on either side of his gilded name. The letters 'SAGE' were simply the remnants of a newsagent's gilded sign.

Rankin lived in Catford, on the eleventh floor of a tower block that overlooked the South Circular Road. On Friday night he'd watched wrestling at the town hall, on Monday he'd gone up the road to a pub to play darts with friends. So much Molly knew from following him home on the train from Victoria, spying on his window with her binoculars from the car she'd hired, following him to the pub and watching him from the other bar while the barman made it clear that women weren't encouraged to drink alone, to the town hall where the tickets were sold out. It wasn't enough, and so she had been driving past the police station for hours, manoeuvring through the streets full of parked cars behind the hotels and back to Bayswater Road, in the hope of finding a way to encounter him.

She had to know more about him. She couldn't just go to his flat and expect to be let in. Posing as someone official might fool many people into inviting her in, but hardly a policeman. She would have to be known to him, and before he had the chance to realize who she was. Every time she followed him put her more in danger of exposure – every time she cruised past the police station because there was nowhere she could park close enough to watch.

The thought of the trophy on the eleventh floor, beyond the curtains that her binoculars could bring close enough to touch, made her feel angry and reckless, if she let herself be. She drove the hired Datsun through the side streets, past parked cars lined up like pegs in a memory game: red, green, red, white, yellow, silver – she knew the order without looking, except that the second red was slewing toward her on a patch of ice. She braked as the red Toyota backed toward her too fast, she drove slowly and breathed deeply when the Toyota had roared away – and almost didn't see that the driver of the police car which was just pulling away from the police station was Rankin.

He was using his lights and his siren to scare pedestrians off the road as he drove through the side streets into Sussex Gardens, and she wasn't sure she would be able to keep up with him. At least he was conspicuous. The police car went screeching onto Westway, and she followed as fast as she dared. On the freeway she was able to match his speed and when he swung off Westway at White City, she followed.

His siren died as he turned onto Du Cane Road and swung into the avenue that led to Wormwood Scrubs. She watched as he was let in through the prison gates, and then she wondered what to do.

It must be visiting time, since there were so many parked cars. She parked in the nearest space she could find, then she walked slowly down the avenue toward the gates in the eighteen-foot walls. She stared up at the firing slits above the names of penal reformers on the towers of the entrance arch, she stared at the oak doors. She couldn't think how to get in or what that would achieve.

The sound of the gates took her unawares. They were letting out the visitors, mostly women, talking in hushed voices as they walked through the cloister of the forecourt. Then she saw Rankin unlocking his car, and her innards clenched. Not only had he seen her, he was locking the door again and making for her.

She turned away quickly and mingled with the crowd. When she looked back, he'd got into his car. Perhaps he hadn't been after her at all. But her skin began to prickle as she heard the car start up, and she was stepping out of its way before she heard the horn. That scattered the visitors to the opposite side of the avenue from Molly. She'd turned her face away, and it wasn't until he wound the offside window down that she realized the car had boxed her in between two trees. 'Why are you following me?' he said.

Her face felt like ice cracking. She had to make something of the situation, it might be her only chance. The visiting women were glancing at her from the far side of the avenue as if she were a criminal. It was only just in time that she realized he couldn't know what her reason was. 'What do you mean?' she said, struggling to think.

His eyes narrowed in his small sharp face. 'I mean what are you doing here, that's what I mean.'

She could only improvise, though she didn't know where it might lead. 'Visiting.'

'You don't say.' His sneer made her panic until she saw that it meant he believed her. 'Who?'

'Just a friend.'

'Is that right.' He turned off the car engine. 'Don't give much away, do you? Does your just a friend have a name?'

'Of course he does,' she said, and wondered if this were a women's prison. No, that was Pentonville, which had somehow got into her head. Or was it Holloway, a short walk from Pentonville?

'Going incognito then, is he? Or maybe you don't want us to get hold of his name?'

She needn't conceal her anger; his treatment would make the character she was trying to play feel like that too. 'His name's Marty,' she said, and wished she'd taken time to think of some other name.

'Not the villain I was interviewing.' It seemed typical of him, or at least of her image of him, that he would use someone's visiting time for questioning. 'And what's yours?'

'Nell.' She added the next name that entered her head. 'Nell Swain.'

'Swain by name, eh? Know what swaining is? They told us once at school.' His expression was more of a leer now. 'So what's your friend in for?'

'Drugs,' she said, which seemed relatively common and harmless.

'Fine friends you have. Coon, is he?'

'He's coloured,' she said, trying to think how she could use all this.

'Thought as much. Does he start them young, your friend? Pushing outside schoolyards, is that his scene?' His sudden fury made him climb red-faced out of the car and slam the door. 'I wouldn't mind a quiet word with him.'

He looked capable of leading her back to the prison. 'He doesn't push, he only uses. He's been arrested several times, that's why he's in here now,' she said, and wondered if that could be enough to get someone locked in Wormwood Scrubs.

'You'll be telling me next he's never given you any.'

'You wouldn't believe me if I did.'

'Truest thing you've said,' he agreed, and for a moment she thought he was on to her. 'Bet you wouldn't like to be searched right now.'

'I wouldn't mind.'

'Turns you on, does it?' He strolled round the car to her. The avenue was deserted now, the oak gates were locked. 'Is that why you like hanging round police? You haven't told me yet why you were following me.'

She had virtually forgotten that question, and wasn't prepared for it to reappear. 'I don't know what you mean.'

'Don't you? Well, I'll tell you something. I never forget a

face.' His was inches from hers now, but still looked small and pinched. 'You were in the pub last night, watching me play darts.'

'What if I was? I live near there.'

'Ah, now she remembers.' He was slapping the car roof lightly; it resounded like a drum. That seemed as much of a threat as the closeness of his face. 'Going to apologize?'

'For what?'

'For acting as if you knew better than me. I know when I'm being followed even if you didn't know you were doing it. Next time don't act as if you're right and I'm wrong.' He leaned his head back a little from her and laid one wiry hand on her shoulder. 'I never forget a face,' he said as if he were quoting a film, 'specially not one that interests me.'

So it hadn't been an interrogation so much as a flirtation. She suspected that he couldn't tell the difference any more than she had been able to. 'I'll buy you a drink in the pub next time if you haven't got yourself locked up by then,' he said, and climbed into the car. 'What did you say your name was? Nelly, that's right. I'll remember.'

He leaned over to wind up the window. 'Just don't try bringing any of your coon friends to the pub,' he said, his face reddening again. 'I don't know what you can see in them, a clever girl like you. Cut six of them open and I'd be surprised if you found a brain, except maybe one they'd been eating. I've known them mistake someone else for their son. And they get stroppy if we say they all look the same to us.'

He was talking about Lenny Bennett's mother, about the unrecognizable smashed face in the film. She managed to look blank and at the same time angry, which seemed safe and which apparently amused him. 'Can't give you a lift unless I arrest you,' he said with a grin, and drove away.

She was making things happen at last. He would recognize her now, and that was the first step to getting herself invited into his flat. As she started the car she wondered if confronting him with the trophy and filming his guilt were bound to happen once she had dreamed of them, unless she prevented them herself. No doubt her dream had exaggerated, as dreams do, but it made her feel powerful, and so did having beguiled Rankin. It was strange and encouraging that she knew his name though she had only heard it in her dreams. She felt sure enough of herself to drive straight to MTV.

Terry Mace wasn't there, nor was Nell. At least Leon was back at last from filming Paddy Shaw. She found him watching the rough cut.

His hair was cropped still closer to his head, which made his face look even chubbier. 'I got the film out before they blew the van up,' he said, 'and we had no trouble at all filming. The Christmas truce, you see. Filming then was one of my better ideas. Sounds as if I had a better time in Belfast than you were having here.'

'Oh, you heard?'

'Eccles couldn't wait to tell me. Martin's in Oxford looking for safe subjects, I suppose.'

'Something like that.'

'That isn't what we brought him here for. It certainly isn't what he should be doing. And all this fucking nonsense about having to broadcast a retraction would only stir things up again. Gould must see that by now. I think it's just a matter of time before they take Martin back. I spoke to him yesterday and he says there's no way they can have him back without you. You can add to that that if they refuse to take both of you back they can do without me as well.'

She couldn't tell him that she didn't think that would be necessary. 'None of this is your fault, Leon. You mustn't think it is,' she said, and gave his soft cheek a kiss before she made her way home.

She drove past Nell's, but nobody was there either, though for a moment she thought she had seen a child's face at the window. It must have been the reflection of a cloud, the way it was changing. Tomorrow she would have to brazen her way into MTV again, to see if she could find out what was wrong at Nell's and to persuade Terry to be ready when she needed him. She parked several streets away from her flat and walked home down the streaming lumpy hill. She was on the steps when she heard her phone ringing.

It was Mrs Wallace. 'Is Martin there?' she shouted faintly. 'I tried the other number.'

'He's away just now. Shall I give you the number or give him a message?'

'I'd appreciate your doing both, Molly. It's his father. The doctor says he hasn't long, maybe just a few days. He wants Martin to come back.'

Molly wasn't sure if she meant his father or the doctor, but she wouldn't have dreamed of asking. 'I'll call him straight away,' she promised. But he wasn't at his Oxford hotel, and the receptionist had no idea when he might be back. Molly left a message for him to call her or his mother. She wished that he weren't in Oxford; it wasn't as if she wanted to know what Stuart had to say. She felt as if she'd made Martin go away purely for her own ends, and she couldn't help dreading the consequences.

'Susan,' Mrs Fisher said, 'will you please stop daydreaming and try to do some work? The holidays are over now, for all of us.' But Susan wasn't dreaming. At last she knew what she must do about Eve. School and the woman with the cats had helped her realize what she could do.

She ducked her head and tried to work with the other children in her group, and wished Lonnie hadn't brought his Space Invaders. Mrs Fisher had set one group of children timing the frequency of spaceships that jittered like insects across the tiny screen while the other groups had to work out the chances of winning. Susan had never been much good with figures, though she was sure that Mummy was spending more on Eve than she could afford, and she could only watch while the others in her group scribbled figures and compared them. Eventually Mrs Fisher came to her. 'What don't you understand, Susan?'

'None of it, miss.'

'Budge over.' Mrs Fisher sat on the corner of Susan's seat and showed her what to do step by step, but Susan couldn't concentrate. Her eyes kept wandering to the initials 'E. V.' carved by the inkwell that she never used. She wouldn't be able to concentrate until she'd done what she had to do about Eve. Mrs Fisher leaned over to look into her eyes just as the bell rang for playtime. 'What's wrong, Susan?' Mrs Fisher said.

She wouldn't believe what was happening. Susan's school friends might, but they couldn't help. There was only one person who could help Susan, and she had to tell that person just enough. 'Nothing, miss,' she said and ran out before Mrs Fisher could stop her, ran downstairs and out of the gates before the teacher on yard duty could demand where she was going.

Frost clung like mould to the roofs of parked cars. She ran grabbing railings that felt soaked and crumbly, she crossed a road and dodged aside from a squashed dead cat, which proved to be a frozen furry newspaper. She was several houses away from the flat when she saw Eve beyond the window.

Susan held onto a gatepost and watched while melting frost trickled down her sleeve. Eve was singing to herself and dancing, pirouetting and writhing her arms. Susan remembered what the woman with the cats had said about the song she'd heard. She tried to focus Eve, who was somehow losing definition even though she was turning

271

more slowly. It must be frost on the window that made her look blurred and pale, so blurred that she no longer looked like a person, a pale blurred shape that seemed to be expanding, filling the window that was writhing too, like the house and the street and the sky where the clouds were exploding outward, impossibly fast. Not only couldn't Susan hear Eve's song, she could hear nothing at all except an enormous stealthy shifting.

She shook her head, wrenched herself away, and ran back toward the school. Now she knew Eve was still in the flat, and she was sure that Eve went to no school. She didn't want to think why.

The bell was ringing for the end of playtime. They all groaned when Mrs Fisher told them to write what they'd done in the holidays. Estelle had had her first period, and Monica was wearing a bra, but Susan didn't think they would be writing about those events any more than she was able to mention Eve, or how Mummy was someone she hardly knew all the time now, or how last night, as she'd lain trying not to think, she'd felt as if Mummy had gone away and left her alone with Eve. She wrote a page and a half about how much she'd enjoyed Christmas in London, mile after mile of Christmas, and almost felt as if Eve hadn't happened after all.

She gobbled lunch in the dining hall, fish fingers and chips of all consistencies, followed by something buried under wobbly custard. She was standing up when Zoe caught her. 'Chloe and me and Estelle are going to play table tennis. Come on or there won't be any tables.'

'Can't, I'm busy.'

'Aw, go on or we won't have a proper game. You're the only one who plays as good as us.' When Susan pushed by, Zoe poked a finger up at her. 'Don't you ever ask us for anything, girl.'

Susan darted through the gates. Boys tried to grab her through the railings as she ran toward Bayswater Road.

She'd forgotten it was early closing day. The post office was closing in ten minutes. At least there wasn't a queue at the phone booths. Directories were spitted spine up near the booths, and she turned up the directory for 'T,' flicked the pages so fast that they almost tore. 'Trading,' 'Travel,' 'Truncheon,' but there was no listing for a truant officer.

She ran to the counter, to a window beyond which a small man with glossy hair and hair cream on his ears was counting stamps. 'No change for the phone,' he grumbled without looking up.

'I've got change,' Susan said indignantly. 'I can't find the number for the truant officer.'

He frowned at her. 'If you were at school you wouldn't need him, would you? Look under "Education." And be quick,' he shouted after her.

Education referred her to yet another directory. She found the number as a woman with a bandaged leg limped out from behind the counter and stood with her hand on the bolt of the door. She was clearly expecting Susan to leave, but Susan ran into the nearest booth with her fistful of change and dialled before anyone could stop her. 'Education Offices,' a brisk voice said.

Susan shoved in a coin. 'Please may I speak to the truant officer?'

'They're probably at lunch. Hold on.' There was total silence for so long that Susan started repeating, 'Hello?' In the glass over the notice above the phone about emergency calls, she could see the woman with the bandaged leg glaring at her. She mouthed into the phone in the hope that would keep the woman away. When a voice said 'Truancy' she jumped and almost couldn't turn her mouthing into speech.

'There's a girl who never goes to school. Her mother thinks she does.' Susan hardly knew whose she meant, hers or Eve's. 'She'll have to be sent away, won't she? She'll have to go to a school where she can't get away.'

'That sounds a bit drastic.' The light voice, which might have been a man's or a woman's, seemed amused. 'How old are you, may we ask?'

'Fourteen.' Susan had anticipated some such question. 'My mum, my mumther told me to call you,' she said, squirming at not having been able to say mother, as a girl of fourteen surely would. 'She can't get out of the house.'

The voice sighed. 'Well, I suppose we must set the machinery in motion. Just a moment.' It went away for considerably longer than that, until Susan felt as if the coins were melting in her fist. 'Will you give me your name first and then your mother's, and your address.'

Susan almost dropped the sweaty coins. She hadn't expected that question, she could think of nothing but the truth. She stuffed the coins into her pocket to keep them safe, and gasped, for that had told her what to say. 'My money's running out,' she gabbled. 'I'll tell you the girl's name first. It's Eve.'

The voice sounded weary. 'Eve what?'

Susan didn't know. 'Eve Verney, I think,' she said, and gave the address.

'All right, I have that. Now your name and address and your mother's.'

'We live at the same address,' Susan said, not caring how stupid she sounded so long as it wasted time. She couldn't have sounded stupid enough, for the voice said, 'The same address as the one you've just given me, you mean?'

'No, as each other.' She was sounding too stupid now, the truant officer might think she was playing a joke and not bother to do anything about Eve, but she couldn't give their real names and address in case the truant officer got in touch with Mummy before calling round to check on Eve. She stared at the glass where the bandaged woman was limping purposefully forward, she tried to think of something reasonable to say to waste time. She said, 'We live across the road,' and then, as if in answer to a prayer she hadn't been able to put into words, the pips began. 'That's all my money,' she said and dropped the receiver into its cradle, 'I'm going now,' she said cheekily to the limping woman and ran back to school. She slipped unnoticed into the schoolyard, and felt as if she were flying. She'd got the better of Eve.

She felt free until she was back at her desk. As the others piled into the classroom and Mrs Fisher told them to make less noise, Estelle came over. 'We saw you creeping out when sir wasn't looking. We're telling miss.'

'See if I care.' But she did, because Mrs Fisher might make her tell where she'd been, she would tell Mummy what Susan had done and then Mummy would protect Eve from the truant officer. All afternoon, every time Zoe or Chloe or Estelle raised a hand, Susan wanted to run out of the classroom, out of the school, except that she had no idea where she would go. 'Now I want you all to paint something you've never seen,' Mrs Fisher said eventually, and Susan wondered if imagining something could make it exist or whether everything that could be imagined already existed, and other things too. The idea of imagining something into existence made her more nervous than she already was, and so she painted an eclipse of the sun, which she had never seen and which was easy to do. 'I would have expected something more imaginative from you, Susan,' was all that Mrs Fisher said before she moved on to Zoe's desk.

Susan held her breath and waited for Zoe to tell on her. She rubbed her slippery palms on her skirt, and then she wondered what she was afraid of. All she had to do was tell Eve the truant officer was coming. Eve wouldn't be able to ask Mummy to hide her unless she admitted she hadn't been going to school, and wouldn't Mummy want to know why? Susan thought she knew: because Eve didn't want too many people to see her, whyever that was. Mrs Fisher was at Chloe's and Estelle's desks now, and they weren't telling on Susan after all, but by now Susan didn't care if they did.

She ran home as soon as school was over. Mummy shouldn't be home for more than an hour, but Susan wanted to make sure of getting to Eve first. The streets seemed to be growing whiter under the darkening sky, though she could hardly see for her white breath. The light was on beyond the dimming window of the flat, which ought to mean that Eve was there. Surely it didn't mean that Mummy had come home early, as she sometimes had on Susan's first days back at school.

Susan turned the key and hurried upstairs into the smell of cats. As she opened the door of the flat she saw Eve sitting watching television, except that it was switched off.

She looked at Susan as if she were the intruder, but Susan wasn't nervous, Eve couldn't stop what was going to happen now that Susan had made the call. 'You didn't go to school today,' Susan said at once.

Eve stared at her, then shrugged. 'Some schools don't go back on the same day as yours.'

'You don't go to school ever.' Susan felt she'd beaten Eve at her own game, especially when Eve didn't answer. 'Why don't you?'

'You know why.'

Did she mean she didn't want to be seen by too many people? Could she really hear what Susan was thinking? It no longer seemed to matter. 'Someone's told the truant officer you don't go to school,' Susan said. 'The teacher told me so. They'll lock you up in a special school if you're still living here when the truant officer comes.'

'Mummy won't like that.' Eve was staring at her with the look she'd had when she crushed the beetle, and not only then. 'Mummy won't like what you did.'

So she knew it was Susan who'd called the truant officer. Perhaps it had been obvious. Susan didn't care, it was done now. She tried not to care when Eve said, 'Mummy said she wanted to see you as soon as you came in.'

That was just like Eve, talking about Mummy as though

she were Eve's and not even telling Susan until now what Mummy had said. 'Where is she?' Susan demanded.

'In the bedroom,' Eve said with an odd lopsided smile, and stood up as Susan made for the hall. She must think Mummy would be on her side, but Susan didn't think so: Mummy wouldn't like the truant officer coming here and asking her why Eve didn't go to school. Maybe it would make her angry, maybe she would take it out on Susan. Anything that Mummy did to Susan would be worth it so long as Eve went out of their lives.

Susan told herself all this as she ventured into the hall, but she couldn't help being afraid. Mummy must be lying down, for the bedroom light was off. 'Mummy?' she said.

When there was no answer, she stepped into the dark. An echo made the boxy space seem larger than it was, an echo of her footsteps and of Mummy moving on the bed in the dark. Susan reached out and pulled the cord, pulled it twice and heard it click, but the light didn't go on. 'I don't want to stay in here, Mummy,' she said, suddenly afraid of the largeness of the movements and of the echoing dark.

She had just reached the doorway, which seemed more distant from the cord than it ought to be, when Eve stepped in front of her and gave her a shove backward. It was so unexpected that Susan stumbled the length of the room, tried to save herself from falling over the end of the bed before she realized it wasn't there. She was still stumbling backward, because there was no wall to stop her. The dark was even larger than it sounded. She threw herself forward, toward the lit doorway in the distance, and only managed to stand still. 'What's happened?' she cried in a voice that didn't sound like hers. 'What have you done with Mummy?'

'She's there with you. She likes the dark.' Eve might have been grinning, as her voice was, but it was impossible to tell, because of what was happening to her face. 'It's time you met her. My Mummy, not yours.'

She was reaching out to close the door in the shaky wall. Susan knew that once the door was closed she would be lost in the total darkness. She was running as she had never run before, running as if she could outrun having to think about what Eve had said, yet the doorway was still impossibly distant, and something else was wrong. At first she thought Eve had shoved the dressing table into the doorway to block her way out, even if she reached it; she thought she was seeing herself in the mirror. Eve closed the door tight and Susan heard the soft unhurried movements that now seemed as large as the dark, the movements and the giggling whisper that were between her and the vanished door. The dark cut her off from the world forever and the last thing she saw was that Eve's face was no longer Eve's. It was her own.

The young woman in the white lab coat who smelled of soap and duplicator paper led Martin through the pale green corridors to the auditorium and showed him a seat at the back. Though a film was being projected on the curtainless screen, all the lights were on, and so he recognized Stuart Hay as soon as the man in the front row turned to glance up the steep rake at him. Hay was quite stout now and had grown a clipped red beard, but there was no mistaking Molly's description of him, his faint superciliously sceptical expression and the appraising glance he gave Martin's escort. He nodded curtly to Martin and turned back to the film. Martin tried to watch it too, to understand what it was supposed to be, to quell his instinctive dislike of Stuart Hay.

Presumably the film was more than nonsense, since the

fifteen or so businessmen in the small auditorium were watching it intently. Some of them were taking notes, flashing gold cuff links and expensive watches. Martin tried to be comfortable on the meagre seat that threatened to fold up if he sat back – presumably the seats were meant to make sure that nobody would fall asleep – and wondered why nobody was laughing at the film. Actors appeared in different scenes with different dubbed voices, a character was driving an invalid car in one scene but walking in the next, a man and woman were clearly married in one scene, but later proved to be married to two other people. 'The End,' a title said, and the film went on. When Martin couldn't suppress a snort of mirth, three businessmen glared at him.

The film broke halfway through a scene. Martin assumed it was a faulty copy until Hay said, 'I'll join you gentlemen in the canteen shortly.' Martin waited as the businessmen climbed the steep steps past him, and then Hay joined him. 'Mr Wallace,' he said and gave Martin a handshake like a handful of firm sponge. 'What did you think of our film?'

'Hard to say without seeing it through.'

'You think so?' His grin seemed somehow too friendly. 'Did it make any sense to you?'

'Some.'

'Really? What sense did it make?'

Martin felt he was being satirized. Under the stubbly red hair Hay's flushed face looked argumentative. 'The technique isn't that radical,' Martin said.

'I suppose not.' His grin wagged the beard, which looked like a brush that had been used to redden his face. 'Sorry about that. I'm not laughing at you. The way people's minds work fascinates me. We set up that film so there was no way it could make sense, yet everyone who sees it tries to reconstruct it and nearly everyone manages to persuade himself he understands it, says scenes are missing or remembers details that weren't there. It's a valuable experience. It gives our subjects an insight into how their minds work.'

'That's what you do now, is it?'

'Right, and there's hardly a one of them doesn't thank us at the end of the course. Ask them if you like.'

He was leading Martin down the corridor to the canteen. His defensiveness only strengthened Martin's resolve not to be distracted. 'I'm not here for that,' Martin said.

'Why are you here, Mr Wallace?'

'I told you on the phone.'

'Tell me again.' His grin was a challenge. 'It was a bad line.'

'You wrote to Molly Wolfe. She sent me to find out what you wanted and why.'

'Faper not fofip, eh?' He held open the canteen door. 'The Foundation for Applied Psychological Research,' he explained when Martin stared at him, 'which was here before the Foundation for Industrial Psychology. That's where you are now.'

Martin felt uneasy and couldn't think why. 'You mean this is where Molly came eleven years ago?'

'That's what I said. Why not?' He slid a tray that bore two plastic cups of muddy coffee along the counter to the till and paid the sniffing cashier. 'Thanks, pet,' he said with a wink, and turned to Martin without warning. 'Haven't I seen you somewhere before?'

'I shouldn't think so.'

'Strange, could have sworn I had.' His grin was even friendlier. He led Martin to a table among the businessmen, who were discussing a computer language and seemed almost to be talking in it. 'Sorry, I've forgotten what you wanted to know.'

Perhaps he thought that sitting with the businessmen would inhibit Martin. 'Molly Wolfe wants to know why you wrote to her after all this time,' Martin said without bothering to lower his voice.

'No particular reason. I just thought it was time to check.'

'After eleven years of not checking? That's not the way your letter reads.'

'It was designed to get a response. Not that it did, except from you.'

'You wrote to everyone who took part in your experiment?'

'Yes, of course. Why would I single out Miss Wolfe?'

Martin suppressed an angry response. 'What after-effects were you expecting?'

'I honestly don't know. Part of the scientific method is not to anticipate.'

'Maybe so, but don't tell me you expected nothing.' Losing his temper wouldn't help Molly. 'You must have expected your original experiment to achieve something.'

'You ought to ask Guilda Kent about that. She was running the show.' He stirred three spoonfuls of sugar into his coffee and sipped before he went on. 'We wanted to look at correlations between the prophetic dreams of different subjects and whether different conditions might affect their dreaming.'

'But did any of the dreams come true?'

Hay looked as if he hadn't expected such a naive question. 'A few seemed specific enough. None of Miss Wolfe's, I'm afraid, at least not so far as I know. Again, Dr Kent would be the one to ask. She took her research with her when faper became fofip. What we're doing here now wasn't for her, she said.'

He swallowed half his coffee in one gulp. 'Five minutes, gentlemen,' he called. 'Will you excuse me now, Mr Wallace? I think I've answered all your questions.'

Martin seized Hay's wrist as he put down the cup, and felt how the bones would creak if he gripped hard. 'You haven't told me what happened here eleven years ago.'

'I'd call it collective hysteria, probably involving hallucination. Would you mind?' He tugged his wrist free, gently but firmly. 'In retrospect it isn't surprising. There was a very strong rapport between the subjects, stronger than they were able to cope with. They did appear to share dreams. I agree we should have had more safeguards, if that's what is on your mind.' He pushed his chair back. 'If you're asking about the subjective experience of what happened, of course I wouldn't know. I should have thought you would have got that from Miss Wolfe.'

Martin opened his mouth, but Hay had been waiting to interrupt him. 'By the way, you've left it a bit late to tell me if she has experienced any after-effects.'

'How should I know which they are?' The implication that he'd been neglectful infuriated Martin. 'She's been having prophetic dreams again, which she says are accurate. She's on edge even though she's sleeping nights. One of the others contacted her and she keeps thinking there's another of them somewhere near. Frankly, I think these are effects of your goddamned letter.'

Stuart's frown had cleared so quickly that Martin wasn't sure what he had said to cause it. 'Who contacted her?'

'I couldn't tell you.'

'Then it looks as if we've told each other all we can.'

Martin doubted that, but Hay was following the businessmen toward the door. 'How can I get in touch with Dr Kent?'

'Good question,' Stuart said approvingly as if it were Martin's first. 'I wish I could tell you. I haven't seen or heard of her for years. I understood she was planning to get closer to the problems of ordinary people.' He turned to Martin before stepping into the auditorium. 'If you should trace her, you might tell her I'd like her to get in touch.'

Martin's anger died as the double doors ceased to swing. He could always confront Hay tomorrow if there was anything Molly wanted him to ask, but he rather felt that Hay had nothing more of significance to offer. He strolled down the pale green corridor and glanced back belatedly at the painting that had looked like a window on a summer landscape, hills and distant Oxford, but there was only a window. No doubt the painting had been in one of the rooms he'd passed.

He was stamping his feet and slapping his forearms by the time the Oxford bus arrived. Nevertheless he left the bus when it reached the outskirts of Oxford, and walked through the elegant streets. Icy winds blew through the quadrangles, in one of which a guided tour had halted, heads tipped back to admire stone figures in their lairs; winds rattled the Georgian windows in the High Street. Domes and cupolas swelled against a sky like a flood of ice, Gothic pinnacles bristled, and Martin kept having to dodge bicycles as he gazed up. It must have been an hour before he reached the Randolph, where the receptionist gave him Molly's message.

He called her and then, with a good deal of transatlantic difficulty, his mother. His father's condition hadn't changed. She said he wanted Martin, and Martin promised to be there as soon as he could. His initial panic was fading now that he knew his father was still alive, but it was giving way to a kind of nervous frustration. Of course he mustn't blame Molly; coming to Oxford had been his idea. All the same, as he hurried out to find a travel agent's he couldn't help growing furious that he had wasted so much time.

Danny sat in the parlour and stared at the aquarium and struggled not to tell his mother where he had been on New Year's Eve. He mustn't care that neither she nor his father had addressed a complete sentence to him since then; he

283

mustn't care that he felt as if he were drowning in their silence and disapproval, felt as if their disapproval were a substance that covered him from head to foot and clogged his ears. He watched the fish swimming through the castle in the aquarium and thought he had never seen anything so stupid: the fish didn't even know what a castle was. Thinking that was no good, because he knew his parents thought that he was even stupider and more contemptible. The only way to prove them wrong would be to tell them where he had been.

When he'd staggered down to Bayswater Road after copying Molly Wolfe's address, he'd found he couldn't afford a taxi. It had taken him nearly three hours to stumble home, he'd been sick all over his new suit outside Regent's Park while revellers had cheered him on and woken all the monkeys in the zoo. When he'd picked up a handful of snow to clean himself he'd discovered that a dog had been there first, and after all that he had realized that Caledonian Road would have been a quicker way home. He'd reeled into the flat to find his mother calling the police. 'Never mind the drunks, they can look after themselves, and it's their own fault if they can't. My son's missing, don't you understand?' When she had seen Danny, she'd walked away to bed, wheezing as if she would never again catch her breath. His father had stared at him until Danny was afraid of falling down from being unable to move. 'By God, your mother was right about you,' was all that his father had said.

Let the spies tell his mother where he'd been on New Year's Eve, she wouldn't listen because she didn't believe in them. All the same they were confusing him, making him feel he mustn't say where he had been, making him forget that telling was the only way to get rid of the disapproval that was suffocating him. He was opening his mouth before he had thought what to say, when his mother said, 'Shall we watch the war film?'

'It isn't a war film, it's some slushy thing,' his father grumbled.

'It must have a battle in it, *The Battle of the Villa Fiorita*.'

'That's a good film.' Danny had remembered what he'd read about it, and his crotch felt warm. 'I'd like to see that,' he said.

His father ignored him, his mother gave him a sad helpless glance. 'Maureen O'Hara's in it,' she told his father. 'You like her. You liked the one where John Wayne drags her to town by her hair.'

'*The Silent Man*,' Danny said.

'That's right, Danny, thank you. We'll watch this one this afternoon then, shall we?'

'You'll do whatever suits you, I expect,' his father growled and stumped away to the bathroom, scratching his stubbly chin so hard that Danny could still hear it in the hall. 'The silent bloody man, good God. Pity there isn't one here.'

'I can watch too, can't I?' Danny said anxiously to his mother. 'I won't distract you or anything.'

'If you say you're sorry and promise you'll never do anything like that again.'

'I'm sorry and I promise.'

'Just never let me down again, Danny. I'm not in the health for it. You were nearly the death of me on New Year's Eve.'

He hadn't been, it wasn't fair. Dr Kent had if anyone had. Could she and Molly Wolfe have taken turns to keep him out so late that worrying would finish off his mother? Dr Kent had said he wouldn't feel free while his mother was alive. But he didn't feel guilty now, because his mother had forgiven him. They had reckoned without her.

Later his father went to the pub so that he could smoke his cigarettes, and came back for lunch. He didn't say a word to Danny while they washed and stacked the dishes, but when Danny joined his parents in front of the television, he growled, 'Got you watching too, has she? At least while you're here you can't do much harm.' Danny thought

285

he could hear how his father felt that at least Danny was being unselfish, keeping his mother company while she watched the kind of film only she liked. Danny smiled at how everything was fitting together on his behalf.

When the film began, his father produced a bag of boiled sweets and gave them to Danny's mother as if he'd bought them from the usherette. She sucked and wheezed and glanced about to make sure nobody was looking while she removed her bottom teeth to which a sweet had stuck, while Maureen O'Hara went to live with a concert pianist in Italy. Their children went on hunger strike to force them not to remarry, and it looked as if the scene was coming: '14-year-old Olivia Hussey goes across Rosanno Brazzi's knee and has her skirt lifted for a few powerful smacks. . . .' That's what the dictionary of spanking films had said. He sat back to give the wriggling in his trousers room.

The fish gulped at their floating food, Danny's mother sucked her sweet and rattled her teeth, Rosanno Brazzi was forcing his daughter to eat. When she spat out her food on her plate, Danny knew this was it, and suddenly realized why he was nervous: suppose his mother saw the movement in his trousers? Brazzi pulled the girl across his knee and spanked her – 'About time too,' Danny's mother said around her sweet – and then it was over, too quickly. She stalked away to a safe distance and began to curse her father in Italian. 'I wouldn't let you get away with that,' Danny muttered.

It looked as if Brazzi had heard him, for the actor jumped up and dragged her back to the chair. He unbuckled his belt before he forced her across his knee and slipped her knickers down. Danny pressed his spine into the easy chair as his penis rose, and could hear nothing but the cracks of the belt and the girl's cries. It wasn't until his mother said, 'Is that the same girl?' that he realized something was wrong.

The scene wasn't meant to go on like this. He was making

it happen somehow. His parents frowned at it and shifted resentfully in their seats as Maureen O'Hara brought Brazzi a cane, and Danny knew what Dr Kent had done: by reminding him of Oxford she'd weakened his hold on things so that they could change. He knew that when the pleading girl raised her face to the camera it would be Dr Kent's or Molly Wolfe's. He was seized by a suffocating fear that his mother would realize he was making the film change. He staggered up from his chair, though his penis almost jerked him back into it, and switched off the television.

He was sitting down again before he saw he had achieved nothing. The girl was screaming as Maureen O'Hara used the cane. He forced himself not to grab the huge painful weight in his trousers as he limped back to the television and wrenched the plug out of the wall. For a moment, or much longer, that seemed to make no difference either, then the picture shrank reluctantly to a fading point of light. He was straightening up from the socket when his father threw him out of the way. 'What the hell do you think you're doing, you damned lunatic? Your mother was watching that and you knew she was.'

Danny limped bewildered to his room and slumped on the bed. His penis was as reluctant to shrink as the picture had been, but eventually it did. Had he been the only one to see the scene in the film? Was that Dr Kent's trick? He squeezed his eyes shut to try and stop his head throbbing. He heard the music at the end of the film, and then his father marched in and threw something on Danny's bed.

It was a letter that had been opened. Danny was afraid to read it, even when his father had gone, in case someone had written to his parents that they had seen him in Soho. Then he realized it was addressed to him. He hadn't received a letter for years, yet his parents were still opening his correspondence as if he hadn't grown up. They were spying on him, just like his enemies. He tore the envelope as he fumbled out the letter, and wished he had something else to tear.

The letter was from Stuart Hay in Oxford, and it had been posted weeks before Christmas. His father must have kept it from him to protect him, and now had given it to him as a rebuke for the way he'd behaved, or because he felt Danny was no longer worth protecting. It wanted to know about after-effects, if what Dr Kent and the others had done was still affecting Danny. If Stuart Hay had known Danny's address for so long, Dr Kent must have known too. Both of them were helping Molly Wolfe try to get hold of his mind.

They might have succeeded if his father hadn't kept his letter. He knew at once what he had to do. The Hercules wouldn't be open for hours. 'I'm going now,' he said when he'd put on his coat, and almost thanked his father until he saw his blank furious look.

He ran through the streets, and half an hour later was in Soho hurrying past a line of disapproving women with placards. Dr Kent opened her door before he reached it, and raised her eyebrows. 'I'm glad you've come back, Danny.'

She wouldn't be for long. Perhaps she sensed his mood, for she sat forward at her desk and gazed sharply at him. 'What makes you keep coming back, do you think?'

For a moment he panicked, thinking that she knew. The draught up the stairs made his soaked feet ache and his ankles tremble. Then he saw that she was only trying to probe his mind. 'I don't want to come here any more,' he said.

'Name your place. Anywhere at all if you think it'll help.'

'The Hercules,' he said.

'Why?'

He had an answer he knew she would like, and so he didn't stammer. 'Because you said the films he makes me show made me how I am. I want you to come and see.'

'You think that may achieve something, do you?'

288

His grin was almost too strong for him, but he managed to keep it inside himself. 'I know it will,' he said.

'Let's both hope so. When?'

He realized just in time that he would need to think of an excuse to stay out late. 'Next week,' he said fiercely, to show he wasn't losing confidence.

'Monday?'

'Tuesday.' Monday seemed dangerously close. 'Tuesday night after he's gone home. I'll meet you outside. Don't come before eleven.' As soon as she agreed, he stood up. 'I've got to go now or I'll be late.'

Nevertheless he dawdled on the stairs once he had closed her door. Her question had got to him after all. Why *did* he keep coming here? It made him feel like his magazines did, excited by what was going to happen but always depressed afterward, disgusted with himself. This time that wouldn't happen. At the Hercules they would be alone with nobody to hear.

He stepped into the court and a flash of light blinded him. A woman had photographed him. He was surrounded by women with prams and placards: 'People Not Pornography,' 'Save Our Soho,' 'Would You Live Next Door to a Whore?' They must think he'd been to a sex shop or a prostitute. 'You mustn't take my picture,' he said as calmly as he could. 'I haven't been to one of those.'

'Lost your way, did you?' said a woman with a baby strapped to her chest.

'No, I come here to see a doctor.'

The women began jeering at him. He was suddenly terrified that they would publish the photograph for his mother to see. 'I want my photograph,' he said loudly.

'Go on, you dirty bugger.' The woman with the camera held it out of reach. 'Lay a finger on me and I'll call the police.'

'I'll bet that's all he can lay,' Danny thought one of them said as he lurched at the camera. The woman stepped back,

289

holding it above her head – stepped back onto a patch of ice. She fell with a thud that sounded to Danny like nothing so much as a bundle of newspapers, and the camera flew out of her hand, under the wheels of a car. The crunch of its destruction was the most satisfying sound he'd ever heard. He stared at her floundering on her back, he thought her face might sound like that if he stood on it, but there was no need to do that; the picture of him was destroyed and there was nothing they could do to him. He strode away, grinning at the threats and insults the woman shouted after him, grinning wider when one of them threw a piece of ice at him that missed and shattered on a passing car. As the driver halted and demanded what they thought they were playing at, Danny began to laugh softly as if he might never stop. The way he'd felt when the camera smashed was nothing to how he would feel next week, alone at last with Dr Kent on his own ground.

The guard marched away from Buckingham Palace. The men's eyes were invisible beneath the furry bullets of their hats, their mouths were almost hidden by their chin straps, and Molly wondered how the band could see the tiny scores clipped to their golden instruments. Terry Mace steadied himself against the balustrade around the Queen Victoria Memorial, zoomed in on the face of a guard and began to film. 'Tell me again,' he said.

At least he wasn't refusing. 'What do you want to know?'

'The whole thing.' As he pressed his eye against the camera, the badges on his creaking jacket scraped together. 'I'll tell you now, I don't want any more trouble with the police.'

Nor, she was sure, did he want to antagonize Gould, who had almost certainly assigned him to this work because he suspected Terry of having been involved in making the Bennett film.

'I never thought I'd hear you say that, Terry,' she said.

His shoulders stiffened. 'I don't need you to tell me what to do about the police.'

'You needn't make it sound as if I don't know what they can be like. I've had trouble with them myself, remember.'

'Yeah, but for the wrong reasons.'

He was taking his resentment out on her. 'That's not for you to judge, Terry.'

'Don't kid me you didn't try to shit on the police so that people would believe Martin Wallace.'

'Would it do any good if I did?'

'Not with me, princess.' To her surprise, he smiled. 'Well, all right,' he said. 'So remind me what happened then.'

'I told you, I went to see them with Oliver Boycott and they proved I couldn't have been arrested when I'd said I was. They sent me out and presumably Oliver persuaded Maitland not to prosecute. And while I was waiting, Rankin came up to me and said what I told you.'

'Come on, twitch, you bugger,' Terry muttered, and it wasn't for a moment that she realized he was talking to the sentry. 'He told you his name, did he?'

'No, someone asked for him by name at the desk while I was there. But I really think he could have told me, he was bold enough.' Telling the lie for the second time was easier. 'He came as close as I am to you and said I was right it was Maitland who gave the nigger the treatment, but he was the one who finished him off.' She'd spent time choosing words that would enrage him. 'He was showing me that he could say what he liked to me,' she went on, while Terry was visibly furious. 'He knew damn well nobody would believe me.'

Terry was zooming in further as if that would make the guardsman twitch. 'So?'

'I told you, I watched the police station and followed him home. I managed to slip into the building one night while he was out and take a look through the letter-box with my binoculars. Lenny Bennett's bracelet is on the mantelpiece in the room at the end of the hall. All it needs is someone to go there and photograph it.'

He adjusted the lever of the zoom lens minutely. 'Someone like cop-hater Mace.'

'You said you wanted power to change things, didn't you? I'd still be taking most of the risks, persuading him to let me into his flat so I could let you in. All you'd have to do would be to film.'

'Yeah, and maybe get my head kicked in.' He glanced suddenly at her. 'There you go,' he said to the sentry. 'Knew you couldn't keep it up.'

He switched off the camera. 'How do you reckon you'd set all that up?' he said.

'Wait until he gets home and go up there at once. You'd follow and wait for me to open the door.'

'You don't fuck around when you get an idea, do you?' He lined up the camera on the other sentry's face. 'All right, princess, you've convinced me. I owe Lenny Bennett that at least, and I wouldn't mind getting back at the pigs either. When do you want to go?'

'Tonight?' she said, suddenly tasting apprehension.

'Monday is better. You're right we should do it as soon as we can, before I change my mind.' He gave her a wink and started the camera. 'It can be my peace offering to Martin for shitting on his work.'

But it couldn't make up for her having kept Martin away from his father until it was too late. 'I'll pick you up Monday afternoon,' she said, and started for home.

Leon had told her Martin had called him and asked that he tell her he would be away for a week or more. His father had died while Martin was on his way home. She wondered if he blamed her for keeping him away. So he should. She wasn't entirely convinced that he'd asked Leon to give her any message.

She shook off her mood when she reached Bayswater Road, and headed for Nell's. At least there she might be able to achieve something. A man went by chatting to the other head on his shoulders, a baby strapped to his back, and Molly felt as if she'd dreamed of someone like that. It must have been years ago, too long ago to make her nervous.

The doorbell brought Nell running down. 'Molly! I hoped it was you.' She turned away, assuming Molly would follow. 'You've time for a coffee, haven't you? Come on up.' She seemed much happier than last time. Nell made coffee and said she hoped Molly would soon be back at work, it didn't seem fair that Molly should have lost her job when she had just got Nell hers. She'd been looking forward to working with her and seeing more of her. Molly felt confident enough to say she might soon be back. They carried their mugs past the closed doors of the bedroom and the bathroom, and Nell said, 'I was meaning to phone you. I wanted to apologize for Susan, for the scene she made on Boxing Day.'

Molly realized what she had been missing without noticing. 'Where is she? Still at school?' she said, though it was late.

'She's in disgrace. She's been behaving very badly since we moved, telling lies and arguing all the time and even stealing. She took the light bulb out of my room for no reason and wouldn't admit she had. Such a stupid lie too, as if anyone else could have. I don't mind telling you, Molly, I was beginning to wonder if she was the same child.'

That made Molly feel strange, she couldn't say why, and she still hadn't learned where Susan was. 'And as if that wasn't enough,' Nell said, 'someone called the truant officer and tried to make out there was another child here who didn't go to school. As if I could afford to keep another child on my salary! I often used to wish I could adopt a child, I used to wish Susan had a sister. Of course they wouldn't let me adopt, they haven't much time for single parents. Still, I've got over that. I have my Susan. Even when she misbehaves I wouldn't change her for anyone else.'

Perhaps it was the born-again gleam in her eyes that was making Molly uncomfortable, that bright unassailable look. 'But I'll tell you, Molly, though I wouldn't tell anyone else, I had to hit her when she wouldn't stop lying. I've never hit her before. At least she's behaved herself since. I suppose it's just growing up and moving to a new place,' Nell said, and paused as they heard a key in the door. 'Here she is now.'

The door opened, and Molly wondered what she was seeing. In the dimness of the landing, Susan's face above the school uniform looked old and sly, and far too large. The girl stepped forward, and of course it was Susan. 'Molly's here. What have you to say to her?' Nell said.

Susan clasped her hands behind her back. 'I'm sorry I made such a fuss when we came to visit you, Molly. I was very rude.'

'I should think so too,' Nell said. 'Is that all?'

'I was just being silly because I was in a new place. There was a girl who kept trying to spoil things for me, but she's gone now.'

'A girl at school, she means.' Both of them were gazing brightly at Molly as if nothing had ever been wrong.

'Thanks for the coffee,' she said, and stood up.

'You'll have to come for dinner soon. And if you ever need a place to stay, you know where it is.'

So Nell was still odd. At least Susan seemed much happier. All the same, Molly felt uneasy as she stepped onto the dim stairs. When a door spilled light onto the landing, she jumped. A woman in a hairnet was beckoning to her from the flat opposite Nell's. 'Are you from the Education?' she hissed.

'Afraid not.'

'Come here anyway. I want to tell you about them.' She was pointing at Nell's. When Molly went to her the woman shuffled quickly backwards, slippers flapping, and gestured her to close the door. 'Do you know them?' she whispered.

'Slightly,' Molly said, holding her breath against the smell of cat turds among the sagging stained chairs.

'They want keeping an eye on. You ought to if you're supposed to be their friend,' the woman said as if she hadn't heard what Molly had said. 'For the child's sake.'

Molly put her hand over her face, as if she were musing, and tried to breathe. 'Why, what's wrong?'

'Her mother sends her to school with the darkeys, for a start. You don't need me to tell you they're bound to be giving her drugs. And half the time she doesn't go to school at all.'

'Is that what you wanted to tell me?'

The woman sat down heavily on a chair, which creaked and wobbled, and stared incredulously at her. 'Isn't it enough?'

'I'll keep it in mind,' Molly said, and opened the door before the woman could invite her to sit down. Once she was in the street she was able to take a deep breath. All the same, she was glad the woman had cornered her. The business of the truant officer and the child in Nell's flat had troubled her, but there was the explanation: the woman who'd called him wasn't quite right in the head. She couldn't help wishing that her problems with Rankin and even with Martin could be resolved as neatly, but that seemed too much even to dream.

Freda was the last to leave the train at Euston. A porter muttered at her that this was the end of the line and went on to the next carriage, grumbling because nobody had left a Sunday paper.

A woman's voice boomed through the hall beyond the barriers, apologizing for the lateness of the train, as if the Sunday journey weren't already long enough – long enough for Freda to lose her reasons along the way. She'd phoned Doreen only to find that she couldn't tell her about Sage over the phone, it had to be face to face, and then she'd spent the week worrying until today, when she could stay overnight because Monday was closing day at the store. As if she hadn't enough to think about, a letter had been waiting among her Christmas cards, a letter from Stuart Hay, the doubter from Oxford. He'd as good as asked if she had started dreaming again, but if she told anyone it certainly wouldn't be him. She'd put his letter out of her mind so as to concentrate on what she would tell Doreen, but now she was nearly there she didn't know what she would tell her, or why.

She went quickly along Euston Road, and wondered why she was hurrying: how could she tell Doreen that Sage had tricked them somehow when the closer she came to it, the less she believed it herself? Was the truth simply that she was jealous of Doreen?

She was walking slower now, to give herself time to think. If anyone had tricked her, surely it was herself. Either his name had happened to coincide with the letters above the shop or it wasn't his name at all; he had never said it was. She had hardly glimpsed the posters on the window the night she'd met him. Either vandals had wrecked the place after he'd left or she had mistaken the street. The one thing she couldn't tell Doreen was that Sage was a charlatan, and it dismayed her to think that perhaps she had meant to try.

She almost turned and made for the station. Instead she turned along Doreen's road, past the locked gate. She couldn't go yet, not when there wasn't a train for hours, not when the thought of seeing Sage made her feel so peaceful.

She climbed the steps to the front door she'd repainted and stood there wondering what else was new. Of course, Doreen had changed the knocker. She must have grown tired of the way the dog-faced knocker was askew, even though Harry had bought it. That showed she was getting over her loss. Freda took hold of the bright new silver bar, but a movement made her glance up. Sage, if that was his name, had come to his window.

As their eyes met, he smiled. On his calm face the faint glad look meant more than astonished delight would have meant on someone else's. He pointed to himself to show that he would let her in, and she closed her eyes, giving thanks that she hadn't managed to warn Doreen. She couldn't believe that anything but jealousy could have made her suspect him.

Doreen came out of her quarters as he opened the front door. She peered along the hall and missed a step as she saw Freda. She ran to her and threw her arms around her. 'Freddy, we were just talking about you. We hardly talk about anything else.'

'How are you, Doreen?'

'Happy, thanks to you.' She ushered Freda to the parlour, where the gas fire parched the air. 'What brought you back so soon? Did you hear me wishing?'

'I just wanted to see you.' Freda couldn't resist adding, a little slyly, 'After staying here it felt strange to be on my own.'

Doreen smiled reminiscently. 'I know what you mean.'

Freda was disconcerted to find herself feeling what she'd thought she was pretending. 'How long are you going to stay this time?' Doreen cried, taking hold of her hands. 'As long as you like.'

'I could stay overnight, if you don't mind. I don't want to put you to any trouble.' Now she felt thoughtless for not letting Doreen know she was coming. 'The Sunday trains take such a time to get anywhere.'

'Don't you dare say another word. We've plenty to eat, and you know your room is made up.' She glanced at Sage, who was stretching his long fingers toward the fire as if he were beckoning the flames into his hands. 'Freddy, would you mind if a friend of mine came over?'

'Should I?'

'She's been a good friend, and I know she wants to meet you. She doesn't want to be alone, you see. You don't need me to tell you how that feels.'

It sounded somehow ominous, but Freda couldn't very well refuse; after all, it was Doreen's house. 'Don't put her off on my account,' she said.

Doreen blinked at her as if she'd missed the point, then went into the hall and closed the door. Freda heard her dialling, heard her saying, 'Freddy's here, Rosie. You must come over tonight,' and would have liked to hear the rest, but Sage sat forward and smiled at her. 'The house has seemed lacking without you,' he said.

She felt the blush spread over her face, and thought it would never stop. Her ears were so hot she had gone deaf. When she said 'I'm glad to be back,' her voice sounded muffled in the cave of her skull. So did Doreen's when eventually Freda was able to hear again, and it wasn't until she heard the closing of the door that Freda realized Doreen had been talking in her bedroom, no longer talking on the phone. After Timothy's death Freda had often caught herself talking to herself.

Soon Doreen wheeled in the trolley bearing her best tea service. 'Rosie's coming tonight. I do appreciate it, Freddy, and so does she. I know you understand.'

Freda was growing less sure that she did, unless she was supposed to comfort Doreen's friend somehow. Surely Sage could do that best, and she told herself he would. She sipped her tea and felt peaceful. There seemed to be no further need to talk.

Sage carried her overnight bag to her room and opened the door for her. She found herself wondering what she would do if he came in with her and closed the door behind him, and she snatched the bag, blushing furiously. 'Thanks,' she muttered as she closed him out, and waited until she heard his descending footsteps. To think she'd meant to ask him if his name was really Sage! She could only scoff at herself and her jumble of feelings.

She dropped her bag beside the dressing table and lay down on the bed. No wonder she was sleepy after so long on the train. She stared up at the crucifix above the bed, then closed her eyes. The miniature figure had seemed to lean forward as if preparing to jump off the cross and onto her pillow. She slept and dreamed she was in prison, endless pale green corridors of cells whose windows looked out on nothing whatsoever. She was glad when a knock at the door woke her up.

It was Sage. 'I am to tell you that dinner is almost served,' he said. She couldn't help smiling, though she didn't think he meant to parody a butler. She washed and changed, she propped the tilting mirror while she inspected herself in her black dress, and then started as she stepped onto the landing, for Sage was waiting for her at the head of the stairs. Didn't he think she could find her own way down? All the same, she felt elegant when he took her arm to escort her to dinner. A twinge of delicious apprehension made her scoff at herself as he ushered her down past his room.

Doreen wheeled in the trolley as soon as they were seated.

She must be expecting her friend Rosie, for there was far too much on the trolley for three. Either Doreen's cooking had improved with her state of mind or Sage was helping her, though there was nothing elaborate: a large boiled ham, baked potatoes, piles of steaming vegetables in serving dishes. Sage carved the ham and served from the dishes, and it wasn't until he passed her the plate that Freda realized the largest helping was for her. 'I don't think I can eat all that,' she protested. 'What do you think I am, the ever-open door?'

'I thought you to have an appetite.'

She remembered the enormous meal she had consumed here after Christmas. All at once the sight of the heaped plate made her feel ravenous. She wolfed down the food while the others ate and smiled at her, Sage encouragingly, Doreen with a kind of awe. She was astonished to find when she'd cleared her plate that she was still hungry. 'Have as much as you need, finish it if you like,' Doreen said, and seemed nervous.

Freda had another helping and was hardly aware of eating as she listened to Sage. The sound of footsteps in the street brought her back to herself. She couldn't remember what he had been saying, she knew only that it had made her feel peaceful. The footsteps outside seemed an intrusion from another world, and so did the knock at the front door.

'Freda, this is Rosie Scatchard.' Doreen stood aside so that her friend, who looked daunted, had to step into the room. The woman had large, very dark eyes in a face that was smiling bravely against its lines, and seemed in awe both of Freda and Sage, of Freda perhaps because she barely came up to her shoulder. Freda noticed that Rosie Scatchard had forgotten to varnish her left little fingernail, flesh-coloured when the others were silver, and the sight made her feel protective. She recognized Rosie as the woman behind the sandwich table at the Spiritualist jumble sale. 'Thank you for letting me come,' Rosie said.

'It wasn't up to me.' Freda felt ashamed at once, though she hadn't meant that as a rebuff. 'This is Sage,' she said, to indicate to Rosie where she ought to direct her hopes.

'Oh . . .' Rosie grew tongue-tied as he shook her hand lightly. Freda sank back into her chair, wondering how she could have eaten so much and why. She closed her eyes as Sage jerked the cords to turn out all the wall lamps except one. He sat beside her, while Rosie seated herself nervously between her and Doreen. She wished the room weren't so stuffy with its floor-length curtains and the trapped heat of the gas fire, but she could hardly ask for a window to be opened just now. She kept her eyes closed and listened to the clock, straining her ears to make sure she didn't lose it, and then she was in the forest where the leaves were all the same. She was running through the aisles of trees, running from whoever was there in the forest with her, but the worst thing was that the forest didn't go on forever. There seemed to be nothing but colourlessness beyond the trees between which she was fleeing, an absence that terrified her so much she couldn't look. Wouldn't any kind of companionship be preferable to this? The thought of choosing terrified her too, for once the choice was made or even thought of it would be irrevocable. The forest was growing swiftly dark, which only threw the nothingness beyond it into sharper relief. There was nowhere to run as the birds started singing, and she cried out as a hand grasped hers. It was Sage. 'It's over now,' he said.

Did he mean the séance, if there had been one, or her dream? Presumably the séance, for there was no sign of Rosie Scatchard. Freda felt too enervated to awaken, and could only blink at the room. 'Rosie asked me to thank you,' Doreen said. 'You can imagine how grateful she is.'

She must be talking to Sage; she could hardly be thanking Freda for falling asleep. Freda felt distant and attenuated and, incredibly, hollow. She stumbled to her feet and

301

clung to her chair. 'I think I'll go to bed, if you don't mind. Sorry I was rude.'

'Allow me.' Sage held her elbow lightly, as if she weighed as little as she felt she did. Doreen was frowning, and seemed not to understand what Freda had said. She came to herself just as Freda reached the door. 'Rosie's staying,' she said. 'She's on your floor, in case you hear her and wonder who it is. She doesn't want to go home, not now.'

Perhaps the séance had aggravated Rosie's nervousness. Freda hoped she wouldn't come to her room in the night for reassurance. Freda laboured up the stairs and staggered into her room, and said 'Good night' firmly as Sage held her arm across the threshold. She sat on her bed for quite a time before she felt able to stand up and undress.

She lay in the cool dark where the crucifix hovered above her head, and heard Rosie mumbling across the landing. When she strained her ears she thought she heard a male voice answering. If Sage was comforting her that was fine, so long as he stayed away from Freda's room while she felt like this.

She woke from dreaming that Pentonville had invaded the house somehow and made it endless. She felt walled in by the dark until she switched on the bedside lamp. She didn't want to risk sleep again until she'd had a talk – perhaps she would feel less on edge if she found out what had happened at the séance while she had been asleep. Doreen ought still to be awake. Freda stood up gingerly and put on her coat over her nightdress, then she ventured onto the landing.

She mustn't be fully awake. For a moment she had the impression that the stairs went up as well as down. She crept downstairs, clinging to the banister, and halted at Sage's floor. Yes, it was his voice she could hear, singing in no language, she felt instinctively. Presumably it was a way of meditating. The song was so convoluted it seemed to have no shape; it made her feel unstable, all the more so

302

because somehow she couldn't judge its distance: it didn't sound close, it sounded distant but very large. She opened her eyes when her foot touched a floor that wasn't stair, and then she began to shiver. She wasn't on the ground floor.

It was tiredness that was making her shiver and imagine things, not his voice. Somehow, with her eyes closed, she had only thought she had gone down a flight of stairs. She was still on his floor, his voice was still as close, and she didn't even glance at the landing or the doors as she went down, opening her eyes so wide that they stung. Here was the ground floor where it ought to be, though Sage's voice above her seemed no more distant, seemed to be permeating the house. At least she knew where he was, and so she didn't knock before easing open the door to Doreen's quarters.

The little sitting room was dark. Doreen must be in bed after all, for Freda heard her sighing. Surely that meant she wasn't asleep. Freda made her way round Harry's sagging chair, supported herself just in time on its creaking back to prevent herself from knocking over the chessboard. She seemed to know this room more vividly than she knew her flat in Blackpool. She tapped softly with her fingernails on Doreen's bedroom door, then inched it open.

At first she could see only the pillow, spotlighted by a streetlamp through a gap between the curtains. Doreen's face was there, upturned so that Freda saw her sighing mouth begin to gasp, and so was something else, something soft and pink. Why was the ridge of bedclothes that hid Doreen's body so large? Why was it heaving? Freda dismissed the possibility that occurred to her, because Sage was upstairs, and stepped forward. The next moment Doreen saw her, and what stopped Freda as though a hammer had struck her on the temple was Doreen's face.

If anything could have started Freda from her paralysis, it would have been the defiance in Doreen's eyes. Freda wanted to turn and run upstairs, take her blushing burning

303

face away, for Sage wasn't in his room after all – it must have been a record or a tape that she'd heard in there. The man in bed with Freda was lifting his soft pink head from the pillow, the bedclothes were slipping off his naked back, and she couldn't flee for the thought of seeing what Sage looked like without his clothes. Surely he ought to look paler than this, surely his head ought to. The hairless pink head bobbed up through the wedge of light, it turned on its neck that was soft as a baby's, and he smiled at Freda. She didn't know if it was his smile that made her want to scream or prevented her from screaming.

She knocked over the chessboard as she stumbled toward the hall. She didn't know how many floors she climbed past, but there were far too many stairs. She had a nightmare fear that if she didn't find her floor she would simply keep on climbing. Her legs were shaking violently by the time she reached her room.

She bolted the door behind her for the first time in her life and felt as if she'd walked into a cell. Sage's voice came seeping up from his room, reaching sinuously for her. He had been in his room ever since she had left hers. The man in Doreen's bedroom, the man who Freda knew suddenly had been there ever since the night of the first séance, the man with the pink newborn face that had given her a smile she couldn't mistake, was Harry.

Half an hour into the examination, one of the industrialists raised his head and glared at Stuart as if the questions were Stuart's revenge on the world for all the examinations he had had to sit. He looked ready to stand up and tell Stuart the examination was useless, they were paying far too much money to be told what they already knew, he was going to make sure the media heard about it and exposed it for what it was. Though Stuart didn't believe any of this, he couldn't help hoping wickedly that the industrialist would make a scene. It would be the first time anyone had.

The industrialist was glaring at the problem, not at him. His eyes didn't move as Stuart strolled down the long green room under the fluorescent tubes and tried to make sure his shadow didn't fall on anyone's desk. Now Stuart knew why proctors paced: not so much to make sure that nobody cheated as because there were few more tedious ways of wasting time than sitting at the proctor's desk and staring at the rows of bent heads, staring until you might have thought you were in a wig factory instead of looking at people.

More of the industrialists were frowning or muttering or scratching their heads. Stuart guessed they'd reached one of the logical problems that didn't make sense, hidden among the problems that were capable of resolution. If anyone protested he knew what to say: science was a matter of discovering and showing, not assuming; what people called common sense was liable to point in opposite directions for different people; the examinees might think they knew how they would respond to the paper in front of them, but they couldn't without going through the experience. Some of them were crossing out the question to show they had deduced it was fake, while their neighbours glanced resentfully at them, unconvinced. At least they might be learning something about themselves.

This afternoon would see the sneakiest routine of all, the slide show. He'd tell them they were about to undergo an experiment in perception, he'd flash up a slide and tell them they hadn't seen what in fact they had, he'd flash the slide again and most of them would see what he had told them they had seen. Sometimes arguments broke out when eventually he held the slide on the screen for as long as it took them to see what was there. He knew how they felt, for the first time he'd shown the slides he had almost seen what the subjects believed they had seen. Nothing was more infectious than belief. Why, the only nightmare that had ever disturbed him he'd experienced while Guilda Kent was pursuing her research here on prophetic dreaming.

There it was: he was back to that again. He went to his desk at the front of the room and dumped himself in his chair. Outside the window, beneath the white sky, the snow had retreated to the tops of hills and into the odd copse. He stared out and wondered what else he could do to find Guilda.

Maybe she had left because she'd wanted to work with ordinary people, but that wasn't the whole truth. She'd left because she'd been disturbed by her research. After the experiment had been terminated so abruptly, she'd wandered the corridors as if she were looking for something, she'd hardly spoken to anyone for weeks, and then one day she had resigned and he had never had the chance to look at the notebook in which she had been scribbling observations ever since the experiment began. He'd had the impression that she was uneasy in this building, though he had never understood why. He rather thought she had resigned in the hope that she would find the problems of ordinary people less disturbing. Of course he hadn't told Martin Wallace any of this – thank whoever made things happen that he read *Private Eye* and had recognized Wallace in time – but Wallace's visit had made him feel even more responsible than he'd grown to feel over the years.

It was no use telling himself that it had been Guilda's project, not his, and he wasn't going to try. Even if he hadn't caused whatever had happened, he felt he had made it worse. Something had caused the subjects to experience collective hysteria and perhaps hallucination – he suspected it had affected Guilda, it had almost affected him – and then by trying to reason the subjects out of their hysteria

306

afterward, back to reality, he'd simply aggravated their condition. He ought to have stuck to handing out tranquillizers. Every time he remembered what he'd said to them, said with the calm of total insensitivity, he squirmed. He'd lost more than one girl friend because they'd said he analysed too much, and by God, he had eleven years ago. Of course remembering so vividly was analysing too, and so was realizing that it was, and his mind would turn into Chinese boxes if he wasn't careful. He'd reached the conclusion that he ought to stop analysing himself long enough to see if he could help.

It didn't seem as if he had. The only letter that had provoked a response was the one to Molly Wolfe, and that had brought him Martin Wallace. Perhaps Wallace was a friend of Wolfe, perhaps he hadn't been wanting to investigate Stuart, but Stuart wasn't fool enough to take the risk. Wallace had left him feeling more responsible and more helpless, for Stuart had gained the impression that Wolfe was still affected by her stay here, though he wasn't clear in what way. Were the others ignoring his letters because they had nothing to tell him, or because they had too much to tell? He'd thought some of them were on the edge of sanity that night eleven years ago.

That thought made him squirm too. Insanity was his secret fear; that was why he felt so bad about having helped put Wolfe's mind and the others at risk. Even now he didn't know what Guilda's research had achieved: they'd found a higher proportion of common dreams than average, there might have been a higher incidence of verifiable or likely prophecies; he was prepared to accept that some form of telepathy had been shown to occur, perhaps even that it had proved too intense for the subjects. All that didn't seem to justify the way the subjects had been put at risk.

The bowed heads lowered even more over the desks. Someone groaned, someone capped and uncapped a pen: pop, pop, pop. Stuart sat up so determinedly that half the heads jerked upright, and the man who'd been playing with his pen started to blush. There was no point in Stuart's blaming himself or Guilda for taking risks that had become apparent only retrospectively, but every point in making sure the subjects didn't need help now. The problem was that he felt Guilda would know better how to help.

He shoved his chair back, its rubber feet juddering on the linoleum, and began to pace again. He'd tried every way he could think of to trace Guilda, but the only research establishment she'd worked for after leaving here hadn't heard of her for years. Perhaps she'd left the country; he was still waiting for replies from Europe and America. He hoped one of them would tell him what he needed to know, hoped that he hadn't acquired this belated concern for her subjects and his only to be unable to help.

The industrialists were turning their papers face down to signify they'd finished, they were gazing expectantly or resentfully at him. Christ only knew how the subjects would look at him if he met them. He must contact Guilda first, maybe persuade her to meet them with him. More and more he was convinced that she and her notebook held the key to what had gone wrong eleven years ago. Besides, he wanted to discuss with her the notion he'd had, not quite strongly or clearly enough to mention it in the letters: that in some way it might now be dangerous for the subjects to dream.

The first person to oust Molly from the phone box was carrying an empty jerrican. Molly stood in the glare of the streetlamp and thought the pavement was whiter than it had been when she'd taken refuge less than ten minutes ago. The night was intensely cold: her hands and the breath in her nostrils began to ache at once. She stamped her feet and peered round the phone box at the tower block and across the South Circular Road at the Datsun. She thought it was empty until the vague dark shape that was Terry Mace raised a hand to acknowledge her. She wasn't on her own yet, but she wondered how long she would be once she was inside the tower block.

The man on the phone told someone twice to start dinner without him and stumped out, grimacing as if it were Molly's fault that the light in the phone box wasn't working. At least that helped her hide and made it easier for her to watch. She dodged back into the phone box, which smelled of petrol now as well as pipe tobacco, and willed Rankin to appear. The longer she waited, the more nervous she would grow. Deep breaths wouldn't help, not with the smells in the box.

When someone jerked open the door she swung round, heart pounding like a wound, fists clenched. It was an old woman with a stick and a fierce fixed stare. 'Who's there?' she cried. 'I want to phone.' As Molly squeezed out past her, she wondered if the diversion could have let Rankin past without her noticing. Surely he couldn't have been so quick. She lurked behind the box while the old woman kept shouting, 'I can't do that, I'm blind,' though her stick wasn't white, and then Molly realized she needn't hide, she could very well be waiting to use the phone. She might fail to see Rankin if she hid behind the box. All the same, when she ventured into the open she felt exposed and vulnerable.

She had to step back when the old lady stormed out of the box, waving her stick. Molly dragged the door shut behind her, since the metal arm was reluctant to do so, and tried running on the spot to tame her shivering. If she wasn't careful it would make her feel she was afraid. And then she caught sight of Rankin crossing the road.

He was beside the Datsun. For a long moment she thought he'd spotted Terry. But Terry was still in the passenger seat, and leaning forward now to watch as Rankin crossed to her side of the street. She ran toward him. 'Mr Rankin,' she cried.

At first she thought he hadn't heard. He continued walking towards the tower block, a leisurely self-assured walk that looked studied. He grasped the handles of the doors as she came into their light. 'After me again, are you?'

'I didn't know if it was you at first. I need to talk to you.'

'That's your story this time, is it?' His small sharp face wore an exasperating grin. 'Just passing by, were you?'

'I was looking for a phone that worked.'

'Well, you can't use mine,' he said, and opened the doors as wide as his arms.

'I wasn't asking to. I just want to talk to you. I can tell you about drugs.'

'Changed your tune, have you? Come and tell me all about it tomorrow at the station.' He turned back as he stepped into the lobby. 'Want to know where it is? On Bayswater Road near the TV station.'

She blocked the doors as they swung in her face. 'I don't want to go there, I can't.'

'Afraid someone'll see you there?' When she followed him he leaned against the wall between the pair of lifts, one of which was out of order. 'You could be right. So tell me now.'

'Not here. Anyone could see us.'

'Anywhere in Britain that does suit you?'

'Couldn't we go upstairs for a few minutes?'

'That's what you're after, is it?' He raised his eyebrows ambiguously and reached inside his overcoat. 'Right enough, nobody's going to follow us up there.'

She glanced through the doors as he turned to the lifts. Terry had got out of the car and was watching across its roof. She willed him not to follow too quickly: he knew where she would be. When she looked back at Rankin she found he was unlocking the lift, first the door and then the controls. 'That's the way to keep the vandals out,' he said. 'Only tenants have a key. My idea.'

Terry would have to walk up. She'd prepared enough of a story to keep Rankin occupied until he did. The lift drudged upward, emitting a creak and a muffled twang at each floor, and she felt trapped in the cramped box with Rankin and his sharp pinched face, his skinny restless hands with their nails pared to the quick. It was too like her dream of the police cell. That dream was dealt with; now all she had to do was keep Rankin talking until it was time for what she had foreseen. When she stepped out on the eleventh floor she couldn't separate her nervousness from her relief.

A token burgundy carpet led past identical doors, featureless except for locks and letterboxes. Rankin selected another key. 'What kind of a place do *you* live in?'

'Pretty much like this.'

He grinned as if that were what he had expected her to say. 'Ever make you think of prison?'

That was exactly what his bunch of keys had made her think of. 'No,' she said, 'it's better than where we used to live,' and was afraid he would ask where that was. All he said as he unlocked his door was, 'Maybe it should.'

Standing aside for her made him visibly resentful, and she wondered why he bothered. She would rather have followed him in, so that he wouldn't see her hesitating, though he could hardly guess it was because the thought of confronting the place she had already seen in her dream was almost paralysing her. She made herself step forward, and there everything was: the chest expanders and the wrestling magazines, the immigration reports under the table, the shelf of horror novels, the low cupboard where she knew the rifle was. Venetian blinds hid the windows, a doorway led to a dark kitchen. Though she hadn't noticed the chairs in her dream, canvas on tubular frames, they looked familiar. None of this mattered as much as the ivory figure on the

311

mantelpiece, the identity bracelet round its neck. She made herself look at anything but that, and was sure the newspaper clipping underneath the figure was about Lenny Bennett too.

Rankin chained the door before he followed her along the hall. He threw his overcoat into the bedroom and came uniformed into the main room, where he sat down on a canvas chair and pointed at the nearest. 'So let's hear your tale. Nobody can see or hear you now but me.' His finger lazily indicated the walls around him. 'Soundproof,' he said.

Her apprehension was sharp as a headache: this hadn't been in the dream. 'Completely?'

'Just about, I reckon. No reason that should bother you, is there?'

'There won't have to be, will there?' She was thinking frantically as she sat down. Terry was supposed to whistle 'Rule Britannia' in the corridor to signal he was there, but they had never considered the possibility that she mightn't be able to hear him. She was trying to plan when Rankin demanded, 'Well?'

She could waste time by acting stupid, but she felt as if she was. 'Well what?'

He sat back and crossed his legs comfortably. 'Well, Nelly. That's what you called yourself, isn't it? Well, Nelly, are you going to tell me what you came up here for?'

She mustn't let him feel he was wasting his time. 'I've come for someone who can't speak for himself.'

'Can't or won't?'

'Whichever.' There was no point in playing with ambiguity when it might trip her up. She must tell her lie straight and trust her dream, trust Terry to realize that she couldn't hear him, if she couldn't, and knock at the door. 'He doesn't like the police,' she said.

'But you do?' His grin was wider, his foot in the air was dancing. 'What's his name?'

'Luther.'

'Not Martin Luther?'

'That's right,' she said, trying to think how she and Terry could make sure of filming if Rankin opened the door to him. 'Don't ask me his last name, he said I mustn't tell.'

'Martin Luther, eh? Wasn't he the one who started the church? You'd wonder where they get these names from. You'd wonder who gave them their names.'

She struggled to keep her lie in mind, for the unnatural quiet of the flat reminded her of those times she had thought so deeply that she'd lost herself in silence. It made her more nervous than he did. 'Well, get on with it,' he said.

'There's going to be a big consignment of resin coming in next week. They're flying it in and Luther knows where. He was going to be involved but now he's got frightened. The consignment's too big and the people involved are.'

'Got out of his depth, has he? You'd be surprised how easy it is to do that when you're committing a crime.'

Not quite so easy, she thought suddenly. She'd heard someone coughing beyond the outer door. For a moment she thought it was Terry, who was starting a cold, then she heard the faint slam of a door. She could hear. 'I suppose so,' she said.

'So where are the drugs going to be landed?'

'I don't know. Luther knows.'

He uncrossed his legs and stood up so abruptly that she jumped. 'No use to me then, are you?'

'He'll tell me if I can tell him he won't get into trouble.' The silence had closed in as if the coughing had never been. How much longer would it take Terry to climb the stairs? 'He's afraid he'll be arrested,' she said.

'Why, because he's black?'

'Maybe.' She resisted glancing at the figure with the bracelet round its neck, made herself stare at the wrestling magazines behind him. 'He wouldn't be arrested, would he?'

'You tell me.' Without warning he stalked forward and

313

stood so close to her that she couldn't get up unless she pushed back the chair. 'No, I know what you can tell me – what you're looking for.'

'What do you mean?'

'You've been looking round ever since you came up here as if I'm hiding something. Let me tell you, I don't need to. Not from you.'

She mustn't move or look away. She had a sudden glimpse of Terry toiling up the stairs, and then she wondered if the street doors could have locked themselves, if Terry wasn't in the building at all. 'I wasn't looking for anything,' she said, 'just at your magazines and things.'

'Wondering what a wanker like me was doing with them, were you?' He stooped and before she could stop him, picked up her handbag and put it on top of the wrestling magazines against the wall. 'I'll show you something. Don't mind if I use this, do you? Haven't got a camera in it, by any chance?'

'No, why should I?' His sceptical look as well as his question made her suddenly more apprehensive. 'What do you need my bag for?'

'Just a little demonstration.' His face looked almost disinterested as his fist shot out and smashed her bag against the wall. She heard her perfume spray break, and something else that must have been her pen. She was on her feet at once, her mouth wide open. She'd forgotten who she was meant to be, but it no longer mattered. 'Not bad for a wanker, eh? They teach you how to handle yourself in the police,' he said. 'Maybe now you'll tell me what you're looking for, Nelly Swain.'

He pronounced the name with such contempt it made her shudder. She mustn't make for the door, she hadn't heard Terry. 'Why did you break my things?' she cried, like her alias or herself. 'You'll have to pay for them.'

'Oh, I'm terrified. I'm shitting myself, can't you smell it?' Suddenly his face was wild, his thick tongue was out more than an inch and licking his lips. 'There's what you came for,' he said, pointing at the mantelpiece. 'Go and see.'

She went, because it put distance between them. She faltered before she reached the mantelpiece. The cutting that was pinned down by one corner by the figure looked familiar, the silence was closing in as if she were losing consciousness. By the time she was close enough to see the rust that was blood on Lenny Bennett's bracelet she had recognized that the cutting was about her, complete with photograph.

'There it is,' he said, 'and there you are. And one more thing in case you don't know it – this is the last time you'll try and make a fool of the police.'

His delighted eyes were almost as moist as his lips and chin. He came towards her with small steps that looked delicate. His fists were half open, beckoning her or ready to seize her. The silence had closed in, and Terry wasn't there. She was stiff with panic, yet somehow she felt the silence was hers if she could only use it. 'Don't you touch me,' she whispered. 'Just you try.'

'Oh, don't scare me. I can't move.' His voice was parodying a wail, his paces towards her were even smaller and more studied; yet it seemed to her as if he were really almost wailing, and that he couldn't walk. She knew suddenly that she had to go towards him, confound him that way. She had taken only one step when he fell.

Perhaps he had tripped on the carpet. Perhaps the excitement of what he meant to do to her had proved too much for him, or the sight of her not cowering but coming towards him had. As she moved to stand beside him, well out of reach, he tried to turn towards her, his face growing an agonized purple. He couldn't even shuffle on his knees; he fell on his side. 'What are you doing?' he snarled.

She hoped she wasn't doing anything. It was enough that he thought she was. Though her heart was pounding so hard she could hear it, she was no longer afraid. Someone was whistling in the corridor, Terry was, and she ran to the door.

Rankin began to scream at her as she opened the door: 'I'll get you for this, you bitch.' Terry gaped at him along the hall. 'Jesus X. Christ,' he said, and had to be told to start filming. The door of the flat opposite wavered and then opened to reveal two middle-aged women in dressing gowns. 'What's wrong with Mr Rankin?' one said hoarsely.

'He wants to tell us something,' Molly said, so convinced of it that she didn't bother to think. Terry turned from filming Rankin – who had levered himself to his knees with an effort that left him panting – and the trophy as the women ventured into the room. He filmed them as Molly said, 'Who killed Lenny Bennett?'

Rankin's mouth was working, perhaps struggling not to answer, as the camera returned to him. His eyes pleaded savagely with the women from across the hall, who stepped back, afraid of him. At last his mouth opened as if someone were prying at it. 'I did,' he mumbled, choking.

It mightn't be enough. 'You did what?'

His streaming eyes were growing red with effort or with hatred. 'I killed Lenny Bennett,' he said in a harsh voice that was almost a shriek. 'But it wasn't only me.'

'Who else?'

'Inspector Maitland.' He seemed to be trying to grin viciously until his mouth shook. 'Stop, stop.'

As Molly turned away to look for the phone, he crumpled and fell into a fetal huddle on his side. 'I'll call a doctor,' she said, and as the women began to retreat, 'We'd all better stay until the doctor comes.'

Terry was still filming as he came over to her. 'That was incredible,' he murmured. 'How did you do it?' She wished he hadn't asked; inexplicably, he had almost made her panic. Suddenly she felt that unknowingly she had started something from which there was no turning back.

Danny gazed through his window at the auditorium. Under the bright lights the faded seats looked like almost white cardboard. Mandy and Karen had chased out the last of the audience, three boys who'd been hiding in the Ladies', and now the girls were searching for lost property. He had plenty of time, nothing was going to go wrong. He'd teach Dr Kent to try and drive him mad. Tonight she would learn how mad he could be.

Mr Pettigrew was padlocking the exit doors beside the screen. As he came towards Danny, before vanishing below his field of vision, he glared up at him as if he meant to keep him back after hours.

Danny didn't care. He would still be in time if he ran. His resentment made him feel clear and intense and purposeful, above being confused.

Seven Sisters Road was black with ice. He felt cold as a knife, and as dangerous. Under the streetlamps everything looked flat and thin and unthreatening, a stage for him. He ran up the concrete staircase to his home.

When he heard the television, he went into the parlour. Sydney Greenstreet was saying, 'You're the man for me, sir,' and Danny saw him swelling like a balloon, saw the seams of his suit begin to give, until he looked away: he mustn't let that happen again, especially not now. 'I'm going straight to bed.'

'That's right, Danny, you try and have a good sleep.' His mother gave him a brave, forgiving smile, his father glowered. Danny slammed his bedroom door to make sure they heard, and thought of sighing loudly as if he had climbed into bed, but decided that was too much. He hauled back the blankets and ran lightly to the wardrobe for the newspapers he'd been begging from his mother all weekend.

He'd already tied the pages in knots. Once he had arranged them on the bed and draped the blankets over them, the shape looked very much like someone asleep, even more so when he turned off the light. He crept out of his room and eased the door shut; he tiptoed along the hall and sneaked out the front door, drawing it toward him with his key so the latch wouldn't click.

He was on his way at last. Waiting through the weekend had given him time to enjoy what was coming. His mother seemed afraid of him ever since he'd disconnected the television to stop things changing, and his father hadn't spoken once to him. His eyes were warning Danny not to upset her again, as if Danny wanted to. Danny no longer minded the helpless anger it made him feel: it was something else for Dr Kent to pay for.

The black street seemed hardly there, it was slipping by so fast. Danny trotted the last few yards and turned the corner. Dr Kent was waiting on the steps of the Hercules. This time she didn't take him by surprise, not like New Year's Eve. He glanced along Seven Sisters Road. The pavements were deserted – it was hardly a night for walking – and there wasn't a car on the move. He selected his key as he strode up the steps to her.

'Well, Danny,' she said, 'you certainly like to keep a lady waiting.'

She couldn't have been waiting that long. If she had, he hoped it had made her shiver. He unlocked the foyer doors and waved her in. 'Quick, before anyone sees.'

'Shouldn't we be here?' she said. For a moment he thought she was going to refuse. 'I hope this is worth it, that's all.'

'It will be, oh yes.' He mustn't let her sense his eagerness. He locked the doors and pushed the keys as deep into his trousers pocket as they would go, and wondered what the smell in the dark foyer was. Of course, it was her coat, which looked like leather but smelled like plastic. 'Steps here,' he said as he found his way up to his box.

He switched on the light and closed the door quickly, since she wasn't following him. When he'd turned on the projector and the auditorium lights, he found she hadn't moved. Had she been growing apprehensive, alone there in the dark? No doubt she thought she could get the better of him, but she wouldn't for much longer. He held the doors open a crack. 'See where you want to sit while I get the film.'

'Have you put the lights on just for me? I'm honoured.' When she went in, looking amused and perhaps a shade wary, he closed the doors at once. Hercules Place led nowhere, nobody was likely to pass by, but there was no point in having light visible from outside. He switched on the light in Mr Pettigrew's office just as he dodged in. This was where Mr Pettigrew would keep the film.

He sat in Mr Pettigrew's chair and put his feet up on the desk. 'Come here, Karen, I'll teach you to wipe your nose,' he growled, wagging his finger at the air. 'And Mandy, I'll give you both a wipe you won't like.' He grabbed his mouth to keep in his laughter, in case Dr Kent heard or he woke up Mr Pettigrew's suit on the back of the door. He got up and punched the jacket in the stomach, in case it was one of her spies, and made his way back to the projection box.

Dr Kent was sitting halfway down the auditorium. The sight made him feel even more powerful than sitting in Mr Pettigrew's chair. She must think he'd gone to Mr Pettigrew's office for the film, perhaps she thought he believed there really was one, but she couldn't confuse him now.

He was still savouring the experience of watching her when she turned and looked at him. She must be wondering why the film hadn't started. Though he felt a twinge of panic, he was excited too: it was time to tell her why she was here. But then she hurried up the aisle. As he pressed his cheek against the window to see where she was going, she opened the door behind him and came into the box.

'You haven't shown me where you work. That's your little spyhole, is it? Let me see.' She squeezed past him in the cramped box, and he jumped when he felt the heat of the projector on his shoulders. 'You can see just about everything and never be noticed, can't you? I'll bet it makes you feel big. But there's one thing I don't see, Danny,' she said turning. 'I don't see you putting on a film.'

He started to grin, even though her taking the initiative had stolen a little of his clarity. She was going to regret forcing the pace. 'There isn't a film, is there?' she said. 'There never was.'

'No, there isn't.'

'And your manager didn't send you to Soho. You went there on your own behalf.'

She was smiling sadly at him. Sweat oozed into his eyes, making him blink and feel like weeping, but he mustn't mop his forehead, that would look as if she were bothering him. 'You aren't in Soho now,' he muttered. 'You're here. You can't bother me.'

'Of course I can, Danny, without trying. All women do. That's why you buy those magazines.' She held up one hand to stifle his denial. 'Tell me something, Danny. What would you do, what would you really do, if you got a woman on her own, all to yourself?'

She'd better take care. She was making him feel trapped in the box where there wasn't room for two people, trapped with the heat and the bulky projector and the plastic stink of her coat. He thought he was managing to smile, to show she couldn't bother him, but something inside him was tightening, tightening. He was forgetting what he'd meant to do.

Then he had an idea that delighted him. He could turn off all the lights and leave her locked in. If she tried to break out he would call the police and say she'd broken in – yes, broken in to hide the magazines that were under the carpet she was standing on, to discredit him with his parents and gain more of a hold over his mind. He was inching backward, toward the light switch and the door, when she said, 'I'll make it easy for you, Danny. I know what you're up to.'

His face stiffened, and then his body. His sweat felt like hot salt water that someone was pouring on his hair. 'You've brought me here and locked us in and now we're on our own,' she said. 'All right, Danny, I'm ready. Show me what you want to do.'

He would have if he could. He had only to reach the light switch and dodge out of the door, to the fuses. But he couldn't move, he could only grow tighter inside as she gazed at him and shrugged. 'Just say it if that's easier.'

She was taunting him, doing her best to make him feel helpless. He needed all his energy to fight his body, make it move. She was shaking her head now, pursing her lips sadly. 'Danny, I don't think we can make any further progress by ourselves. I think we have to involve your parents.'

She stepped forward as if she meant to go straight to them. Even if he couldn't move, she wouldn't get past him or the projector. She hadn't reached him when she stopped and looked down at the carpet. Sweat crawled under all his clothes. She had found the magazines.

If she pulled back the carpet, the first thing she would see would be the picture onto which he'd stuck Molly Wolfe's face. He wanted her to know he had seen through them both, knew they were in league, but he couldn't bear the shame of her seeing the picture. His expression must have betrayed his fear, for she was stooping. 'Leave that,' he screamed, and darted forward, shoving her away from the magazines.

His scream had jerked her to her feet but she was off balance as he reached her. Somehow, as if he had dreamed it and forgotten, he knew what was going to happen a moment before it did. He heard it first, the sound of meat thrown into a hot pan, and yet he couldn't quite believe what he was seeing, not until her desperately flailing hands made it clear what it meant for her to fall with the side of her face against the projector.

He backed away towards the door. He couldn't have touched her even if he had wanted to save her, he could only watch. It seemed a long time before she was able to hurl herself backward, crashing into the wall, and he was dismayed by how much of her face she had left on the hot metal. He was still watching when she struggled away from the wall and came towards him.

The sight of her made him cringe inside. Her raw face disgusted him. He would have fled into the foyer, except that she was already too close; he hadn't room to open the door. He couldn't touch her, he could only dodge around the projector.

She was stumbling, hands outstretched, towards where he had just been. He knew what to do without even thinking. He braced his back against the wall and shoved the heels of his shoes against the projector.

When it began to rock, it felt so heavy that he was afraid it would topple towards him. He could feel his shoes beginning to stick to the metal. He shoved with all his strength as it rocked away from him, as Dr Kent turned what was left of her face towards him to see what he was doing. She hadn't time even to throw up her hands before the projector fell, pinning her to the floor.

Though there was room for him to escape, he had to see what happened. Her face and most of her torso were under the projector. Her hands kept trying to claw at it then recoiling, bruising their knuckles against the floor, clawing wildly at the air. The cramped room began to stink of burning plastic and then of something worse. Eventually her legs gave a shove, so violently that her heels tore the

322

carpet, and fell apart limply. After that she didn't move. Nevertheless Danny watched for a while to make sure that she wasn't playing another of her tricks.

The way the metal burned deeper into her fascinated him, but when she or her coat began to bubble like a slug, he clapped his hand over his mouth and hurried into the foyer. When at last he took his hand away he found he was grinning. He had never expected to get rid of her so completely. He dug out his keys and jingled them like bells, and was unlocking the foyer doors before he wondered what he was going to do with her body. He wanted desperately to flee while there was nobody to see him, but he couldn't just leave her for Mr Pettigrew to find. It wasn't even her that bothered him so much, it was his magazines that were under her and the carpet.

He crept back to the projection box and stood outside the door. Perhaps Dr Kent hadn't really been here after all, perhaps she had just been one of the things they put into his mind. When he pushed open the door he was hoping the projector would still be upright, the box would be empty. But her arms and legs were protruding from beneath the metal, the room was full of smoke and an abominable smell.

He slammed the door and thought of the smoke. All at once he knew what to do. He ran into the auditorium to one of the rickety rows of seats. It took him a few minutes to tear a dozen loose.

He couldn't bear the thought of going near whatever was left of Dr Kent until he had to. He climbed on a pile of seats and used one to smash his window. He was retching with the smell before he'd cleared the frame of broken glass. At least the seats would go through diagonally. He posted them all through the window and pulled a few more loose to follow them, then he ran into the foyer, to the counter.

Two columns of the plastic display case were full of matchboxes; the rest held packets of cigarettes. He took one pile of match boxes to the steps outside the projection box.

By now his arms were trembling. He pushed the door open, to see what he needed to do.

The smoke was thicker. Most of the seats that had fallen on or against the projector were smouldering, and so was the carpet; he thought he heard the crackle of wood. The heat made him nervous about going in. He began to throw boxes of matches onto the projector, and he'd thrown about a dozen when the first exploded. Flames sprouted from the nearest seats and raced towards the others, and he flung the remaining boxes into the flames and slammed the door.

He ran into the auditorium. Flames were snaking out of his window, reaching towards the roof like ivy in a gale; the wall above the window was already black. As he watched, the projector's window shattered, releasing flames that clawed at the roof. The fire needed no more help from him. Mr Pettigrew would have to open a video library now. He locked the doors behind him, and grinned with astonishment at how much he'd achieved in one night. He welcomed back his sense of power. He'd dealt with Dr Kent, and soon there would be nobody to confuse him. He only had to deal with Molly Wolfe.

The sound of Joyce's voice woke Geoffrey. When he realized she had been saying good-bye, he struggled out of bed and groped his way into his dressing gown, then he stumbled dozily towards the landing. He shook his head irritably, but nothing seemed to move in there, neither his blood nor his thoughts.

Joyce was emerging from the old lady's room. She gave his arm a squeeze and kissed his cheek. 'I'm in a rush to get started on the painting. You'll be all right if I go now, won't you?'

'I'll cope.' But he clung to the banister and hobbled downstairs after her as quickly as he could. 'How long will it be now?'

'Are you getting fed up, poor old thing? Not long, I promise. They've put the new floor in, and we were only waiting for the plasterers to finish. I won't be any longer painting than I have to be. I want it to look nice and bright for my old folk.' As she opened the front door, she gave him a sympathetic almost guilty look. 'I know you're missing auctions. You won't miss many more.'

His doubts must have shown on his face, for she came back along the hall. 'I'm not hurting your business, am I, Geoffrey? You mustn't ever let me do that. You're more important to me than my old folk are, you're the only one who is.'

'We're doing all right. It's just that I'm selling more than I'm buying. I don't like to do that for too long.'

'I can understand that, Geoffrey. I'll be back as quick as I can.' She leaned towards him to whisper, 'You won't be looking after her much longer. Sometimes I feel we've no time to ourselves any more, don't you? I tell you what,' she said more normally, 'when I've got things running smoothly we'll go away somewhere, shall we? Go somewhere we've never been before.'

'I'd like that. Let's do it soon.' He watched from the front door as she hurried away. A few scraps of snow lay here and there in gardens, and made him think of his dream of the pats of flesh. He shivered and stepped back into the house.

He stumbled blinking to the kitchen. He could bathe and dress later, when the unpleasant part of the morning was over. When he opened the refrigerator, at first he couldn't see the old lady's bowl of mush. Left-over vegetables, a plateful of steak which, as he squinted at it, looked dusty and unreal; for a moment he thought it was the plastic steak from the day centre that had previously been a butcher's. He shook his head as if he could shake out the thought; he was imagining too much these days. He found the old lady's bowl, put it with a spoon on a tray, and carried them upstairs.

He had been feeding her most days since Christmas. When she had refused to come downstairs, they'd taken Christmas to her, first the dinner and then the games. They'd played alphabet games and rhyming games, and when they'd played opposites she'd said the opposite of 'dream' was 'brain.' 'That's clever, isn't it, Geoffrey?' Joyce had said, kicking him surreptitiously when he failed to respond.

It was surprising how quickly he'd grown used to the task, which was almost part of his day now. He knocked at her door, though she couldn't be out of bed. 'Who's there?' she piped nervously. When he went in she said 'Oh, it's Geoffrey' as if she were telling someone else, and he wondered if she were growing worse.

Her head lolled back on the pillow as he set the tray down by the bed, lolled so heavily that he saw the ends of the pillow draw in. As soon as he picked up the spoon her mouth opened wide, displaying her almost white gums and tongue. Apart from saying 'thank you' after each mouthful of mush, she said nothing – had said nothing else to him for days. It seemed her personality was vanishing beneath her fat, which he was sure was growing. He stared into her colourless eyes to avoid looking into her mouth, and wondered what colour her eyes had once been. Every time she said 'thank you,' he filled her mouth again at once, for gazing into her eyes while he listened to her breathing kept making him feel sleepier, in danger of nodding forward, too close to her face.

The scrape of the spoon on the empty bowl made him start. Her lips and eyes were sagging closed. Her brows were so fat now they overhung her eyes; no wonder it was a strain

326

for her to raise her furrowed lids. He laid the spoon in the bowl and held the tray on his lap, and stared at her as her breathing grew deeper. He didn't know how long he sat there, thinking of nothing at all, before the phone rang.

He dumped the tray on the landing and hurried into his office. Once he'd picked up the receiver, he held it while he thought of what to say. 'Geoffrey Churchill,' he said.

At first he thought it was a fault on the line. 'M-m-m – '

Eventually he realized. 'Mr Pelham. What can I do for you?'

'Are you all r – ' Mr Pelham said, and after a few attempts, began again. 'Are you a-a-a – '

'I'm fine, thank you, Mr Pelham. I know I should have visited the lady whose address you gave me before now. Do tell her I'll price her collection soon.'

'I was calling to t-t-*tell* you that the collection has been s-s-s –' It seemed minutes before he managed to pronounce 'sold.'

'Oh, I see. Well, thank you for letting me know, Mr Pelham. I expect I'll see you at an auction soon.' Geoffrey replaced the receiver and wondered why he should feel so relieved that he needn't go to Canterbury, needn't go out at all. Whenever he thought of leaving the old lady on her own he felt the stirring of panic. He could only hope that was all it was, hope that the habit of staying at home hadn't somehow made him nervous of going out. Joyce had enough problems without him.

He unlocked his desk and lifted out the sheets of the new issue she'd brought home yesterday for him from the post office. He ran his ruler down the sheets to help him spot imperfections, but he hadn't examined three sheets before he found his eyes were blurring. He closed them and opened them, gazed at the paintings on the stamps, miniature English landscapes above which the queen's obligatory head was floating in eyeless profile, but that didn't help him rest his eyes; if anything, it seemed to strain them, for he felt as if he were gazing not at the stamps but into them, into tiny windows or screens. Suddenly the landscapes seemed to have too much depth.

When he found he was moving his head back and forth as if he might see around the edges of the paintings, he stood up quickly. Apart from anything else, he needed a bath. He would be letting himself go unless he was careful. He mustn't be a burden on Joyce.

The old lady's breathing followed him into the bathroom. He was so used to its presence everywhere in the house that noticing it came as a shock. He shaved before he ran his bath, so that steam wouldn't fog the mirror, but still the mirror didn't seem clear; he couldn't recall the last time it had. He brushed his hair and went into his office, and then he stood staring.

The old lady must have begun to snore. That was what the squeaking was. It wasn't the sound of a chorus of tiny voices, it couldn't be, yet he could see the heads moving. He made himself go to his desk to prove that nothing was. But all the queen's heads on the topmost sheet of stamps were mouthing and squeaking as they began to float across the tiny landscapes. Though they were all in profile, they were turning towards him.

He grabbed the sheet of stamps and crumpled it between his hands. Something struggled in his fists while the sheet he had exposed began to move. Clouds drifted over the tiny landscapes, the floating heads were chattering excitedly in mousy voices. He gasped and swept all the sheets off the desk, flinging the crumpled sheet after them, and ran downstairs.

At the front door he faltered. It wasn't just the thought of leaving the old lady that stopped him, it was a sudden terrible fear that if he fled he might not be able to find his way back home. Everything stable seemed to be crumbling at once. He must control himself, mustn't let Joyce see what was wrong with him; he simply hadn't realized how much stress he was suffering, what with being unable to leave the house and caring for the old lady and his fears for Joyce. Surely he was too young to be senile. He had managed to calm down and was making his way upstairs for the tray he had left on the landing when someone knocked at the front door.

Geoffrey had to search his mind before he recognized the bony, sensitive face and the single earring. It was Mark, the young poet who'd helped Joyce at her old day centre. 'Joyce is out, I'm afraid,' Geoffrey said.

'I know. Can I talk to you?'

'Of course you may,' Geoffrey said automatically. 'Please do come in.' At least Mark would be company of a kind, though he glanced up nervously at the old lady's breathing. Geoffrey closed the door of the living room after them, but that didn't help much. 'Sit yourself down,' he said. 'Can I offer you a cup of something?'

'No thanks, I'd better not.' He seemed prepared to sit and clasp his bony hands and stare at them.

'Are you still in the same line of work?' Geoffrey prompted.

'Old people, you mean. Yes.'

'Joyce found a new centre, you know,' Geoffrey said.

'Did she?' His face brightened, looked relieved. 'When?'

'Before Christmas. She's been refurbishing it ever since.' Geoffrey faltered. 'What on earth is wrong?'

'Mr Churchill, I don't quite know how to say this, but – have you been to see her new place?'

'Not yet, no. I've been looking after one of her old people, as a matter of fact. Why?'

'Please don't be angry, Mr Churchill.' Mark pulled at his cheeks with his knuckly fingers, peeling the flesh of his cheeks from his eyes. 'I work in the West End now,' he said as if this were an answer. 'I take the bus past Hyde Park every morning, and the same way home at night – I like the trees.' He gazed harder at his clasped hands.

'What I'm trying to say is, most days I see Mrs Churchill. Joyce.'

'What, near Hyde Park?'

'On Bayswater Road.'

Geoffrey shook his head. 'You must be mistaken. That isn't where she's working.'

'I thought I was mistaken too. I got off the bus the day before yesterday to make sure. It really was Mrs Churchill. Yesterday I tried to talk to her, but she didn't know me. Mr Churchill, she hasn't found a new centre at all. She just wanders up and down Bayswater Road as if she's waiting for someone.'

What drugs have you been taking? Geoffrey wanted to demand. You look the type . . . But he wasn't quite sure enough of himself to ask. Suppose Joyce had finally gone the way he'd been afraid she would after Oxford? 'Are you saying she's there now?'

'I'm sure she is, Mr Churchill. I'm sorry.'

'Don't be. You can help instead.' Geoffrey stood up and held the door open. Now that his fears had come true he felt almost relieved; at least it seemed he could do something. 'I told you one of the old ladies you used to look after is staying. If you'll keep an eye on her, I'll find Joyce. I'll be as quick as I can.'

As soon as Mark came into the hall, Geoffrey hurried upstairs. When he reached the top, Mark was hesitating halfway up, gazing towards the breathing. 'Which old lady?' Mark whispered.

'I don't know her name, and I don't think she does. You'll know her when you see her.' Geoffrey was murmuring impatiently through his cupped hands so that she wouldn't hear. 'Very fat and almost bald.'

Mark stared at him. 'There was never anyone like that.'

'Of course there was. Don't be absurd.' Geoffrey was sure he'd seen her at the centre. 'Please be quick. I must find Joyce.'

He opened the door of the old lady's room as Mark ventured onto the landing. Geoffrey had to beckon him before he would step forward. 'That's the old lady I mean,' Geoffrey murmured. 'Recognize her now?'

Mark barely glanced into the room before he recoiled. Geoffrey wouldn't have believed he was capable of turning so much whiter. 'I can't go in there. It isn't – ' Mark muttered as if he didn't care if he were heard or didn't know what he was saying. 'I did my best, Mr Churchill. I told you about Joyce.'

Geoffrey glanced into the room as Mark fled towards the stairs. For a moment he could see only something pale and very large that hung down from the bed in several places. He squeezed his eyes shut and opened them, and there was the old lady asleep. He must have been seeing the blankets. A moment after the thud of Mark's feet at the bottom of the stairs, Geoffrey heard the slam of the front door.

Mark must be on drugs, Geoffrey thought. But did that invalidate everything Mark had said? Geoffrey wasn't sure. He put on his overcoat, but by the time he'd buttoned it and taken hold of the lock of the front door he knew he couldn't go. He couldn't leave the old lady by herself.

He didn't need to go to Joyce, he could talk to her when she came home. He hung his coat on the hallstand and climbed the stairs into the slow deep breathing. The sheets of the new issue were waiting on his desk. Perhaps he wouldn't tell her about Mark after all, it would only disturb her unnecessarily, and in any case he had almost forgotten what Mark had said – something about the old lady, some nonsense. Mark shouldn't be looking after old people if that was how he felt about them. The breathing settled around Geoffrey, slow and heavy and somehow vulnerable, as he drew the ruler down the first of the sheets. If Joyce mentioned Mark he would tell her what had happened, warn her against him. If there was one thing besides the stamps he was sure of, it was that he didn't want Mark working with her in her new place.

As Molly went into Mrs Shankar's grocery shop a woman said, 'If you ask me, they gave him drugs.'

Her friend or her daughter, whose headscarf just reached around her piled hair and her chin, disagreed. 'Why should they want to do that?'

'To make him say those things. Don't try and tell me he'd have said them otherwise. You can't believe a word someone says under drugs.'

Mrs Shankar gave Molly a shrug as if the women were nothing to do with her, but Molly couldn't see why it should matter. 'Just some glue,' Molly said, and Mrs Shankar went into the back room, where she kept glue so as to be able to tell children she hadn't any. The older woman came to the counter at once and stood tapping her toe irritably, as if she had been ready to be served when Molly had jumped the queue. 'Are you asking me to believe that a policeman – a *policeman*, mind you – would confess all that in front of a camera?' she demanded, and Molly realized what the shrug had referred to.

'He might if he'd felt guilty.'

'Never. Never in this world, Irene. You've been seeing too many films. If you ask me, these television people faked this film just like they did the other one.'

I wasn't directed at Molly, whom she clearly didn't recognize: there was no reason why she should. Mrs Shankar appeared with the glue and another shrug. 'I never was convinced they faked the other one,' Irene said.

'Then you need your head examining.'

'Says you. Who said it was fake? Only the police. They

said the writing on the wall couldn't have been there, but they would, wouldn't they?'

Molly intervened before she knew she meant to. 'Actually, it wasn't only the police.'

Irene gave her a resentful glance. 'So they scared someone into saying it. You would if the police got hold of you, wouldn't you?'

'No,' Molly said.

Irene looked disbelieving beyond words as she turned her back on Molly. 'And that policeman saying he was in church all the time. The cheek of him, saying he was in church.'

Molly couldn't stop herself. 'But he was.'

Both women turned on her. 'What do you know about it?'

'It isn't worth it, Molly,' Mrs Shankar said as she handed over the tube of glue, and Molly had to agree, though the women were nodding as if they thought Mrs Shankar was talking about her prices. As Molly went out Irene said loudly, 'Some people will say anything to get attention.'

The street was growing colder. It had been shady all day, since the January sun couldn't crane above the roofs. The conversation in the shop had made her nervous, with its fantasies of what had happened, for she wasn't sure what had happened at Rankin's herself. It must have been real – enough people had said so, including the police – but she was beginning to wonder if anything was.

She let herself into her flat and glued together the kitchen drawer that had fallen to pieces. She held pieces together while they adhered, and wished that she could put her life together that simply too. She'd thought of nothing but the episode at Rankin's for days, though thinking was hardly the word. Couldn't he have suffered some kind of nervous paralysis – the doctor had said so – perhaps brought on by guilt, and couldn't he have confessed out of terror? He had certainly seemed unstable enough. All the same, her doubts about precisely what she had achieved and how were among the reasons she hadn't yet called Martin to tell him his reputation was secured. Besides, she thought it would be like offering him compensation for his father's death.

Later she met Leon and his lover in a restaurant that overlooked Tower Bridge. Rain streamed like ink down the windows, the bascules of the bridge rose into the dripping night as strips of bright windows were drawn silently through, ebony funnels glistening. Molly sipped her Harvey Wallbanger and wondered why Leon's lover, Michael, a graceful young man with oval eyes that looked Oriental and large pink delicate ears, had taken an instant dislike to her.

'Have you heard from Martin?' Leon said.

'Michael glanced sharply at him. 'Not yet,' Molly said.

'Nor I. And you haven't called him? You don't want me to, do you?'

'Not unless you want to,' she said.

'You should, even if it's just to say how are things. He may be waiting to hear from you. And you'd have good news,' he said, draining his tall glass of gin and bitters, 'on the whole. They've got to take him back now, they just want it to seem like their idea. It's best he waits while they come up with a way that will save their faces and get them the most pulicity, of course.'

'If he still wants to come back.'

'I hope he does. I near as dammit told them they could stuff my job if they took their mistakes out on him.'

'I'm sure he's grateful to you, Leon.'

'So long as he is to you.' He sat forward and squeezed her hand. 'You really shook them up, you know. They don't know what to do with you. I think they'd like to have you as an investigative reporter, except for Eccles and except they're afraid you might investigate too much. Their story is you're so *unstable*, of course,' he said, breaking suddenly into camp, 'she can't be *trusted*, we don't know what she might *do*. They'll take you back as Martin's assistant, no doubt, and probably make reluctant noises. My advice is you should start finding out who else might take you on as a reporter. I'm surprised you haven't been approached already.'

Michael looked offended by Leon's display of camp. 'Leon must be very fond of both of you to go to so much trouble,' he said.

'God, you're a jealous bitch sometimes.' Leon grasped Michael's hand in both of his until Michael managed to smile at him and stopped trying to pull away. 'Listen, I'm not *interested* in Martin, in case that's what you think. Anyway he's a good straight Southern boy. It's this lady here I'm trying to look out for, more than Martin. I just want to be sure things stay good for her now.'

'I expect they'll work out, Leon. Maybe I'll call him later,' she said, though she didn't think she would: she didn't think she would be able to avoid trying to explain what she had done to Rankin, and the strain would only make her unhappier if she restrained herself. All at once, out of desperation, she said, 'I dreamed all that about Rankin before it happened, you know.'

Michael clicked his tongue at her. 'Good heavens, aren't you already famous enough?'

'Tell me about it,' Leon said.

She might as well now, though she wished she didn't have to convince Michael too. 'I've been able to forsee things ever since I can remember.'

'You never told me.'

He sounded accusing. 'By the time I knew you,' she said, 'I thought I'd lost the knack.'

'But you haven't?'

'Apparently not. As I said, I dreamed I saw Lenny Bennett's identity bracelet in Rankin's flat.'

'I wondered how you knew. Christ, was *that* how?' His eyes were wide, his gaze held hers. 'You're not just spinning us a yarn? It's the truth, hand on heart?'

'I promise.'

'Jesus. It does make sense, it's the only explanation that does. You couldn't have known any other way. I wonder what it tells us that nobody thought to ask how you knew.' He rubbed his temples. 'This is quite a shock. Give me a few minutes to take it in.'

Michael was staring at her with undisguised scepticism. 'Be careful, Leon. Don't go rushing into anything.'

Leon patted Michael's hand. 'Would you be willing to talk about it, Molly?'

'I am. I haven't finished. I'm not sure that I'm just foreseeing things any longer. I feel as if my dream somehow made Rankin confess.'

'I can't imagine how you could feel that way,' Leon said. 'But what I meant, Molly, was would you be willing to talk about it to the camera?'

'I don't know. Suppose the police tried to use it to discredit us?'

'Fair question. I don't see how they could, but on the other hand, you'd be making a claim you couldn't prove. All right, that wouldn't be a good idea.' His tentative smile was a plea. 'But I'll tell you, Molly, I'd love to make a film about you.'

'That's very flattering, Leon, but – '

'It's not flattering at all after what you've just been saying. I'd like to start filming now, this week. Do you remember most of your dreams, or do you think you could?'

'I suppose so,' she said, remembering Oxford. 'I used to be able to.'

'Maybe you could write them down as soon as you wake and then we'd film you talking about them, say once a week. We'd date the sessions so that nobody could argue later. Can you tell at the time which dreams will be prophetic?'

'They're more real,' she said, which seemed inadequate.

'Of course we'd check all of them, and if enough of them

proved accurate, maybe you could talk about Rankin after all. Will you think about what I've said, Molly? I'd take it as a great favour. I realize you might not want that kind of exposure. I'll respect your decision if eventually you say no.'

'I will think about it.'

On her way home, Molly wondered if Leon's proposal might help her achieve whatever she was capable of. She made her way down her frosty steps and selected her key, which burned like ice. She was slipping it into the lock when she hesitated. Was someone waiting in the flat for her?

It must be Martin, for nobody else knew where she kept the spare key, but why would he be waiting for her in the dark? She felt as if the apprehension she'd experienced the first time she had seen him had reached its point at last. Of course, he must be sleeping after his flight. She let herself in and went into the bedroom. But her bed was empty and so, when she switched on all the lights, was her flat.

She was almost asleep when she realized the flaw in Leon's proposal. If they broadcast her talking about her dreams, mightn't the others who had been at Oxford contact her? She still felt they should stay away from one another. All the same, if MTV reinstated her she must try to get Joyce on the air despite Ben Eccles.

She felt asleep happily, only to dream that the others had found her and they were all dreaming together. She had to stop dreaming before it was too late. She struggled to wake, and then she was afraid to, because whatever was waiting for her to awaken was worse. She couldn't prevent herself from wakening now that she'd fought the dream. She jerked and awoke.

Surely it had only been the dream that had made her afraid of waking. She opened her eyes and saw her room, the dim patch of light that seeped through the curtains and hovered on the wall, the leg of her old toy monkey poking out from under the pillow. She turned over to put herself back to sleep, and froze. A man was standing in the doorway of her bedroom.

A pulse began to pound in her throat, which seemed to be swelling up; she felt she might never draw another breath. Her nightmare had come true at once, and all she could think was that she'd had years to move the phone into her bedroom from the hall, where it was useless now. She was inching out of bed and trying to think what she could grab for a weapon when he switched on the light. It wasn't Danny after all, and how could it have been? 'Oh, Martin,' she cried, 'thank God it's you.'

His face went blank so quickly she couldn't tell what his expression had been. 'Who were you expecting?'

'Nobody really. I was just dreaming.'

'Sure you were. Seems as if you don't do much else.'

She knew he blamed her, she could hear it in his voice, and she didn't know if going to him would simply antagonize him further. 'Have you just go in?' she said, ignoring his coldness. 'I'll make some coffee.'

'Forget it. Stay where you are.'

She'd expected blame, but this felt more like hatred. 'Martin, what's wrong?'

'What's wrong?' He raised his hands as if to spread them incredulously, except that they were fists. 'Now what do you think could be wrong? My father's dead. Try that for openers.'

'I know.' She couldn't let him stand so far from her and work himself into a rage. She swung her legs off the bed. 'I'm sorry.'

'Stay there!' Rage convulsed his face. 'Goddam it, why the good Christ did you have to wake up? I just wanted to see how I felt about you after your crazy damned dreams kept me away from my father.'

'Martin, I tried to stop you going to Oxford, if you remember. I know you went for me, and I'm sorry. I don't

338

know what else to say.' She held out her hands as if that would open his fists. 'Won't you come here? You look so tired. When did you last sleep?'

'What the fuck does that matter?' The blankness of his face was worse than his rage; it looked as if he had no feeling left for her. 'Maybe I should go to sleep and dream I got to my father in time, okay? Maybe for you it would be just like the real thing.'

'Stop it, Martin. You're only hurting yourself.' She stood up. 'Or say it if it makes you feel better. Just don't tell me to stay away. You mustn't tell me what to do in my own flat.'

If she went to him and touched him, he would have to respond somehow. She crossed the room to him. 'Martin,' she said gently, and reached out for his hands.

He spoke before he moved. 'Know why I had to come back here last time? Because you wouldn't even leave me alone when I was with my father. All that shit about the film got me so confused I ended up telling him about it and that was the last I ever saw of him, you fucked-up, meddling bitch.'

The only warning she had was a gleam in his eyes, so harsh that it made them look blank. She thought he was lifting his fists out of her reach until he punched her in the face.

She staggered back against the wall; her shoulders felt as if someone had hit them with a plank. Her left eye was already puffing up and closing. The sight of him through one eye made him seem even more unreal than his action had. He was grinning as if to control an atrocious pain. 'That's what reality feels like,' he snarled. 'You never would believe I had a temper, would you?' Before she could say anything, he punched her in the mouth. She didn't know how many more times he hit her before a blow to her chin smashed her head against the wall and into blackness.

44

Eventually Mr Pettigrew gave up trying to persuade Danny's mother to leave them alone. 'If you can't say whatever you have to say in front of me,' she told him, 'you shouldn't be saying it at all.' He sat with his back to the aquarium while Danny's father stood beside it, and both of them glared at Danny. At last Mr Pettigrew said, 'Well, what about it?' in a voice that shook with suppressed fury.

His arrival had been almost a relief. Now at least Danny could talk about the Hercules. When he'd woken this morning, an hour later than usual, he'd had to pretend it was like any other morning, he'd had to get dressed and behave as if he were getting ready for work. He'd been so on edge that he had thought the knock at the door was the police. When he'd heard Mr Petigrew saying that the cinema had burnt down last night, he'd felt clear and refreshed, just as he'd felt on waking. They couldn't prove anything.

'What about what?' he said.

'What did you leave on the projector last night?'

'I didn't leave anything.' Danny looked innocent, and why shouldn't he? Mr Pettigrew was trying to make out he'd left something there that had caught fire, but all he had left on it was some of Dr Kent's face. 'You'd have seen if I had, wouldn't you?' he said with sudden delighted cunning. 'You were going round checking when I left.'

'That's right,' his mother said fiercely. 'Of course Mr Pettigrew would.'

The manager glared at Danny as if he wanted to glare at her. A fish sailed up behind his head like a thought in a cartoon.

'Fires don't just start,' he muttered. 'Someone or something started this one.'

'Oh, I'm sure you're right,' Danny's mother said.

Danny waited for her to go on. When he realized she had no more to say he said, 'I know who might have.'

'There, you see,' his mother said. 'Just give Danny a chance and listen to him for a change.'

The experience of being listened to by both his father and Mr Pettigrew was so novel that Danny almost forgot to go on. 'Those boys who went in the Ladies' last night, they were throwing cigarettes before.'

'They ought to be horsewhipped,' his mother said – it wasn't clear for which offence.

'What did they look like?' Mr Pettigrew demanded.

'I didn't really see,' Danny said.

'The girls must have. I'll ask them. By God, if it turns out to be those little bastards – excuse me, Mrs Swain – but if it turns out to be those sweet little darlings I'll see that they wish they'd never been born. And their parents. I'll get them in the papers, by God. I bought that place forty years ago and I've run it ever since. It was more my home than anywhere else ever was. It had a personality, didn't it, John? Insurance won't bring that back.'

'I thought you were thinking of selling it,' his mother said, and started at his father when he grimaced at her. 'You mightn't have got so much for it if you'd sold it.'

The manager opened his mouth and closed it again, and shook his head as if she couldn't be expected to understand. 'We'll take a look at what's left if you're ready, John,' he said to Danny's father. 'Danny, the police are over there sorting through what's left. They want a word with you.'

'So long as it's in front of me,' Danny's mother said and could hardly wait until the men left before she turned furiously to him. 'I don't know how he dared, as good as saying you started the fire. We could take him to court for libel if we wanted to.' She came to Danny and held him by the shoulders, knelt down in front of his chair, so that her face was level with his. 'Tell me the truth, Danny. You didn't have anything to do with it, did you?'

Her breathing was growing wheezier, he thought she was going to have an attack before he could make himself say, 'No.'

'Of course you didn't. You mustn't think I thought you did, I just wanted to hear you say it. I'll tell you who I think started the fire – he did, to get the insurance money. That's why he tried to make out it was you. Did you notice he could hardly look at me? That's why, you mark my words.'

Danny was glad when she let go of him. 'I'll have a lie down,' he said. When she looked anxious he added, 'Since I haven't got to go to work.'

'That's right, you have a rest so you'll have your wits about you for the police.'

He wanted to get away from her, for her protectiveness wouldn't let him think. Something Mr Pettigrew had said was troubling him, but he'd forgotten what it was. He sat and gazed through his bedroom window at the shades of grey that seemed to be merging above Seven Sisters Road, and then at his wardrobe. Was there a clue in there? He opened the doors and found his extra suit. It looked like a hanged monkey, dangling arms and short legs, another hollow figure that his enemies could hide in to spy on him. It wasn't until he tore at the buttons and threw the jacket open so that nobody could hide in there that he remembered the letter in the breast pocket.

He unfolded it and read it again before he put it back. He was pleased to have remembered it; Stuart Hay would have to be dealt with as well. He was obviously in league with Molly Wolfe. All the same, the letter was confusing him. He felt as if it ought to help him remember what Mr Pettigrew had said.

He went to the window, as if that might open up his mind.

Two policemen came strolling along Seven Sisters Road from the direction of the Hercules, and Danny dug his fingertips into the edges of the window frame so that he wouldn't panic. He had to remember, because he thought they would ask him about it, whatever it was. Should he say that the boys had started the fire or that Mr Pettigrew had? They couldn't blame Danny – his father had said the place could catch fire and he wouldn't notice. It was Mr Pettigrew's fault for not having the extractor fan fixed. Perhaps he'd left it because he was hoping the place would catch fire. That must be the truth, and Danny would tell the police so; his mother would back him up. Still, he didn't feel safe any more; he couldn't remember what they were going to ask him.

It couldn't be about Stuart Hay. It was even less likely to be about Dr Kent, when she was out of the way for good. The two policemen were staring up the path at him, and he didn't care if they could see that he was grinning defiantly. Then his head jerked back as if someone had seized him by the neck, arrested him. He had remembered.

Mr Pettigrew had as good as told him. He'd said the police would want a word with him once they'd looked at what was left. The police must have seen what was left of Dr Kent. They must have found her bones.

He began to dodge round the room, his knuckles pressing into the sides of his skull as if the pain might somehow control the writhing of his mind. He was dodging from corner to corner with no idea where he was going. He kept hurrying to the door and flinching away, his head tightening. He wanted to tell his mother what he'd done to Dr Kent and why, tell her before the police did, but he had no time. When he looked out of the window there was no sign of the police. They must already be on their way up.

His mother mustn't know. That seemed to clear his mind. He must say he wouldn't talk until they took him to the police station. He would have to insist that they took only him. She would try to stop him, perhaps she'd say that she would never speak to him again, but he was doing it for her; he mustn't let her change his mind. As soon as the police took him outside he would get away somehow, to deal with Stuart Hay and Molly Wolfe. He mustn't let himself be locked up until he had finished off his enemies.

He ought to go to the front door, to be ready to let the police in. He opened the wardrobe and lifted his overcoat from its round wooden shoulders. Shouldn't the police be at the door by now? Or maybe they were still at the Hercules.

He hung up his coat and slumped on the bed, and then he made himself sit up. He ought to go to the Hercules so that they wouldn't need to come to him. He must, because then his mother wouldn't see them. He was rubbing his forehead savagely as if that would stop it tightening when someone knocked at the front door.

The next he knew, he was crouching in a corner of the room, hugging himself with his crossed arms, clawing at himself. Even when he heard his mother going to the door, he couldn't move. He heard the front door open. When he cried, 'Who is it?' it was almost a scream.

He heard his mother's footsteps in the hall, and managed to shove himself away from the walls. He dug his hands into his pockets so violently that the material felt in danger of tearing. Perhaps he looked all right now. But she didn't come in when she opened the door. 'It's a doctor,' she said.

He thought he was going to be sick with relief. Only a doctor, and past time she saw one. He was glad when he heard her close the front door, for it had let in a stench of burning that made him choke. She and the doctor were coming down the hall – a woman doctor, if the footsteps were anything to go by. She would keep his mother busy while he slipped out to the Hercules, to the police. He bit his lip and made himself stop wondering how long it might be before he saw his mother again, and where.

But his mother was opening his bedroom door. The doctor had halted outside too. The stench of burning must be overpowering, to have lingered so strongly; as the door opened he had to press one hand over his mouth and nose. It couldn't be doing his mother's chest any good, but as she came in quickly and closed the door behind her, she only seemed a little awed. 'She wants to see you,' she whispered.

'Who does?'

'The doctor. She won't tell me what she wants. She seems very nice, polite, and everything.' His mother stepped away from the door and reached for the knob. 'She says she's Dr Guilda Kent from Oxford.'

His mother couldn't have said that. She had been facing away from him. His mind was playing tricks on him, or somebody was. But the smell of charred meat flooded into the room as his mother opened the door wide, the smell he'd tried to close in the projection box, and he would have backed into the corner and covered his face except that his mother would see. She stood aside, and Dr Kent came in.

'Well, Danny, this is a surprise, isn't it,' Dr Kent said. 'I expect you thought you would never see me again.'

She wasn't marked at all. She was smiling at him as if she wanted him to see the joke. He clenched his teeth until they throbbed, but his lips were twitching; he was afraid he was going either to laugh or to scream.

Dr Kent looked disappointed. 'Nothing to say for yourself?' She glanced pointedly at his mother and back at him. 'If I were you I shouldn't leave all the talking to me.'

Even if he found words, he couldn't bear to open his mouth while the stench filled the room. The throbbing of his mouth was spreading into his skull and down his neck. Either she hadn't been real last night or she wasn't real now, he told himself over and over. It didn't help. His mother frowned and nodded at him to tell him he was being rude, to make him speak.

'Is it how I look that's bothering you, Danny?' Dr Kent

pointed at the side of her face. 'A woman's secret, that's all. We both know I don't really look like this.'

Danny ground his knuckles into his lips. Her face was blackening, her eyes had started to glaze and swell, first the left and now the right. He didn't know if his mother was able to see this, but even if she wasn't, she would soon know what he had done. He would have to tell her everything once he began to scream.

He was stumbling towards her before he realized what he meant to do. Above all he couldn't bear her knowing. Her neck would be thin between his hands, he wouldn't need to squeeze for long, she wouldn't have time to feel much pain, she had enough trouble breathing as it was. Anything was better than the pain and shame of her knowing.

He reached for her, and then he threw himself aside, clenching his hands into his fists. Good God, what had he almost done? He was as crazy as they wanted him to think he was. He screamed at the door as he wrenched at it, managed to turn the doorknob and flee along the hall, away from his mother's anxious face and reaching hands and something blackened beside her with no eyes. They'd made him crazy at last, Dr Kent and her fellow conspirators.

Perhaps they hadn't quite. Now he was out of the building, away from the threat of his mother, his mind was clearing. He couldn't go back home, but then he had been planning to leave anyway when Dr Kent had appeared. It occurred to him that Dr Kent had been intended to keep him away from Molly Wolfe. They hadn't confused him, they had been too clever for their own good. They had shown him the truth.

By the time he reached the pavement he was almost calm. He had eleven years' experience of resisting nightmares. He strode towards the station as if he were out for a walk, and ignored the people who stared at him. They must be wondering why he was out without a coat on such a wintry day.

Saving his mother, or getting away from her, had made him sure of himself. He knew where he was going. He caught the train to Oxford Circus and then to Notting Hill Gate, and didn't look behind him once. When he emerged onto Bayswater Road he made his way past the estate agent's, up the slope of the side street, down the steps beyond the railings, and stooped to the niche where he'd seen Molly Wolfe find the key. It was there. He let himself into her flat without making a noise and tiptoed quickly into the nearest room, the bedroom, eager to begin.

The room was empty. So was the rest of the flat. It was a few minutes past eleven in the morning; she must be out at work. He could wait, he would enjoy waiting, planning what to do to her. Tonight wouldn't be like last night with Dr Kent, over too quickly. He was going to take his time in making sure that Molly Wolfe was real.

45

Molly came to herself slowly, and wasn't sure that she was. How could her bedroom seem so distant and somehow muffled, even if she couldn't open her left eye? It took her a while before she realized she was lying on the floor in a corner of the room. When she made to get to her feet she cried out. It was pain that was between her and the room.

He mouth felt huge and misshapen and immovable, and she was afraid to touch her teeth, even with her tongue. Her left eye felt as if it were swelling out of the socket. Now that she'd moved she could hardly breathe for the pain in her ribs. She stumbled into the hall, holding onto the wall, and made herself look in the mirror.

Her lips were twice the size they ought to be, her eye was black and swollen shut, her body was a mass of bruises. It took her minutes of touching herself gingerly and resisting the instinct to bite her lip before she was sure that her ribs weren't broken. Martin had done all this to her, Martin as he really was and had warned her he was – and then she saw that he'd ripped the telephone cord out of the wall.

Was he still in the flat? The thought – the fear it seized her with – was worse than the pain. She went through the flat, every step an agony, and flung open all the doors. She was alone. She bolted the front door and limped into the bathroom, expecting the pain to make her sick.

She couldn't think about last night. Even to begin to think about it made her weep, made her swollen eye sting horribly. She had to get away, that was all she could think of, before he came back.

She must go to her parents. She hobbled into the bedroom. Getting dressed took half an hour, and she didn't care if the secretaries upstairs heard her cries. Then she remembered that Leon was waiting to hear from her about his proposal. She'd go to him on her way to Kings Cross. He ought to be at work now, it was after ten o'clock. She realized she wanted him to see what had been done to her.

She thought she would fall before she reached the foot of the hill. At least a taxi for hire was passing on Bayswater Road, and screeched to a halt at once. 'My God, love, you've been in the wars,' the driver said angrily. 'Which hospital?'

Molly had to tell her twice that she wanted to go to MTV. 'I work there,' she said, which seemed so grotesque she didn't know whether to laugh or sob. Her mouth reminded her not to do either.

The taxi made a U-turn and sped towards Marble Arch. The driver helped her out onto the MTV forecourt. Molly would have asked her to wait, except that it might take a while to find Leon.

Several reporters piled after her into the lift, almost crushing her until they saw her condition. 'That'll teach you to wear your seat belt,' one said. As she got out on the fourth floor she heard another saying, 'I wouldn't put it past her to have beaten herself up.'

She found Leon in the studio, chatting to a tall man with a brush of grey hair at last six inches high. As soon as Leon saw her through the glass he jumped up. He looked appalled and then dangerous as he excused himself and came out to her. 'Molly, who did that to you? Those fucking police?'

His assistant had run to her with a chair. 'It was Martin,' she said.

'Martin *Wallace*?' She heard him grind his teeth. 'Why?'

There was so much anger and despair in that one word that she was nervous about replying. 'He lost his temper. He was always telling me he would.'

Leon turned to his assistant, perhaps to get control over himself. 'Tell our friend I'll be a few minutes and then you could get the first-aid box, there's a dear.' He lost control again as soon as he looked at Molly. 'Martin isn't here yet, I don't think,' he said , 'but when I see him – by fuck, when I do . . .'

'You mustn't do anything you'll regret, Leon. It's over, that's all.'

'I won't regret it, believe me. If I don't do it for you, I'll do it for myself. I'll make sure the bastard stays away from you if I do nothing else. Will you have someone to stay with you in the flat?'

'No, I'm going to my parents.'

'At least you'll be out of the way, thank God.' He followed her as she limped after his assistant to the nearest dressing room. 'Was that what you wanted to tell me?' he said hopefully.

'And that I'd really rather not make that film. You understand, don't you?'

'You didn't come here just to tell me that – ' He gazed at her bruises when she took off her sweater. 'My God, Molly, oh, Jesus.'

'Look, it was my fault as much as anyone's. I'll tell you why one day.'

'All right, stay here while I interview this bloody poet. I'll get rid of him as soon as I can and take you to the station. Half an hour. You can rest on the couch.'

'Thanks, Leon, but I want to get going. The sooner I'm home the better I'll feel.'

'Martin won't find you here, I promise.'

'I know.' Nevertheless that was what she was determined to avoid. 'I'll be all right. I got here on my own, didn't I?' Nothing he could say would persuade her. As soon as his assistant had finished, Molly got dressed with her help and kissed Leon's cheek before she limped away.

She felt easier once she was out of the building, but not for long. Not only were there no taxis to be had, she now realized she had no clothes to take with her. She would have to go back to the flat. It was after eleven, there would be plenty of people about. There was no reason to suppose Martin would be there; now she thought about it, the key had been in the niche under the steps. She wished she had taken it with her, but surely he wouldn't come back. In any case, if he did no doubt he would be desperately contrite. He'd better leave at once, that was all.

She limped home, the air smarting her bruised face. Once she reached the shops, there were crowds. She passed W. H. Smith's and made for the path between the traffic lights, then she grabbed the pole of the nearest to stop herself. Martin was standing on the corner of her hill.

He didn't look at all contrite. His face was dark with fury – he must have gone back to her flat and found she wasn't there. His father's death must have driven him crazy. She limped into the nearest side street for fear that he would see her and come running.

It led to Nell's. The thought of explaining her state depressed her, but where else except Nell's could she hide until Martin gave up? She went as fast as she could, she was ringing the doorbell before the pain gave her the chance to realize that Nell would be at work.

She was turning to hobble away when the door opened. It was Susan. 'Oh, poor Molly,' the child said. Perhaps she was home from school because it was lunchtime, or perhaps she was ill; Molly was too relieved to care. Susan let Molly in and matched her pace on the stairs. Either she didn't want to know what had happened or felt she was too young to ask. Her disinterest was so welcome that Molly felt like weeping.

The green room was cool and calming. Susan stood by the couch to show her where to lie down. 'Better not have anything to drink just yet,' she said, and Molly marvelled at how old the child seemed. She lay down and closed her eyes, and felt safe. She thought that Susan had begun to whisper to her, or perhaps even to sing her a lullaby, as she fell into a peaceful sleep.

Martin disembarked at Heathrow in the early afternoon. The Customs officers clearly knew who he was, and one kept him waiting while another took his passport away. Eventually they gave it back and let him go, having made sure he understood that he was in the country only by their leave. Their eyes were blank as cameras. So long as he saw Molly first, he didn't care if they sent him back.

The Underground took most of an hour to get him to Gloucester Road. Daylight made him blink and grin. On his way to Kensington High Street he decided he would call Molly as soon as he'd dumped his luggage.

He wished he could have called her from Chapel Hill. But he hadn't wanted his mother to hear him telling Molly that he didn't blame her for keeping him away until it was too late. Of course she hadn't, he'd done it to himself, out of aimlessness as much as anything. He'd begun fiercely to resent her when he had learned that his father was dead, but he'd dealt with that feeling. If he was seeking anything to blame, he would have to start years earlier, pick through the whole unsatisfactory jumble of his life.

He let himself into the mansions and pressed the button to call the lift. The faint squeak of the descending cage caught his throat; the empty sound reminded him how empty his mother's house was now. He'd held her last night as she wept and he'd wept himself, for her and his father and Larry and lost opportunities. 'Come back soon' was the last thing she had said to him. 'You have to bring Molly to see me, you hear?'

He hadn't liked to leave her, though her friends visited constantly, though she had insisted. 'You go back to that girl of yours before someone steals her,' she'd said. He hoped to take Molly home soon – perhaps they could find work in America. He no longer felt so inhibited about making films there. He'd realized why his English work was so unsatisfactory: he had been too concerned what his father might think, no longer able to trust his own instincts.

He clashed the gates together, unlocked his door, and went into the bedroom to dump his luggage. Someone, two people, was in the four-poster bed.

The girl's face peered shocked around the man's hairy shoulder. She looked remarkably young, especially next to the man's long white hair. As he turned towards Martin his face went pink, red, purple. 'Who the devil are you?' he shouted. 'What do you mean by walking in here?'

Martin felt a wild urge to act out the situation as comedy: do a double take, retreat to the outer door to see if the number was right, go to the mirror to see if he was someone else . . . But the long-haired man had recognized him.

'Oh, I see,' he said contemptuously. 'You must be the American.'

'One of them,' Martin admitted as the girl hid her face behind the man's shoulder.

'I'm assuming you were not told this is no longer your flat. Presumably the message went astray.' He glared at Martin with a coldness that almost managed to seem righteous. 'Will you please leave? You can see you are causing embarrassment. If it's your belongings that concern you, they have been moved. I have no idea where.'

Martin gazed at the couple in the bed he'd shared with Molly, and somehow couldn't look away until he knew what they meant to him.

'What do you want?' the man spluttered.

'Maybe just to know who you are, since you know me.'

'Never mind who I am. Have the goodness to leave before I call the police.' Then his pride got the better of his caution. 'That is who I am,' he said ominously, pointing to a National Theatre poster he had stuck to the wall. 'I wrote that and other plays you may have seen on Broadway. I mean to write a play for television, but by heaven, I won't be doing so if this is an example of the treatment I can expect from your people.'

'They aren't my people.' Martin had tired of him. 'May I use your phone, the phone?'

'If you must.'

Martin went into the hall and dialled Molly's number, but it was unobtainable. He knocked on the bedroom door and called, 'Enjoy the accommodation,' before heading for Bayswater Road.

When he rang Molly's bell, there was no reply. The key had gone from its niche under the steps. He rang the bell again, for it made him a little uneasy that the curtains were drawn. Eventually he made for MTV, reminding himself to find out where he'd been rehoused.

Leon wasn't in his office. Martin looked into his own in

case Molly might be there, but there was nothing to be noticed in the room except a faint musty smell. He ought to go up and find out where he was living now, except that he was growing anxious about Molly, he didn't know why. He went down to the studios and found Leon in the middle of an interview.

Leon caught sight of him through the glass. 'You fucker,' Leon mouthed.

He couldn't be serious. Martin had enough to deal with already without this. 'How do you mean?' he mouthed back.

'How do I mean?' Leon was shouting now. He turned to his interviewee, a man with a shock of grey hair: 'Look, this isn't working. Too many interruptions. Let's do it in the open, all right? Film you in your countryside. I'll be in touch.' He stalked out while the man gaped after him, and advanced on Martin so violently that Martin had to make himself stand his ground. 'What do you want here? Looking for Molly?'

'Sure, if she's here.' Why should that make Leon shake with rage? Martin was suddenly afraid for her. 'What's the matter, Leon?'

'What's the matter? You shit, you fucking shit.' He beckoned his assistant with a gesture that came close to scratching Martin's face. 'You saw Molly Wolfe. Know what this bastard just asked me? He asked me if anything's wrong.'

His assistant, a motherly Cockney who could outswear anyone in the building, gave Martin a single contemptuous glance and grasped Leon's arm in her large hand. 'Ignore him, Leon. He isn't worth it. Let the police have him.'

'She'd have been better off with Ben Eccles. To think I persuaded her to work with this . . .' Leon looked as if he could weep with rage. 'I need my fucking head examined.'

Martin was losing his temper. 'Look here, Leon, I don't

354

know what you're talking about. What's wrong with Molly?'

'What's wrong with her?' It was somewhere between a scream and a humourless laugh. 'Jesus Christ, what's wrong with her as far as you're concerned is that she's still alive, I should think.'

'Leon,' Martin said as calmly as he could, 'I give you my word that I don't know why you're talking to me like this. Has Molly tried to harm herself?'

Leon actually screamed. 'Has she what? Right, of course, why didn't I think of that? No wonder she looked such a mess if she had to punch herself in the face until she knocked herself out. All the same, it must have been hard for her to kick herself in the ribs.'

Martin felt as if a band were tightening on his skull. 'You're saying *I* did that to her?'

'I'm saying it? No, you cunt, you turd, you shit. It's what Molly said.'

For a moment Martin almost felt he might have done everything he was accused of. If Molly believed he had, wasn't that as bad or even worse? He couldn't speak, couldn't think. Leon seemed to have lost impetus too. 'Why did you do it, Martin?' he said almost sadly. 'Because she got you back your job? Because she tracked down the cop who killed Lenny Bennett all by herself so that our bosses would have to admit you were right after all? Didn't you want her to help?'

It was too much all at once. Martin was beginning to wonder if Leon had flipped. 'I didn't know about any of this.'

'She wanted to wait and tell you when you came back. And you never even gave her the chance, did you, you fucker.'

'Leon, I haven't seen her for more than a week. I only got back here a couple of hours ago. If she really thinks I hurt her, I mean if she thinks she actually saw me, things must have got too much for her, these dreams and all that stuff.

355

She seemed pretty close to the edge when I went away. I wouldn't have gone, except I had to.'

Leon looked as if he could spit in his face. 'Christ, you'd say anything, wouldn't you?'

Martin almost tore his pocket as he dragged out his passport. 'Leon, will you look. There's the date I came back, on the visa. Today's date.'

'Right, today's date. The day you beat her up. It doesn't prove a fucking thing, mate. Pity they let you back in.'

'Leon, I came in less than three hours ago. For God's sake, if you don't believe me, call Heathrow.'

For the first time Leon seemed doubtful. 'Maybe I will. Just go away now, Martin, all right? Maybe I'll be in touch.' He shook his head as he realized what Martin was thinking. 'Don't go looking for Molly. You won't find her.'

'Take me to her, Leon. You must. I give you my word she'll be safe.' Martin hardly knew what he was saying. 'She needs help.'

Leon stared blankly at him. 'I've no idea where she is, Martin, and if I had I wouldn't tell you.'

Martin turned away, because he felt ready to grab Leon and choke him. He headed for the lifts and out of the building. Though he was hardly aware of his surroundings, he knew where he was going. It wasn't only the thought of the drawn curtains that was driving him back to Molly's, it was the belated impression that he'd heard someone moving stealthily beyond them.

The key still wasn't under the steps. She must have taken it from its niche to prevent him from going in to her. He tapped gently on the window. 'Molly,' he said, trying to keep his voice low, 'it's Martin. Please let me see you. If you won't open the door then come to the window.' He was still knocking on the glass when the van screeched to a halt by the railings and two burly policemen came clattering down the steps. 'Don't try anything, mister,' one said. 'Just get in the van.'

Martin controlled himself as he never had before. 'I can explain. Just let me explain,' he said as they took hold of him. 'My girl friend's in there. She needs help.'

'We know all about her. It isn't help she needs.'

'My God, you've been watching the place because of what she did.' Martin forced himself not to struggle. 'Look, I'm sure she's in there. If she isn't, you know where she is, right? I need to see her, she's in trouble. You've nothing to arrest me for.'

'She's in trouble and so are you.' Their grasp was bruising his arms. 'As for the rest of it, neither of you are that important, if you want to know. The neighbours called us because someone was breaking in down here, and that's why we are formally arresting you.'

It might be true, for Martin heard a window slam on the second floor. The realization came too late. Everything that had been happening to him exploded all at once. 'Goddamn it, you know where she is,' he yelled. 'I have to go to her.'

They mustn't have expected him to struggle, for suddenly he was free and lurching towards the steps, so fast that one of the policemen tripped on them and fell. Martin didn't get far, A blow on the back of his head with a truncheon knocked him down, the weapon was heavier than it looked. Though the women on the second floor were watching, the policemen clubbed him twice as they dragged him up the steps to the van.

Geoffrey was cutting himself a piece of bread when he heard the knock at the front door. It threw him. He stared around the kitchen and couldn't recall where he'd put the butter, couldn't even remember which meal he was trying to make himself. Outside the window the light of the flat sky was neutral, which seemed to suggest noon. Presumably he was making lunch, though he couldn't recall when he had last eaten: sometime yesterday, he must assume, after he'd come home from visiting Joyce's new day centre. Hadn't that been the dinner at which the meat in the stew had tasted like plastic? He must have been tired, that was all; he still was. It took a repetition of the knocking to remind him that someone was at the front door.

He dusted crumbs from his dressing gown as he made his way along the hall, and had to switch the knife from hand to hand. He mustn't rush, he wasn't getting any younger, and it annoyed him when his visitor knocked a third time. 'Yes, yes,' Geoffrey muttered angrily. Perhaps it was his peevishness, or the sight of the knife in his hand, that made Mr Rowley step back.

'Oh, Mr Rowley.' Geoffrey just managed not to admit he'd forgotten that Mr Rowley had made an appointment; it was enough of a shock to himself. 'Do come in.'

The stamp dealer looked troubled as he ventured into the hall. 'I was just preparing lunch if you'd like some,' Geoffrey said, hoping there would be enough bread and cheese for them both. Mr Rowley shook his head, and still seemed troubled. Perhaps the old lady's breathing was bothering him.

Geoffrey let him go first up the stairs. 'You know the way, Mr Rowley. I have to take my time.' He expected Mr Rowley to go into the office, but the dealer waited for him at the top of the stairs. 'Forgive me prying,' he murmured, 'but what's wrong with Mrs Churchill?'

'Nothing at all. Why do you ask?' Of course, he meant the breathing. 'That isn't Joyce, it's an invalid lady we're taking care of.'

He found the key of the safe in the pocket of his dressing grown and stooped to the lock. He carried Mr Rowley's stamps to the desk. He turned back to close the safe, and then he clung to the edge of the open door. There was something in the safe it was crucial to remember.

He was still peering into the safe when Mr Rowley finished examining the stamps. 'These are highly satisfactory, Mr Churchill,' he said, and cleared his throat. 'I hope you won't think me presumptuous, but we've known each other for a number of years. May I ask if you've been to see a doctor? You don't look at all well.'

Geoffrey was touched, knowing what an effort Mr Rowley must have made to break through his reserve. 'Just tiredness, Mr Rowley. Nothing to worry about.' He hoped he didn't sound abrupt, but he'd realized what was in the safe: Stuart Hay's letter. He needed to remember what that meant, what it should remind him of. 'May we talk business now?' he said.

Mr Rowley named a price. 'Fine,' Geoffrey said, but Mr Rowley looked more dismayed than he had at the front door. 'Perhaps you could hold on to the stamps for me, Mr Churchill. I have to come to London for a sale next week.'

'I assure you, Mr Rowley, your price is quite acceptable. It always is.' Geoffrey didn't want to be distracted from the letter in the safe, not even by haggling. 'By all means write me a cheque.'

Mr Rowley did so reluctantly. He locked the album in his briefcase and gazed at Geoffrey while Geoffrey willed him to leave, twisting the cord of the dressing gown in his fists. At the front door he said, 'I do hope you will consider my advice, Mr Churchill. Surely it will do no harm to consult a doctor.'

'You have my word I'll think about it. I do appreciate your concern.' Geoffrey closed the front door and trudged upstairs, wondering what possible use a doctor could be.

In his office he found he'd left the safe open. That showed

359

how tired he was. Nobody could have got into it while he was downstairs but all the same, his carelessness dismayed him. He stepped forward to close the safe.

He was too eager and too exhausted. As he pushed the heavy door he lost his balance. Without thinking, he grabbed the upper edge of the safe, and the door closed on his thumbnail. He snatched out his thumb before it could take the full weight of the door, but even so the pain made him dizzy so that he fell into his chair by the desk. The pain jarred him out of his stupor: he had meant to leave the safe open to remind him what it contained.

He made himself get up immediately and grope in the safe with his left hand. He couldn't use his other hand; the nail was black, his thumb felt like a rotten tooth. When he found the envelope, he didn't need to look inside. It was reminder enough by itself of all that had happened eleven years ago, and of why he was staying at home: to make certain that Stuart Hay didn't trouble Joyce. He mustn't leave it on his desk in case she saw it. He felt calm as the breathing that seemed to fill the house. He levered himself to his feet with his good hand, to replace the letter in the safe.

But the pain in his nail was nagging at his calm. It felt worse now that he'd stood up. He sat down again hurriedly. Now the letter was nagging at him. All at once he dragged back the flap with his good hand and fumbled out the letter.

He read it slowly and shook his head. He read it again and wondered why he should have thought it could tell him anything. Either his concentration or the slow calm breathing was making him forget the pain in his thumb. He had been right before: the letter was eleven years out of date. He pushed it back into the envelope. Thank heaven Joyce hadn't seen it, it would only make her worse – and then he remembered why the letter was crucial: it reminded him that something was wrong with Joyce.

360

He clutched the sides of the desk as memory came flooding back. The pain was helping him now. There was no day centre: Joyce went out every day to wander the streets. He couldn't have seen the day centre; he must have dreamed he had. He wondered dizzily what else he might have dreamed, but he had no time to wonder. He must think what to do about Joyce.

The breathing stifled his attempts to think. He closed his eyes exhausted and thought of what Mr Rowley had said. He wished he could thank the dealer for telling him what to do. He reached for the phone to call the doctor.

The holes in the dial felt too small, seemed not to be where his eyes told him they were. He could use his right hand, his fingers weren't injured, but now the holes felt even smaller, and he could hardly make out the numbers. The plastic of the receiver had begun to feel soft as the breathing that surrounded him. He managed at last to dig his forefinger into one of the holes, he squinted to see which number it was, and then he cried out. He'd forgotten the doctor's number – there was nothing in his head except the sound of breathing.

He threw the receiver on the desk, hoping the thump would waken the old lady, but the breathing never faltered. He found the address book in his desk drawer and thumbed through the pages with his left hand – the pain in his injured hand was growing worse – until he turned up the number at last. It was no use. The phone felt soft as old flesh into which his fingers were sinking. He flung it away, onto the floor, and stumbled out to his bedroom.

Even the jangling crash of the phone hadn't disturbed the breathing. As he struggled to dress, the inescapable slow sound kept making him forget what he was doing. He was dressing, he couldn't sit round all day in his dressing gown. Hadn't he forgotten to wash? He hadn't time now, he must go down the hill to the doctor's, except that now he had forgotten why.

He lurched ouf of the room, his shirt half-buttoned inside his jacket, his belt so loose he felt starved, and was almost at the old lady's door before he realized what he meant to do. He couldn't stand her breathing any longer, he had to stop it somehow. Gasping, appalled, he reeled away to his office.

The letter was still on his desk. That was why he must go to the doctor's, to ask him to come and see Joyce. Not only Joyce – Geoffrey needed treatment himself – he must, to have such feelings about the old lady. He had to get out of the house before he could harm her. He crumpled the letter in his hand so as not to forget what he was doing – he must tell the doctor about his lapses of memory too – and made for the stairs. He had just reached them when the old lady called, 'Geoffrey.'

She sounded weak and plaintive and afraid. How could she know he meant to leave her? How could he be so callous as even to consider doing so? Then he remembered what he might have done to her, remembered the doctor, and he fled downstairs, almost falling headlong. He shrugged on his overcoat so hastily that the sleeve caught his injured nail and made him scream. He opened the front door with his good hand, and stumbled along the path. He was at the gate when he saw Joyce.

She came running to him from the end of the street. 'Are you going out?' she demanded. 'I had a feeling you were.'

She couldn't mean that the feeling had brought her home. 'Just to get the doctor,' he mumbled.

'Why, what's wrong?' When he hesitated, not knowing what to say, she cried. 'What's wrong with her?'

'Nothing. I'm the one who needs the doctor.'

'I can't see anything wrong with you, Geoffrey. You look fine, tip-top.' She was rubbing her hands, against the cold or nervousness. 'If you need him, call him. I have to go straight back to the centre.'

Which centre? The question might have destroyed her

362

pretence, and her with it. He would have died rather than ask. He found he was shaking. 'You'll have to stay in the house for a few minutes,' he said. 'I'll be as quick as I can.'

When he tried to sidle round her, she stepped in his way. 'I can't wait, Geoffrey. They need me right now. I shouldn't have come away at all.' Perhaps she could see that he didn't believe her, but did she believe herself? All he could see was that she was desperate. 'At least come in the house and tell me what's supposed to be wrong with you that you need the doctor. We don't need to argue out here.'

'I haven't time to argue at all.' The thought of going back in the house made him panic. 'The sooner I go, the sooner I'll be back. Look, this needs seeing to.'

He held out his injured thumb and realized that he was still clutching Hay's letter. He hid it behind his back, swallowing the terror that the possibility of her seeing it had brought to his throat. She was holding his right hand gently, turning it over to examine the thumb. 'Good heavens, Geoffrey, that's nothing. I can bandage that for you.'

'It's worse than it looks.'

'I didn't mean the pain. I know it's painful. I know you're a soldier, you always were. I can treat it for you, that's all I'm saying. I did use to be a nurse, you know. Or don't you think I'm any use any more?'

Her look and her voice made him want to weep. He was screwing up the letter behind his back. He'd throw it away, make sure she never saw it; she must never realize what was happening to her mind. But he knew suddenly that unless he went to the doctor now, unless he got away from the house, he never would. 'It isn't just my thumb,' he stammered. 'I only did that because I was so tired. I need a tonic to buck me up.'

'You don't need to go to the surgery for that. I'll get you one from the chemist's. I know the best one, I was a nurse.' She was crying the words after him as he stumbled out of reach towards Highgate Hill. He couldn't look back until he reached the corner of the street, in case the sight of her made it impossible for him to go on: she was unlocking the front door. Absurdly, he thought he heard the old lady's breathing.

The High Street plunged toward the steeper slope of Highgate Hill. Both seemed dauntingly steep, far more so than he remembered; his legs were already aching. If he couldn't walk home he would hire a taxi.

He stumbled downhill. His steps felt awkward, uncontrollable, as if the slope were already too steep for him to be able to stop walking. He clutched the letter more tightly to make sure he didn't forget where he was going. He hardly noticed the crowds he was weaving through, the shops that rose past him.

Each step made his ankles throb, and he had yet to reach the steepest part of the hill. He glanced round at the noise of cars, the noise that seemed almost as regular as breathing, but there was never a taxi. It dismayed him to think he was looking for one to take him downhill. He must need a tonic more than he'd realized.

He turned away from looking, and felt dizzy. He was going so fast now he thought he would never be able to stop. It was as if the thaw hadn't happened, as if the cold that was making him shiver had turned the slope into ice. He grabbed the corner of a shop front and lurched to a halt in the doorway. He stepped back at once, to make way for the old man who came limping out of the shop.

But there was nobody. The shop was locked. The glass of the door was reflecting the street and himself, limping backwards, backing away from the sight of himself. He turned away choking and almost fell. He couldn't really have looked like that, it had been only a glimpse. He stumbled away wildly, away from the reflection, away from the slow regular sound of cars passing that made him unable to think, that seemed almost to be stealing his breath.

Before he knew it he was past the shops, on Highgate Hill. The slope seemed almost vertical. He grabbed railings to slow himself down, and soon his good hand was bruised. Why did he bruise so easily now? At least his pains were bearable, perhaps because the slow regular sound of the traffic blotted them out somehow; it was almost suffocating. He looked round uneasily, wondering how it could be when so few vehicles were passing.

Suddenly he was in Hornsey Lane, where there was no traffic. The relief of walking on a level pavement was blissful, and he was nearly at the viaduct before he realized the sound hadn't faded at all. It was behind him, all around him. He felt as if he were in someone's dream, could hear their breathing. He fled to the viaduct and clung to the railing, but even the view was no use. Nothing seemed real, not even the dome of St Paul's. Nothing was real but the breathing, nothing could keep it away.

It had blotted out his thoughts, driven him off course. But it hadn't won yet – he still knew where he had to go. He must go down to get help. When he glanced over the railing, it didn't look too far. He must do it, for Joyce as well as for himself.

At first he couldn't. It was too much of a struggle to shake off the breathing, to move in its midst at all. He tried again, dragging at the railing with both hands. His legs were agony, the stonework scraped his ankles as his feet slipped, but now one foot was over, the rail was digging into his groin. He had only to step down, he could do it easily, and he would have left the breathing behind. Someone was shouting, perhaps at him, but he lifted the other leg over the rail and let go with his hands. The rush of air swept the breathing from his ears at once, but he couldn't understand at first why it was taking him so long to touch the ground – long enough to realize that he wasn't going to fall on the pavement but among the traffic lanes, where the lorries were thundering by. Long before he got there, he was trying to take his fall back.

Molly dreamed she could change everything. There would be no more poverty, no more wars, no more famine or disease or any kind of suffering. Tall graceful buildings shone above the wide streets full of smiling people, fields and forests glowed on the hills, rivers glittered on the mountains. She climbed the highest mountain and stood on a rock amid the dazzling snow and ice while mirages of all the cities in the world came riding the clouds for her to see. Each one looked perfect, each omen made her feel even happier. She knew she was dreaming: she had to know, to be able to dream everything right. She would have to dream everything constantly, never letting up for an instant; she would have to dream everything in the world simultaneously. Now she could feel the indescribable burden of all that responsibility, the strain of having to sustain that dream, and then she realized that was what she was doing. The idea was so terrifying that she woke.

Thank God it had been only a dream – but she wasn't in her room. Or if it was, it had changed. It was green and full of plants. Perhaps her dream had made them grow. She widened her eyes and turned her head desperately, then she let out a shuddering sigh of relief. Susan and Nell were sitting opposite her, watching. Of course, this was Nell's flat, not hers.

Looking around had made her face ache. It felt like a mask that was too small for her, particularly around the right eye and the jaw. When she sat up she felt as if metal bars were locked around her body, tightening when she breathed. She remembered why. 'How long have I been here?' she cried.

Nell sat forward reassuringly. 'Just a couple of days.'

'Good God, I didn't meant to stay that long. I mean, thank you for letting me stay, but I've got to go now. I'll feel better once I'm there.'

'Where, with your parents? You don't want them to see you looking like that, do you?'

Molly couldn't recall saying she was going to her parents; she could remember nothing after lying down here on the couch. At least her head felt clear for having slept, despite her aching body. Perhaps she had talked in he sleep. 'Do I look that bad?'

When she made to push back the blankets, Susan jumped up. 'I'll get a mirror.'

She brought a hand miror and squatted down with it in front of Molly. The bruised face in the mirror looked even less like Molly than she'd felt. She looked away before she could start weeping with dismay and rage and weakness. 'The doctor said it looked worse than it was,' Nell said.

'Which doctor?'

'He only woke you for a moment. I'm not surprised you don't remember. He examined you the day you came here. He said all you need is to rest for a few days.'

Perhaps she did, for she kept thinking it was Susan, not Nell, who was speaking. 'Stay over the weekend,' Nell said. 'There won't be many trains, and they'll be crowded.'

'When's the weekend?'

'Now.'

That didn't sound right, but then neither did the impression of two voices speaking, Nell's after Susan's. 'It's very kind of you, Nell,' she said and stared at herself, at everything Martin had done. She stared for so long that Nell said anxiously, 'Do you want to talk about it?'

'Just what you'd assume, Nell. Someone I thought I was safe with.' Again she felt in danger of weeping, though it infuriated her that she should. It must be exhaustion, not grief. She musn't break down in front of the child, and so she looked away towards the mantelpiece, at a photograph of Susan in her first school uniform. The face in the photograph looked oddly unlike the Susan who was watching her now. 'I know there are men who think we're for knocking about when things go wrong for them, but I never thought I'd get involved with one. They think we're their property to do as they like with.' She remembered Nell was divorced. 'I don't suppose I'm telling you anything you don't already know.'

She began to breathe deeply, to calm herself down. Nothing was wrong with the photograph now that she looked again; clearly nothing could have been – it could hardly have changed. Susan seemed to know what her breathing was for – Molly wondered how she could – but Nell said, 'Are you all right?'

Molly let out a breath with a gasp; she'd forgotten how bruised her ribs were. 'It's just a way of breathing. I learned it years ago, after – ' She was tempted to take Nell into her confidence, tell her about Oxford and her dreams, but she didn't know how Nell would take it; nor could she see how it could help. 'When I went to a meditation class,' she said.

'That's what you need,' Nell cried – Nell, not Susan. 'That would help you get over what happened. I know where there's someone who's meant to be excellent.'

'I'd just like to rest, Nell, since you offered. I don't feel up to going anywhere.'

'I don't mean now.' Molly thought Susan was shaking her head too, until she glanced at the child. 'Before you go home,' Nell said.

'I think when I go I'd like to go straight home.'

'Which way will you go? Which station.'

'Kings Cross.'

'Well, there you are,' Nell said triumphantly. 'The place I heard about is just near Kings Cross. You could go there on your way, on Monday.'

'I don't think so, Nell. Thanks for the thought.'

Nell seemed determined to keep on, until she glanced at Susan. 'I've got to go shopping,' she said, sounding surprised. 'Susan will stay with you, won't you, Susan?' Molly must have looked nervous, for Nell said, 'You'll be all right, don't worry. We'll make sure he never finds you.'

Molly stood up to go to the bathroom and cried out, her legs were so stiff. Walking was painful, sitting down was worse, and she remembered only just in time not to bite her swollen lip. When she returned to the couch, Nell was gone. Susan watched as Molly eased herself under the blankets. 'I'll read to you if you like,' the child said.

'That would be nice.' Molly was touched by the child's concern for her, though she would have liked to select the reading matter herself. It seemed to be a book of fairy tales. Before long she found her attention was wandering, even though she enjoyed the sound of the child's quiet confident voice: she read like someone much older than her years. Molly gave up trying to follow the story and closed her eyes. She could imagine she was a child again, being read a bedtime story. That would help her rest, she could already feel how deeply. As she dozed she felt very much like a child, long before Oxford and self-consciousness. This was peace, and she had almost forgotten what it was like – this eagerness to dream, this sense that dreams were the most natural thing in the world and capable of anything. If she let herself, she could imagine that that was exactly what Susan was reading to her, but she wasn't going to struggle awake just to prove her imagination wrong. As she drifted into sleep, she was smiling.

When she had finished dressing, Freda realized she was afraid to go downstairs. She lingered at the mirror as if she wanted to make sure of her appearance, as if she were really going down to dinner. If she met anyone, she told herself, they would think she was; they would think she needed feeding – her face had never been so thin. She stared at her starved face until she realized it wasn't the mirror that concerned her, it was the window. She was listening for sounds of the street, but she could hear no sound out there at all.

The street was out there. She mustn't indulge her fear, mustn't part the curtains to prove it was still there. She must get out of the house while she had the strength.

If she still had. As soon as she turned off the gas fire she began shivering. It might well be colder outside, yet she couldn't wear a coat in case someone saw her on her way down. She didn't know where she would make for once she was out of the house, she could only tell herself she would know what to do once she was. She felt as if the house itself were making her unable to think of leaving it, the house and Sage and the suffocating happiness and peace.

She gazed at the crucifix above her bed as if that might help. All that pain and suffering seemed unnecessary, beside the point, despite everything it promised. Christ had had to go through all that to make sure he was remembered, to convince people there was a life after death, but now there was no need to take it on trust: Sage was here to show that there was.

That was what Sage wanted them to think. She wished she could feel more ashamed, more sacrilegious, for that might keep her mind clear. She placed her hand on the nailed feet as if that would give her faith. She couldn't ask for much, not when she hardly ever went to church, but surely God would come to her aid now if he existed. Surely he would want her to escape the house and its temptation.

The crucifix felt like wood and cold metal. Her lack of response did make her a little ashamed. As a child she'd believed God was in every image of himself, even before she'd learned that he was supposed to be in every wafer at

370

Communion. Trying to imagine how it must be for him to be in so many places at once had made her head spin. She wished she could recapture that awe, just for a few minutes, just to concentrate her mind until she was out of Doreen's house.

It wasn't Doreen's house now, it was Sage's. If there was still a crucifix in his room, what might it have turned into? The idea terrified her; she didn't know where it had come from, didn't want to glimpse what it suggested. She let go of the nailed feet, ran out of the cold room to the stairs, and started down at once. Somewhere voices were murmuring, but otherwise there was no sound except for the creak of a stair. She mustn't tiptoe in case she was seen, she must walk down as though she were on her way to Doreen's quarters, walk down the cheerful stairs with their green carpet, their polished banisters that gleamed under the bright lights. Except that the stairs didn't look cheerful now, but harsh, unfamiliar, menacing. If she met anyone she dreaded, she would be able to see far too much under the lights.

Perhaps it would be Sage. Suppose he already knew where she was going? She could imagine how gently and irresistibly he would ask her to stay – his eyes had been telling her for days how much he and the others needed her, how important she was. Her fear might help her resist him, make her able to dodge past him. But it wasn't Sage she was most frightened of. She was afraid of meeting Harry on the bright deserted stairs.

She ought to be overjoyed Harry had come back. But that was the trouble: apparitions never lasted longer than the séance that produced them, she knew that much. And she didn't want to be a medium for what Sage was doing.

But what was that exactly? If he was giving people what they most wanted – giving the bereaved their loved ones, giving her a peace she could find nowhere else – what did *he* want? She could no longer believe he wanted purely to help people. They were giving something to him that he needed, and never noticing that he was taking it from them.

She wouldn't be a party to it any longer. Freda hushed her thoughts, for she was nearly at Sage's floor – the floor below hers. She made to step down, then she clung to the banisters and began to shiver. The floor that was just a step out of reach wasn't Sage's floor.

It was even more brightly lit than the stairs. She could smell the new green carpet that covered the landing from wall to wall; she could see beyond the open doors into the empty rooms, if they were empty. She hung on to the banister with both hands and made herself look down the narrow stairwell. She looked once, she looked away and tried again, and at last she clambered backward up the stairs, never letting go of the banister. There were so many floors down the well she couldn't count them.

She didn't dare risk getting lost in a house that was turning into something else. She realized suddenly that since the night she'd gone down to Doreen, someone had always taken her downstairs to her meals and ushered her back to her floor. She fled into her room without looking to see if the stairs continued upward, for she was almost sure they did.

She sat on her bed and told herself that when they next took her downstairs she would make a run for the street. She'd meant to do that every time, she had tried walking towards it until they steered her gently away. They could be gentle, since the séances had left her with so little strength. But perhaps she could reach the front door if she took them unawares.

All at once she remembered that Harry was supposed to have got lost too, on the day he'd died – got lost not a mile from his home, in streets he had known for years. Had he been made to get lost? Could his heart attack have been meant to bring her to London? She was trying to think about it when her thoughts froze. Someone was coming upstairs to her floor.

She tried to hush her thoughts, praying Sage hadn't overheard them and was coming up to deal with her. Perhaps he'd sent the pink creature with Harry's face or whatever was sharing Rosie Scatchard's room. She was round the far side of the bed and reaching for the crucifix, whether as protection or to use as a weapon, when the doorknob turned stealthily. But it was Doreen. 'Oh, you're awake,' Doreen said.

It wasn't relief Freda felt so much as the impossibility of telling Doreen what she thought. 'Would you rather I wasn't?' she said, more sharply than she would have wanted to.

'Of course not, Freddy. What a thing to say!' She looked sympathetic and forgiving. 'You've seemed tired, that's all. I'm not surprised, with all you've been taking on.' Even the hint of that subject must have embarrassed her, for she went on quickly, 'I just came to tell you dinner's nearly ready. Come down now if you like.'

'Come in for a moment and close the door. I want to talk to you.'

Doreen looked reluctant to listen but she closed the door and sat in the chair by the bed. 'What's wrong, Freddy?'

'What do you think is wrong?'

'Nothing,' Doreen said brightly. 'Nothing at all.'

'How can you say that, Doreen? What about the way your house has changed?'

'What about it?' Doreen was defiant. 'It's happier, that's all.'

'It isn't only happier. It isn't the same house.'

'Oh, Freddy, can't you see that doesn't matter? It's more than it was, don't you see? It has to be.'

Freda wondered if they were talking about the same thing. She had to say what she dreaded to say, to break through Doreen's faith. 'Why are you so happy, Doreen?'

'You know, Freddy. You know if anyone does.'

'But I don't. I'm not sure. I want you to tell me.'

'Oh, Freddy, you make me feel almost ashamed to be happy sometimes. I wish you could have what I have. I don't see why you can't.'

'But what *have* you got? What do you think it is?'

'Happiness, Freddy. Happiness and peace and never having to be alone again.'

It was like talking to a machine – like being unable to ask a question until you hit on the key word. 'But what has that to do with me?'

'You know.' She was visibly uncomfortable. 'It couldn't have happened without you.'

'What couldn't?'

'You know perfectly well.' She jumped up at once and clasped Freda's hands. 'Oh, I'm sorry. I shouldn't snap, at you of all people. Sage told us you didn't know what you were capable of until that night. It must take some getting used to. Just try and remember how much happiness you've been responsible for.'

'But I *still* don't know what I'm capable of. What *have* I done?' It was less a question than a cry of desperation.

'I wish you could see. But it's – private. You understand.'

Freda was struggling not to reveal what she'd seen in Doreen's bedroom, in her bed. 'You think I'm a medium, don't you? I'm not. Not in the way you think.'

'What other way is there?'

'Sage's way. He's using me to make these things.' She didn't care if that offended Doreen or upset her, she was so desperate, but Doreen only looked forgiving. 'It's like being made to give birth against your will, can you imagine that? He never even asked me. I hate it, Doreen, it's horrible, it's not fair. I won't be made to do it again. I want to leave.'

'He *needs* you, Freddy. That's not the same as using you, you mustn't think it is. And I do.' She held Freda's hands more tightly when they tried to pull away. 'You mustn't go yet, you've so much still to give. You wouldn't deny people that, would you? You wouldn't have denied me. He can't do without you.' She looked away from Freda, towards the door. 'You tell her,' she said.

374

Sage was in the doorway. 'I heard my name,' he said. 'I thought it best to come.'

'I'll go and help Rosie with dinner.' Before Freda could stop her, Doreen had gone. Freda stared at him, at his calm deep eyes, then looked away in case they overwhelmed her. 'Did you hear what I was saying?' she demanded.

'I did.' His voice was untroubled, reassuring. 'I think you know it is no longer possible.'

'You'll see whether it is.' No, she ought to let him think she had given up all hope of escaping. 'What do you want of me?'

'Only what you want yourself.'

'No it isn't.' She thought of Timothy, forced herself to remember how he had died. 'Don't you say that,' she cried.

'I think you see its truth.'

'I'm going downstairs. Don't you come in my room again without being invited.' She was so angry and dismayed that she forgot how the house had changed until she went onto the landing. The stairs went up as well as down. She wondered if he would try to stop her if she headed upward, and then she realized that he wanted her to go up, to see what was there. The bright deserted stairs above looked quite as real as those below. All at once she was dizzy and falling, until he took her arm.

They descended the stairs, through floor after floor. She lost count of the empty rooms. Beyond one open door she thought she saw a crucifix, except that the small figure was moving, growing brighter, reaching out its arms. Everything was too bright; her eyes were stinging. She closed her eyes and kept walking, since there was nothing else to do, and said, 'Why have you made all this?'

'Not I.' He seemed surprised. 'All this is yours.'

'So that's why you need me,' she said, understanding nothing.

'To an extent, and for the moment. Soon there will be less strain on you.'

He sounded sympathetic, which dismayed her more than ever. Whatever he meant, it sounded so ominous that she couldn't question him. They were on the last flight now, and he was holding her arm lightly. She ought to be able to break away, run for the front door. Where would she go? Who would believe what she had to tell? Even if she managed to bring someone here, what was there to see? Her eyes were so dazzled by the parade of floors that she could hardly see the front door or the smooth pink face of the figure that stood in front of it, smiling with teeth white as neon. She fled towards the dining room.

Doreen and Rosie were already seated, and Freda's plate was piled high. 'I can't eat all that, don't be ridiculous,' she said, wondering if she could eat at all.

'Do your best, Freddy. You need to eat,' Doreen said, but Freda was sure that they needed her to. It was the séances that were taking so much out of her. If she didn't eat they couldn't very well expect her to continue acting as a medium, but if she didn't eat she would be too weak to resist anything. Above all, she was famished. Nobody spoke until she had almost cleared her plate.

'You aren't still thinking of going back, are you?'

'Not yet,' she said.

'That's right. You look after yourself for a change, you've done enough for us.' When Freda had finished, Doreen said, 'You'll feel better for that. Come and watch television and relax.'

Were they getting her ready for another séance? They couldn't make her do it, that was one thing they couldn't do. She sat with Sage while the women washed up, and wished she were anywhere but in the parlour, so close to Doreen's bedroom that was Harry's again now. Suppose she got up before Sage could prevent her, ran across the hall into the sitting room, and threw open the bedroom door? What would Harry, or the thing with Harry's face, do? What would Doreen do if she couldn't pretend that her companion didn't exist? She was almost grateful when Doreen turned on the news and she could stop thinking.

There was unrest at Holloway Prison as well as Pentonville now. Prison officers were locking prisoners in their cells for twenty-three hours a day. Realizing both prisons were less than a mile away made Freda feel imprisoned herself. Had Sage let her go home so that she would see the derelict shop, because he knew it would make her come back? She thought of being locked in a cell, of looking out at walls of blank windows, and wondered if she already had. The house was turning into a prison full of empty cells, and only she realized they were prisoners. Though Doreen had the gas fire on full, she couldn't stop shivering.

She hardly noticed the next news item, about the death of a London stamp dealer named Churchill. The name took her back to the war, to Timothy – dangling from the parachute as the German flare struck him, writhing helplessly and screaming as he drifted down . . . She dragged her attention back to the news, for all at once, though she wasn't sure why, it seemed vital that she should.

The inquest into the death of Geoffrey Churchill was to be held next week. Mr Churchill had fallen from the viaduct at Hornsey Lane. Freda was trying to think what his name should mean and growing afraid that thinking would distract her from that very information on the news. Now there was something about Mr Churchill's wife, Joyce. Surely not the Joyce Churchill she remembered? Then there was a brief shot of her at the viaduct, and the glimpse of her face was like the answer to a prayer. 'I know her!' Freda cried.

'You know her?' Doreen demanded. 'The lady who's lost her husband?'

Freda mustn't seem too eager, the plan that was forming mustn't seem to come from her. 'Yes.'

'You know what she needs, don't you?'

'No,' Freda said, 'you tell me.'

'She needs to come here. She needs you.'

'You know what I said about all that to you, Doreen.' Freda's reluctance was quite real. 'But she is a friend of mine,' she admitted. 'She did look so alone.'

'That's how it feels, Freddy. You remember, don't you?' Doreen gazed moist-eyed at her. 'Call her, Freddy. Call her now.'

'I can't. I've forgotten the number.'

'Look it up.' Doreen obviously thought that Freda was trying to avoid calling. She hurried back from the hall with the directory. 'Don't leave her suffering, Freddy. Help her like you helped me.'

Freda turned the pages shakily until she found the Churchills. Joyce was the only person she could think of who might believe what was happening here, who might see what was wrong with it and not be seduced by it. Joyce had the strength Freda needed, she would know what to do and not be daunted; surely she was still like that. Here was G. Churchill, Stamp Dealer, and of course the 'G' was for Geoffrey. She suppressed her excitement. 'I've got it,' she said.

'Call her, Freddy. Do it now before you change your mind.' Doreen turned to Sage as if she'd forgotten him. 'It'll be all right, won't it?'

Freda held her breath. 'Please do,' he said.

He couldn't read her mind! If she'd been alone she would have laughed aloud at herself. 'All right, I will.'

As soon as she left the gas fire for the hall, she began to shiver in earnest. She could ignore that, and the stairs that went up forever; she must. She dialled while Doreen held the directory for her. The phone at the other end rang, went on ringing. Seconds passed before a woman's voice said, 'Yes?'

'Joyce Churchill?'

'Yes?'

'This is Freda Beeching. We met at Oxford.' That was all she had time to say before she was cut off. She stared at the buzzing receiver and then at Doreen. 'She hung up.'

Doreen looked dubious. 'You don't seem to know her that well.'

'Let me have another try.'

This time it seemed the phone would never stop ringing. She imagined Joyce willing it to stop, to be left alone with her grief. Freda was close to hating herself, but where else could she seek help? She swallowed when the ringing was cut off.

'What is it now?' Joyce said harshly.

'It's Freda, Joyce. Please don't hang up until you've heard what I have to say.'

'I'm sorry if I seemed rude. I lost my husband recently. I don't feel like talking just now.'

'I know you have, Joyce. I saw it on the news. That's why I'm calling.' For a moment Freda didn't think she would be able to go on. 'Would you like to see your husband again?'

The silence lasted so long she thought Joyce had walked away from the phone, but Joyce must have been fighting to keep control of herself. 'I'm sorry, Freda, I've given all that up. Oxford finished it for me. I'm sticking with reality, however hard it is.'

Freda heard a stifled sob. How could she persist when she didn't believe what she was saying, when she hated herself for distressing Joyce? Then Sage came softly out of the parlour to watch her, standing between her and the front door. She had to go on, she knew this was her last chance. 'This is real, Joyce. I give you my word,' she said, and writhed inside herself for lying. 'I've done it for other people who've lost their loved ones. Let me do it for you.'

'I've given you my answer,' Joyce said. 'He's gone and that's all. You don't come back when you've fallen that far, when you've given up. Please leave me alone to live with that. I'm sorry, you aren't helping at all. If you phone again you won't get through.'

Freda clung to the phone as if it could stop her shivering, and gazed up the endless stairs. She tried to dial again, but when her shivery fingers succeeded at last the line was engaged: Joyce had taken the phone off the hook. She stared hopelessly at Doreen, and might have rushed Sage to get to the front door if she'd had any strength. It was Sage who broke the empty silence. 'Perhaps it was too delicate to discuss over the phone.'

Could he really be handing her the solution? She bit the inside of her lip to keep her mouth shut until she had suppressed her eagerness. 'I think you're right. I'll go and see her first thing tomorrow.'

Doreen began to protest, but Sage shook his head. Could he really not see that he would be letting Freda out of the house, into the fresh air that would clear her head at last, clear away his influence for long enough to let her fight back? He was leading her back into the parlour. But as she sank into her chair, he nodded approvingly at her. 'Yes,' he said with that faint calm smile. 'A visit ought to be just what is needed.'

Martin's new flat was on Earl's Court Road. The kitchen and the bathroom put together weren't much more spacious than the cell the police had kept him in overnight. His feet were aching from days of trudging from hospital to hospital. Molly's parents hadn't known where she was, and all he'd done was to make them worry. Leon wouldn't help him find her, and he could certainly expect no help from the police. He mustn't let any of this get through to him. He went to the phone, the one bright new object in the flat, at once.

He didn't want to see Molly if she didn't want to see him. He just wanted to know that she was all right. He wanted to be sure of that before he was forced to go back to America, if that was what they meant to do to him. Yesterday several members of Parliament had been asking why he was allowed to stay in Britain; so had some of the newspapers. He didn't know how easy it would be for the police to have him extradited, but they had certainly given him the impression that they meant to try, even though for the moment they weren't pressing charges against him. It felt as if the whole of Great Britain was against him, but he hadn't time to brood over that. He was too worried that Molly was hiding somewhere, with nobody to help her or even aware that she needed help.

There was someone who ought to be aware, and by Christ, Martin would make sure he was. This time Stuart Hay would help, by God he would, because he was responsible for Molly's breakdown. Martin had to believe that was what she'd suffered – that she'd injured herself and, for whatever reason, convinced herself that he'd injured her. The thought made him clench his fists until the receiver creaked. 'Foundation for Industrial Psychology,' a voice eventually said.

'Stuart Hay, please.'

'I'm afraid he isn't here just now.'

'Then I need to know where to get in touch with him.'

'I'm afraid I don't know.'

'It's extremely urgent,' Martin said, closing his aching eyes. 'I'll need to know his home address.'

'I'm sorry, sir, I'm not allowed to give out that information.'

It was unbearably predictable. 'Then put me through to someone who is,' Martin said with an edge to his voice.

When a donnish-sounding woman asked him briskly what he wanted, he didn't give her a chance. 'Stuart Hay wanted to know whether a friend of mine had been affected by an experiment he ran. Well, she has, so badly that she can't call him herself. I need to get in touch with him right now, but I don't know where he lives.'

'We don't give out private addresses without the permission of the persons concerned.'

'Either I call him or I get the police to find him. It's up to you.'

'You were proposing to call him or visit him?'

'Call him, obviously. What else?'

'Since the circumstances are so unusual,' she said reluctantly, 'I can give you the phone number but not the address.'

He scribbled the number, cut the connection, and dialled. This phone was in Oxford too, but sounded fainter. Shouting to be heard might drain some of his rage – but it was a woman's voice that answered. 'Stuart Hay,' Martin demanded.

'He's gone away.'

No longer there, did she mean? Martin's fists clenched again. 'Where to?'

'London. Just for the day, I think. I'm expecting him back this evening.'

'Back where?'

'Back home. Oh, you mean the address? Here you go,' she said, and gave it to him. 'Who shall I say called?'

'Don't bother,' Martin said, and cut her off, as much to make sure he didn't take out his frustration on her as anything. He grabbed his overcoat. He wouldn't call Hay, he would confront him. Never mind that he'd promised the police he wouldn't leave this address. He didn't care what he risked so long as he was sure that Molly was taken care of.

Stuart had almost passed the site of the cinema before he realized what it was. A few heaps of rubble, bony with timber, surrounded a blackened patch of earth. Two grubby boys were digging a half-melted Exit sign out of one of the heaps, but ran away when they saw him watching. He stood and wondered what could have made Danny Swain do such a thing, wondered what the others might be capable of. They might be well adjusted socially by now; it would be wrong to assume anything else. When a wind blew ash and the stench of burning towards him, he went on quickly to the police station.

'Stuart Hay to see Inspector Hackett,' Stuart said to the desk sergeant.

'That's him,' a woman's voice said. 'Stuart Hay, that's what he said.'

It was a middle-aged woman. Suddenly he knew who she and her companion were — would have known even if they hadn't been staring at him with such dislike. He went over to them. 'You must be Mr and Mrs Swain.'

'Look at him, look at the cheek of him.' Mrs Swain glared up at him with eyes that were red from weeping. 'Coming straight up to us, bold as you please. Hasn't even the decency to pretend he's not here.'

'That wouldn't really make much sense, would it?' Stuart said, as gently as he could.

Mr Swain got to his feet, his eyes narrowing, and Stuart had to step back. 'We don't need you to tell us what makes sense, lad. It's you who filled our boy's head with nonsense and worse. Proud of that, are you? You've got his mother afraid to stay at home in case he comes back.'

She was clutching at her husband's arm and shaking her head tearfully when the desk sergeant beckoned Stuart. 'Inspector Hackett can see you now.'

'And us.' Mrs Swain used her husband to drag herself to her feet. 'I want to hear what you've got to say.'

'I don't mind if they come in,' Stuart said.

He might learn something that way. The desk sergeant looked dubious, but when he came back, he seemed surprised. 'The inspector will see all of you.'

The inspector was a thickset man with curly hair. Two chairs waited to the right of the inspector's desk, one to the left. When everyone was seated the inspector said, 'Well, Mr Hay, what do you know about all this?'

'I'm not sure I know anything.'

'Come now. You certainly know what you were told. You know Daniel Swain set fire to the cinema where he worked, shortly after he received your letter.'

'I wouldn't say shortly after. It must have been a few weeks.'

'No, it was a few days.' The inspector held up one hand to forestall Mr Swain from interrupting. 'Mr Swain kept the letter from him for several weeks because he feared it might have a bad effect on Daniel's mind. It rather seems his fears were justified. Would you agree?'

Stuart felt as if he were on trial. 'You're sure it was Danny who set fire to the cinema?'

'I'm afraid so. The fire was started in the projection box. He used seats to start the fire, and' – he glanced at Mrs Swain, and away – 'we found his fingerprints on the remains of some magazines he must have set light to. And there is the way he behaved afterwards.'

'That's what you did to him.' Mrs Swain was struggling to get to Stuart, while her husband held her in the chair. 'You drove him mad and made him run away. He's out there somewhere with nobody to look after him and the Lord God only knows what he may do.' She was weeping and furious that he should see. 'What did you mean by it? What were you trying to do to him?'

'You really must allow me to ask the questions at this stage,' the inspector said. 'By all means have your say when I've finished.' He gazed coolly at Stuart. 'All the same, the question stands. Exactly what did you want with Swain?'

'Just what I said in the letter. You'll have read it, won't you?' When the policeman simply stared at him, Stuart had to go on: 'Just to find out how he was.' That sounded grotesquely insensitive under the circumstances. 'I don't know if you're aware that he volunteered for a research project I helped run. This was years ago, in Oxford. He claimed he could see the future.'

'And you encouraged him, didn't you?' Mr Swain's eyes were narrowing dangerously. 'You must have had less bloody sense than him. Couldn't you see how he was? Meddling in people's minds. Your sort wants locking up.'

'I was only the assistant, you know.' Stuart resented being made to feel defensive. 'It was Dr Kent's project.'

'Who?'

Stuart started, for all three of them had asked the question. 'Guilda Kent,' he said.

Danny's mother clutched her husband. 'That's who she said she was.'

'Or your son did.' The inspector spoke slowly and clearly. 'I think we talked that through, Mrs Swain. It couldn't have been Dr Kent, we've established that, and there would have been no reason for the woman who came to your house to say that she was, now would there?'

'I suppose not. Maybe Danny said it. I can't remember, and I'm not surprised,' she said, glaring at Stuart. 'I'd still like to know who she was.'

'I assure you we're working on that, but since you can't remember what she looked like . . .' He turned back to Stuart. 'All the same, Mrs Swain, it's significant that your son should have taken her for Dr Kent if Dr Kent was responsible for his delusions.'

'You've lost me,' Stuart said, feeling edgy and denied some vital piece of information. 'Who did he say was Guilda Kent? How do you know she wasn't?'

'A woman visited Mr and Mrs Swain's flat just before Daniel ran away. We have no idea of who she was or whether it was her visit that made him run away. If he took her for your colleague, then I shouldn't be surprised. But she wasn't Dr Kent. We've traced Dr Kent to a mental hospital in Norfolk. She's been there for years.'

'Best place for her,' Mr Swain muttered. 'Best place for both of you.'

So that was why Stuart hadn't been able to trace her:

because she had changed her profession. He hadn't realized she was qualified to work in hospitals, but perhaps she had qualified since Oxford.

'If the sight of someone he believed to be your colleague was enough to make him flee,' the inspector said, 'there's little doubt in my mind that your project was responsible for his mental state.'

'Maybe. I've had my doubts about the project myself.' At least Stuart could answer the questions he could see in their eyes. 'Dr Kent wanted to monitor the dreams of several people who claimed they could dream of the future. What happened ultimately was that they affected one another with a kind of mass hysteria, and the experiment was terminated.'

If anything, the Swains looked even more hostile. The inspector seemed to be waiting for more. 'Really, Guilda Kent is the person you should talk to,' Stuart said. 'Have you been in touch with her?'

'Not yet.' The inspector began to search among his papers. 'Perhaps you should, Mr Hay.'

'I'd very much like to if you'll give me the address.'

The inspector copied it onto a pad and tore off the page for Stuart. 'Any questions you would like to ask him?' he said to the Swains.

'I'd like to tell him what I think of him,' was all Mrs Swain said.

'He's not worth it,' her husband growled, then came to stand over Stuart. 'Go off to your loony bin and stay there. And if Danny has to go in, I hope they put you all in the same cell.'

The possibility of a mental hospital seemed only now to have occurred to Danny's mother. 'Oh, don't say that,' she sobbed.

'You can go,' the inspector said to Stuart. 'If we should need you again, we'll know where to find you.' To judge by the Swains' faces, that might have been under a stone.

Stuart felt he'd been let off lightly. He was at the door when the inspector said, 'Just a minute.'

He was writing on his pad again. 'You might as well have this. Swain had written it down. We found it among his clothes.'

It was an address in W.1: Guilda Kent's address. Stuart stared bewildered at it. '*Danny* had this, you say?' he said, and when the inspector nodded curtly, 'this is her London address?'

'Form your own judgment. We've checked it, of course.'

'Am I likely to find her there, do you think?'

The inspector seemed to lose interest. 'Find out for yourself.'

On his way out Stuart asked the desk sergeant where the address was.

He rode the train to Oxford Circus and hoped the address would be genuine and Guilda would be there. Undoubtedly he was being paranoid because he felt he deserved to be punished. Even if there were no proof, he was responsible for Danny's breakdown, his instincts told him that he was – that his letter had been. He couldn't even recall why he'd sent the letters, except that memories of Guilda's project wouldn't leave him alone. He was beginning to wonder anxiously what effect the other letters might have had.

Crowds were still converging on the January sales. In Wardour Street, dragons and spaceships had taken over most of the posters for forthcoming films. Soon the film distributors gave way to cinemas, their frontage papered with stills of women wearing only round censorious black patches that seemed to invite you to peel them off. How could Guilda live somewhere like this? Most of the neon signs were already lit, as if to bring on the night early, and even more of them said 'Love' than 'Sex.' He was ready to head back to Oxford Street; Danny's fantasy seemed obvious enough – he had been obsessed with Guilda. But there on the far side of a crossroads was St Quentin's Court, and now he could see an open door bearing the number Danny had written down.

He made his way across the junction, willing her to be there so that he wouldn't have to wait all the way to Norfolk. When he reached the pavement and stepped into the court, he saw that there was no open door after all, at least where he had thought he'd seen one, and no doors that bore the number Hackett had given him. He prowled round the court, in case he'd misread the inspector's handwriting or the policeman had made a mistake. Staircases led up beyond the open doors; cards on which women's names were written, barely legibly, were tacked above doorbells. He'd been wondering if a name could have started Danny's fantasy, but none of the names was Guilda. He was making for the street when he saw the mark on the wall.

It looked very like a leaning 8, or infinity rising. Of course, that was what he must have seen, and a shadow had made that patch of wall look like a door. Perhaps it had to Danny too. A lorry was labouring along the street as Stuart came abreast of the mark. As the shadow of the lorry crept over the wall he saw how the illusion had worked, for now the mark appeared to be a number on an open door. Not only that: the door seemed to open on a staircase that led up to another door, which was opening. He could even see the figure that was opening it, if he let his imagination loose, but of course none of that was there; he knew it was only a blank wall without turning his head to look. All the same, he felt easier once he was out of the court, for sharing Danny's illusion had made him wonder momentarily about his own mind. He shook off that doubt and headed towards Oxford Street looking for a taxi. The sooner he was in Norfolk and talking to Guilda, the happier he would be.

A knock at the door woke Freda, who struggled out of bed at once. It must be time to go to Joyce's. She'd wanted to be ready but had overslept instead. She stumbled to the door and called 'just a minute' as she grabbed the dressing gown Doreen had lent her. She was tying the cord when she heard the rattle and thump of the breakfast tray as it was set down on the landing.

She stepped back instinctively, shivering to think that she had almost opened the door. So they weren't letting her go downstairs for breakfast now. She waited until the soft footsteps were well on their way down before she took in the tray. She was tempted to go to the stairs and see who had brought it, but it wasn't only the thought of seeing that daunted her, it was the idea of watching the head bob down, and down, and down . . . She lifted the tray shakily and kicked the door shut behind her.

She ate quickly, though there was so much of it, and put the tray out at once for fear that if she kept it in her room the owner of the soft footsteps would come in for it. How could she be frightened of anything so banal? But it was the banality that frightened her, the way Sage's creatures were becoming part of the everyday life of the house. Thank God she had Sage's promise that she was going to Joyce's. Once she was out of the house she would be able to think what to do.

She washed and dressed, and then she waited. It seemed for hours but there was no way of telling; her watch had stopped days ago, the little gold watch Timothy had given her, that had kept time ever since. It must be late morning, to judge by the light through the curtains. A few specks of dust caught fire in the beam of sunlight that slipped through the crack between the curtains, and she felt as if everything were as slow as the dust was moving.

She waited. The bar of sunlight thinned, went out. All at once her room seemed much darker and colder. They were going to leave her up here, they weren't going to take her to Joyce. This was certainly not first thing in the morning. Sage must have deduced her plan after all.

She went to the curtains in case she was wrong about the time of day. Perhaps the sun had only gone behind a cloud. She peered through the crack, then she turned away, shaking. She couldn't even see the sky now, the walls and their ranks of cramped windows had grown so high.

She mustn't think of that. She was making the walls more real – that was a vital insight. The sun had been shining into her room, after all; she must believe it had, believe the walls weren't real enough to block it out. She could believe that when she kept her back to the window, though the effort of believing made her shake.

Perhaps it was her fear of the multiplying floors that made them real, too. None of this might have made sense to her if she had thought about it, but her mind was so tired that it did. Couldn't she go down if she suppressed her fear, hurry down to the front door and out of the house? She was growing sure that nobody would come to take her down.

She snatched her overcoat from the hanger in the wardrobe and stuffed her fists into the sleeves as she hurried to the stairwell. She closed her eyes while she told herself that there would be no more flights than there ought to be, and then she looked. There didn't seem to be as many as last night, there mustn't be. She started down at once.

The smell of newness came to meet her, and so did the silence. Now she was descending a flight that oughtn't to exist, and her footsteps might have been the only sound in the world. Though they and their echoes were intensely clear, they seemed tiny as a small child's, and as halting.

How could she not believe in the stairs on which she was walking? She heard her footsteps echoing through all that silence, losing themselves among the empty rooms, and now she dared not look into the stairwell. She could walk forever, she would never get out of the house by herself. 'Doreen,' she cried, and fled upstairs while her legs could still carry her.

She heard her voice dwindling through the floors as she called again from the landing outside her room. Could Doreen hear her all the way up here? Suppose someone else could, someone nearer? Suppose not all the new rooms were still empty? She listened to the silence down there, then slammed her door and held it shut. It was a long time before she felt able to move away and sit on the chair by the bed.

She was praying that her heartbeat would slow down and let her hear if anyone was on the stairs, when Doreen came in. 'Put on the fire for heaven's sake, Freddy,' she cried when she saw Freda in her overcoat. 'Did you think we'd forgotten you?'

Freda heaved herself to her feet. 'I didn't know what to think.'

'You poor thing, have you been sitting up here all by yourself worrying about your friend Joyce? Well, you can stop worrying. Come on, I'll take you down.'

They meant to let her go after all. She'd had too much time to brood, to invent reasons to be suspicious and fearful. She took Doreen's arm as they made for the stairs. 'You won't need your coat,' Doreen said.

Surely the weather hadn't changed that much. 'I'll keep it on for now.'

'Are you sure you feel up to this, Freddy?'

'I'm fine. Just a bit exhausted.' Freda was suddenly afraid that Doreen's concern would rob her of her last chance to escape. She hurried them both to the stairs, went down blindly, clinging to Doreen's arm, and they seemed to be downstairs far sooner than she feared. She made to wait by the front door as Doreen headed for the parlour until Doreen turned back to her. 'Come on, Freddy,' she said.

Freda wished she could stay by the front door, but she mustn't behave suspiciously now. Doreen must want to tell Sage they were going to Joyce's, and Freda had only to say good-bye innocently to him. She followed Doreen into the hot cluttered stuffy room.

At least, she followed as far as the doorway, where she found that she couldn't go in. Sage and Rosie were in there, but so was someone else; she could see a hand resting on the arm of the chair that stood with its back to her. The thought of seeing one of Sage's creatures accepted as just another guest was more than she could bear. She backed away, but her legs were so shaky that Doreen caught her before she had taken two steps. 'Lean on me, Freddy, you'll be all right,' Doreen promised, and the woman in the chair stood up and turned round. It was Joyce.

She looked nervous but determined to keep smiling. 'Freda, how are you? I'm sorry I was so curt on the phone. I couldn't talk to anyone just then, you understand. But thank you for changing my mind. Thank you for sending –' She glanced at Sage, a little uneasily. 'Thank you for sending this gentleman to me.'

So that was what Sage had meant by a visit. He'd known all along what Freda planned. She tried to struggle free of Doreen's ushering, but Doreen went on leading her to a chair and sitting her down – seemed not even to notice her reluctance. 'What did he tell you, Joyce?' Freda said desperately.

'He didn't tell me, he showed me.' Joyce's eyes brightened, too intensely. 'The morgue say they've got Geoffrey but *they* can't show me. I know which I believe.'

Sage and Doreen and Rosie were watching, and Freda felt as if they were stealing her breath. 'I want to talk to Joyce by herself.'

'Of course.' Sage beckoned the women out with him. 'Now she is here you may talk to her all you wish.'

As soon as the door closed, she leaned forward to whisper. 'Joyce, what do you think is going on here?'

Joyce was unbuttoning her cardigan and mopping her forehead. 'Really, Freda, I think you should know more about that than I do.'

'You're right. I've seen how it works. I started out feeling as you must be feeling now, but I've seen too much of it. It isn't real, Joyce. I don't know what it is, but it isn't real.'

'Oh, Freda, don't say that. They told me you were depressed. I know you must have doubts sometimes, we all do, but try and buck up. Just think of Doreen and her friend. You brought their loved ones back when they thought they had lost them forever. If that isn't real, you tell me what is.'

So Doreen and Rosie were openly discussing their companions now. 'Have you seen them?'

'Not yet.' She gave Freda a long pleading look. 'You know who I want to see.'

Freda couldn't break through her faith. 'Are you too hot, Joyce?' she said with sudden desperate cunning, and prayed that the idea hadn't occurred to her too late. 'Let's go for a walk. Just down to the canal. That'll cheer me up if anything does.'

'Better not just now, dear. They said you need to rest.'

'I need to go out. I haven't been out for days.' Freda struggled to keep her voice neutral. 'I know what I need, Joyce – fresh air. Come on and then we can talk.'

'All right.' Joyce lifted her coat from the back of a chair. 'I don't suppose a short walk can hurt. I'll just tell him we're going.'

'No, don't do that, don't disturb him.' Freda swallowed her panic. 'Good heavens, Joyce, I don't have to ask permission to go for a walk.'

'Of course you don't.' But she laid her coat over the chair.

393

'I'd just feel easier if they know where we are, just in case you're taken ill. I won't be a moment.'

'Wait, Joyce, listen to me,' Freda whispered. 'Never mind the walk. We wouldn't have got far, they wouldn't have let me. Do something for me, I'm begging you. They can't stop you, they won't dare. Go straight to the police and tell them I'm being kept here against my will. They'll have to come. Do it for me, for pity's sake.'

Joyce gazed at her until Freda's head began to swim with the breath she was holding. Joyce was biting her lip and looked near to tears. At last she said, 'Oh, you poor thing, you *do* need rest. Never mind me. I can wait until you're fit again.'

Freda let out her breath, which sounded more like a scream. Joyce was making for the hall, and Freda's cry sent her running. Freda listened to her murmuring to the others, murmuring with a concern that was more stifling than the room, then suddenly she was on her feet and tiptoeing quickly to the front door. Her legs were trembling, but if she didn't do it now, she never would.

Sage and the women were by the stairs talking about her. With all the force of her painfully held breath, she willed them not to turn as she dodged stealthily into the hall and ran toward the front door. But Harry and another man were in her way, their faces too pink, their eyes and wide smiles unnaturally bright and fixed. They would have looked unreal as window dummies, except that they stretched out their hands to her. She staggered, making a sound too outraged to be a scream.

The women gathered around her at once, murmuring, 'Come on, dear, come and sit down,' while Sage looked patient and untroubled. All of them seemed to take the presence of the men for granted. Freda wrenched herself out of the women's hands and stumbled up the stairs. 'I won't do it!' she cried. 'You won't make me, now or ever. I'll die first, I'll starve myself.' With that she dragged herself upstairs.

They let her go. She staggered onto the first floor, which Rosie shared with Sage now, and clung to the banisters as she heaved herself up and up. She could barely see the floors or the stairs; her exertion was blinding her, her brain had no energy to spare for seeing. It seemed hours before she reached her landing.

She tottered the few steps to her door and then to the bed. She slumped onto Doreen's patchwork quilt and drew into herself, shivering from head to foot, trying to catch her breath. Then Sage and the women came into the room.

When Doreen stooped and tried to touch her comfortingly, Freda writhed away to the far side of the bed. 'Freddy, I'm sorry,' Doreen said. The worst of it was her expression, that look of knowing how Freda felt.

Joyce and Rosie were carrying in chairs from the other rooms on the floor. Freda wanted to demand what they thought they were doing, but Doreen was speaking. 'I blame myself for being so selfish. You've done so much for me and Rosie and yet we've never tried to help you in return. Just close your eyes now. Sage says it'll be all right. Close your eyes.'

They were drawing the chairs close to the bed, so close that two of them could grab her if she tried to slip away. They were bringing the séance into her room. She threw herself toward the foot of the bed. Sage watched.

Perhaps he knew he needn't take hold of her, that it was his gaze that had drained her of so much strength that she collapsed head first over the end of the bed, her forehead thumping the floor. Rosie and Doreen helped her up, ignoring her attempts to struggle, and laid her gently on the quilt. 'It's all right, I'm here,' Doreen murmured.

Freda lay on the bed and glared fiercely at the faces that surrounded her. The women's eyes were comforting, encouraging, almost prayerful; Sage's were unreadably calm. She could still fight them, prevent the séance from happening. 'No, no, no,' she began to scream.

'It's all right.' Not only Doreen but all the women were murmuring now, a kind of litany of concern, unbearably monotonous, almost hypnotic. Freda tried to scream louder, she closed her eyes as if that might help, but her voice seemed to be receding. Each scream felt as if it would have to be the last, they exhausted her so much. Soon her throat felt as distant as her voice, and then she was asleep.

She dreamed she was running away from the house, running between two buildings whose walls would never end, whose ranks of identical windows climbed until they were lost in the clouds. She couldn't bear that, she had to see light somehow. At once the identical windows were the identical leaves of the forest through which she was running. She hadn't escaped the dream; by manipulating it she had made it more real. Suddenly she knew that was part of the answer: by coming true for people the dream gained strength, and Joyce had made it stronger. She must have gasped aloud, for the sound woke her.

She had to tell Joyce now, before the insight faded like a dream. Joyce would know what she meant, and help her think it out. She blinked and opened her eyes wide, but the séance was over, and she was alone. Sage must have given up. She'd beaten him.

She must conserve her strength to talk to Joyce. She must lie still and hold on to what she'd realized about the dream. She blinked at the dark one last time and raised her head to make sure the door was shut; and then she stared, though her neck began to ache. There was something in the chair at the foot of the bed.

Perhaps it was clothes. She must have left her suit there last night, it must be the buttons of the jacket that looked like eyes, glinting at her from the dark – and then she realized she was wearing her suit. She'd put it on when she had thought she was going to visit Joyce.

She grabbed the dark in search of the light cord, praying desperately there would be nothing to fear because she couldn't imagine what she would be able to do, all the way up here, if there were. She had the cord now and pulled.

The sudden light made her close her eyes and fear kept them closed, fear that would paralyse her if she didn't look. She forced them open and raised her head on its throbbing neck, and then she shrank back against the wall under the crucifix, a sound filling her throat until she thought it would choke her. Something was watching her from the chair.

It looked unfinished. Its clothes and its flesh seemed to be composed of the same substance, for they were of the same indeterminate colour. The hands and face looked not so much plump as puffy. Yet there was no mistaking the face, the high forehead, the jutting chin, above all the deep brown eyes, gentle but strong. They were watching her from a face that looked as if it were in the process of being shaped from putty: Timothy's face.

She couldn't move until the figure nodded towards her on the chair, until the mouth began to smile uncertainly as if the lips were stuck together, hadn't yet been separated, and then she lurched off the bed and stumbled choking toward the door. Before she reached it she lost her balance, plunged forward with nothing to hold onto, smashed her forehead against the door. Then there was only dark.

She came out of the dark and wished she could go back. Someone was stroking her forehead, so gently that the touch of the hand soothed her bruise. At last she opened her eyes a slit. Timothy was sitting beside her, stroking her forehead.

It couldn't be Timothy. She knew that much, though trying to remember why made her head throb horribly. She wished it were, as she had never wished for anything. She lay on the bed and would have been happy for this dream never to end, this dream of his loving touch, and then he gazed into her eyes and smiled his smile that was like no other, a smile that recalled everything they had done together, everything they had been to each other. The flood of emotion was so great she thought it would shake her to pieces. 'Oh, Timothy,' she cried in a pale voice she hardly recognized, 'it *is* you.'

'Of course it is, old girl. Who were you expecting? Friend Adolf? That's all done with. There's nothing to keep us apart now.' He sat back, almost imperceptibly but she felt as if he were suddenly miles away. 'That is,' he said shyly, 'if you still want me.'

'Oh, Timothy, if you only knew how much . . .' She reached out her shaky arms to him, and all at once he picked her up, even more effortlessly than he had used to. She'd loved to be held over streams, even once over the edge of a cliff; she'd loved the girlish excitement, the security of knowing he would never let her fall. She wanted him to kiss her, she raised her face to his as best she could, and it was a long time before their faces parted. His lips were so soft, it was like a dream.

He carried her onto the landing as if she weighed nothing at all. 'I'll take you down,' he said. 'He'll see to your head.' As they descended she felt she was flying. It no longer mattered that there were so many floors, not when she was in Timothy's arms. She was flying like an angel, and if this wasn't heaven, she was glad there was no such place.

By the time the train left Norwich, night was falling. Bare trees cracked the sunset, pools and streams glowed like lava among the fields; on both sides of the line there was nothing higher than a hedge between the train and the horizon. Stuart gazed out until his reflection was clearer than the landscape and was tempted to make faces at himself to while the dawdling journey away.

He hadn't been able to get through to the hospital from

Norwich to arrange to meet Guilda somewhere away from where she worked. He hoped he wouldn't have to encounter any of her patients. Insanity dismayed him; just the thought of that loss of mental control did. He could only admire Guilda and anyone else who tried to help.

The train was emptying. By the time Stuart got out at his stop, there was only the ticket collector on the platform. 'How do I get to the hospital?' Stuart said.

'Afraid you haven't much choice. You walk.' The ticket collector frowned at the swaying metal shades of the lamps as they clattered with the first large drops of rain. 'Wait though, he's going that way.' He went to the fence between the platform and the car park. 'Can you drop our friend here at the hospital?'

'Why not,' a man said cheerfully. 'Jump in before you get wet,' he told Stuart as the fields began to hiss.

It was only when he realized the country house that glimmered through the rain was in fact the hospital that he deduced the last few hundred tree-lined yards must have been an avenue leading into the grounds. 'Thank you very much,' he shouted as he dodged under the wide stone porch, but the car was already speeding away.

Dripping urns and stone lions stood among the frantic trees and bushes. Soon a balding young male nurse opened the oak doors. 'I'd like to speak to Guilda Kent,' Stuart said.

The nurse let him in before answering. 'Have you an appointment?'

'I couldn't get through on the phone. It's pretty urgent. I assisted Dr Kent on a research project some years back, and now there's been a new development.'

The nurse stared at him. 'You'll have to speak to Dr Lovell.'

'Isn't Dr Kent here?'

The nurse's face went blank. 'Dr Lovell will explain,' he said, and having ascertained Stuart's name, went away.

The rain that had caught Stuart in the porch began to trickle down his neck and into his shoes. When he peeled off his coat and stood with it over his arm, rain seeped through the sleeve of his jacket. By the time the nurse came back, Stuart was in no mood to be hindered. 'Dr Lovell will see you,' the nurse said.

Couldn't he just say Guilda wasn't here? It was all this protocol that irritated Stuart. He marched after the nurse into Dr Lovell's office, a high-ceilinged white room with French windows. A large painting of a darker room hung on the wall. The painting was signed Lovell, whom he took to be the doctor, a thin middle-aged woman with grey hair clipped close to her head. She gazed at him over her steel-rimmed spectacles, whose lenses were scarcely larger than her eyes. 'What can I do for you?'

He restrained himself from saying 'Not much.' 'I asked to see Dr Kent,' he said.

After a pause she said patiently, 'Why?'

'About a project we were both involved in.'

She pursed her lips. 'Look, you'll have to tell me more than that.'

He was losing the little patience he'd had to begin with. 'It dates from before she came here, you know.'

'I should hope it does.'

Something in her tone disturbed him. 'So why should you need to know about it?'

'Perhaps you aren't familiar with our procedures, though I should have thought they were obvious enough. You are going to have to show me good reason to let you see her at all.'

She couldn't mean what she seemed to mean. 'You're in charge here, aren't you? You mean she's been taken ill?'

'I'm in charge if you want to put it that way, yes. I'm the RMO.'

'The responsible medical officer?' He was still trying to believe he'd misunderstood. 'Responsible for – '

'For Guilda Kent, of course. Every patient has an RMO.' She stared at him and said more gently, 'You didn't think she *worked* here, did you?'

His face must have said it all. 'Dear me,' she said. 'In that case I'm sorry. I thought you were trying to bluff your way in to her. She's been a patient here for years.'

Stuart turned away toward the windows, but the shifting dark was no relief. 'What's wrong with her?' he said, having swallowed twice.

'Acute paranoid schizophrenia.'

'But she was never like that. She was absolutely rational. Are you sure it's the same Guilda Kent?'

'Is your Guilda Kent the one who conducted research into dreaming? Then I'm afraid this is she. It seems to have been her research that affected her mind or at least worked on some dormant tendency in it.'

He didn't want to hear any more, yet he had to know. 'But she seemed all right afterwards,' he protested, then remembered Guilda wandering the deserted corridors of the Foundation as if she were looking for something.

'You assisted her in Oxford?'

'That's right.' Admitting it made him feel almost guilty, and so did saying, 'When she left Oxford we lost touch.'

'She worked for a while on the effects of stress on factory workers. Hardly the best line of work for her to choose under the circumstances. Meanwhile she was reading everything she could get her hands on about dreams. A few months later she went into a rest home.'

Each question was harder to ask. 'Was she paranoid then?'

'Very much so. If she hadn't gone in voluntarily, I think her colleagues would have taken steps. She'd developed a habit of looking around her, as if she were trying to take something unawares, I gather. Sometimes she'd refuse to go through doorways, sometimes she'd insist they led somewhere other than where they did. Mind you, that wasn't why she went into the rest home.'

'Why did she?'

'Apparently because she was convinced some people might try to find her. She gave instructions that they had to be turned away if they came looking for her, she wanted them to be told she wasn't there. She wouldn't give their names in case that somehow brought them to her. Well, that kind of delusory system isn't uncommon, and neither was the outcome, unfortunately. Eventually she forgot their names herself, and then became obsessed with the idea that they were somewhere in the building with her. When she started turning violent and the rest home couldn't cope with her, she came here.'

Stuart wondered if he was one of the people Guilda had been hiding from. 'Why did you want to see her?' Dr Lovell said.

'About her research. I've been wondering about the way it may still be affecting her subjects.' Reluctantly he added, 'One of them is insane.'

'Really. Do you find that more significant now?'

'I don't know,' Stuart said resentfully.

'You're right, we should be cautious in our thinking. I take it you wanted to find out if Kent had any further thoughts about her research. Well, would you like to see her?'

'Can I?' Stuart said, but it felt like, 'Do I have to?'

'It might be helpful. You might pick up allusions she makes that I've overlooked. Don't expect too much. She's sedated, you realize,' Dr Lovell said, and opened the door.

He followed her across the lobby, into the opposite wing. Apart from the pale green walls and carpets, it might almost have been a hotel. There were no uniforms and seemed to be no locks. People sat in a television lounge, watching the news: people were disappearing in London, someone whose name he didn't catch who worked in television and a cinema projectionist, wanted by the police for questioning in connection with a fire – Danny Swain. Someone was praying so fast in a room that at first Stuart thought it was a speeding tape; an old woman stared at him from her bed beyond a doorway and went on masturbating. Dr Lovell beckoned a nurse to go in to her, and another woman Stuart had taken for a nurse stepped in front of him and caught his arm. 'Are you from them?' she whispered.

Stuart forced himself not to back away. 'I'm afraid not, sorry.'

'They put me in here to find out what was going on. I'm not a patient, I had to pretend I was. They were supposed to take me out when I'd found out what they wanted to know, but I think they've forgotten I'm here. You'll tell them, won't you?'

At first he couldn't open his mouth. 'If I see them,' he mumbled.

'You have the touch,' Dr Lovell said approvingly as they made their way to the end of the corridor, 'though we try not to encourage their delusions. Ever considered this line of work? We're always looking for the right kind of person. Here we are. Someone to see you, Guilda,' she said as she opened the last door.

When Stuart stepped forward he found he was shuffling, for fear of what he might see. But Guilda looked healthier than he remembered; her long cheeks were pink, her eyes were bright, if a little glazed. 'How are you this wet evening?' Dr Lovell said.

'Oh, fine. Just resting.'

'You remember Stuart Hay, don't you?'

'Certainly do.' Guilda sat up on the bed. 'You're looking well, Stuart. Still at the Foundation?'

'The new Foundation, yes.' There was an awkward silence until Dr Lovell said, 'I'll leave you to it, then.'

When Stuart stayed by the door of the almost bare room – a green carpet, a night table, a bell push by the headboard of the bed – Guilda patted the mattress next to her. 'Sit by me so I don't have to shout. I don't want them to hear.'

At least she didn't think the room was bugged. He sat on the end of the bed. 'You won't catch anything from me, you know,' she said with a wry smile at the space between them, and then she grew conspiratorial. 'Thank God you've come at last. You'll vouch for me, won't you?'

'Vouch for you how?'

'For my sanity, of course.'

She did seem like the Guilda he remembered. He didn't know which was more dismaying, her being insane or his inability to tell. 'I can't hold on much longer,' Guilda hissed.

'Hold on to what?'

'To reality, what do you think? Could you if you were shut up in here?'

He wished she'd asked him anything but that. She must have been unbalanced when she had been brought here, but suppose she had regained her sanity and couldn't persuade the authorities that she had? The idea appalled him, and he could tell from her voice that she felt she'd scored a point. 'The dreams are getting stronger,' she said as if that followed logically.

'Your dreams?'

'My dreams and everyone else's. We've allowed them to grow stronger by trying to explain them away, don't you understand? Don't you know yet what dreams are?'

The fanatical gleam in her eyes made him afraid she would grab him, but he was already as far from her on the bed as he could go. Still, she was calming down. 'Don't answer that,' she said. 'The trouble is, we thought we knew. Science thinks it can distinguish between reality and dreaming. People who can't are locked up in places like this. You can't lock dreams up. All that does is make them stronger.'

'But the people in here aren't just dreaming,' he protested before he could think. 'They're – '

'Crazy? What's the difference between dreams and hallucinations, Stuart? Only that you can make hallucinations go away with tranquillizers. All that does is turn them back into dreams.'

'Even if that's true,' he said, trying to argue with her as if she were as sane as he was, 'isn't it preferable?'

'Stuart, hallucinations are just glimpses of what might be. That's why they're easy to control. At least this place has taught me that much. Hallucinations are glimpses of dreams, don't you understand? Dreaming isn't a state of mind, but we scientists have lulled people into thinking it is. God knows what we're responsible for.' The gleam was back in her eyes; he wondered if the sedatives were wearing off. 'It isn't a state of mind, it's a state of being.'

He had to keep her talking in case, in the midst of all this, she told him something he needed to know. 'You kept up your research after you left the Foundation, didn't you?'

'You're humouring me.' Her gaze was keen and rather sad. 'You think I'm being irrational. Preserve us from rationalism, that's all I can say. It's at the root of all our troubles.'

Hearing her say that shocked him as deeply as finding out she was an inmate. 'Do you know that up to the seventeenth century,' she said, 'people believed dreams were real? Then along came rationalism to tell them they were wrong. And then there was Freud claiming that dreams were internal and subjective. Jung was closer to the truth.'

'What truth?'

'Don't you even remember? He thought we dreamed continuously, even while awake. Remember now?' She held up a hand to ward off his protest. 'Yes, I know it's been demonstrated in the laboratory that we don't dream continuously at all. But suppose we used to? Suppose it's all the explaining away that's stopped us? Or suppose it's driven the dreams into hiding, where they can't be measured?'

He felt depressed and weary. 'You can suppose anything that way.'

'Then suppose along with me, just for a few minutes.

405

Humour me, for old times' sake.' She looked as if she wanted to move closer but was afraid that he would flinch away. 'If you don't like the idea that dreams are a state of being, call it the collective subconscious. It's where Mozart's music came from, you know, and Frankenstein, and Jekyll and Hyde: all dreams. Do you realize how many horror writers dreamed their material? Lovecraft and Wandrei and Edward Lucas White, and Le Fanu had a nightmare that finally killed him . . .' She must have felt she'd lost him, for she said, 'Tell me something, Stuart. Do you dream?'

'Almost never.'

'You do, you know. All the time.' Again she looked sad, and grotesquely reasonable. 'That's part of the problem. We've told people that not everyone dreams, we've given them the chance to believe that of themselves. We've let them ignore their night selves, even though we know that whatever is repressed grows stronger and more difficult to cope with. Ignoring dreams doesn't make them go away – at least, it doesn't make them disappear.'

'Then where do they go?'

He'd asked out of weariness, and only because she had paused, but she was so delighted it was pitiful. 'That's right, Stuart. My point exactly. Where *do* they? They must go somewhere, and how can that not be real? Do you know that in the seventeenth century some authorities believed that dreams came from the life after death? I wonder if they found out how right they were.'

She grinned at his dismay. 'No, I haven't got religion. We're still talking science. When you die you die, but your dreams don't. How could they? They stay in the dream place, they feed it and grow. Our dreams and nightmares are what live after death.'

Her grin had vanished. 'For God's sake believe me, Stuart. We haven't much time. We've made people think their dreams can be measured and explained and controlled

406

and that maybe they don't even dream, and everything we've led people to believe has let it grow stronger.'

'What?' Stuart demanded. His forehead was tightening, beginning to ache.

'The dream place, the collective unconscious.' Then she shook her head. 'No, I'm not being honest with you. I call it the dream thing. It's alive, I'm sure it is. It wants to feed on what we call reality, feed on it so it can take its place. We've given it that strength, we even helped it gain a hold. That time at Oxford let it break through.'

'That's what you think happened at Oxford?'

'Of course. Stuart, you were there. Can you honestly tell me it could have been anything else?' The gleam in her eyes was beginning to look dangerous. 'They undermined reality, this reality, the one we take for granted. What do you think holds reality together if not our shared perception of it? They shared a perception of something else and made it stronger.' She drew a long loud breath. 'I'll tell you something I've never told anyone else, because I think you'll see it's true if you give it a chance. I don't think our subjects at Oxford foresaw the future – not always, anyway, and not all of them. I think sometimes some of them made it happen by dreaming of it.'

He would have got up and left her, but his fatigue that was so like dread wouldn't let him. 'Thank God at least they were so frightened,' she said. 'At least they aren't likely to meet again.'

'You think they shouldn't? Why?'

'Stuart, what have I been telling you? Haven't you been listening? If they meet they'll focus it, they'll give it a chance to come through. They're its doors, don't you see?' She shoved her hair back from her forehead, so wildly that she scratched herself. 'It tries to break through wherever reality is weakest. That's why you must get me out of here.'

'I'll have a word with Dr Lovell,' he said, and managed to stand up. When she stood up too he was afraid she would turn violent once she found she couldn't leave with him. Perhaps she only pretended to take the tranquillizers. 'You'll have to wait here,' he said hastily.

'I know. Just please don't make me wait long.' She glanced at the flooded window. 'It's out there somewhere, I know it is,' she murmured to herself. 'No wonder, with so many schizophrenics on the loose. One in ten, isn't it? And locking them up together gives it a chance to come through. It used to, you know, I'm sure of it. Succubi and incubi – we've forgotten so much. They weren't only said to come to you in your sleep, they were supposed to be the same creature every time. The same creature, that could be either sex or anywhere. Can you imagine that power? And that's only how it starts to break through . . .'

'Thanks for talking to me,' Stuart muttered, and fled. He was almost at the tall front doors of the lobby when Dr Lovell came hurrying after him. 'Did you learn anything?' she said.

'She's crazy,' he said, and didn't care that he sounded accusing. He threw the doors open and stepped into the downpour. A train from Norwich clattered by in the distance, showing him where the station was. In a minute his hair was dripping. He would be drenched before he got there. Nevertheless he didn't mean to stay at the hospital a moment longer; he wanted to put Guilda and her ravings behind him. Her project had destroyed her mind just as it had destroyed Danny Swain's, and there were four others unaccounted for. For his peace of mind, they were going to have to stay that way. Until tonight he hadn't fully realized how much even the threat of insanity terrified him.

Molly lingered in front of the mirror, to be sure of what she was seeing. Apart from her black eye, which looked no worse than an accident with mascara by now, her face was hardly marked. Her jaw was stiff, but that didn't show. At this rate it wouldn't be long before she would begin to think Martin hadn't touched her at all, that it had simply been another dream.

She grimaced at that, realizing how much she wished she could believe it, and took a deep breath. When the twinge of her bruised ribs made her falter, she tried again, sucked in as much of the soapy perfumed bathroom air as her lungs would hold, to prove to herself that she could. She was well enough to go to her parents, and the aching of her ribs would make sure she didn't have second thoughts. She gave her face a final scrutiny, then she went out to Nell. 'Thanks for putting up with me,' she said.

Nell was pulling on her mittens and matching hat. 'I know what it's like to need someone you can trust,' she said as she opened the door to the landing. 'You stay as long as you like.'

'I have done, thanks, Nell. I'll keep in touch.'

Nell had seemed in a hurry to get to work, but now she closed the door. 'You aren't thinking of going yet, are you?'

'I need to be at home, Nell. No reflection at all on you, you couldn't have been kinder, but I'll feel better once I'm with my family.' She felt almost as if she were trying to persuade Nell to let her go, which was silly; Nell might be leaning against the door as Maitland had blocked the doorway of the police cell, but that was no reason for Molly to feel like a prisoner. 'I'm fit to travel, don't worry,' she said.

Nell certainly seemed worried, so much so that she was at a

loss what to say. Susan came into the room, and Nell began abruptly to speak. 'You'll want to get your things from your flat, won't you?'

'Yes, of course,' Molly said, anticipating the luxury of having her own change of clothes.

'You can't go there by yourself, in case he's there.' Nell seemed so relieved it looked like triumph. If Molly was growing paranoid, that was another reason for her to go home. 'I'll be back from work as soon as I can,' Nell said. 'You'll wait, won't you?'

Her eyes were glistening with anxiety. Molly couldn't wait for her to finish work, it would lose her most of the day. She was opening her mouth to refuse when Nell said, 'I can make sure he's at work, out of the way.'

That did seem reassuring. There was no point in Molly's growing nervous about confronting Martin if all the time he was at MTV. She could deal with him, but it would be unpleasant in she didn't know how many different ways. 'All right,' she said reluctantly, and headed for the bathroom, to waste some of the time in a leisurely bath.

She lay in the steaming water and felt herself float up, first her legs and then her arms. She was drifting – had been for days. She was grateful to Nell, but all the same, she would be happier once she was in charge of herself again. Perhaps then she would know where she was going.

She wouldn't be returning to MTV. She couldn't bear to imagine what Gould must think of her and her relations with filmmakers, first Ben Eccles and now Martin. The thought that Martin must be back at work made her shaky with rage and injustice, but getting angry wouldn't help her think. Just now she seemed unable to. She hoped going to her parents wasn't the same as trying to walk away from her problems.

She climbed out of the bath at last, dried herself and put on the clothes she'd arrived in, and wandered into the green room in search of the hairbrush in her handbag. She

410

couldn't help jumping when she saw Susan. 'Won't you be late for school?'

'We're off today,' the child said, looking innocently at her. 'It's a saint's day.'

'Which saint?'

Susan murmured something Molly didn't quite hear. She went into the bathroom to brush her hair and tried to avoid her own eyes in the mirror. Had Susan said St Quentin? She didn't believe it was a saint's day at all, but what business was it of hers if Susan was playing truant? Perhaps she was staying off school to keep her company. She brushed her hair quickly and told herself she mustn't let Susan make her uneasy, for that made her uneasy about herself.

But that was how Susan affected her. She hadn't been with the child for a quarter of an hour when she found she had run out of conversation. She kept recalling the day Susan had come to her in Hyde Park, had begged her to help. It would be cruelly insensitive to remind Susan of that, and yet she couldn't quite believe that whatever had been wrong then had been put right so simply and completely. Susan was looking expectantly at her. 'Shall we watch television?' Molly said.

'You can if you like.'

At least it would save Molly from struggling to talk. She switched channels in search of a newscast, but all she found were programmes for schools and students. She settled for an undersea documentary, which might be the kind of programme Susan liked. Fish swam through dimness miles deep, their great blank eyes reminding Molly that they were said never to dream. Perhaps their lives were already like dreams, she thought, for their slow progress through the massive water made her feel as if she were there too. It could hardly be Susan who was making her feel sleepy, even though the child seemed to be watching her. She must be, for all at once she said, 'You can lie down in her room if you want.'

Molly started, and felt angry. 'Whose room?'

For a moment the child looked caught out. 'My mother's. Mummy's,' she said.

'I'm fine here, thank you, Susan.' But she wasn't. She mustn't keep glancing at the child, but keeping her gaze on the screen only made her more aware of Susan, made her feel as if the child kept saying things to her she couldn't quite hear. She could almost believe that the face at the edge of her vision wasn't Susan's at all, that the green room around her was changing. She'd had enough. She needed to be at home, especially since she seemed to be in no fit state to be left alone with a child. She shook her head to clear it, and stood up. 'Thank your mother for me when she comes home, but tell her I couldn't wait.'

Susan was on her feet at once. 'You can't go by yourself.'

'Why can't I?' Molly said, with a laugh that was meant to hide her feelings but which came out nervous.

'Mummy said. He might be there.'

'Who?' Molly demanded, in a tone that ought to put her in her place.

'The man who hurt you.' Susan's eyes widened. 'I know, I'll go and see if he's there. I only have to ring your bell and say I was looking for you if he is,' she said, and was out of the door.

Molly felt touched, and ashamed of having been unfair. She listened to the footsteps running down and the slam of the door, she watched Susan hurry towards Bayswater Road. She switched off the television and settled down to wait.

But not for long, for she was waking up. How could she have let the child go? Suppose Martin was there and lost his temper with her? Perhaps it had been her nervousness with Susan that had made Molly unable to think, but that was no excuse.

She grabbed her coat and was opening the door when she thought of her handbag. She might need her keys. She snatched her bag from beside the couch and wished she had time to search for a key to Nell's flat too. Suppose she missed Susan? The child might not have taken a key. She ran once through the flat, but couldn't see one. Surely she wouldn't miss Susan, surely they would use the same route. Getting out was the important thing, getting out and finding Susan. She raced back through the shaky hall, and was on the landing when she caught sight of Susan on the stairs.

Though the sight of the child was a relief, Molly felt all at once nervous. She blocked the closing door and waited. 'Well?' she said as Susan stepped on to the landing.

'Someone's in your flat, but they wouldn't come to the door. I saw them watching through the curtains.'

So they would have to wait for Nell. If Molly tried to go now, Susan would insist on accompanying her. She couldn't put the child further at risk. She went back into Nell's flat and sank onto a chair. She must need more rest than she thought, for she was growing irrational. For a moment Susan had made her remember the dream she'd had before Martin had attacked her. For a moment she'd thought that the man Susan had glimpsed in her flat might not be Martin but Danny Swain.

Stuart couldn't taste breakfast. Walking to the station last night in the rain had given him the worst cold he'd had for years. He drank all the coffee he could take, then he got his coat from his room and went out of the hotel in the hope that a walk around Norwich might clear his head.

He wandered through the sainted streets and down the sloping alleys, past the cathedral and its brood of churches, back and forth across the bridges over the Wensum, past

413

fragments of the Roman wall. When it occurred to him that he wasn't trying to clear his head so much as to evade what he must do, he went back to his room at the hotel.

He shrugged off his coat and stared at the phone. He had to call home, in case there was something he should know. There was no escaping his responsibility. All that his encounter with Guilda had told him was that he was on his own.

At least, so far as he knew – but perhaps he was being too pessimistic. That none of the Oxford subjects had replied to his letters didn't mean they'd gone the way of Guilda and Danny Swain. Perhaps some of them might even help him, especially if the others needed help. He'd woken that morning convinced of all this, but nevertheless, as he dialled home, he began to hope that nobody had been in touch.

Trina, the landlady, answered. 'I thought you were coming back last night,' she said when she recognized his clogged voice.

'Sorry to disappoint you.' He wasn't entirely joking, for she did sound a little piqued. She had the longest legs he'd ever seen on a woman, and now and then she gave him the impression that one day he might find out where they led. 'Any letters for me?'

'Not even one. Nobody must love you today.'

'Anyone been in touch?'

'Yes,' she said, and his heart lurched; he hadn't realized how apprehensive he was. 'An American. Friend of yours?'

'I haven't any American friends.'

'Pity. He was quite a charmer. I'd have liked to get to know him better. I must say he seemed to have a temper on him, though. Maybe it was because you kept him waiting.'

'He isn't there now?'

'No, though I did my best. I wish I'd had a spare room. I ought to have given him yours,' she said, a playful rebuke. 'He's still here in Oxford. Hang on, it's all written down.'

She came back amid a rustling of paper. 'He's at the Randolph. Nothing under four stars for these Americans. Want the number?' She rattled it off before Stuart could ask. 'I'll see you tonight perhaps, shall I?' she said, and quickly, 'Oh, I haven't told you his name, have I? Martin Wallace.'

She rang off as he cleared his throat. He'd wanted to ask her to use her key and fetch his address book so that she could read him the addresses of the subjects who were living in London, so that he could visit them. He still did. The last thing he needed was Wallace's interference – but suppose Wallace had news of Molly Wolfe? Suppose it was information he should have? As he dialled the code for Oxford, he wasn't sure if he meant to call Trina or the hotel.

It was early afternoon when Susan began to grow restless. Molly had heard children coming home for lunch, and now she heard them going back to school. Perhaps only Susan's school had the day off, or only Susan herself. It wouldn't have mattered to her, except that Susan was aggravating her nervousness, making it harder for her to steel herself for the confrontation at her flat. She was beginning to wonder why Susan had stayed home at all.

She leafed through the encyclopaedias on the shelf above the plants and tried to ignore Susan, who kept turning her head as if she could hear someone on the stairs. Molly tried to distract herself with the encyclopaedias, but every subject seemed to hide a meaning: music was Stravinsky who had based his octet on a dream, Shakespeare seemed to have beeen obsessed with dreams when she thought about it, universities were Oxford . . . She sat down and worked on her breathing instead.

Susan went to the window. She stood there, arms straight down by her sides, and watched for Nell. This was even more nerve-racking than her restlessness had been, this obsessive stillness that looked like a ritual. When Molly glanced at Susan's reflection in the window, all she could see were the child's eyes. They looked huge. Molly turned away, telling herself it must be a flaw in the glass. 'I'm sure your mother will come home as soon as she can. You won't make her come any sooner.'

'I know she will.'

The child's voice sounded almost as if she were saying she could bring Nell home, whatever Molly thought. Her eyes in the reflection were impossibly huge and bright. 'What's wrong?' Molly demanded. 'What can't you wait for?'

'*You* said you wanted to go home.'

'So I did. But I can wait, Susan. Don't work yourself up on my behalf.'

She'd hoped her lightness of tone, forced though it was, would make Susan turn. When the child didn't move she tried again. 'You're a strange child, do you know that?'

Susan stiffened. 'Strange how?'

'Why, all that you said to me around Christmas, for one thing. About having power over people, remember? You were going to tell me more about that, but you never did. You hardly seem like the same person.'

She wondered if she'd said too much, for Susan's hands were clenching at her sides. All at once she turned round. She had the look of a child who could no longer keep a secret, yet her face was more threatening than her voice had been. Molly wanted to laugh, but something prevented her, made her too breathless to speak.

'There was a girl who didn't want me to live here,' Susan said in a low voice. 'Do you know what I did?'

Molly tried to smile. 'You tell me.'

'I put her in Mummy's room where there aren't any windows. When I opened the door, she was still lost in the

416

dark where the light couldn't reach. I made it that big. Shall I tell you what was in there with her?' she whispered, just as they heard Nell on the stairs.

Nell seemed to have been running. 'He isn't at the studios,' she said when she caught her breath.

'I know. He's at my place,' Molly said, feeling guilty that Susan had found out on her behalf.

'You won't want to go just yet then, will you?'

'Certainly. Alone, if I have to.'

'Oh, no, we'll come with you,' Nell said hastily. 'We both will.' For a moment she seemed unable to think why. 'Susan can stay outside in case she has to run for help.'

Molly would rather have had Susan stay here, but arguing would only waste more time. She was halfway downstairs before she had buttoned her coat. Her first step on the path felt like escaping – escaping after having been cooped up for years.

When she saw her curtains were closed, though she had left them open, she realized she'd been hoping Susan was mistaken. So much the worse for him. Just let him try to make trouble in front of Nell, when Susan had only to run down to Bayswater Road and cry for help. She unlocked the door and faltered on the threshold, for the walls of the hall were fluttering and rustling.

It was newspaper. He'd taped sheets of it over all the mirrors on both walls. If that was meant to express contempt of her decor, it seemed both feeble and obscure. It didn't seem like Martin, until she reminded herself that once he'd lost his temper she hadn't known him. It had to be Martin, nobody else could be using her flat. 'Come in while I pack,' she said loudly to Nell, for him to hear.

Perhaps he wasn't in the flat now. She went into the kitchen first, and was appalled by how much of a slob he was. Some of the remains of food on the dirty plates piled in the sink were barely cooked. He had virtually emptied the fridge and the freezer. She hoped the undercooked food had

417

given him indigestion. She went into the living room, and let out a gasp so furious she hadn't time to fit a word to it. Her video cassettes were strewn over the floor, and one blank tape had been ripped out of its case. She stalked into her bedroom, to see what havoc he had wreaked in there.

He was using her bed. Instinct told her not to look too closely at the rumpled sheets. She wondered if he'd imagined beating her up to help him masturbate. 'Looks as if we've got the place to ourselves after all,' she told Nell, and went quickly to the wardrobe. Her dresses lay in a heap beneath the hangers, but that seemed to have been the extent of his inventiveness. She packed as many of the dresses as she had room for, and was starting on the chest of drawers when she saw her old toy monkey under the bed.

Its limbs had been torn off, its eyes gouged out. One socket and the area around it was stained with semen. Molly backed away from the idea of touching the monkey, and felt sick. She twitched at a blanket so that it hid the monkey from Nell. She piled the contents of the drawers into her second suitcase, and hurried to the bathroom to collect her toiletries, to be out of the flat as soon as she could.

The bathroom door wouldn't open. At first she thought it had jammed. She threw her weight against it, and then she heard a thud at the far end of the bathroom. The toilet seat had fallen on the pan. 'Come out of there,' she cried in a rage that made her throat and her head ache. 'I want my things.'

There was silence. Did he think she would go away if he didn't answer? Nell came into the hall as Molly began to pound on the door. 'Get out of here, you shit,' Molly cried, 'and don't try anything. There's someone here with me. You tell him, Nell.'

'That's right,' Nell said reluctantly.

'Someone you know, and she knows you. She knows all about you.' The silence enraged her. 'What are you doing in there, playing with yourself again? Seeing how much more of a mess you can make? Get out of my flat right now or I'll bring the police.'

She heard a clatter of glass jars, and then glass smashed. 'That's right, you find something else to break,' she cried. 'All right, I've had enough. Come on, we'll break this door down and find out what he's up to.'

Nell looked wary. Did she think he had broken the jar to use against them? Molly threw her weight against the door and felt the flimsy bolt jerk in its socket. 'Come on,' she said, cold with anger, to Nell. 'I'm not leaving him in here.'

She stared at Nell until Nell moved. They attacked the door together, and Molly heard wood splintering. The screws of the bolt must be loosening. One more combined onslaught and the door would give. She heard the gnash of broken glass under his feet, and Nell's apprehension almost infected her, but she wanted him out of her flat. The renewed pain of her bruises only made her more determined. Just then Susan started clattering the letter box and crying, 'What's wrong?'

'You are,' Molly muttered, and hoped Nell hadn't heard. She couldn't risk driving him out now when the child was so near. Her rage was fading again, her throbbing arm made her bite her lip. She felt stupidly revengeful. 'Never mind,' she murmured to Nell. 'I can buy toilet things when I get home.'

But she didn't mean to leave him in residence, by God. 'Don't get too comfortable in there,' she shouted as she left, and banged on the bathroom door. 'We're going for the police right now.' As she reached Bayswater Road she thought she heard her front door slamming, but Nell and Susan were hurrying across to the far pavement, bearing her suitcases which they'd insisted on carrying. She followed them in search of a cab. She felt wistful and homeless, robbed of all her years in her flat, but at least she was out of Nell's. At last she was on her way.

Once Martin had ascertained that Molly wasn't at MTV, there was little he could do except wait in Reception. It shouldn't take Stuart Hay much longer to get here from Norwich than it had taken Martin from Oxford. It better hadn't, for Hay's sake.

Few of the people who passed through the lobby seemed to recognize Martin. Those who must have didn't acknowledge him, except for the odd double take. All the same, they made him nervous in case someone like Ben Eccles thought of calling the police. Suppose the police were looking for him so as to serve their papers on him? Now that Hay had rekindled his hope, however faint, of finding Molly, extradition seemed a real threat.

Martin had had all he could take, both of worrying about the police and of wasting his time. He left a message at the desk for Stuart Hay to wait, that he was going over to Molly Wolfe's.

The afternoon was growing colder. The bare trees of Hyde Park were caught in the blue ice of the sky. Everything looked sharp and clear and detailed, and quite beside the point. All he wanted was to see that Molly was well, and then he would leave her alone. It was no longer important what she believed about him, only that she was all right now. He hurried past the police station, cursing the police for their part in her breakdown, and was almost at the pedestrian crossing when he saw her across the road.

He was lurching in front of the speeding traffic until he stopped himself – of course it couldn't have been Molly. Why would she have been with a woman and a young girl who were both carrying suitcases? He'd hardly glimpsed her face as she vanished down the steps into the Underground. He ran across when the traffic lights allowed him to, but there was no sign of the three even when he ventured down the steps. As he headed back up, he had to step aside for a pale man with angry pimples and spiky hair, who looked as if he were chasing someone into the Underground. One glance at his face convinced Martin that he wouldn't like to be whoever the man was chasing, especially not when he caught them. He ran up the steps, and up the hill to Molly's.

He could see from the street that she'd gone. Now the curtains were open, he saw at once that her wardrobe and chest of drawers had been emptied. He rang the bell anyway, hopelessly, and thought that she must have been in the flat when the police had dragged him away. Perhaps it had been his attempt to speak to her that had made her go into hiding. All the way back to MTV that thought aggravated his rage. And so did the sight of Stuart Hay getting up from a Reception chair and ambling towards him.

Stuart halted only inches from him. 'I want to be straight with you right away,' he croaked, then had to clear his throat elaborately. 'I went to see Guilda Kent, who ran the Oxford project, and she's out of her head. So is Danny Swain who was one of our subjects.'

Clenching his fists hard let Martin speak. 'And you're still saying you aren't responsible?'

'No, I think I'm the only one left who is.'

This was so unlike his attitude in Oxford that again Martin was speechless. 'I take it she wasn't at home,' Stuart said.

'No.' Martin wasn't ready to give up his resentment. 'I've no idea where she is,' he said accusingly.

'Perhaps she's already over the worst of it. She seemed a lot more stable than Swain, as I remember.'

'Look, don't presume, all right?' Martin lowered his

421

voice as people turned, hoping for a scene. 'You don't know what sort of state she's in, and neither do I.'

'As you like. I was going to suggest that as long as we don't know where she is, we should go and see Joyce Churchill. She's the other subject who lives in London.'

'What, the woman who looks after old people? She contacted Molly a few weeks ago.' Martin tried not to be too hopeful. 'I suppose Molly could be with her.'

'It isn't far. We'll take a cab.' He stood aside for Martin at the revolving doors. 'I'll pay,' he said as if that made things right.

Martin didn't talk to him once they were in the taxi; for the moment there seemed to be nothing to say. He stared out at Regent's Park and Kentish Town as Stuart blew his nose and snuffled. When the taxi drew up before a Georgian house on the brow of the hill, Martin hurried down the short path to ring the bell.

There was no reply. He rang again as Stuart, having paid the driver, followed him. The neat flower beds beside the path were growing unkempt, and Martin thought that Joyce Churchill had left home too. He tried knocking, the last hope, and the door swung open. It had been left minutely ajar.

Perhaps she was at a neighbour's or round the corner at the shops, or perhaps she thought she'd closed the door. Martin and Stuart listened then knocked again loudly, they glanced at each other and nodded, and then they went in. Somewhere above them in the house was the slowest, thickest breathing Martin had ever heard.

Molly ran up the steps and out of the Underground and into Kings Cross Station. The sooner she was out of London, the safer she would feel – safe from what, she didn't know.

She struggled through the crowd to the shortest of the shuffling queues for the ticket windows, and glanced around. Of course she wasn't being followed, except by Nell and Susan.

Didn't anyone have cash? Everyone paid by credit card, which added minutes to each transaction. She watched Nell dumping the cases beside Susan and hurrying to the departure board. She willed the queue, five people ahead of her, to shuffle faster, for God's sake move. Nell made her way over to Molly. 'Your train's just gone.'

'Did you notice when the next one is?' Molly said.

'Not for almost two hours.'

'Bloody hell.' At least she would be able to call her parents to let them know she was coming, once she got her breath back. The queue shuffled grudgingly forward, and when at last she reached the window with her handful of banknotes, she had to close her eyes before she could think of her destination. She stuffed the ticket into her handbag and headed for her suitcases, which were somewhere to sit down.

Sitting down made her feel no better; she still felt as if Susan were watching her, even though the child's face was turned away. She couldn't be watching, nor could whoever had followed Molly out of the Underground, for nobody had. Molly rubbed her prickling forehead with her sleeve. 'Aren't you feeling well?' Nell said.

'No, not very. I'll be all right soon.'

'I know someone not far from here who used to be a nurse,' said Nell.

'Oh, I don't think I'm that bad.' But perhaps she was, for the crowd seemed to be closing in on her, the uproar of trains and amplified voices was growing unbearable. Perhaps once she was out of the station she would feel better – with all those faces she couldn't be sure that one of them wasn't watching her – and perhaps the ex-nurse could give her something to perk her up. 'How far from here?' she said.

'Just a few minutes' walk. Come on, we've plenty of time.' Nell was already helping her up and so was Susan. As soon as Molly was on her feet, they picked up the suitcases and pushed through the crowd, and she could only follow.

Nell and Susan hurried her alongside the station, and in a few minutes the crowds and the lights had fallen behind and they were walking along a dark street where there seemed to be no houses. Down what she took at first to be an alley a canal lapped, a treacly sound in the dark. She glanced back towards the lights of Kings Cross and saw a man coming after her, quite fast. She ran to keep up with Nell and Susan. She'd meant to ask them to slow down, though the icy night air had revived her somewhat, but decided that she wouldn't after all.

Now there were windows. Nell was leading her along a road between tenements. Lights went on here and there, drawn curtains coloured the lights, and Molly wondered why the sight of so many windows made her nervous. She hurried past the Lewis Carroll Library that was the ground floor of a tenement, she had to look twice at a maisonette before she realized it was a church, and then she saw that Nell had brought her to Caledonian Road.

'Nearly there,' Nell said.

They turned along a side street that was closed by a gate. Saplings grew from gaps the size of flagstones in front of the terraced houses. It must be the night that massed above the roofs, though to Molly it felt like enormous walls. She felt edgy at the thought of meeting whoever Nell had in store for her. She would much rather head for the nearest pub.

But Nell had halted in front of a house, and now she was climbing the steps to the front door. Suddenly Molly didn't want to go into that house. It must be shyness that her exhaustion made feel like panic, but she didn't care. She ran to the steps and tried to clear her dry throat, to say she'd changed her mind. Too late. Nell was rapping at the yellow door with the shiny silver bar of the knocker. Before Molly could say a word, a woman opened the door.

She obviously didn't recognize Nell, who seemed at a loss what to do. 'Can I help you?' the woman said. That spurred Nell, who grabbed both cases and marched into the house, followed by Susan. Both of them turned to wait for Molly.

Molly was as bewildered as the woman looked. The woman turned sharply to Nell as someone came out of a room at the end of the hall, beyond the stairs. He was dressed in black, his pale oval face was calm as a mask. 'All right, Doreen,' he said. 'They are expected.'

All at once Molly was breathless with panic. She felt as if she had been here before and forgotten, as if it were more than life was worth to step over the threshold. Susan and the man in black were watching her, and she had a sudden nightmare impression that they were watching her with the same eyes. She turned to hurry down to the pavement – and then she froze. Lurching at her up the steps, his face distorted by hatred and triumph, was Danny Swain.

59

As soon as they were in the house and had closed the door, Stuart called, 'Is anyone there?' It seemed odd to Martin, since someone audibly was. Perhaps Stuart's cold had made

425

him deaf, or perhaps he didn't think the slow thick sound upstairs was breathing. But it couldn't be anything else, though it made Martin think of waves – the waves of a sea that was thicker than water. He followed Stuart towards the nearest room, a living room with paintings of children and cats on the walls. 'You could check upstairs while I look around down here,' Stuart said.

Did he think Martin was used to prying, or was he secretly uneasy about the breathing? Still, if they split up it might take less time to find something that would help them. Perhaps whoever was sleeping upstairs might be able to tell them where Molly was. Martin started up the stairs, calling 'Hello.'

The breathing didn't falter. It made him feel suffocated, and so, as he climbed, did the growing smell. Something smelled unhealthily old. He made as much noise on the stairs as he could, for fear that the sleeper would wake at the last moment and start screaming. 'Hello there,' he shouted.

All of the doors on the landing were open but one. There was a bathroom, a bedroom with an unmade double bed, an office with a desk and a safe and a shelf of philatelic catalogues. All three rooms were deserted. Now there was only the closed door, and he felt less enthusiastic about waking the sleeper; the smell up here was overpowering, as if something had been left for too long. He went to the top of the stairs and called to Stuart, but his voice was swallowed up by the breathing. He felt as if it were swallowing him. 'Stuart,' he called more loudly, and the breathing ceased.

So did Martin's. He stood staring at the closed door with one hand pressed over his mouth and nose, and couldn't think what to do. All they needed was for the sleeper to start screaming burglars, screaming for the police. His head was beginning to throb when he heard whoever was beyond the door suck in a breath, and a voice piped nervously, 'Is that you, Joyce?'

So it wasn't Joyce in that room, and certainly not Molly.

It was nobody who could help. 'No,' Martin called, cursing himself.

'Who then? Is it Geoffrey?' The sexless piping voice was trembling, and sounded near to hysteria. 'It can't be Geoffrey. Come in so I know who you are.'

Martin wanted nothing so much as to steal away. Everything – the breathing that had turned irregular and laborious, the threat of hysteria in the voice, the festering smell – made him unwilling to go into the room. But he couldn't leave the person in such a state when he had been the cause of it. He listened in the hope that Stuart had heard him, but could hear no sound downstairs. He stepped forward quickly and opened the door.

The room was dark. The smell was considerably worse. The light from the landing fell short, so that all he could make out was a pale shape that looked as if it were overflowing the double bed. At least he must be visible, which allowed him to hope he could explain without going into the room that he'd been looking for Joyce and had found the front door ajar. Then the voice came out of the dark. 'Who is it?' it piped, nearer still to hysteria, and there was nothing to be done except switch on the light in the room.

When he reached in and found the switch, the light came on so brightly that he wasn't immediately sure of what he was seeing. Some of the mound that was overflowing the bed was blankets, but he could see that the form under the blankets was very large. He had to stare to convince himself that the two whitish objects near the top of the bed were arms, lying on the blankets, for they looked soft and shapeless as enormous ropes of dough. They had to be arms, for above them on the pillow was the head they belonged to.

It was bald and white and puffy. It looked as if it would quiver like jelly from its scalp to its chin if it wobbled up on its neck. If its toothless mouth hadn't been opening and closing he might not have realized it was a head, for the features were almost lost in fat. But the whitish tongue was fluttering sluggishly about the mouth as the voice piped, 'What do you want? Who are you?'

'I was looking for Joyce Churchill.' Martin had to clap one hand over his nose and draw breath before he went on, 'I don't suppose you know where she is.'

'He took her away, he made her forget about me. I'm not wanted any more. They've left me here by myself. I've been alone for days.' One arm wavered up from the blankets and reached blindly towards him. 'You'll stay with me, won't you? I can't look after myself. I'm all alone in the world.'

Martin couldn't answer. He stared in fascinated horror at her hand. The fingers must be squeezed together, but it looked like a single lump of flesh, hardly recognizable as a hand except for the fingernails that were almost buried in its edges. 'Don't leave me,' the voice piped shrilly, 'let me see if you're as kind as you sound,' and the fat of the arms lolled back and forth as both hands groped towards the face.

They were reaching for the eyes. Martin saw that the fat had forced the eyelids shut until they could no longer open by themselves. He stepped forward instinctively to help, compelled by an appalled pity, but once he was close enough to help he couldn't bring himself to try. The skin of the face looked thin as paper, ready to split at a touch, burst open. He was struggling to overcome his revulsion when the groping hands managed to pry open the left eye.

Martin stumbled backwards, clutching at his mouth, trying to swallow. There was no eye beneath the eyelid, only a swelling of whitish flesh. 'Don't leave me,' the voice piped desperately as he staggered out of the room and held on to the doorframe. 'Stuart,' he shouted, 'can you come up here right now?'

He tried to keep his gaze on the stairs so as not to look back into the room. One glance showed him the hands digging at the right eye, the nails trying to lift the eyelid. As he shoved himself away from the doorframe, he thought he glimpsed a flood of white engulfing the pillow and then the bed. 'Stuart,' he called from the top of the stairs, his voice cracking.

When at last Stuart came up to him he could only point towards the room. 'In there,' he muttered, swallowing. The breathing had ceased as he'd left the doorway. Stuart hurried into the room, and emerged a few moments later, looking impatient. 'Well, what did you want me to see?' he said.

It was Nell and the man with the oval face who helped Molly upstairs, though helped was hardly the word. The woman of the house had slammed the front door in Danny's face, but perhaps they wanted to put as much distance between him and Molly as possible, or thought that Molly did. Of course she did, but she wished they wouldn't hurry her so fast up the stairs, and it seemed they would never stop climbing. They were marching her upwards, each holding one of her arms, giving her no time to catch her breath, and she had barely enough energy to wonder how they had managed to slip through into a different building, into this house with so many floors. They were virtually carrying her by the time the man with the oval face said, 'This will be far enough.'

They could hardly have gone much further. As far as Molly could see, there was only one more floor above, which was dark. He opened a door and switched on the light in the room, a boardinghouse room with heavy curtains over the window, a new green carpet on the floor, a crucifix above the bed with its neatly turned-down sheets. Molly

429

was marched into the room, where they dumped her cases on the floor and lowered her onto the bed. 'You must fear nothing now,' the man with the oval face said.

It was all very well for him to say that, even if it was meant to be reassuring. Molly felt as if she'd left her thoughts and feelings behind on the climb, along with her breath. She lay panting on the bed while they watched her solicitously. As soon as she could speak she said accusingly to Nell, 'You said there was a nurse.'

Nell looked relieved when the man intervened. 'What is it you need?'

'I need to go home.' Reaction overtook her, and she began to tremble. 'My God, I don't know what's happening. That crazy man you saw just now, he's been following me for weeks. What in Christ's name does he want? What has he got against me?'

'We shall deal with him, I give you my word. I imagine you will see that for a time it is best you stay here.'

His calm voice and his deliberate sentences seemed almost hypnotic. At least she would be staying only until Danny was out of the way, she thought; the dumping of the suitcases in the room had seemed ominous.

'You'll send the nurse up, will you?'

'She has not been a nurse for some years. Let me see what I can do.' He laid his hand on her forehead. His touch felt cool, gentle, still. She hardly knew when he began to massage her temples, he was making her feel so restful. All her memories of panic were fading. She felt safe, cared for, home at last.

She was willing him to go on when he took his hand away. She kept her eyes closed, to hold on to the calm. 'I shall come up for you when matters are under control,' he murmured, 'but call on me if you should feel you need me. Call me Sage.'

The door closed softly, and she listened to his and Nell's footsteps descending until she could no longer hear them.

She let the silence float her mind away. Though she could hardly believe it after all that had happened, she felt ready to sleep, even to dream. If she could feel safe to dream anywhere now, it would be here. A dream that would be larger than any she'd experienced was waiting. She breathed deeply and gently, until she was no longer aware of breathing.

She wasn't sure what jerked her awake from the first split second of dreaming. Surely the impression that something had shifted near her in the room must be part of the dream. She opened her eyes as little as possible, doing her best to cling to sleep. Her eyes were closing as she glanced up at the crucifix.

She frowned at it and then, impatiently, sat up. It didn't look very conventional, but why should that bother her? It could hardly have turned its head to grin down at her as she lay on the bed. It wasn't grinning, only smiling widely, though surely that was unusual. If the eyes appeared to be watching her, that was a trick you could find in hundreds of paintings and posters. There was no point in imagining that the eyes looked familiar. If she was going to make herself nervous, perhaps she had better call Sage.

Some instinct restrained her. He'd said that she must fear nothing now. Suddenly that seemed less a reassurance than a suggestion of what might lie ahead.

She jumped up and went to the door. The landing with its new green carpet was deserted, and all the other doors were closed. She went quickly to the stairwell and glanced up at the dark floor above her, then she looked down.

It couldn't be the house with the yellow front door. There were too many floors – so many that she was afraid even to start counting. No point in speculating, no point in making herself more uneasy. All she knew was that she didn't mean to be left alone up here, so far from everyone, and she was about to start down when she heard voices. They must be at the bottom of the stairs, they were so minute, but a quirk of

431

the acoustics let her hear every word. 'We are not quite ready,' Sage was saying.

He was talking to the landlady, for Molly heard her say, 'Are you the one who's lost her husband?'

'Yes,' came Nell's voice, 'and I don't want him back.'

'No, that is not why Helen came here. It is no longer a question of that kind of bereavement. But the lost shall be restored, I promise you. You will not be disappointed.' Sage's voice was moving away. 'Now I think we have left Mrs Churchill by herself for long enough,' he said, and shortly there came the closing of a door.

Molly stared down the impossible distance, then retreated into her room. She couldn't have heard what she'd thought she'd heard. Churchill was a common name, and Nell sounded very much like Helen; why, they were the same name really. But Joyce Churchill had been a nurse eleven years ago, and why should Nell have concealed her real name?

Something was very wrong here, and she meant to find out what it was: anything rather than stay up here in the room that felt as if nobody had used it before her with the crucified figure that, if she let her imagination loose, she could imagine had turned its gleeful head to watch her. She went back onto the landing and winced as the door slammed behind her. She was steeling herself for the descent when a voice spoke to her, whispered to her: 'Don't go down.'

There was someone above her, in the dark. For a moment Molly wanted to run, run and fall if she had to, until she reached the ground floor. But the voice sounded desperate, and almost drained of strength. 'Please don't go,' it said, 'please help me, whoever you are,' sounding like a prisoner who had been kept up there for years. Molly couldn't resist so desperate a plea. She glanced unhappily down the stairs and then she went up.

Even though Stuart looked impatient and puzzled, some time passed before Martin could make himself go into the room. One of his fears was that he might see something in there that Stuart wasn't seeing, and what would that mean? At last he shoved himself away from the banister and went quickly if unsteadily to join Stuart. The bed looked sodden, but it was empty, and so was the room. 'There was someone in here,' Martin cried.

'Not recently.'

'Yes, recently. Just now. I saw them on the bed.'

'You saw them?' Stuart was ready to grin, as if that would bring Martin out of it. 'How many?'

'Just one, God damn it.' Martin was very close to losing his temper. 'I don't know if it was a man or a woman, but it was there, no question of it. I was near enough to touch it,' he said, and shuddered. 'My God, I almost did.'

'Why didn't you?'

'Because it didn't look – because it looked as if – ' He didn't like the ideas that suggested themselves. 'Why are you trying to tell me there was nobody? You heard the breathing when we came in.'

'I may have heard something that sounded like breathing. That's why you expected to see someone, and that's why you did. It's nothing to be ashamed of, Martin. We can all do it. Just for a moment when I looked in here I thought I saw someone on the bed myself.'

'What did you see?' Martin demanded.

'Nothing that could have been a human being, believe me. Obviously it was the blankets.'

'Then what's this?' Martin forced himself to go to the

bed, and pointed at the pillow. The wetness was seeping into the pillow, disappearing altogether too quickly, but it still glistened in the enormous indentation left by the head. 'Explain that, if you can.'

'Do you really want me to? Is it really that important to you, when we're trying to find your girl friend and the others?' Stuart squeezed his arm as if the ache might bring him back to reality. 'We can stand here all night arguing about whether you did or did not see someone, but what on earth can it have to do with what we're supposed to be doing?'

Until that moment Martin would have seen no connection at all, but now Stuart had made him feel he should. 'Molly said something once,' he said almost to himself, 'about dreams that were so intense she couldn't tell they weren't real.'

'In that case who was dreaming just now? Are you saying we both were?' As Martin glanced at the pillow, Stuart said, 'Dreams don't leave traces in reality, Martin. We both saw what we expected to see, that's all. Always trust the simplest explanation that fits all the facts unless there's a damn good reason not to do so.'

Martin made himself stay in the room. The bright light on the marks on the pillow only made them more threatening, for the smell was still in the air. Of course Stuart wouldn't notice with his cold. The smell had faded, but now Martin had the uneasy notion that it was growing stronger. 'You haven't explained that stuff on the bed,' he protested nervously. 'That's a fact, if you'll only look.'

'Leave it, Martin, all right? Don't crack up, not now. Enough people have.'

He must have seen how close that came to enraging Martin, for he said hastily, 'You'll agree we've drawn a blank here. I think the best thing is for me to approach the police. They ought to help me even if they won't help you. They can trace Mrs Churchill while we're contacting the others. Maybe they'll find Miss Wolfe as well.'

Martin wanted to get out of the room and the house before he panicked, get away from the moribund smell, but suppose they had overlooked something? He went dizzily onto the landing, sucked in a breath from the stairwell, and went into the philatelist's office. The telephone – a message pad on the desk. He hurried to it. 'What about this?' he called, forcing himself not to whisper.

Stuart came to see. It was a scribbled address, surrounded by jagged doodles. 'It might be worth checking, if it's in London,' Stuart admitted. 'We need an A to Zed.'

'An A to Zee? I saw one. There it is.' Martin grabbed it from beside the stamp catalogues and leafed through the index, so roughly that a page tore. For a moment he'd thought he heard breathing in the house. 'Okay, there's a street of that name,' he said, and turned hastily to the map, peered wildly at the small print. 'It's off Caledonian Road.'

'You think we should go there, do you?'

'Yes.' Anywhere that was out of this house, where now he thought he could hear movement in the next room.

'All right, we'll go as soon as I've called the police.'

Stuart was reaching for the phone, and Martin was almost sure he heard movement, a creaking of the bed. 'Shouldn't we see if she's at this address first?'

Stuart peered sharply at him, wondering why he was so nervous. 'All right,' Stuart said, 'I don't suppose we want to risk wasting police time.' Martin headed for the stairs at once. When he opened the front door, the night air felt welcome as a cold bath in a heat wave, but he couldn't breathe properly until Stuart was safely out as well. Martin closed the door and felt the bolt snap into place. He thought of asking Stuart if he'd seen or heard anything as they came downstairs, but Stuart would only deny it, and the question would only make him more dubious about Martin. Perhaps Martin had seen nothing, perhaps it was just a fear. But that was bad enough, for he couldn't shake it off: the impression of something struggling to take shape again under the mound of blankets.

Molly was almost at the top before she saw the woman who had called to her, a tall stooped woman who was supporting herself on the banister. She looked starved and old, but Molly could tell that she was younger than she looked. Molly ran up the last few stairs, because the woman seemed in danger of falling headlong. But as soon as the woman saw her face she began to back away along the landing, shaking her head as if it would never stop.

Molly halted three stairs down. Dismay had frozen her. The woman peered at Molly's face as if she hoped she didn't know her, shaking her head as if that would grant her wish. At last she said, 'Tell me quickly, what's your name?'

She must have recognized her from the newspaper, Molly tried to tell herself, and yet she thought she knew the stooped woman. 'Molly Wolfe,' she said.

The woman put her hand over her mouth. 'Weren't you at Oxford?'

'At the university, you mean?' It was Molly's last pathetic hope.

'No, at the research place. Where they were doing research into dreams.' She looked as hopeless as Molly felt. 'You do remember me, don't you? Freda Beeching.'

Now that her half-defined fears were confirmed, Molly felt oddly resigned. 'My God, we aren't the only ones here, are we?'

'That's right. He tricked me into bringing Joyce Churchill here.'

So Joyce Churchill was the ex-nurse, and everything was coming true. 'Helen Verney brought me here, and Danny Swain followed us,' Molly said, and then what Freda had said caught up with her. 'You say someone tricked you? You know who's behind all this?'

'Sage.'

'Who is he?' Molly whispered.

'I don't know. I try not to wonder.'

Perhaps Freda had good reason to be fearful, but it infuriated Molly. 'Why should he want to bring us all together?'

'Don't you remember?'

All at once Molly was as near to panic as Freda sounded. 'Remember what?'

'The dream.'

'I'm not sure I want to,' Molly said.

'Remembering doesn't matter now,' Freda said. 'It's grown too strong to be stopped. I started dreaming it again last night and I haven't dared sleep since. You do remember how it was, don't you? You must remember.' But she looked terrified that Molly would say she did. 'How nobody will be sure what's behind a door until they open it, and how you'll never know where any street leads, and the worst thing you can do will be to ask someone the way . . .' Her hands were digging at her cheeks.

'You need to sit down,' Molly said, struggling to quiet the memories Freda had revived. 'Let's go in your room where we can talk properly.'

'We mustn't go in there,' Freda whispered shrilly. 'We mustn't wake him.'

Molly didn't want to know why Freda was afraid. 'All right, we won't go in your room,' she said, and suddenly was grateful to have been diverted. 'Do you think you can walk down?'

Freda glanced unhappily down the stairwell. 'Can you?'

'If I came up I can go down,' Molly said, not looking.

'Listen, Freda, I think we still have a chance. If we've been brought here for the reason you think, then Sage must need all of us. We have to get out before Danny Swain gets in.'

Freda stumbled as she ventured on the first stair and would have plunged headlong if Molly hadn't grabbed her. 'I'll be all right,' Freda murmured, 'as long as I take it slowly.' Molly suppressed the thought that slowly was the last way she wanted to go down.

Freda kept glancing back at the closed door of her room until they reached Molly's floor, then she began to peer nervously down the stairwell. Molly kept her own gaze away from there. She needed all her energy to avoid making a noise on the stairs. At least Freda seemed to weigh almost nothing.

The floors were trooping past, bright and bare and featureless except for their closed doors. The smell of the new carpet was so overpowering it was beginning to make her feel sick. She wondered if she ought to count the floors, to give herself something to do. The idea came too late, for she'd forgotten how many floors they had already passed.

Perhaps counting the floors would only have made them more real. If the floors and the stairs weren't real, what was she walking on? But if they were real, how could they be in the house with the yellow front door? By now, dismayingly, she knew she hadn't been taken into another building. She mustn't speculate, mustn't think about the stairs at all, just walk. Yet it troubled her deeply that the stairs seemed somehow generalized, as if they were an idea that wasn't yet fully expressed. Worst of all was their utter meaninglessness.

The dream she'd shared with Freda and the others was coming true at last. She couldn't help suspecting that if she was afraid of it, that added to its power. Hadn't Sage told her she must fear nothing? But controlling her fear wasn't taking them downstairs any sooner: on the contrary, the stairs and the floors seemed to be growing more real, more

438

specific; she stumbled on a tack that had bent instead of penetrating the stair, and there was a landing where the carpet didn't quite reach the wall. She was holding tight to Freda's bony arm, since Freda and her laborious descent had to be most real, when she heard a door open and close.

Freda clutched at her so violently that Molly almost lost her balance. 'Where was that?' Freda cried.

'Down there.' Molly put her finger to her lips. She'd remembered how sounds carried on the staircase. Below them, stairs were creaking. Someone trying to be stealthy was coming up from the downstairs hall.

Molly risked a glance over the banister and almost cried out – not because she saw anyone, but because she and Freda were only a few floors up. Just a couple of minutes more and they could have been out of the house. Now she could see a hand on the banister, two floors below. She hurried Freda up to the nearest room. 'Someone's coming,' she whispered urgently. 'We'll hide in here.'

When Freda stared nervously at the door, Molly reached past her and turned the handle. She switched on the light in the room, which looked very much like the one she had been taken into, and quickly led Freda forward. For a moment, to her dismay, she found herself wishing her parents would come for her, wishing that she wouldn't be alone with all this any longer, that they would be in the room. She remembered imagining that they were in her flat. All at once she knew that if they had ever appeared there, they would have had the same eyes as Sage – for those eyes were watching her across the empty room.

They were the eyes of the crucifix. She saw the end of the movement as its head turned to watch. She felt Freda stiffening. She couldn't have forced her into the room, weak as Freda was, even if she had wanted to. They backed out and Molly fumbled the door shut just as the man on the stairs reached the landing. It was Danny.

Before Molly could move, he was between her and the

stairs. The triumph and the hatred in his eyes looked crazier, more dangerous: he wasn't going to be tricked twice. As he stretched out his arms on both sides of him, the light gleamed through his nails. Perhaps he'd kept them long and cruel especially for her.

Her heart was pounding violently, her dry throat was closing up, but she had to make him see he'd been tricked. 'Listen, Danny, we've all been lured here. Wait, let me finish,' she cried, for he was still advancing as if he were determined not to hear, eyes narrowing, hands like claws, and she could only back away to give herself time to finish. 'You remember what we dreamed in Oxford, don't you? It's here now. This is where it begins. We're all needed to make it happen. Someone let you in, didn't they? That's why. If we can get out of here and stay away from one another, perhaps it won't be able to.'

She was nearly at the wall opposite the stairs, and then there would be nowhere to go. Freda plucked at his arm as he stalked past her, ignoring her. 'She's telling the truth,' Freda said. 'Don't you recognize me? He needs me too. If you'll only – '

He threw her off with such force that she thudded against the wall and slumped there, looking stunned, yet it seemed almost casual, something he'd done without thinking to get rid of the hindrance on his way to Molly. 'Don't try and use your eyes on me,' he hissed at Molly, saliva spraying from his mouth. 'Your friend Guilda tried, and you know what happened to her. You won't have them to ruin people's minds with for much longer.'

He'd backed her into a corner, his hands reaching for her face with an accuracy and skill that she could see must be the product of days of insane anticipation and planning – and suddenly she felt calm. Perhaps that was the most terrible thing of all. She was safe, because she knew what was going to happen; she had seen what would happen to Danny eleven years ago, in the dream. She gazed at Danny

440

as his nails reached for her eyes. The stillness of her imagination was a wall that nobody and nothing could breach.

At first Danny didn't realize what was happening. He was stretching his hands out for her eyes, he was stepping closer, yet they didn't reach. Even when his hands withdrew beyond his cuffs, even when he thrust the flapping ends of his sleeves towards her face, he still seemed unaware of how he was changing. It was the sudden appalled look that appeared on his face a moment before he looked down at himself that proved too much for her. She dodged around him and went to Freda, and tried not to watch.

But she couldn't look away. The sleeves where his forearms should be were empty now, and there was only a wormlike writhing in the upper sleeves. In a moment that shrank, and his sleeves hung flat by his sides. He gazed down at them, then he began to scream.

Molly couldn't bear it. She thought of restoring him, wished wildly that she could, in the hope that he would be too shocked to think of harming her, but she knew that was a trap: it would give even more strength to the dream. Perhaps it was already too strong for her, perhaps it had been ever since Rankin's, where it had no longer needed her to be asleep. She mustn't think, in case that trapped her too. She must get Freda out of the house.

Freda winced when Molly helped her up by her bruised shoulders, but seemed otherwise unhurt. She stared back at Danny as if she couldn't take in the sight as Molly hurried her to the stairs. He was staggering back and forth, moaning as if he were choking on his horror. His empty sleeves flapped as he smashed his incomplete body against the walls. At least he wasn't screaming now, but was it possible that his screams hadn't been heard downstairs? She could only pray that it was as she hurried Freda down. One flight of stairs, two, and she heard soft footsteps coming down from the top of the house.

Freda hadn't heard them. 'Not too fast,' she protested weakly, 'or I'll fall.' Molly touched her lips for silence and held on to Freda more tightly as she quickened her pace. She wanted to be out of the house and the dream; she didn't want to see who Freda had been afraid to waken. Six more flights to the downstairs hall now, five, and someone knocked loudly at the front door.

What must she do? Run down with Freda so that they would be there when the door was opened, or stay out of sight of whoever went to the door? Of course they must go down, but Freda was shrinking against the wall, refusing to move, tugging Molly back out of sight. When they heard footsteps hurrying to the door, Freda ventured to look. 'Doreen,' she whispered.

'Is Joyce Churchill here?' a man said. When the landlady nodded he stepped into the house, into view. In a moment Molly would have recognized him, stout face and clipped red beard, but another voice said, 'And Molly Wolfe.'

Martin had found her. At once she remembered the nightmares she'd had about him, and realized at last that she'd dreamed of him eleven years ago – dreamed how the dream would change him. It served him right for the way he'd attacked her, she thought, even though it made her shudder; it had a horrible kind of justice. She made herself remember how he'd injured her, how he'd seemed capable of killing her, so that she wouldn't care what happened now, since it was beyond being stopped. Then, too late, she realized what had been wrong with him the night he'd attacked her: his eyes.

It hadn't been Martin. It had been the thing that had fastened on all of them, on Freda and Helen and presumably the others. Too late she realized why she had experienced panic the first time she'd seen him. She hadn't been frightened of him but for him. 'Martin,' she cried, 'don't come in whatever you do, please don't come into this

442

house, you mustn't come in,' and then she cried out
helplessly, for the sound of her voice had made him step
into the house.

Martin strode along the hall towards the stairs. Nothing and
nobody would stop him from going to Molly: not the
landlady nor Stuart, whom Molly's cries seemed to have
made nervous, and least of all Molly herself. It didn't matter
what she said. She sounded terrified, and he meant to find
out what was wrong.

At least nobody seemed prepared to get in his way. A tall
man in black with an oval face had come out of a room at the
end of the hall, but he folded his arms and stood watching
Martin, smiling faintly. Martin ignored him, for now he was
at the foot of the stairs and could see Molly on a landing two
floors up. She was helping a woman who looked hardly able
to stand. 'Molly, I'm here with Stuart Hay,' he called. 'If
you won't talk to me, talk to him.'

She looked down and saw him. Her expression halted
him as he made to step on the first stair – he had never seen
such terror on anyone's face. 'I'm all right, Martin,' she
cried in a voice that said the opposite. 'You're the one who's
in danger. For God's sake leave while you can.'

He suddenly had the impression that above her the floors
went up and up. It was impossible – and beside the point
anyway. He was on the first stairs when someone grabbed
his left shoulder.

That was how it felt. Someone had grabbed him to try to
stop him, so fiercely that the seam of his coat tore as he refused to be hindered. But nobody was near enough to have
touched him. Molly was clutching her temples as if she

443

wished she could shut out what she was seeing. Now he knew. From her look and the growing ache in his shoulder he deduced that someone had shot him or thrown a weapon at him.

Who? The man with the oval face hadn't moved, neither his folded arms nor his faint smile, and there was nobody else but the landlady and Stuart, who would certainly have come to him if he had been attacked. Martin seized the banister and was starting determinedly upstairs when the cloth at his shoulder tore again and something touched his left cheek.

It was soft and cold and heavy. When he swung round furiously, nothing was there. Molly's cry of horror twisted him back again, so hurriedly that he almost lost his footing on the stair, but nothing had seized her except horror at what she was seeing. She was gazing at him, at his shoulder. He was turning his head painfully to look when something pale lolled against his face.

It must be a bird of some kind. That explained the ache where its claws had fastened on his shoulder through the torn cloth, and the weight, which he had been confusing with the ache. What kind of bird was as large as his head, what kind of bird felt like cold puffy flesh? It was too close for him to make out any of its features, and he was reaching gingerly to touch it when its mouth opened. It was not a bird: no bird could mimic terror so intensely, even if it were somehow able to imitate his father's voice. 'Where am I?' it cried.

For a moment Martin felt he'd gone mad. His head felt thin as shell and cracking with horror. At least being mad would mean this wasn't really happening – and then the object on his shoulder lolled against his cheek again, as if it had hardly anything to support it. It wasn't perched on his shoulder, it was growing there. 'I don't know where I am,' his father's voice cried. 'Help me.'

Perhaps he'd sounded like that on his deathbed. There was a moment, or however long it was, during which Martin was insane, convinced he was at his father's bedside and reaching to touch his father's face. His hands recoiled just in time. He wanted to tear at the thing on his shoulder, shred it into tiny pieces – it felt soft enough – but how could he when it might be in some sense his father? 'Help me, for God's sake do something,' it cried, and at last Martin had his secret wish: he was hearing his father own up to weakness, to fear.

He didn't want it now. He didn't want it to come true, above all not in this nightmare way. Nightmare – yes, it was like Molly's idea of dreams that were indistinguishable from reality. By God, that must be what was happening, and his rage at whoever was causing it blazed through him, all the fiercer because he couldn't tell where it should be directed. It was blinding him; he no longer knew where he was. He was stumbling off the stairs in his rage, reaching for the pleading object on his shoulder and failing to touch it, stumbling wildly as if he could outrun the nightmare. But that wasn't the way, he knew suddenly. He'd been too late to be with his father at the last, he couldn't dream him up to give himself a second chance, and he'd known that all the time; perhaps his rejection of the dream come true had caused his father to appear in such a hideous form. He had to live with the knowledge that he'd been too late, there was no other way for him – certainly not the parody of his father that was slumping helplessly against his cheek. His rage was beyond control now, his rage at the dream that had fastened on his shoulder, at the very idea of it. He reached to tear it off his shoulder, and all at once it wasn't there.

Nor was the house. At some point in his blind rage, he'd stumbled into the open night. He staggered out of an alley into a street full of small shops and their customers, and it wasn't until he found a sign that he identified it as Caledonian Road. The night air chilled his shoulder where his coat was torn. He must have torn it on something in the alley; any other explanation was already out of reach. His rage had let him fight his way out of the dream, too well. He had no idea where he had been, nor where he had been going.

445

Molly saw him fumble at the latch and drag open the front door and stagger out into the night, the thing with the hint of a face flopping on his shoulder. She could only pray that he'd got out in time, that he had fought off the dream. Praying wasn't enough. She had to know that she hadn't changed him irrevocably into her nightmare, she had to find him. While Stuart Hay was here, surely she had a chance to get out of the house.

He was staring bewildered after Martin. The landlady gave Molly a smile that said everything was all right now. There was no sign of anyone else. She had to go now, while Sage was out of the way, and take Freda with her – but she was so appalled by what had happened to Martin that she couldn't move.

She heard the soft tread still coming down from the top of the house, and then she could move, if only to save Freda from whatever she feared up there. Molly took her arm and hurried unsteadily downstairs, wishing she could hold on to the banister herself. A minute later they were in the hall.

'Stuart, we have to leave at once,' she said, trying to hold her voice steady. 'This is Freda Beeching, and you know who I am. You bring Joyce Churchill. She has to leave too.'

The landlady moved between them and the door. 'You can't take Freddy, she's ill.'

'It's being here that's made her ill,' Molly said, desperately willing Stuart to help.

'It's all right, Doreen.' Freda managed to stand up straight by clinging to Molly's arm. 'I want to leave. I have to.'

'That's settled then,' Molly said, but staring at Doreen didn't move her out of the way. 'Where's Joyce?'

Doreen folded her arms. 'Sage is fetching her.'

Freda's hand tightened on Molly's arm, and Molly covered the hand with her own, to communicate a reassurance she was very far from feeling. 'Don't let him talk you round, Stuart. Don't let him stop you from taking Joyce. He's behind everything that's happening.'

Stuart had been frowning at her; now his frown deepened. 'What is?'

She didn't want to go into it while they were in the house – she feared that doing so might give power to the dream – but she had to convince him. She had a sudden intuition that otherwise he might refuse to leave until he'd questioned Sage. 'You saw what happened to Martin,' she said.

'I saw him get out when you told him to. Isn't that what you wanted?'

Unbelievably, he looked secretly amused. If he hadn't seen Martin's transformation it must be because he hadn't wanted to see it. She wanted to tell him so, she felt like screaming it, but what use would that be? She wished she hadn't mentioned Sage; she must have roused Stuart's interest. She had to make him promise to take Joyce out of the house – surely Joyce would want to leave, she'd said she was finished with dreaming – and she was about to demand it of him when he started. He was gazing up the stairs.

She was afraid to look. When she made herself follow his gaze, her stomach flinched. Danny had lurched into view on the fourth landing up. He came swaying down the stairs, thumping himself against the wall at every step as if that was the only way he could keep his balance. At each step his empty sleeves flapped. Molly turned to Stuart, away from the sight of Danny's fixed eyes and drooling mouth. 'That's what I mean. You can see *that*, can't you?'

'I'm not with you.' Incomprehension made Stuart's face look heavy and sluggish and dull. 'You mean someone did that to him?'

How could she say that she had? Even if she managed to

447

admit it, she could see he would never believe her. A door opened at the end of the hall and Sage came out with Nell, who was Helen, and Joyce.

He was ushering each of them by an arm, but now he let go. 'I think you recognize your visitor,' he said lightly.

'I certainly do.' Joyce's cheeks turned pink, then red. 'He's the one who nearly ruined my mind.'

Helen said nothing. She looked aimless, not quite sure what was happening. Molly found herself wondering how much of Helen's behaviour had had the sole aim of bringing them both here, but she hadn't time to sort out the implications. 'Joyce, you know me, don't you? Molly Wolfe. And that's Helen, if you hadn't recognized her. It wasn't Stuart who brought us all together this time, it was him.'

Sage continued smiling, rather sadly, as she pointed at him. Joyce looked ready to be suspicious, but her suspicion focused on Molly. 'How?' she demanded.

'It doesn't matter how.' She mustn't be trapped into trying to explain, not when Danny was only three flights up. 'We've all been brought here, you can't deny that, and I give you my word it wasn't Stuart's doing. We have to get out of here, Joyce. We're in terrible danger, and not only us.' Her voice was growing louder. 'He can't stop all of us. Surely you see there must be something wrong if he wants to.'

'I would not dream of it.' Sage gave the two women a gentle push towards her. 'Doreen, please do not stand in their way. Let them do what they wish. Mr Hay, please do open the door.'

His gentleness, his apparent indifference, were terrifying. Doreen stepped reluctantly aside as the others moved towards her. Danny came reeling down the last flight of stairs, and all at once Molly knew what would be outside when Stuart opened the door: walls, endless walls. She wanted to stop him as he turned the latch, but what else

448

could they do? The door opened and she heard the others gasp, but she had closed her eyes. It took her some time to open them, to see the walls.

There were no walls, nor was there a street. The door gave onto the beginning of an avenue. Here and there between the trees she glimpsed stone lions and ornamental urns, while at the far end of the avenue she saw a country house with a wide porch, long windows splashing lawns with light. She couldn't speak, she couldn't think except to realize that the dream had come true. They had been tricked into letting it in.

It was Stuart who broke the silence. 'My God, it's Norfolk. It's the mental hospital where Guilda Kent is.'

Speaking released him from looking, and he swung round. When he read in their eyes that they were all seeing it too, his face wavered, but only for a moment. He threw up his hands as if he could block their view. 'Listen, it isn't real. We're sharing a hallucination, that's all. It isn't the first time for you.'

He glanced back hopefully over his shoulder. While he had distracted them, the hospital appeared to have moved closer. It must have, because now they could see a face at a window, glaring at them. He turned away quickly, his hands at his eyes. Molly had the impression that he couldn't close them.

'That isn't Guilda Kent.' He'd lowered his voice as if that might convince them. 'You're only seeing her because I have. There's nothing out there that shouldn't be. Come out with me and I'll show you.'

His hands were faltering again towards his weeping eyes. He couldn't close them, couldn't stop seeing. Of course, that had been in the dream eleven years ago – and suddenly, hopelessly, Molly realized something else. Sage had been waiting for him.

He had been waiting for Stuart to take them to Guilda. Of course both Stuart and Guilda had been touched by the dream in Oxford; they must have shared it even if they had never admitted it to themselves. The dream needed them as much as it needed the others, and she had realized too late.

Perhaps Guilda had realized too, for her eyes had filled with terror. She appeared to be struggling to turn away so as not to see them in the doorway, so as to be able to believe they weren't there. Stuart was still trying to believe the same of her. He'd turned his back on her again and was waving his hands near his eyes. 'Come out with me,' he said, low and intense. 'It'll go away, I promise you. All we have to do is show we don't believe in it. It can't last, these things never do. So long as we stay together none of us will be in danger. Trust me.' Perhaps it was only fierceness, at them or at the way the sight beyond the doorway was persisting that made his voice waver as he beckoned to Danny. 'You too,' he said, 'whoever you are.'

Danny had been leaning against the post at the foot of the banister, grinding his spine against it as if the pain might restore reality. 'No, you don't,' he snarled. 'You and your friend there want to get me into the nuthouse. You can't trick me any more. Don't try.'

Even if he hadn't been nodding his head viciously at her, Molly would have known he was accusing her. Stuart went towards him. 'Please trust me. Nobody wants to harm you. It isn't real, it can't be. Come with us and you'll see.'

Danny lurched aside. He was performing a grotesque dance to keep his armless body from losing its balance, and Molly could hardly bear to watch. 'You got your hands on me once,' he screamed. 'You won't this time. You leave my mind alone.'

Stuart faltered, staring at his face, his armless torso. 'You can't be Danny Swain.'

'Can't I? Thought you'd destroyed my mind already, did you? I'm still here and still sane too, and you'd better give up. You've been trying to drive me crazy for eleven years, but you never will. Don't close that door!' he screamed.

Molly had been reaching for it, in case closing out the sight of Guilda might weaken the dream a little. She dodged as he came lurching towards her, for he looked capable of falling on her, tearing at her with his teeth, since that was all that was left to him. But he fled out of the doorway, onto the avenue.

For a moment he glared wildly about, almost falling headlong. Perhaps he had been hoping Stuart was right after all. He lurched between the trees, away from the hospital. 'Come back,' Stuart cried. 'It isn't real. My God, we can't let him go out there alone, he must think that's where he is. Anything might happen to him.' He was looking to the others for support, but nobody moved; Molly couldn't have. With a despairing gesture, he ran out after Danny.

They heard his footsteps on the avenue, which sounded nothing like the pavement that ought to have been there. A breeze swayed the trees, dislodging a few raindrops. He shook his head impatiently as a drop fell on his scalp, and peered between the trees. He must have seen Danny, for he ran between two of them, thumping his elbow against the right-hand trunk.

He faltered and stared at the tree, then he began to shake his head. Molly knew instinctively that he was telling himself whatever it looked and felt like, it must be something else or not there at all. He ran between the trees, out of sight. 'Wait, Danny,' he was calling, as reassuringly as he could. 'Don't run. We can deal with this together, trust me.' At intervals they heard him calling, more and more distant, eventually so distant it made Molly catch her breath. His voice was at the limit of audibility when, without warning, both men began to scream.

Even at that distance their terror was unbearable. Molly would have blocked her ears if she had been able to move. It seemed a very long time before the screams became inaudible. But their inaudibility was no relief. There was still

451

Guilda's terror, so intense it felt as if both it and her glaring eyes were inside Molly's head. The hospital was much closer. Soon there would be no avenue at all.

Then Joyce stepped forward, her face red with anger. 'No you don't,' she cried fiercely at Guilda. 'Not this time.' She slammed the door with such force that Molly felt the house shake.

Molly stared at the front door, wondering what closing it could have achieved. Joyce had shut out the sight of Guilda, but hadn't Guilda already completed the dreadful reunion? Could Joyce really have broken the dream? Opening the door would answer that, but Molly stepped back to make sure she wasn't tempted to try.

There was one other way to find out. Eventually she made herself go to the foot of the stairs. Joyce was staring at the front door as if she could hold it shut by the force of her gaze, Freda was leaning exhausted against the wall and looked unable to take any more, Helen seemed utterly bewildered. Doreen had closed her eyes for what appeared to be a silent prayer, and Molly could only will it to come true, whatever it was. She gripped the post at the end of the banister, which surely had always been real, and looked up. Her fists clenched, she let out a shuddering breath. The multitude of floors was still there, the soft footsteps were descending.

Sage watched her from beyond the staircase. His faint smile looked sympathetic, a shade pitying – the smile of someone watching a child who had to learn for herself. She turned on him. 'You're doing all this. You'd better stop it right now. There's several of us and only one of you.'

'I think you understand that I could not stop it now even should I wish to.' His face was growing calmer, as if she were helping him somehow. 'That moment passed eleven years ago.'

'You'll never make me believe that,' she said, but what was the use? Of course she was helping him, by believing in him, since he was part of the dream. How could she not believe in him? How would it be to their advantage to try? He looked as if he were following her thoughts, waiting for her to agree with him. 'Open the door and see what is there,' he said gently. 'There is nothing to fear unless you make it so.'

She was struggling to believe the street would be out there, but she knew it was the last thing she would find. Refusing to believe hadn't helped Stuart. All the same, remembering Stuart gave her the strength to hate Sage. 'If you're real,' she said desperately, 'you can feel pain. Maybe that'll make you change your mind and stop this.'

His eyes told her to try if she felt she must. At least that helped her hate him, and she was stepping forward, with no idea of what she meant to do to him or even if she could, when Freda cried out inarticulately. She was gazing at the stairs.

Molly forced herself to turn to see at last what Freda was afraid of. The man who had almost reached the hall didn't look in any way frightening: high forehead, strong chin, deep brown eyes – he looked almost too good to be true. It was that thought, not his babyish complexion, that made Molly shiver.

Freda drew herself up straight, though she had to lean against the wall to do so. She took a deep breath and stared levelly at him. 'Stay away from me. You aren't Timothy,' she said.

'Don't say that, old girl.' He looked determined not to be hurt by her rebuff. 'You haven't been well, you don't know what you're saying. Let me take you up to your room for a bit of a rest.'

'You won't be taking me anywhere. Just lay a finger on me

and see what happens.' Freda laughed bitterly, near to hysteria. 'You can't. You've been dead for thirty years.'

'I can't blame you for feeling that way, Freddy. It must seem like that to you.' He came to the foot of the stairs and lifted his hands towards her, let them fall. 'I'd have come to you sooner if I could have.'

'That isn't it, and you know it isn't.' Freda faltered, just as Molly urged her silently to go on. There was something wrong with the man's soft skin and unblemished complexion, something horrible about it that made Molly want to reach out and tear. Freda knew what it was, but now she was hesitating – because she must have realized that perhaps he didn't know there was anything wrong about him.

He stepped forward a pace, and Freda stiffened. 'Timothy was burned alive in the war,' she said as if each word hurt her throat. 'If you're Timothy, you can't look like that. That isn't the way you are.'

'All sorts of rumours came out of the war, old girl. If you heard that about me – '

'No, that wasn't a rumour. That was the truth.' She shook her fist at him. 'How dare you pretend you're my Timothy! You ought to suffer what he suffered, that's what you deserve.'

'You shouldn't say things like that, Freddy.' He frowned as he held out his hands. 'I know you don't realize what you're saying. Let me take care of you. Just let me – '

'I'll let you nothing.' She'd seen what Molly had: the hint of fear in his eyes. 'My God, when I think of what I've already let you do, you – you *thing*.' She was growing incoherent, but Molly was nodding wildly; if Freda ran out of words, she'd take over if she could, for she had glimpsed the most hopeful development of all: Sage was growing uneasy. 'What are you?' Freda cried. 'I'll teach you to pretend you're Timothy. Let's see how you like being burned alive. Go on, you fake, you dummy, be what you're pretending to be. Burn!'

She screamed the last word with such hatred that Molly shuddered, even as she willed Freda to succeed. Doreen was staring aghast at Freda. Helen and Sage were converging on her until Molly stepped in Helen's way. Only Joyce watched Freda as if some of the truth was beginning to filter through to her, and even she flinched back as the face of the man at the bottom of the stairs began to smoulder.

His eyes glazed almost at once. When he opened his mouth to scream, smoke poured out with a stench that made Molly's stomach heave. He fell back on the stairs, writhing and shrivelling and blackening. 'My God, my God,' Freda sobbed, 'die, just die.' Suddenly the parlour door opened beyond the stairs.

Three men and Susan crowded into the hall. The child ran to Helen and clung to her, dragging at her as if she were so desperately frightened she couldn't put her plea into words. Molly noticed this only peripherally as she shrank away from the three men, their soft tread, their faces that were too pink. They looked frantic, and were almost running. Not until they surrounded Freda did she realize they weren't fleeing the house.

At first she thought they meant to suffocate her, they were pressing around her so closely. The charred shape on the stairs was dwarfishly shrunken now, but it was still writhing. Freda cried out with disgust and tried to push them away as they clustered softly about her, while Molly dragged vainly at them, at their shoulders which gave like putty inside their clothes. Without warning they abandoned whatever they were trying to do to Freda and ran instead to Sage.

His calm wavered as they closed in; he tried to ward them off. 'Trust me,' he murmured, 'you are in no danger,' but his voice wasn't quite steady. He'd begun to back away towards the parlour when Susan let go of her mother and ran to him. As she grabbed his arm and hung on desperately, the three men reached him.

455

'No,' Sage said in a last attempt at calm, and then he shrieked it. In a moment Molly saw why he was screaming, saw and tried not to believe what she was seeing. She was grateful for the distraction, however brief, when a woman came running out of the parlour. 'What's wrong, Doreen? What's going on?' she demanded, and dodged aside, her face crumpling with disbelief as Sage and the others crowded past her towards the parlour. Sage was being forced backwards by what they were doing to him, and he could do nothing but scream.

Molly watched as the mass of bodies squeezed through the parlour doorway. They were achieving what they hadn't managed to achieve with Freda, what the thing that looked like Susan hadn't been able to get from Helen. They were surrounding him like terrified animals burrowing into their mother. Pressing close to him wasn't enough. They were merging together, merging with him.

Molly listened to the sounds from the parlour as long as she could, then she made herself go to the doorway. She had to see what happened, to be certain. It was the parlour she remembered from the dream – heavy curtains, antimacassars, a gas fire parching the air – but there was little further similarity to the scene she'd feared for eleven years, though there was something quite as terrible. Something large and pale with several faces was struggling on the floor.

She made herself watch while it heaved and mouthed and tore itself apart into pieces that no longer resembled bodies, and merged again. She was willing it to finish, and eventually it did. There was one last violent merging, mouths gaping like lockjaw, and it burst, strewing the floor with a soft substance that gradually seeped into the carpet. Until they vanished, the fragments were still twitching and struggling. One of them almost reached her.

She closed her eyes when it seemed safe to do so and clung to the doorframe until she felt capable of venturing back along the hall. As soon as she reached the banister she made herself look up. There was nothing on the stairs now, and there were just two floors above.

For a long time there was silence. Nobody seemed to want to look at anyone else or at anything. Without warning Joyce shook from head to foot and burst into tears. 'I knew it wasn't Geoffrey.'

Molly went to her and held her shoulders. Helen seemed the most shocked, her eyes dull and uncomprehending. Doreen demanded, 'What were they, Freddy? What was he? You must know.'

'They were dreams, as near as I can tell. It's wrong to want dreams to come true,' Freda said miserably. 'I'm sorry, Doreen. It's all my fault. I wish I'd never come.'

She reached to cover her face but had to grab at the wall, for reaction had seized her and she was falling, grey-faced. Doreen supported her just in time. 'She needs a doctor,' Molly said.

'You call him, Rosie. The number's by the phone.' Doreen gripped Freda's hands. 'Don't blame yourself, Freddy. Don't work yourself into a state, I'd never forgive myself. The doctor's coming.'

The woman called Rosie picked up the phone by the stairs and dialled. The silence was so eloquent that she hardly needed to say, 'It isn't working.'

'I'll take her to the doctor,' Molly said. All at once she felt capable of taking charge, felt as if she were the only person there who was. 'Which way?'

'Along Caledonian Road and over the bridge, nearly to Kings Cross.' Doreen's directions seemed so incongruous and yet so reassuring that Molly didn't know if she were stifling laughter or tears. 'It's a house on the left with a big brass plate. Can you manage on your own?'

'I'll come with you,' Joyce said, and strode upstairs as if she were daring anything to be there. Molly couldn't help holding her breath until Joyce came down, buttoning her coat. 'Can I come too?' Helen said in a small voice.

457

'Yes, you'd better.' Certainly she would need the doctor. Molly took one of Freda's arms, Joyce the other, and Helen trailed behind as they supported Freda along the hall. As soon as they reached the front door, Molly opened it at once.

The street was there. Freda's sigh of relief was so profound it made Molly tremble too. 'Let's step out,' Joyce said, and Molly thought she was impatient with herself, with her own unnecessary secret fear.

They helped Freda past the locked gate and onto Caledonian Road. The deserted streets made Molly wonder how late it was; it looked as though they would have to get the doctor out of bed. Beneath the streetlamps the shops looked unreal, their windows blank with glaring light. She wished it weren't so silent – just the sound of a car would have helped.

Tenements massed along a side street, and not a window was lit. Nothing moved, not a breeze, not a scrap of litter in sight. They were crossing the bridge now, over the canal that was still as ice. The open sky at the bridge showed only unbroken blackness.

They must be nearly at the doctor's, nearly at Kings Cross. The bridge sank behind them, and Molly strained her ears for cars, trains, taxis. Why did the streets appear to continue into the distance, walls and blank windows and never a main road? Freda was slowing now, dragging them to a halt, glancing up at the cloudless black sky and then around at the streets. It's all right, Molly tried to tell her by squeezing her arm, we'll be all right, please don't say it, please don't ask –

'Where are we?' Freda said.

66

'We must have taken a wrong turning,' Helen said.

'Of course we have,' Joyce agreed fiercely, as if that would make it so. 'We'll go back.' She was turning Freda, who seemed all at once drained of strength, and Molly had to follow. She held Freda's arm – that was real – and tried not to grasp too hard. They must go back to Doreen's and start again, she told herself as they turned towards the shops.

But there were no shops. There were only identical terraces of identical dilapidated Victorian houses dwindling into the distance until the street vanished into its perspective. Identical streets crossed it at regular intervals. In the light of the few streetlamps, doors and windows gleamed like knives. The lightless sky pressed close above the worn roofs.

Freda's fingers dug into Molly's wrist, but Molly was beyond noticing the pain. Freda must be realizing what Molly had realized: they hadn't come out of Doreen's into the street after all, but into a dream of the street. They had stepped into the dream and made it more real. 'It's happening,' Freda said in a dull despairing voice.

'I don't know what you mean. We can't be very lost, we haven't come that far.' Joyce urged them forwards, glancing back sharply to make sure Helen was still following, urged them so fast that she left Freda no breath to protest. She was glaring about, challenging the familiar streets not to reappear, until Molly wondered if she was actually not seeing the identical seedy houses. Perhaps Joyce had no time to see, but Molly was seeing too much: glimpses of unlit rooms beyond the uncurtained windows, glimpses of shapes that might have been furniture or figures but which moved like neither. She didn't know if she was more afraid that all the houses were empty or that a face might look out of a window, perhaps out of all of them. Most of all she was afraid that one of the doors might open as she passed.

Their footsteps rang flatly beneath the featureless sky. Molly had lost count of the number of roads they had crossed. 'I know what I'm looking for,' Joyce said angrily as if someone had suggested she did not, and at the next intersection she pointed. 'There we are.'

It was a telephone box at the far end of the terrace, on the corner of an intersection exactly like the one where they were standing. It looked heart-breakingly real, the bright red box with its beckoning light and waiting phone and even a directory on the shelf beneath. Joyce was already making for the phone box, supporting Freda when she stumbled, but there was at least one question that needed to be asked. 'Who do you mean to call?' Molly demanded.

Joyce stared at her as if she were being facetious. 'The police, of course.'

It wasn't clear how much sense of the situation she had. Perhaps the dream had got inside her, perhaps she was beginning to behave as people did in dreams, or could her proposal be the answer, however grotesquely out of touch it seemed? Surely the dream could reach only so far – perhaps the phone could reach further. Molly had a sudden inkling that she could limit the dream, if she could think how.

Joyce pulled open the door of the phone box and beckoned Helen to take Freda's arm. The creak of the door in the midst of the empty streets was shockingly loud. She left the door open as she lifted the receiver. The sound of the bell echoed through the streets. Before she could dial, a voice spoke on the phone. 'Joyce, it's Geoffrey. Come home.'

'No,' Joyce cried and dropped the receiver as if it were crawling with insects. She stared at it as it lay in its cradle and then, though she was shaking, she picked it up again. 'Please, Joyce, I'm all alone,' the voice said at once. 'Leave the others, they won't let me come to you, they'll try and tell you I'm not who I am. Just start walking and I'll come to you.'

'No!' It was almost a scream. Joyce backed out of the phone box, still clinging to the receiver, and wrenched the cord out of the body of the phone. She stared at the receiver in her hand, then she flung it clattering along the deserted street. She stared furiously after it. Molly was searching for something to say when Freda murmured, 'Look up there at the lights. That's where we should go.'

She was pointing feebly along the street at right angles to the one they had just taken. On the horizon, beyond the multitude of roofs, lights were shining – lit windows. They must be beyond the reach of the dream.

Again Molly felt as if she had it in her to limit that reach. Molly helped Freda away from the phone box, and Helen had to follow. This time it was Joyce who lagged behind, glaring about the cloned streets as if she had only just realized what was wrong with them. When Molly called to her, she came hurrying.

The houses progressed slowly past them, every door a threat. There were fewer streetlamps now. It occurred to Molly that the streets were in some sense their fears, hers and Freda's and Helen's and Joyce's. 'You must fear nothing now,' Sage had said. She could change the streets, she realized, but then she saw the trap: if she made the streets familiar they would change behind her back, just as they had when she'd left Doreen's house, and in any case by changing them she would be giving more power to the dream. There was no way out through her own mind.

The street was heading uphill. Her legs and her feet were aching. The distant lights were a little closer, only a little. She wondered if it was possible to die in the dream, and knew all at once that they never would. Nor would they ever sleep, for there was no longer any need.

Helen was suddenly urging them faster. At first Molly couldn't see what had changed. The identical houses crowded the pavements, which were deserted except for the streetlamps. Only when she saw the first lamp go out did she realize how much the dark had already closed in.

She matched Helen's pace on the sloping pavement, and avoided her eyes. It seemed they had all agreed tacitly not to discuss what was happening, as if that might help. They were virtually carrying Freda now, and Molly was tempted to slow down for her sake when she heard sounds above the hollow clatter of their footsteps. Doors were opening beyond the lit streetlamps, footsteps were converging on the women from the dark.

Joyce was turning furiously to see what could be there, and Molly urged her to keep up. Inside her head she could hear how insane and pitiful she would sound if she began whistling, as some trapped part of her mind wanted her to do. The hill was growing steeper. The lights ahead had come closer unnoticed, but more of the lamps behind and around the women were being extinguished, more doors opening in the dark. The noises of pursuit sounded less like a marching crowd than one huge sluggish deliberate mass.

'Up there,' Freda was pleading, nodding her head at the top of the hill. They were nearly at the summit, on which stood a church. The church was dark. Nevertheless Freda's instinct seemed to be right, for as they laboured up the hill and came abreast of the churchyard gates the sounds of pursuit stayed down below. What was more, they could see the lights.

The lights of London began at the foot of the hill and reached to the horizon across the Thames. A ship full of lights was sailing past the luminous Houses of Parliament, and Molly could even make out the face of Big Ben: it was almost four in the morning. The lights of a plane blinked across the sky where she felt there might be stars, the lit windows of tower blocks south of the river reached their broken lines into the sky. She stood on the summit and drank in their randomness, the randomness of all the lights. It was life, the opposite of the dream.

The women gazed at the lightscape. Nobody spoke, but now their silence wasn't caused by a fear of speaking. Molly was listening to the murmur of the city, the murmur that proved beyond any doubt that the city never slept, when a light went out between the hill and the river.

Molly took a deeper breath. Of course lights were going out here and there, it would be unnatural if they did not, and soon lights would come on as people woke. She had almost calmed herself when the next few lights went out, and then a line of them. Some of them were windows, all of them were at the foot of the hill. Darkness was spreading like a stain from the hill on which she was standing.

Freda had seen it too. 'Let's go in here,' she pleaded, pointing at the church. 'I want to rest now.' Molly knew that she was thinking they could never outdistance the dream or escape the night. The dream would simply engulf the world ahead of them.

She gave the lights one last yearning look, then turned quickly away. Perhaps watching was spreading the dream. She pushed open the gates, which scraped over the concrete path as if they had never been opened before. 'Help me,' she said urgently to the others as she led Freda towards the church.

Helen took Freda's arm, but Joyce was lagging again, gazing wistfully towards the lights. 'Come on, Joyce,' Molly called, fighting to keep her voice steady. 'Let's not split up. Freda can't walk any further just now.' She'd begun to suspect something else: perhaps each unlit window meant someone dreaming the dream, perhaps she and the others had spread the infection of it as they wandered, changing the streets of London into the streets they'd seen.

463

The doors opened when she turned the knob, and showed her a dim unlit porch. By the glow that hovered on the clouds over London, she made out that the porch was quite bare. It didn't matter, the church was a refuge, and even if she didn't like the coldness of the place, Freda was stumbling determinedly into the porch. Freda opened the doors into the body of the church just as Molly found the light switch beside them.

The other women hurried to support Freda as the lights came on. Molly thought she heard one of them groan with dismay. But there was nothing to fear in the church: there was nothing at all – no altar, no pews, no furniture of any kind. A few bare light bulbs dangled from the unadorned ceiling and glared on the cold white naked walls and grey flagstones.

Freda slumped into a sitting position on a flagstone, which tipped up an inch or so with a scraping of mortar, and there was nothing for Molly to do but close the doors. She squatted beside Freda and tried to understand what she was capable of doing.

Nobody spoke or looked at anyone else. The church felt like a cave far smaller than it was. It wasn't the refuge that a church was supposed to be, and that was why Molly shrank into herself as she heard the sounds outside. The pursuit had come up the hill.

She heard the gates scrape over the concrete and the outer doors open. Soft sounds crossed the porch, and then the inner doors squeaked inward. But Helen's cry was so violent that Molly twisted round. Susan was in the door-way.

Or rather, something that was pretending to be Susan. Whatever was behind it, in the porch and beyond, was very large and dim, but Helen saw only the child. 'Oh, Susan, thank God,' she cried. 'I thought you'd – I don't know. Thank God you're all right.'

Molly realized Helen had never been able to accept she'd

been tricked. 'It isn't Susan,' she said and, irrationally, felt cruel. 'Look at her eyes.'

Then both women faltered, for Susan ignored Helen and walked up to Molly. 'Yes, look at them,' she said. 'You look.'

'Get out of here and leave us alone,' Joyce shouted. 'You can't frighten us.'

Molly stared at Sage's eyes in the child's face. 'You can't hypnotize me,' she muttered. 'There's nothing you can do to us now.'

'We never did,' Susan said.

'What do you mean, we?' Molly demanded. 'There's only one of you.'

'Yes, only one.' It was Sage's voice now. 'But you must see who it is.' The child reached into a handbag she was carrying. Her hand emerged, and something flashed towards Molly's face. The flash was so bright that she recoiled, squeezing her eyes shut in case they were in danger. She opened them, expecting to see a knife. 'Look at the eyes,' the child said in Sage's calm voice.

It was a mirror. She looked into it, looked away quickly and glared at the sight of the child with Sage's eyes, glanced reluctantly back at the mirror, at herself with – 'It's a trick,' she said flatly.

'No,' Sage's voice was almost sad. 'At last you are seeing the truth.'

How could a mirror in a dream tell the truth? How could it be? She stared at the sight of herself with Sage's eyes, and then she saw the truth, remembered it. The dream couldn't have changed her memory. The reflection was not a trick. At last she saw that Sage's eyes, and the eyes of the others from the dream, had always been her own.

'Yes.' Sage's voice, and the eyes in the child's face, were gentle now, encouraging. 'You made us. You are us. You must not deny all this any longer.' The child's hands gestured gracefully at the church and implied everything

465

that was outside the walls. 'You are only harming your friends,' the child said in Susan's voice.

'You leave us out of this,' Joyce shouted. 'Just get out, whatever you are. Nobody here wants you.'

But Helen was sidling towards the child. She looked bewildered and hurt by being ignored. 'Don't try to use Helen,' Molly whispered furiously. 'Haven't you harmed her enough?'

'Haven't you?' Momentarily the child's voice was sharp. 'You will not be able to bear this forever,' she said more gently, glancing at the walls of the church as if she could see through them. 'There will come the moment when you cannot stop yourself.'

'You wait and see,' Molly cried, but her words sounded as empty as the church. She didn't need the child with her eyes to tell her that sooner or later she would have to give in, for the sake of the others if not for herself; she couldn't condemn them to eternity in the dead place on the hill, with only the interminable dilapidated streets and whatever lived there to go out to. If she even wished they could change, they would. That would feed the dream, but she knew she couldn't stop herself wishing, not for long, not for ever. Why couldn't she have suppressed the power in herself once and for all years ago, while she still had the chance? That was one wish she couldn't grant herself, to go back all those years to a point where she could have been stopped.

Then she had a thought that sent a shudder through her from her feet to her head. At last she saw how she could limit the dream. It must be true, for the child's eyes flickered. The thing that looked like Susan was suddenly afraid. If any change that Molly imagined would come to pass, couldn't she imagine herself incapable of ever changing anything again?

Again the child's eyes, her eyes, flickered. The thing with Susan's face knew she could do it. What would happen then? Would Susan and the restlessness beyond the doors vanish, or would the women be trapped here forever, since it would never change? Molly didn't care; the secret fear in the eyes was giving her strength. She closed her eyes, she reached deep into her mind and pushed the power away from her.

She opened her eyes, and Susan was smiling. It couldn't be done that way, there was something undermining Molly's wish. Molly thought of the real world, of how much she and the others might already have infected as they wandered, how many people might be in danger of waking and finding themselves still in the dream. She thought of what she'd done to Martin, and cast off the power violently, glaring into the eyes in Susan's face. Saving the world must give her the strength.

Susan smiled more widely, sympathetically. 'You cannot do it. You know what would happen. Nobody has that strength.'

Molly did know, deep in herself. Before she was conscious of what she feared it had saved her from her wish. If she gave up her power, she and the others would be trapped in the dead place forever. She would never see Martin again, or her parents, or any human being except Joyce and Helen and Freda. She had to do it, if she didn't condemn herself and the others she would be condemning the world, but the fear of eternity had paralysed her will. They would never die, but one by one they would certainly go mad.

How could she condemn the others to that without consulting them first? But how could she consult the world? Her choice was clear again, clear and so simple that she grew absolutely calm. She glimpsed the flicker of fear in Susan's eyes, her own eyes in Susan's face. Her own fear was there outside her, unable to daunt her. The next moment she had made her choice, let go of the dream and her power over it, and her choice could never be taken back.

The child stared at her, a terrified accusation, then fled out of the church. She dodged whatever was outside, but

467

Molly heard it start after her, a huge purposeful movement that left the concrete path and rushed down the hill. Molly stood there like a cardboard figure, listening helplessly to the receding sounds, until she was hurled to the stone floor. Helen had knocked her down, and gave her a look of pure hatred as she ran out, crying 'Susan!'

'It isn't Susan! Helen, for God's sake come back!' But Helen had slammed the doors before Joyce helped Molly to her feet, and by the time Molly reached the gate Helen's cries and the other sounds were far down the hill, lost in the maze of streets that led towards the lights. There was nothing to be seen up here, but perhaps soon there would be. The few belated stars in the eastern sky looked faded, not only because of the lights of London. Dawn was near.

Joyce came out, supporting Freda. 'We don't want to stay in there,' Joyce said with a hint of her old fierceness. She glared towards the lights, challenging anyone to stop her from heading for them.

'We can't go down there,' Molly said wearily. She wasn't even sure they weren't still carriers of the dream.

Freda shushed them, until they all heard the massive sounds ranging about the streets above the lights. 'No, we can't,' Freda said, drawing a shaky breath. 'We'll have to go back.'

None of them looked at one another as Molly and Joyce helped Freda down the hill. Ahead their shadows under the few streetlamps seemed more distorted than they ought to be.

The lamps at the foot of the hill were still dark, and so were all the windows. Freda strained forward as if she knew where to go, and there seemed no reason to doubt her route was as good as any.

Once they thought they heard someone, perhaps a great many people, pacing them in the next street over. They stood and tried not even to breathe until Freda said it was an echo, but Molly wasn't sure it had been. Once they heard what sounded like a distant car, and Molly glimpsed a face at an upper window, round, with too much mouth. Dawn was growing, seeping into all the streets.

The roofs were lightening, as the upper storeys were. Night wasn't endless here after all, but Molly was beginning to wish that it were. The colourless light showed her glimpses of herself and her companions, distorted glimpses that looked worse and worse. It was showing her the revenge of the dream.

The streets ahead were quite visible now, interminable colourless terraces. Freda urged them forward, though at times she almost fell, and Molly let her lead, though the urgency seemed pitiful: they could never outrun the dawn.

Then she realized that Freda wasn't trying to. The streets in the distance weren't only brighter, they were different. As well as the dawn, there were lights, and now Molly saw that some of them were moving. They weren't streetlamps, they were car headlights. It was a main road.

She wanted to hang back in case it was another trick, but Freda was running or falling forward, and she had to follow. Now they could hear the sounds of the main road, the roar of the traffic, people hurrying past the junction, many people. They must be on their way to work.

She and Joyce were stumbling almost as much as Freda by now – was that a hint of how much the dream had crippled them? She mustn't look, mustn't think, only hope. The dead streets coursed by, their silence giving way to the sounds of traffic ahead, and she was suddenly afraid that the main road would prove to be a mirage, the first of an eternity of cruel tricks. When at last they reached the main road, Molly was too afraid to set foot on it, in case it vanished instantly, but Joyce and Freda dragged her forward.

She stepped on the pavement, and nothing happened. Traffic roared by, two workmen in overalls sidled around the three women. She found herself reading all the names of shops, devouring them: Fig Leaf of Covent Garden, Kebab Machine, Burger Delight, Model Railways, Bureau de Change, Tattoo Studio, Sure Square Deal & Co . . . She made herself turn and look back. The interminable streets had gone: the road from which they had emerged led between a tobacconist's and a newsagent's, and people were walking on its uneven pavements, past its motley houses. All the same, it wasn't until several passersby had glanced at her and the others with no more than mild curiosity that she was able to look down at herself.

There was nothing wrong with her, nor with Freda or Joyce. Her wish had come true after all: the world out here had overcome the dream. The dream had closed in on itself. It must still be somewhere, wherever Helen was. She wished she had destroyed it while she'd had the chance, and then she thought she must have had the power to dream that nobody would ever dream again, which seemed unspeakably terrifying. 'Oh, my God,' she said, shaking with relief, and was all at once so dizzy that she had to grab the nearest lamp-post to stop herself falling in front of the traffic.

When she was steady she found that the others were staring up the road, towards an intersection where traffic was converging along several roads. 'It's Kings Cross,' she said with a delight that felt close to hysteria.

'I want to see how Doreen is,' Freda said as firmly as she could.

'Yes, we should.' It was rather Doreen's house that Molly wanted to make sure of. They headed along Caledonian Road, the three of them staggering like all-night alcoholics, and didn't mind the laughter and comments that followed them. The sight of the shops beyond the canal made Molly want to cry with relief.

She was first up the steps to the yellow front door, to prove she could. She felt a lingering nervousness as she hammered the knocker on its silver plate, but that was why she had to be sure. Doreen came almost at once, and looked ready to weep when she saw Freda. 'Did the police find you?'

'No,' Freda said, and looked at her two companions. The next moment all three of them began to laugh, so hysterically that it seemed they would never stop.

When at last they did, gulping air and dabbing at their eyes, Doreen said reprovingly, 'The doctor's here, Freda. You come in and sit down.'

She led them into the parlour, where Molly glanced quickly at the carpet to make sure it was unmarked. Doreen's friend Rosie was sitting in an armchair. Her eyes were red, and both she and Doreen looked as if they had been up all night talking, weeping, helping each other back to reality. 'I'll have to tell the police you're here,' Doreen said, fussing around Freda. 'I had them looking for all of you and they found hardly anyone.' She turned suddenly to Molly. 'Can you go up and tell the doctor Freda's here? First door on the right on the first floor.'

Molly couldn't believe how small the house felt as she made her way up. She wasn't even sure how that made her feel, because she thought she knew what Doreen had been telling her, why she had sent her upstairs. She knew it before she opened the bedroom door and saw Martin lying on the bed.

The doctor was closing his bag. 'Doreen asked me to tell you Freda's downstairs,' Molly said. Even when the doctor had gone down she wasn't sure what to say to Martin or whether to go to him. He was buttoning his shirt after the examination, and all at once the meaning of his unmarked shoulders overwhelmed her. 'Thank God you're safe,' she said.

He was gazing sadly at her. 'You know it wasn't me that night.'

'Yes.' Still she couldn't quite go to him. 'Oh, Martin, I'm so sorry. I don't know how I could ever have thought it was.'

471

'I'm nothing special. I should have been out looking for you right now.' He reached out to her, then let his hands fall as if he didn't have the right. 'I must have been wandering all night. I didn't know where I was going until the police found me and mentioned Doreen. I've been lying here waiting for the doctor when I should have been looking for you. I'm not much of anything, I can tell you.'

That made her run to him, cling to him, squeezing the breath out of him. 'What happened last night? Where did you go?' he gasped, but she was almost speechless with the feel of him that she had nearly forgotten, the most real thing in the world. 'Don't ask me now, just hold me,' she said, and settled herself in his arms. 'It's all over,' she said, knowing that the dream had less power over them now than over anyone else in the world.

67

She never quite got used to being called Molly Wallace, and she didn't think she would want to. If people smiled at it, that made her smile too. Two years and two codirected films later, she and Martin were already being referred to in film journals as the Wallaces, and she thought she liked that most of all. Their Chapel Hill film was to be shown at Cannes. Martin often said that it was her delight at living in America that gave their films the human warmth his work had always needed. Sometimes they argued over that all evening.

She'd stayed in England for a while, for Joyce's sake. When Molly had gone home with her, Joyce wouldn't cross the threshold. Molly had never been sure why, and hadn't wanted to ask. Joyce had stayed at Molly's while she'd sold the house and bought herself a flat with enough money left over to buy a long lease on accommodation for a new day centre. Molly had waited to be sure Joyce settled back into her work, which certainly seemed to be what she needed, then at last she'd joined Martin, breathing a sigh of relief that the months of living with Joyce and her relentless helpfulness were over. As soon as she met Martin's mother, they liked each other so much –

'That they all lived happily ever after,' Guilda snarled.

Dr Lovell was taken aback by her sudden viciousness, even though she ought to be used to it by now. 'I suppose you could put it that way.'

'I don't want to put it any way. I'm not interested, can't you understand? Why are you making me listen to all this?'

'Because you asked me to find out,' Dr Lovell said patiently.

'I most certainly did not. What are you trying to do to me?' Guilda plucked at the bedclothes as the sedative took hold. 'They told you to tell them where I was, didn't they?' she cried, her voice trying to rise to a shriek.

'No, Guilda, not at all. Nobody wants anything of you except that you get well. Try and sleep now. I'm sorry I disturbed you.'

'Try and sleep? Why, you crazy woman, don't you understand – ' But Dr Lovell had closed the door and was walking away from the muffled voice. Certainly Guilda was the most difficult patient she had ever had to deal with, even now that they'd discovered Guilda had only been pretending to swallow her sedatives. Dr Lovell disliked authorizing injections against the patient's will, disliked the screams and struggles and the patient's loss of dignity, but in a case like this it was the only answer.

She looked in on some of her other patients and chatted to one of the nurses and then went to her office, still thinking about Guilda. One thing Guilda never failed to do was to make Dr Lovell feel unsure of herself. It was a talent schizophrenics had, but she was immune to it in all the others. Of course Guilda had asked her to write to Molly Wallace and the rest of them; otherwise, obviously, she would never have done so. It didn't matter that she couldn't recall being asked.

She gazed through her window at the dark grounds under the black sky. She hadn't intended to tell Guilda much more in any case. Of the people she had tried to contact, only Molly Wallace had replied – rather warily, Dr Lovell noticed, for she hadn't given a return address. She wouldn't have told Guilda that, except for Joyce Churchill and Freda Beeching, who had last been heard of in a rest home somewhere up north, all the others were missing, still sought by the police: Danny Swain, Helen Verney and her child, even Stuart Hay. Dr Lovell didn't know what to make of it herself.

She wasn't sure how long she had been standing at the window when it occurred to her to wonder what she was looking for. Of course, she was trying to recapture the momentary impression she'd had from Guilda's window that there was something unfamiliar at the far end of the avenue. She could see nothing there that shouldn't be. Either it had been heavy traffic on the road or she was tired; in fact, she undoubtedly was. That was Guilda's other little talent: whether or not she was sedated, she always left Dr Lovell feeling she could sleep for hours. Just now there was no reason why not. Dr Lovell was asleep almost as soon as she sat at her desk, and before long she began to dream.

Afterword

Incarnate was the novel where I threw away my sketch map and set off into the unknown. I had already published eight novels – four signed, one under as undeceptive a pseudonym as I could invent, three under a house name – all of which had been written from preconceived plots. Indeed, I didn't feel safe in beginning a novel until I knew or thought I knew what every chapter would contain. My first two novels hardly deviated from the chapter breakdowns I'd prepared in advance, except in the final chapters (the preconceived endings acting as a kind of safety net, allowing me to reassure myself that I had a way of finishing the book if I couldn't think of anything better), and the same is true of the early drafts of those which followed, though I later cut approximately forty thousand words from the first revision of *The Parasite* and substituted about twelve new chapters at the same stage of reworking the pseudonymous book. By then I must have known that preconceiving the plot wasn't the ideal way for me to approach the writing of a novel, but perhaps it was a habit which I needed help in breaking. Hurrah for George Walsh.

He was then my editor at Macmillan in New York, and saw five of my books into print, starting with *The Parasite*. By the time of which I'm speaking he had started to commission my books in advance. This entailed my sending him a synopsis of what I had in mind. For various reasons, *Incarnate* had been blundering around inside by head for some years – indeed, it had begun as a treatment of quite a different theme, until the plot was so thoroughly hijacked by the notion of the experiment in dreaming and its aftermath that the original theme was left behind, perhaps still to be turned into a novel of mine – and so the synopsis was almost as detailed as a chapter breakdown. George, let me say, was very much a gentleman, and he presented his criticisms of the synopsis to me as no more than suggestions I might like to consider. He felt that instead of having several plots which only very gradually intersected I might want to make one character somehow more central, and he thought that to have the characters converge on a particular location would give more unity of place. Minor changes, I thought, and ones I would have no difficulty in accommodating – but I had scarcely begun to write the novel when they took over. The ideas they brought to life were so much livelier than those I'd written down for George that I don't think I consulted the synopsis again for the year and a half I spent on the book. Appropriately enough, none of my other novels has felt so like a dream I was having at my desk.

Now, that was happening alongside events I discuss in the introduction to *The Face That Must Die* ('So began the worst year of my life . . .'). I used to believe that *Incarnate* was somewhere I could go during that period and still be in control, but it seems more likely that the book was somewhere I could lose control, at least in some senses, as part of the process of letting the book and its structure be themselves. I wouldn't want this to read like yet another admission of guilt on my part; I don't believe any writer should feel guilty about the compulsion to write or to look upon their life as the raw material of their art. In some cases, indeed, that compulsion may be a way of retaining sanity, and I rather think this was true in my case.

One consequence of allowing the book to explore itself was that it was much longer than the book you're holding. Even the edited typescript I delivered to Macmillan was over 750 pages long. Macmillan, however, were extremely enthusiastic – so enthusiastic that they wanted to be into print with the book in time to display copies at the American Booksellers Association (much like the Frankfurt Book Fair) that year. They edited the typescript for the printer and sent it for my approval, as any good publisher will. It arrived on a Friday, and I had until Monday to read it. I think that's the only period in which I've lost my voice from snarling and screaming even though I was by myself in the room.

Don't assume that I'm about to take revenge on George Walsh or on his consistently helpful assistant, Ilka Shore Cooper, with whom I had a prolonged transatlantic conversation that Monday afternoon. When I needed a break from reading the typescript over the weekend I found myself leafing through Tom Dardis' *Some Time In The Sun*, an account of the experiences of novelists in Hollywood, and chancing upon F. Scott Fitzgerald's plaintive protest to Joseph Mankiewicz: 'I'm a good writer, honest . . . Can't producers ever be wrong?' To judge by some of the material Mankiewicz cut from Fitzgerald's script for *Three Comrades*, any writer can sometimes use an objective opinion of their work, but I still wished that if (as was certainly the case) *Incarnate* needed further cutting, I had been given time to carry out the rewriting myself.

The book has seen several editions since then, all of them based on the Macmillan version, which was the product of my discussion with Ilka of the changes I agreed with and those I wouldn't countenance. By now I regard it as the authorised version, more or less. Two cuts have always bothered me, and so the cut material appears in the present edition. The first passage occurs at the beginning of chapter 43 – the scene in Mrs Shankar's shop – and I've never quite understood why anyone should want to cut it, given the themes of the book. The other, however, is almost a complete chapter, and I'm appending it here, because while I think it gives one kind of strength to the book, its absence is responsible for another kind, insofar as Martin remains an ambiguous figure until much later in the book. It should follow chapter 15, and here it is, to be fitted into the jigsaw if

477

the reader wishes. It's your book as well as mine – you shape it . . .

It was late afternoon when Martin returned to Chapel Hill. Fall had turned the mountains all the colours of firelight and embers, but the fires were dying now. Leaves gathered in the long shadows of the Memorial Cemetery, drifted across the shopping plazas and the front yards on Franklin Street as the taxi cruised by. A truck loaded with windows swung off Franklin toward Hoot Owl in Hidden Hills, and all the other names he had made into stories once as he rode on his father's shoulders came back to him: Fox Run and Possum Place and Wild Turkey on the far side of town, Tinkerbell Road staight out of *Peter Pan*, Gimghoul which he'd thought was Grimghoul, because he had been reading horror comics when the soda jerk wasn't looking. Mounds of leaves sat in the empty ampitheatre, a daylight moon hung like a wafer of cloud in the blue sky above the Planetarium and made him think of Molly back in England, where night had fallen hours ago. He hoped they wouldn't use the Bennett film before he went back to England. Coming home for him to cope with.

Squirrels red as the bricks of the campus buildings scurried across the grassy quadrangle, white pillars gleamed in front of the Wilson Library and above the Old Well, gargoyles craned their crumbling necks. The taxi passed the sprawl of the Medical Centre, and Martin was almost in Westwood. 'I'll walk from here,' he said.

When the taxi had murmured away, striped by the lengthening shadows, he walked down into Westwood. A few hundred yards and his pace slowed, so much was coming back to him: The narrow hilly streets that looped back on themselves, the faint scent of pine in the shade of the slim trees that grew in front of the two-storey houses, the English ivy that covered the ground of many of the yards.

478

An old couple walked a small dog through the leaves where a sidewalk would have been, and the only sound was the whisper of footsteps. He wanted to stroll until the Indian summer evening kindled the porch lights, but he knew he was putting off his return home. When he reached it, he stepped down to the house.

The yard smelled like no other. Dogwood bushes sprouted from the ivy beneath the tulip poplars, but he could never quite locate the smoky scent that made him think of raked leaves and backyard fires and barbecues. Leaves covered the roof of his father's Ford at the side of the house, beyond which a frayed swing was still tied to a branch. He and Larry had sat on it years after they ought to have been too heavy, but it had always held. The sight of it made his throat close up. He managed to swallow and strode to the porch.

His mother answered the bell. Her delicate face was lined now, white china beginning to crack; her blue eyes looked bright with unshed tears. She hugged him on the porch, but not for long. 'Come in,' she said, with a fierceness that seemed ominous. 'This is your home.'

The years seemed hardly to have touched the living room. The heating still sounded as if it harboured mice. The dark leather furniture was piled with books and papers now, but everything else was unchanged – his mother's mountain landscapes and his father's citations and diplomas on the panelled walls, the warm tobacco-smelling dimness that made him think of a clubroom. His father was levering himself out of the chair whose arms were grey with decades of spilled ash. His broad shoulders sagged very little. His shock of hair was even whiter than his moustache, his eyes were sharp as quartz, his face was deeply lined, old bark. His presence was so large that Martin was almost able not to notice he was leaning on a stick.

He looked Martin up and down, then he nodded to himself, unsmiling. Abruptly he stuck out his free hand.

479

Martin grasped it – it was cold and rough and felt like a bundle of sinews – but his father let go after one hard shake. 'Let's not pretend with each other. I'm too God-damned old for pretence.'

'I'm not pretending.'

'Then I've got one thing to say to you: I wonder why.' He turned from Martin to his mother. 'All right, let's get this shindy over with and then maybe we can talk.'

'I'll tell them.'

'In a pig's eye you will. I can still walk,' he said, thumping the pine floor with the rubber tip of his stick, 'and climb all the hills God made.'

He shoved the stick under his arm and made for the porch, gripping the backs of chairs to support himself. Martin saw that he leaned on the stick once he reached the path. He hadn't realized he would find that so dismaying. He cleared papers from the chair by the window, Larry's chair that had been moved from the corner under the deer's head, and sat down. 'What shindy?' he said.

'Just a few of our friends who've been missing you. Lester Craxton got his best chef to make the hors d'oeuvres. You know Lester, he'd have been hurt if we'd refused, and we invited a few people so he wouldn't feel out of place. It'll be like a real homecoming.'

He noticed that she didn't try to tell him that it was. He glanced about at the books and papers. 'What's happening here?'

'Your father plans to write his history of Chapel Hill now he's retired. I'm sure he could right now if he would only get started. Talk to him about it, Martin. Maybe he'll take notice of you now that you've achieved so much.'

'Maybe.'

'Talk to him anyway.' She clasped his hands, pulled at them. 'Promise me you won't fight any more. He can't take it any more, don't let him fool you into thinking he can. I don't want to lose him. We've lost enough.'

Did she blame him for Larry too? 'I haven't come home to make trouble,' he said.

'I'm sure. We're all older and wiser now. Your father doesn't want to fight you either. He loves you, Martin, but he's afraid to let you see. You know that, don't you?'

'I guess.'

'Be patient with him. Let him know you love him, you don't have to say it. You still do love him, don't you?'

'That's why I came home.'

'Exactly what I told him.'

Martin had to smile. 'How did he take it?'

'Can't you just hear him? "I don't need my own Goddamned son to do me any favours." But you're still his son, you see. He said that wasn't how he meant it, but you and I know better. It's going to be all right now, I know it is. I've been praying for this for years.'

She let go of his hands at last and went to the window. 'Lester must be giving him a drink before they come by the house. He won't listen to me or the doctor about drinking. Maybe he'll listen to you.' She laughed nervously and surveyed the room. 'That Lester, I've never known a man so shy. Even takes a drink before he can visit his own hotels. So much for your father clearing up his papers before the company arrives.'

Martin was helping her stack the books and papers on the roll-top desk in the study when Martin's father and his friend came in. 'God *damn* it, boy, I had those how I wanted them.' When she pointed out that they'd kept the piles separate he shrugged. 'Don't let it gripe you. I don't even know if it's worth doing.'

Martin saw a chance to make contact. 'I feel like that sometimes.'

His father stared at him. 'You should.'

Lester was lingering by the door, a bottle of vintage champagne in each hand, his face growing redder. 'I just need to bring the hors d'oeuvres. There are a couple of trays.'

'I'll help.' Martin thought it best to walk away from the first skirmish. Streetlamps lit their canopies of branches, a breeze crept through the ivy, and Martin told himself as he carried a loaded tray down the hill that he must keep the peace. His mother was holding open the porch door for the other guests. Perhaps they would help.

'Martin, you remember Professor Fuller and his wife. And this is David Wess and –'

'Rosemary,' the young woman said. She was twenty years younger than Wess and, clearly, unexpected. Her large brown eyes were gazing speculatively at Martin when Lisa Fuller said, 'Come on, Dorothy, we'll leave them to it,' and herded them both to the kitchen, calling, 'We'll leave you boys alone except when we want a drink.'

David Wess proved to have written two books that had been filmed and wanted Martin's advice about scriptwriting. Jonathan Fuller told Martin's father stories of the campus while Lester wandered about, leafing through books and peering at the mountain landscapes as if he had never seen them before, and at last reminded everyone diffidently about the hors d'oeuvres. 'Lester, what must you think of us,' cried Lisa, shooing everyone to the round oak table that was laid with Martin's great-grandmother's tablecloth. 'Why don't you sit by our host,' she said when Rosemary made to sit opposite Martin. 'I want to hear all Martin's news.'

'They tell me you direct movies in England,' Rosemary said as his father opened the champagne. 'Do you think I could get into them some day?'

'They're not that kind of film, dear,' Dorothy said.

Rosemary ignored her. 'I used to win all the acting prizes at high school.'

'I just make documentaries.'

'Well, David Wess, you might have made that clear. He never tells me anything, just sits at his big old desk switching his typewriter on and off. Can't even spare the time to show me round Chapel Hill.' She leaned toward Martin and extended one bare arm from her filmy blouse for a glass of champagne his father was pouring. 'Maybe you can show me something you think I'd like, Martin.'

He found it easier to grin than speak. 'Did you meet any nice English girls?' Lisa asked.

'As a matter of fact I did.' He glanced at his father. 'I said I'd phone her later. I hope you don't mind.'

'You should have brought her home with you,' Lisa protested. 'You fly her over to meet us all, you hear? And if Dick gives you a hard time, you just come and use our phone.'

'I guess he'll do as he pleases,' his father said, not looking at him.

'I guess he will, Dick Wallace, just like you. And I guess you wouldn't have much use for him if he didn't, am I right?'

Martin's father muttered something that Martin managed not to hear. 'Well, Martin,' Lisa said, 'tell us all about yourself now you're famous.'

'I think I'm pretty much the same as I used to be. Sometimes I feel out of my depth, especially now I'm working for television instead of myself . . .' He told them as much as he could while the party demolished his mother's ham and pork roast and sweet potatoes, and realized how much he had to leave out: whatever he might have said about Lenny Bennett would simply have confirmed his father's worst opinion of him. At least he could say he would be filming in the House of Commons and tell them about Molly, but all at once the meal was over, Lisa was leading the parade of dishes to the kitchen and organizing Jonathan and David at the sink, and no time seemed to pass before she was ushering Lester away. 'Shoo now, Lester, they want to be alone.' Lester shook Martin's hand – 'It's good you're back, Martin,' he murmured quickly as if to outrun his shyness, 'Dick and Dorothy's house feels like a home again.' – and then everyone was leaving, until Lisa halted in the porch and shook a finger at Martin. 'You stay now you're home, you hear? Fly your girl out here if she means as much to you as I think she does. And just you make him welcome, Dick Wallace. You know you want him to stay. You aren't fooling anyone except maybe yourself.'

Martin's father closed the door when the path was clear. 'I'm going to tell you, it's a good thing those folk are my friends, otherwise there's some of them would have me reaching for my shotgun as soon as they set foot on the path.'

'Oh, Dick, do try for once in your life not to be such a grouch.'

He stared at her, then he took her hand. 'Don't mind me. You know good and well it was a damn fine party, you can cook the whole lot of Lester's Paree chefs out of the kitchen and stuff them too.' He was guiding her toward the stairs. 'You ought to get your rest now.'

She glanced anxiously at Martin. 'I don't mind staying up if you want to talk.'

'Why don't you leave us to say what we have to say. Go ahead, we can take care of ourselves.'

Martin saw that was what she was afraid of, but he felt almost at ease now. 'We can talk in the morning,' he told her.

'Well, all right. I am tired. Just be kind to each other.' On the stairs she stopped to catch her breath. 'Don't either of you drink too much.'

His father lowered himelf into his chair as if he were sitting down in a very hot bath. When at last he was seated he reached back and produced a bottle of Beam's Choice. 'Do you use this or do you just drink wine like a woman?'

'I'd be glad to join you.'

'I don't doubt it.' His father's eyes narrowed. 'Well, get the glasses. I guess you still know where they are.'

Martin found the glasses in the cupboard next to the

oven. His father was pulling up his trousers from the knees, and Martin saw how thin his ankles were now. The sight of the old man in the room that smelled like Martin's childhood – pipe tobacco, old books, his mother's delicate scent – released a flood of memories: His father and Larry competing to push him higher on the swing, his six-year-old shouts up in the branches; Larry shooting the white-tailed deer among the leaves that were beginning to glow yellow while Martin, even with his father's hands on the gun, had managed to shoot nothing but a treetrunk; the moonshiner rocking on his porch deep in the mountains, ready to lean back and lift down his shotgun from inside the doorway. They'd rested by a stream on the way home, Martin's father hunkering down for a handful of water, sunlit drops glittering on his moustache. 'I'm going to tell you what an old black man said to me once: Mr Wallace, he said, when a man's got a wife like I got he don't need no French cook, he don't need no other kind of woman a-tall. Well, I didn't stop until I found me a wife like that and don't you settle for less,' he'd said, gazing at Martin. 'That's what you're worth. Both of you,' he'd added, almost quickly enough, and Martin could see Larry's instant self-depreciating smile, the rippling of sunlight on the water, stones shining through the ripples, until his father's voice broke in. 'You going to be all night finding those glasses? At this rate I'll be dead before I get a drink.'

He took a glass from Martin and tried to pour. Bottle and glass were trembling, clinking together, but when Martin made to hold the glass his father jerked it away, spilling bourbon down himself, 'God damn it, when I want your help I'll tell you.'

Nothing had changed between them. Martin felt his helpless rage beginning to crawl in his scalp. He musn't lose his temper. He took the glass when at last it was filled and sipped it as he sat in Larry's chair. His father drained his own glass and gave a heartfelt sigh. 'That's what I call a drink. I remember killing a litre one night with your brother. About time he came home.'

Martin's eyes were stinging, and he didn't know what to say. 'That Lisa Fuller,' his father mumbled, refilling his glass, 'still has a mouth you could fall into, always had. Fall in and get lost until Thanksgiving.' All at once he glared narrowly at Martin. 'Well, what do you have to say to me?'

'I'm sorry,' Martin said, and wished he could take his hand. 'I hope we can still be friends.'

'Sorry for what?'

After the way his father had spoken of Larry, Martin wasn't sure what to say. 'Offending you, I guess.'

'Offending me? Is that all you think you've done?'

'I hoped it might be after all this time.'

'Hoped the old fool might be losing his memory is more like it. You'd better believe I remember, and I'm not likely to forget.' He put down the Beam's Choice with a thud that almost knocked it over. 'I remember having the police come here because of you, I remember how you went to college just to make trouble, I remember how you wouldn't fight for your country even after those Goddamned slanteyes killed your brother. You've never even visited his grave, have you? You put his name on that piece of shit you call a film instead. Sometimes when folks have asked after you I've wanted to go up in the mountains with my gun and end it right there.'

'You wouldn't do that and you know it. You wouldn't leave my mother on her own.'

'You're saying that to me? Why, you damned traitor, what do you think you've done except left her with nothing? You've pissed your life away and made us so we got to hoping people had forgotten you. You had everything going for you and Larry had nothing, but he achieved more than you ever will.'

'I don't think my mother feels that way.' The day that Larry had enlisted and Martin had returned to the peace marches she said that if Martin was forbidden to come back she would leave home too. 'And Larry had a lot going for him. You just treated him as if he hadn't.'

His father glared across the bottle and the glass. 'How the hell do you know what she feels? You haven't seen her for years.'

'Only because I thought I wouldn't be welcome.'

'Then you were right for once. You aren't welcome now. If I had the strength I'd throw you out, mister.'

Martin was cursing himself. 'And you listen to me,' his father said, setting the bottle down with a care that seemed threatening. 'Don't you dare tell me how I treated your brother. At least I never wanted to get rid of him.'

Martin stared. 'Nor did I.'

'Maybe you didn't know it, maybe you had that much of an excuse. Not much of an excuse at all. Listen here, you must have known, you were never that stupid. You must have known when you caused that scene that he would never come back. Or were you so Goddamned self-righteous that you didn't even realize he thought it was his fault?'

It had been in this room. Martin had knocked his father down for calling Larry a dumb mechanic. The rage that felt like insects in his scalp had finally got the better of him, the years being used against Larry had been all at once unbearable, expressible only as rage. He hadn't told Molly that, he was still too ashamed. 'He had no reason to believe it was his fault,' he said, and couldn't stop himself for anger. 'And if he felt that any of us wanted to get rid of him, it wouldn't have been me.'

His father's fist was clenching, and Martin was afraid the glass it held might break. 'Why, you damned shit-eating pigfucker, are you telling me I did?'

'No, of course not. I'm sorry.' Martin made to get up; words were worse than useless, they were dangerous; if only they could touch . . . 'I know you couldn't have.'

'Stay away from me. I don't want to fight you, because of your mother, but by God, I can still knock you down. Don't come crawling round me like the prodigal son. I've had years to think on what you did while you've been trying to forget, and I say that's why you've come back now, to make sure you get the house and everything.'

'That's ridiculous. Look, maybe we should go to bed.'

'That's all you have to say? Can't sound like much, even to you. Well, let me tell you something so you'll know: I'd give this house to a nigra before I'd let you inherit it, and that's the truth.'

'You don't know what you're saying,' Martin muttered, and wished he hadn't spoken.

'The old fool doesn't know what he's saying? He knows enough to make a fool of you, boy. Want to know something? You thought I was getting senile when I said it was time he came home, didn't you? Why, you damned ninny, I said that to see how you'd react. I know he's dead, and by God I know who wanted him to die.'

Martin wondered if he really had known all the time that Larry was dead, but it no longer seemed to matter. He drained his glass and stood up. 'I hope you don't mind if I stay under your roof for the night. I'll leave in the morning.'

'You'll sit there and listen to me, by God. I haven't finished.' He lurched to his feet and made a grab for Martin with one hand, for his stick with the other. He missed both, and fell. Suddenly Martin saw him clearly, a dying old man trying to hold his mind together, finding little to hold onto except grief and helpless rage. He saw how alike they were, he glimpsed the extent of his father's loss. He stepped forward to help him up, unable to speak, but his father shoved himself back toward the chair. 'I told you to stay away from me. I don't want you hanging around to watch me die.'

He had his stick now, and heaved himself back into his chair. 'One more thing before you go creeping off to bed.

David Wess is a friend of mine. He didn't like you making eyes at his girl, and nor do I.'

Martin halted at the foot of the stairs. 'That's bullshit and you know it. I wasn't encouraging her, I was fighting her off.'

'By God, you really think a lot of yourself, the world-famous film director every women drops her pants for.'

'That isn't what I meant and you know damn well it isn't. My impression of his girl was she'd rub up against a bedpost if she couldn't find a man.'

'Well, I believe you're right.' Suddenly, incredibly, there was the hint of a twinkle in his father's eyes. 'But David doesn't see it that way, and I won't be the one to tell him. Just you keep away from her.'

Before Martin could be sure of the look in his eyes, his father glanced toward the stairs. Martin's mother was halfway down them. 'That's enough, Dick,' she said, her voice trembling. 'You've said enough. Just you come to bed.'

'I'll tell you, Dorothy, I don't think he needs you to fight his battles. I guess he can look after himself.' He turned to Martin. 'Well, we can't talk that way in front of your mother. Another night we'll do without all that Goddamned wine. We can't leave things as they are now,' he said ominously. 'There are things that need to be talked out.'

Nevertheless there had been grudging admiration in his voice, and as much of an invitation to stay as he was able to give. When his parents had closed their bedroom door, Martin went outside. Wind breathed in the trees, crickets in a shed sounded like a band of children playing combs. He sat on the swing, though the branch creaked, and felt there might be hope. Had anything besides his father's pretence of senility, if it was a pretence, been meant to make him react? He could only wait for the morning.

He ought to go to bed, though he didn't feel tired. 'It was past two by his watch, sevenish in England. Would he wake

Molly if he called now? After all, it was Saturday morning. Still, he thought she would want him to call, and he went in to the phone.

He had to dial three times before her phone rang. He shouldn't sound too optimistic in case his father overheard and thought that Martin felt he'd won. The phone had rung only once, startlingly close, when Molly demanded, 'Who's there?'

'Martin. How are you?'

'Oh, surviving. Are you home now? How did you get on with your father?'

'Better than I thought I would.' He had lowered his voice, not only to say that but because he was growing uneasy; there was an edge to her voice he didn't like. 'Everything all right over there?'

Her silence lasted so long that he was about to repeat the question. 'No,' she said across Atlantic waves of static, 'but don't worry. We were acting in good faith, that must count in our favour. If we didn't take risks in our business we wouldn't be doing our job.'

His scalp was crawling again. 'What are you talking about? What's wrong?'

'Look, you mustn't worry. I wish I hadn't even mentioned it. I can handle it, trust me. You stay there as long as you need to and leave the situation here to me.' At last she said, 'Ben Eccles used the Lenny Bennett film and what you said about it, and now it's proved to be fake.'